C.S.A.

CONFEDERATE STATES OF AMERICA

C.S.A.

CONFEDERATE STATES

OF AMERICA

A NOVEL BY

HOWARD MEANS

WILLIAM MORROW AND COMPANY, INC.

NEW YORK

It is the policy of William Morrow and Company, and its imprints and affiliates, recognizing the importance of preserving what has been written, to print the books we publish on acid-free paper, and we exert our best efforts to that end.

Library of Congress Cataloging-in-Publication Data
Means, Howard B.
C.S.A.—Confederate States of America : a novel / by Howard Means.
p.   cm.
ISBN 0-688-16187-1
I. Title.
PS3563.E196C2   1998
813'.54—dc21   98-27461
CIP

Printed in the United States of America

First Edition

1   2   3   4   5   6   7   8   9   10

BOOK DESIGN BY DEBBIE GLASSERMAN

www.williammorrow.com

TO NATHAN AND IHRIE

ACKNOWLEDGEMENTS

This is a work of fiction. As such, it takes liberties with the course of a war that claimed more than half a million American lives. No disrespect is meant. Thanks are owed to my agent, Rafe Sagalyn, and his assistant Ethan Kline, and to Paul Bresnick, my editor at William Morrow, and Casey Fuetsch. Thanks, as well, to Jack Limpert and *Washingtonian* magazine for granting me a leave of absence. Most of all, thanks to my wife, Candy, for enduring the creation of this book.

Finally, a request: Please keep in mind as you read this that the winners get to write the history.

C.S.A.

CONFEDERATE STATES OF AMERICA

PROLOGUE

RICHMOND, VIRGINIA
APRIL 1, 1866

"GENERAL LEE?"

He awoke with a start, utterly lost. What year was it? What place? He'd been dreaming of Alexandria, of dances on verandas that over-looked the Potomac, of rooms filled with laughter, tinkling glasses, the scent of jasmine. Now he struggled to right himself in the desk chair he'd been dozing in, struggled once again to ground himself in the here and now, and as he did so, he realized: He'd been dream-ing of a time when it was possible to be young again. And not just him. Not just him. Lord in heaven, the cost!

"General Lee? It's the people, sir. The line extends back Franklin Street almost to the edge of the city, I'm told. May I send the first of them in?"

It was Walker, his aide, practically the last of them at the end who wasn't little more than a boy.

"Not yet, Colonel. A moment more. Allow me to finish this cor-respondence. Please."

Walker saluted with his left arm—his right one gone at the el-bow since Cold Harbor—turned on his heel, and pulled the door behind him. As he did so, the general picked up the letter he'd been reading, brought it to his good eye, and turned to take advantage of the morning sun.

"Dear General Lee," it began. "I beseech you yet again, sir, in the name of all that is right, all that is decent, all that is proper in the eyes of God, to free my Abraham. Permit him to return to the bosom of his family; to the children whom he loves and who love and deeply miss their father; to the wife, sir, who is haunted by dreams of his abuse, the wife who cannot sleep, the wife for whom there will be no rest—none!—until this unlawful imprisonment is remedied.

"Surely, General Lee, you, you of all people, must know how madness threatens to engulf me in my grief.

"Sincerely," the letter was signed, "Mary Todd Lincoln."

Sincerely indeed, the general thought. He had heard, of course, what was being said in those last months: that he himself was mad, that grief had driven him beyond reason, that the war finally had broken even him. Well, maybe it had, and why not? The fight had seemed at first a matter of simple honor: his honor as a gentleman and a soldier; the honor he felt as a Virginian, which had led him to answer the Confederate call to duty. Later, he had come to think of it more as a war of "if only's." If only the Fifteenth Alabama could have slipped around the Twentieth Maine at Little Round Top; if only the English had joined the cause sooner; if only Johnston had survived Shiloh, Jackson had survived Chancellorsville. He'd lost a daughter to typhoid fever during the war, a grandson to bad intestines. If only they had survived. If only. Pure futility. Finally, he had come to see the war for what it was: blood, slaughter, trenches filled with human offal.

It was the men under Pemberton's command at Vicksburg, reduced to a diet of rats and frogs in their last days, whom he had in mind when he ordered New York City burned and the generals who had defended it hanged. It was the boys he had left dead in the foothills of Pennsylvania in those last months—literal boys, still in knee pants, all who were left to fight—that he was thinking of when he torched Trenton and drove the Federal soldiers in Philadelphia into the icy Delaware to seek the mercy of the British gunboat captains rather than face his wrath. It was Richmond he saw as he entered Washington City on Christmas Day—what?—only a little more than three months ago. How could it be? Richmond burned nearly to the ground, Jefferson Davis incinerated by his own hand. In truth, he had no idea what he intended to do when he rode into the White House on Traveller that day. Had Lincoln begged, had he cowered, had he so much as asked for a single ounce of mercy, the general supposed he would have left with the Union president on the point of his sword. Instead, he ordered him thrown in chains, and there Mr. Lincoln remained to this day.

The general looked out his study window now, saw the burned-out hulk of the Capitol looming on Shockoe Hill—Thomas Jefferson's Capitol, almost the last thing standing—and thought as he always did of the terrible price his friend Jefferson Davis had paid. How does a man do it? How does a man set himself on fire? How? And why? The latter is what truly haunted him: Why? Was he braver than I? the general wondered. Or just more mad? A question never to be answered on this side of eternity.

Richmond. It was a capital itself these days, and not just of a state, not just of a rebellious Confederacy, but of a sprawling nation. Secession had proved impossible; the South had to conquer the Union to leave it. The general assumed some version of the old capital's vanities would come to infect this new one: an infatuation with its own grandeur—a weakness Richmond always had. There was talk already of turning the charred terrain of Shockoe Hill into a new national mall, bedecked with the usual statuary, with the wreck of the old Capitol as its centerpiece. At least, the general thought, he would not be around to suffer it.

He reached for a piece of stationery, laid his left hand heavily on it to hold the paper in place, and began to write:

"My dear Mrs. Lincoln,

"I have talked only yesterday with President Forrest, and he has agreed with me that your husband be released from his present confinement and allowed to join you and your family at Springfield. You may expect him to arrive by train, under guard, within a fortnight of your receiving this correspondence.

"I must warn you that should he ever attempt to leave Springfield during the remainder of his life, he will be hunted down and recaptured, and he and you and all your family members—every child and every grandchild that may be—shall be summarily put to death.

"Respectfully,

"Robt. E. Lee"

He blotted the paper carefully, set it at the side of his desk for his secretary to copy for his signature, and rang the sterling-silver dinner bell he used to summon Walker. Forrest had agreed with him: An eternity with Mrs. Lincoln was punishment enough for any man.

"Sir?"

"I'm ready, Colonel."

Walker turned the desk chair so the sun caught the right side of the general's face, then covered his shoulders with a simple gray blanket. In civilian clothes, the general looked like a circuit preacher rather than a military commander, although perhaps that was more the white beard and the fire that seemed to burn like an eternal light in his dead left eye.

"I think, sir, that should do it."

The general merely nodded this time, worn out before the day had begun. He watched as Walker swung the door open and drew the velvet rope across the entrance.

"General Lee, sir," the first visitor called from the doorway. "I have come from Camden, down in South Carolina, to offer the congratulations of my state and people. You, sir, have delivered us from evil even as the Bible foretells."

The general merely nodded as Walker gently urged the man onward so the next visitor could take his place. There was no time, and no point in speaking even if there had been. Since the stroke, not even his wife—no one save for Walker—seemed able to understand a word he said. Maybe, he thought, Jefferson Davis had had a simpler reason for setting himself on fire. Maybe he knew that had he lived, he would have been reduced to either a prisoner or this: a museum piece, barely removed from a circus sideshow, entrapped by endless admiration and love. Robert E. Lee longed suddenly for the plantation at Stratford, longed for solitude, longed to be merely human, and he knew that he would never again see his birthplace, never again know the peace of his own companionship, never again be merely a man of woman born.

PART I

APRIL 20, 2000

THE MALL,
WASHINGTON, D.C.

SOMEDAY SOON, THE man thought, the living dead will all become the dead dead, and this city will become what it has so long been heading toward: a necropolis, a city of the dead, a place where death, not life, is taken for granted.

He was standing on the crumbling wall of the Washington City Canal. Five blocks to the east, what remained of the canal ran behind what remained of the crumbling City Market, deserted now forty years. There was talk of tourists and "adaptive reuse," but there was always talk of "adaptive reuse" in Washington, and nothing ever came of anything. Tourists showed up only once if they bothered to come at all: to what had once been the home of presidents, to see the shackles that had bound Abraham Lincoln to his bedroom in the first months after the war had ended; and to Blair House across the street, where the war had come full circle. It was there that Robert E. Lee had first spurned Lincoln's offer to command the Federal army; there, too, that Lee had presided as Ulysses Grant signed the articles of capitulation on behalf of the defeated Union. At the far eastern end of the Mall, the unlit dome of what had once been the American Capitol pierced the sky, lit by a full moon. Once, the Capitol had housed Daniel Webster, Henry Clay, the raw, impassioned debate of a raw and forming nation. Now its rotunda, its chambers, the small side offices where deals had been cut and reputations made or broken, were regularly swept by a D.C. police detachment, rounding up the addicts, the whores, the homeless, those

who could slip through a crack no wider than a knife blade. About
police the man knew something, and about evil too. In Washington,
he had long ago decided, evil didn't happen; evil simply appeared.
It materialized out of the air, the water, the ground.

To the west, the Potomac had run over its banks four days earlier,
swollen by winter snows and early spring rains. He could almost
hear the river, three blocks away, as it lapped against Seventeenth
Street. For once, the canal had a wash running through it—less than
a flow, more than a trickle. For the tens of thousands of rats who
called the canal home, it was bath day, party time.

Overhead, the elevated Fourteenth Street Expressway hummed
like a giant angry mosquito—its flow of eighteen-wheelers constant.
Midnight to six, the freeways from the Potomac to Canada belonged
by government decree to the semis; southward, the truckers had to
share the highways with whatever traffic dared to travel at those
hours. The man tracked the trestles as they disappeared across the
river into the night. To his west, set on an ancient high bluff of the
Potomac, the Custis-Lee Mansion glowed in its undying light. But
that was Virginia, and for more than one hundred thirty-four years
now, Virginia, not Washington, had been the whole point.

Washington was a city of grand ambitions that had not prospered
long enough to achieve them. Its brush with history, *real* history, ran
the gauntlet from the great general and first president for whom it
had been named to the Great Satan who had interred its hopes and
dreams, and nearly, too, the hopes and dreams of the Founding
Fathers who had created this haggard shell of a place. This Mall said
it all, this graveyard of ambition—this Mall and the shining lights
on the hill across the river.

For what he thought must be the ten thousandth time, the man
wondered why he didn't pick up stakes, follow the lights toward a
different future. Only an accident of birth had landed him in Washington: His father, dead now fifteen years, had come here out of
college to help manage the forms that were the city's lifeblood—a
bad career choice from which he had never recovered. As for himself,
only an accident of schooling had made him a cop: He'd ignored his
classes, run with the wrong crowd, found a bar his junior year that
opened the same time as Algebra II was scheduled, and decided to
concentrate on pool instead of college prep. By the time he'd gotten

his feet back under him, police work seemed high ambition. Still, he'd learned on the job. He might have a bad attitude, but after twenty years on the force, he knew he was a good cop, a cop who wouldn't let go. And in the Confederate States of America, a good cop would never want for work.

Why not just go, then? Light out for Richmond, the West, the territories? The Caribbean Corporation bombarded beat policemen, detectives like himself, the whole range of law enforcement officials, with help wanted ads: "See sunny Grenada!" "Come to Cuba!" All you had to be willing to do was hunt down Patriation workers who had run away and enforce an existence that he imagined was barely any existence yet held what was said to be the greatest promise: citizenship of the Confederacy, this America.

Why not leave? Because, he thought, his mother couldn't survive without him. Because his sister would feel his absence like a great hole in her life and never understand why he had gone. Because even his ex-wife needed someone close by to despise. And then there were the two patrolmen to consider, the ones he had brought to this far corner of civilization. They could barely feed and clothe themselves without him.

"FOR CRISSAKE, JENKINS, Flannerty—you've got to go *down* there. Those bodies aren't going to come *up* to you."

For the last half hour, the two patrolmen had been using poles and a makeshift lifesaving crook to try to prod the two bodies onto a rope-and-tarpaulin stretcher.

"We've just about got the tall one, Lieutenant," Jenkins said.

"You've just about rendered him useless for forensics purposes is what you mean, Jenkins."

"Lieutenant, give us a break. It's wall-to-wall vermin down there." Flannerty was the whiner.

The lieutenant unsheathed a nine-millimeter pistol and fired half a clip into the dirt bottom of the canal, just beyond where the bodies lay, facedown. The rats, which had been risking the dim illumination thrown by the portable spotlights, scuttled to the edge of the shadows.

"Gentlemen, a cordon sanitaire. Now."

Before he lowered himself over the side, Flannerty looked at the lieutenant as if he were crazy. Jenkins didn't look at all. He'd been a uniformed patrolman for fifteen years and would never be anything else. Crazy is what the job made you, and Christ, the *noise*—he'd be deaf for half a week now.

The lieutenant had just fit a new clip in his pistol when Flannerty came scrambling up the canal wall.

"Ready to haul number one," he said, already out of breath. As the two of them pulled the rope in, hand over hand, the lieutenant could hear a head pounding against the limestone embankment.

"You might try to keep the face clear, Jenkins. Just in case we have to make an identification. Or at least catch the fucking teeth as they pop out."

"Jesus, Lieutenant, these rats. They won't—"

"You've got a service pistol, Jenkins. You're a trained professional. Defend yourself."

TEN MINUTES LATER, the two bodies lay side by side on the gravel path that paralleled the canal. Number one was a white male, approximately six feet four inches, long and lean. The lieutenant put his age at late thirties, early forties. While Jenkins and Flannerty sat on the canal wall, exploding vermin, the lieutenant rolled the man on his side and bent down with his flashlight for a look. The bullet had entered at the base of the neck from close range—powder burns splayed away from a small, almost blackish-red circle. As always, the lieutenant was astounded by how delicately a bullet can slip into a body. From here, he guessed, the slug had shattered the spine and broken apart. He leaned around to the front of the corpse now. The man's neck looked as if it had been ripped out by a wild animal. Tendon and nerve endings hung out of the hole where his throat had been. A .22? the lieutenant wondered. With a long-rifle bullet for punch?

Number two was nearly a head shorter and forty pounds heavier—a black male, deeply muscled, with what seemed to the lieutenant a massive cranium. He'd been shot once, through the forehead. Again, the entry hole was clean—too clean, maybe, for a Saturday-night special. With a skull this thick, a .22 would probably explode on impact. The lieutenant had to put his weight into rolling number two; he seemed to be held to the earth. When he finally got him on his side, he shone his flashlight on the rear of the man's head and saw almost nothing. The back of his skull had been blown away. His brains, the lieutenant imagined, were lying in the canal or dripping along the wall. The lieutenant guessed the murders had been done with a nine-millimeter pistol like his own—lots of wallop for the load. He fought back the urge to throw up.

"No wallet, Lieutenant. No nothing," Flannerty called over his shoulder. Either his brown hair was too long or his hat was too small. Whichever it was, he looked to the lieutenant like a clown cop. "We checked them both before we brought 'em up. Didn't want anything to drop out of their pockets."

"You're a paragon of thoroughness, Flannerty. A model to be admired."

"All in a day's work," Flannerty called back, enormously satisfied.

Clueless, the lieutenant thought. Police work was the black hole of irony, but irony was all that made the job bearable.

"What do you figure brought them here, Lieutenant?" It was Jenkins this time. "The usual?"

"Would you be referring to Section Twelve, Subsection Seven, Articles C and D of the Criminal Code of the Confederate States of America, Patrolman Jenkins?"

"Lieutenant?"

"Crimes against nature, Patrolman. 'Thou shalt not lie down with thine own, nor shalt thou lie down with what is not thine own.' Seems to leave a fairly narrow window for fun, doesn't it?"

"You're losing me, Lieutenant."

"I was giving the code its biblical rendering, Jenkins. The Good Book. The statutes pertain to what you were referring to when you asked if our friends here had chosen to visit the Mall in pursuit of 'the usual'—that is, the coming together for the purpose of sexual gratification of persons of the same sex or of different races."

Jenkins at least had a glimmer of understanding in his eye. Beside him, a few inches taller and ten years younger, Flannerty looked at the lieutenant as if he'd been speaking in Urdu.

"In short, Patrolman Flannerty, cross-racial screwing, same-sex humping, both of which, you will recall, are grounds for expulsion from our fair Confederacy, much as Adam and Eve were expelled from the Garden of Eden and forced into this world of sin and sorrow. To return again to the Good Book. In this instance, of course, someone seems to have pre-expelled our lovers."

Shut up, the lieutenant told himself. Shut up. It was the trouble with men who spent so much time alone: Once they started talking, they wore out their audience. He shone his flashlight on the two faces—the cranium destroyed in the one, the almost delicate entry hole of the other—and as he did so, he tried to imagine what set of circumstances might have brought these bodies to him.

Was it the love that dared not speak its name? Certainly, that was a best first guess. The laws against homosexuality were rooted, like so much of the criminal code, in a rigid reading of Scripture, but for decades now they had been enforced only when the police had no choice but to notice. The Mall was a tempting trysting ground for homosexuals—the grass was mowed at best every two months; the shrubbery was overgrown. Unless they were summoned, policemen tended to give it a good leaving alone. But what made the Mall attractive for illicit lovers also made it a tempting target for the blackmailers, thugs, and worse who preyed on them. Half or more of the beatings, muggings, even murders, logged in this tiny patch of hell began in the pursuit of the little death, not the big one.

Perhaps, then, this was nothing more than a lovers' quarrel gone bad—a murder-suicide. Not the first of those, either, or the last. The lieutenant was holding his nine-millimeter at arm's length in front of him, pointing it at the center of his forehead. Maybe, he thought, if you pushed the trigger with your thumb. And had nerves of steel. And were from the planet Woo-Woo.

"Makes you wonder, doesn't it, Lieutenant?" Jenkins called over from the canal wall.

"Wonder?"

"I mean, having sex with a guy is strange enough, but having sex with, you know, a guy who's not even your same race—that's going way off the charts."

Way off was right, the lieutenant thought. Race was the defining distinction of the Confederacy, the divide around which the entire nation had been built. To cross it like this was beyond even his imagination, but maybe that was just him.

"Who knows, Jenkins," he finally said. "Maybe taboos like this are paper thin. After you break them, you might not remember they were there. Hell, it might even be fun."

The lieutenant could see Jenkins's red hair bobbing as he crossed himself.

AS THE LIEUTENANT bent down to look at the ankles of the corpses, he felt his belt press heavily against his stomach, his stomach rise up into his chest. He was forty-one years old and already inhabiting the body of a fifty-year-old. By the time he got to fifty, his body would be dying of old age.

Rope had been used to bind the two men, he guessed. A deep wrinkle line ran around the base of both their trousers. He slid his flashlight along the black man's body to his wrists. They'd been wired, it seemed, and tightly. A crust of blood circled each of them, scabrous bracelets, still crimson. This was new death, fresh horror. And then he noticed what he told himself he should have seen when both men were first brought out of the canal, and at least the suicide part of the murder-suicide became a moot point. And probably love as well.

"Jenkins, Flannerty, you two highly paid crime stoppers didn't happen to notice a bolt cutter when you were down there, did you?"

"It's a goddamn trash dump down there, Lieutenant. There's all sorts of shit—"

"I'm not interested in all sorts of shit, Flannerty. I'm interested in one piece of it: a bolt cutter. Two handles, probably vinyl-coated, a—"

"There it is. You want it?"

The lieutenant could see Jenkins's flashlight playing up the canal bed to the right.

"Come here first."

As the two patrolmen looked on, the lieutenant held up each of the victims' hands and washed them with his flashlight. All twenty fingers had been sheared off at the second joint.

"Jesus," Flannerty finally asked. "What's that about?"

It would take half a week at best to make a match from dental records, maybe two days if headquarters pushed it. And two dead men in the Washington City Canal weren't likely to make anyone's priority list.

"Fingerprints, Flannerty," the lieutenant said, "so we couldn't do a quick ID on them. My guess is that someone has borrowed their identity, just for a short time."

"Uh, Lieutenant, you want me to look for, you know, *body parts* while I'm down there? Maybe we could make a match from that." It was Jenkins this time, getting ready to lower himself into the canal while Flannerty peppered the path to the bolt cutter with gunshot.

"Vienna sausages," the lieutenant answered, half to himself.

"Sausages, Lieutenant?"

"You want to get rid of fingertips, Jenkins, you can't do much better than serve them up as hors d'oeuvres at a rat party."

FLANNERTY AND JENKINS were bagging and tagging the bolt cutter when the van finally arrived from the medical examiner's office.

"Another crime of passion, Lieutenant Haddon?" Like the lieutenant, the assistant medical examiner was an insomniac who would rather be out in the night than staring at a ceiling.

"Maybe, but with extenuating circumstances."

"As always."

The soft breeze of earlier in the night had given up, and with it had gone the full moon and clear air. The lights of the van cut barely thirty feet into the dark now. Once, two-story-high carnivores had prowled this territory, along with vegetarians tall as trees. There had been nodosaurs, twenty-foot-long armored beasts that walked on all fours; ostrich-like ornithomimids, eleven feet long and fast as a horse; the bird-like coelurosaur, another meat eater; the one-ton tenontosaurus; and more. The lieutenant knew something just as fearsome was headed this way again, and soon. Well into the nineteenth century, these lowlands of Washington had been malarial swamps. That they would be swamp once again—and pestilential too—the lieutenant had no doubt. Washington was sinking back into its own primal ooze.

Somewhere beyond the hazy arc of light cast by the van, something scuttled, squirmed. Two-foot or four-foot, vermin or human? The lieutenant couldn't say. Just as Washington was a place where evil simply appeared out of the air, so it was a place where life just washed up. The movers and shakers, the dealmakers and manipulators, went elsewhere—to the great cities of the South and Midwest and West, bursting with the energy of this energy-driven nation; even to Baltimore, just to the north, a frontier town, poised on the edge of an industrial wilderness. Washington was a city more than a century into its penance, a city on its knees in an atonement that would never be enough. Such a place attracted people with much to be forgiven.

If the lieutenant were to empty a clip from his service pistol randomly into this darkness, he might well put more than one troubled soul out of its misery. Not for the first time, he wondered how such cynicism was possible—in himself, in his colleagues, in anyone—in a land where everything was so close to being so absolutely right.

2

THE OVAL OFFICE

UNEASY LIES THE head, et cetera, he thought. But why is it always the et ceteras that wear you down so.

In the hallway outside, Spencer Lee could hear the usual morning shuffle. There was a press briefing at ten, the New Zealand agricultural minister at noon for lunch. At three o'clock, sure as a migraine, Toby Burke, the House Speaker, and Senate Majority Leader Willard Wilson would arrive. Budget issues needed to be addressed; the question of statehood for Mexico had to be resolved sooner or later. There were debts to be paid in both the House and the Senate; chits were being called in, as they always were in politics. At four, the new Canadian ambassador would be presenting her credentials, undoubtedly along with a few well-chosen words from her masters in Ottawa. Canada was rattling its saber again, screwing down the border, telling anyone who cared to listen that its neighbor to the south was an environmental time bomb waiting to explode. Happily, the President had managed to serve seven years in office without ever once setting foot north of the border. Long, dark winters must feed such apocalyptic visions, he thought. He himself preferred to pass what part of the winter months he could golfing in the Carolinas or fishing along the Gulf.

What else? Spencer checked the typed schedule on embossed stationery that Kay always included with the silver coffee service before Manzini brought it in—two cups, two beautifully wrought pots, one full strength, one decaffeinated. How did Nathan survive on such

thin stimulation? There was a photo op at nine with the preservationists: That meant Waddell and a stern lecture. Reporters from
Atlanta and Birmingham would be staying on after the ten o'clock
briefing for a tête-à-tête, stalwart supporters both. If Wormley were
less of a mother hen, he would have scheduled the meeting for six
tomorrow, when there would have been time to break out the bourbon. But Wormley, bless him, had been fretting about the President's
health ever since Frannie died. The New Zealand minister would
be shooed out the door by two, an hour to prepare for the honorable
gentlemen from the Capitol. The honorable gentlemen would be
shooed out by four; the new Canadian ambassador by five. In between would be the usual hubbub of life in Richmond—the lobbyists,
the flatterers, the influence peddlers, all cramming to get in his door.
Thank God for Kay, who ran the outer office. Thank God for
Wormley, his scheduler, who blocked out his life in fifteen-minute
grids. They were all that held the floodwaters back. Without them,
he'd be swept away. Still, there would be debris to deal with after
five as well—the crisis management and press strategy that took up
the tail end of every day.

In all, the President calculated, he would have no more than an
hour left at day's end to jog on the Mall, shower, and change before
the dinner at the Hotel Richmond, honoring the completion of the
InterAmerican Waterway, the capstone of his and his predecessor's
administrations. An hour wasn't enough.

He walked over to his desk and punched the button on the intercom.

"Mr. Wormley?"

"Sir?"

"Cancel the House Speaker, please. And call the Senate Majority
Leader and tell him that he needn't show either."

"But, sir, we've canceled Mr. Burke twice before."

"Well, three's the charm, Mr. Wormley. I'm going to jog instead.
And Kay?" The two of them—Wormley and Kay—took their
coffee together each morning in Kay's office, just outside the President's own.

"Yes, Mr. President?"

"Would you be so kind as to call Alice and ask her if she can join
me for the dinner tonight."

"Alice is in England, Mr. President."

Too much. Too much. How could he have forgotten where his baby sister was?

"So she is." Eternally grateful, England had turned itself into a lovely little theme park for America.

"Jason?"

His son was in college, no more than seventy miles away from Richmond. He could send the helicopter and have Jason here in half an hour. He hated to do it—Jason would despise the commotion, the spotlight trained even so briefly on him. The President's son seemed to be devoting his college career to not being noticed. At the moment, though, the thought of sitting down at the waterway dinner without any family member by his side was appalling.

"Midterms, Mr. President. We've arranged for Miss Barnes to accompany you tonight."

That would be Wormley's work. The irreproachable daughter of the irreproachable late secretary of state, Margaret Barnes was a woman of fierce moderation in drink, food, conversation, opinions, even looks. Even, he assumed, sex. The very thought caused him to shrivel.

"Mr. Wormley?"

"Sir?"

"Your attention to my needs shall not go unrewarded."

"Thank you, sir. I think."

The President wondered what he would do with his time, his life, when his second term was finally completed and there was no more Kay in the anteroom, no more Wormley waiting and worrying. The farm took care of itself. So did the trust fund. So would his place in "history," a word he never thought of without ironic quote marks: History, he knew, had people like him for lunch.

Would he be one of those prematurely rich, prematurely retired men who wake up each morning and see a desert of time stretching in front of them before lunch, a golf date, maybe, the cocktail rituals of six and later? Dear God, he thought, what if I have to spend the rest of my life chairing blue-ribbon commissions just so I have something to do? I'll be only fifty-three when this is through; not quite a spring chicken, but still . . .

"Mr. President?" Kay had stuck her head in at the door, knowing how much Spencer hated to hear the intercom at this early hour. She had her hair drawn back in a bun. If she hadn't been an executive secretary, the President supposed she would have joined the church and become a bride of Christ. "It's Carruthers, on line one. He says it's urgent."

"No," Spencer said. "No." Alton Carruthers was his chief of staff, one of the few personnel blunders of this second term. The President kept him as far out of the loop as possible, hoping that even at this late date he might resign.

"And, sir, it's time for the daily."

"Ah! Space agents on patrol."

Spencer sipped his coffee and watched the two Secret Service agents probe the Oval Office for electronic bugs, as they did every day. One was carrying a miniature satellite dish; the other searched the carpet and baseboards with what looked like a personal mine sweeper.

"No new infestations, Mr. Pignon?" Spencer asked as the sweeper passed his chair.

"Not yet, sir."

What could he possibly say in this office, the President wondered, that would be worth such an effort? After all this time, he couldn't have a secret left.

Spencer looked at his watch as the agents closed the door behind them: 7:55. Nathan would be here in five minutes, soon enough to save him from self-pity. He supposed that should be part of the job description of every Vice President.

BEFORE HE SAT again, Spencer drew back the gauze curtains so that he could see unimpeded the great stretch of green that ran from his office to the river. The sun was climbing to his left, lighting the equestrian statue of George Washington that had been unveiled in 1858, just before the bottom seemed to fall out of history. Opposite it, on the east side of the Mall, Madison Tompkins—as imposing in bronze as he had been in life—stood on a marble pedestal in all his oratorical splendor, ready to deliver the speech that would help piece history back together. Between the two statues, a block closer to the President, towered the twin obelisks to his own ancestors—the agents of history, the ones who had carried it from before to after, the ones without whom history would simply have ceased to exist. No wonder the obelisks looked so much like lightning bolts striking eternally into the earth. We live in the past, the President told himself; that's why history has us for lunch. But we have no choice.

From these third-floor windows of the White House, the joggers and lollygaggers along the Mall, the self-important lawyers and bureaucrats scurrying back and forth from government building to office complex, appeared like nothing so much as ants. Were they to see him seated in his wing chair, gazing at them as they looked at him, he would seem like an ant as well—a favored ant, an opulent and pampered one, an ant in chief, but an ant just the same. All in all, it was a useful perspective.

BEHIND HIM, HE heard the doorknob turn.

"Mr. Vice President."

"Mr. President, suh."

As Nathan Winston settled heavily into the wing chair beside him, the President poured him a cup of decaffeinated coffee, sweetened it with two sugar cubes, topped the cup off with whole cream, and waited for Nathan to cross his legs and adjust his cuffs—left over right, always left over right.

"Sightseeing?" the Vice President asked, accepting his morning coffee.

"It *is* a sight. You sound tired."

"I should have married younger, Spencer; had my children when I had the strength to deal with them."

"John Henry?"

"He and Lucinda were at it again yesterday. She was still upset when we talked a little while ago. The subject this time was the Patriation Program—John Henry seems to think it's enslavement."

"He's seventeen, Nathan. The world looks simple when you're young."

"And I'm sixty-five. Almost nothing seems simple anymore, not even tying my shoes." The Vice President patted his broad girth as he spoke. "Maybe if I argued more with John Henry myself, I'd eat less. It seems to work for Lucinda. There's barely anything to her."

"Lucy?"

"Oh, Lucy helps when she's there. John Henry's never been able to stay angry at her. But she's only twenty, Spencer, and she's never been interested in these kinds of issues. Lucy accepts the world as it is. I try to referee when I'm home, but Lucinda and John Henry are so much like each other, if only they would recognize it. Neither is willing to yield an inch of ground."

"He'll grow up, Nathan. Time will take care of things."

"Or he'll be the death of us while we're waiting. Did Jason go through anything like this?"

"He doesn't talk about issues, about politics. He's heard too much about both his whole life, and I think he's still busy getting over his mother's death. But—"

The President stopped, stared off in the distance, down the Mall to the twin obelisks.

"But, Spencer?"

"I think he worries that he won't be able to be himself, to just be Jason. I think maybe he's terrified that people will try to make him into another me."

"There will be that temptation. We Confederates hate to let a bloodline like yours just die out."

Silently now, they sipped their coffee. The President was dressed in blue pinstripes, a crisp white shirt, as always the red-white-and-blue tie—his signature. The Vice President, beside him, was in three-piece charcoal gray, a deep-blue shirt, his tie a rich solid purple. A matching foulard peeped from the breast pocket of his jacket. They had been together now through two campaigns and for nearly two terms in office. Like an old married couple, they thought they could read each other's minds and moods.

"I'd like for you to be here this afternoon when the new Canadian ambassador shows up."

The Vice President's schedule was on the silver coffee tray as well. He picked it up and scanned it.

"The trade minister from Greater Germany is due in at four."

"Let Sumner take care of him."

"Gladly. I seem to bring out the worst in the Germans."

"It's easy to do. By the way, I canceled Toby Burke at three."

"Toby will be unhappy, Spencer. He has the impression that you're ducking him."

"I am. Like the plague. But Willard Wilson and I are sitting with him at the waterway dinner tonight, and I can't deal with Toby more than once a day. Besides, I'd rather have him buttonholing me in front of a cast of hundreds than in private. It'll keep the histrionics down—both his and Willard's."

Spencer refilled his coffee cup, only halfway up this time, and leaned back in his chair.

"Toby will want something for the waterway, now that it's done, Nathan. He delivered; now we'll have to pay him."

"Mexico?"

"Maybe, if I can convince him that I give a damn for the statehood initiative. But I think he already knows I'd just as soon see it quashed."

"The old Capitol, then?"

"More likely, I'd think—bulldozers, a cloud of dust, obliterated from memory."

They both shifted slightly in their chairs. From where they sat, the old Capitol was perfectly framed between the twin obelisks, with the statues of Washington and Tompkins on either wing and the Mall falling away to the river beyond it. Already, twenty minutes before it opened, a queue of tourists waited to get inside. Sharply downhill from the old Capitol, the top stories of the "new" Capitol, more than one hundred thirty years old, stood gleaming white in the morning sun.

"Do you think I should do it, Nathan? You think I should let them have the old warhorse torn down?"

"I think, Mr. President, that you are the only one who *could* do it."

"A perfectly diplomatic response. I should appoint you ambassador to the Court of St. James's before our terms are up."

"I would prefer France."

"There is no France."

"A perfect job, then. I accept."

They retreated a last time to silence, each studying the scene. The President imagined the James River waiting at the far end of the Mall, lit like a silver thread as it wound its way southeast from the Blue Ridge to the Atlantic. As was more and more the case in this final year of his final term, Spencer longed to follow the river—in a raft, a canoe, it didn't matter—straight out to the sea.

"After the meeting with the Canadian ambassador, I want you to go home for the night, Nathan. Take the helicopter. Spend the night

with Lucinda; have a good talk with John Henry. You can't raise a
son by telephone. It's the work that separates you, not the age."

"With your permission, Mr. President, I think I'll do just that."
Nathan had put down his coffee cup and was rising slowly to his
feet. "And thank you."

"It is I, sir, who thank you. Always," the President said, stealing
a last look at his morning schedule as he stood. Nathan's internal
clock never failed to astound him. Just as he came to full height,
Kay was knocking on the door.

"MR. PRESIDENT, MAY I have the honor of presenting—"

"Mrs. Bryce Dinsmore needs no introduction in this office, Kay.
She practically raised me."

"I did no such thing, Spencer Lee. You boys lived like wild animals on that farm. You all just raised yourselves."

The small group Waddell Dinsmore had entered with—a half
dozen dowagers and retirees, though none nearly so old and wizened
as she—gasped at the informality.

"Oh, for heaven's sake," she called over her shoulder, "don't be
such a bunch of fuddy-duddies. I've known this handsome young
man all his life. I have no intention of calling him Mr. President.
We must be related somehow. Everyone is."

"Second cousins, I believe it is, Waddell, twice removed. I think
it would be safe for us to marry."

"I'm through with marrying, Spencer. We'll just have to have an
affair."

Behind her, more shuffling, an embarrassed cough. Waddell Dinsmore was in her element. The President was bending to give her a
kiss when he saw Nathan Winston trying to slip through the door
into Kay's office.

"Mr. Vice President, please. A last few moments of your time."

As the President introduced Nathan to Waddell, the Vice President bent deeply at the waist and took her fragile hand in his large
and beefy one, an ambassador already.

"Mrs. Dinsmore, a supreme pleasure. I've long admired the work
of your group. Now perhaps you'd do us the honor of introducing
your committee members."

"Dear God." The President slapped his head. "My manners."

"I told you," Waddell said. "The whole lot of them were raised by wolves." She beamed up at the burly, impeccably tailored black man looming agreeably above her. "Thank God someone in this administration is a gentleman."

Thus the dance of governance.

THEY SAT AT the rosewood table in the alcove on the west side of the office, endorsing proclamations declaring Historic Preservation Week, listening as each of the half dozen committee members described a favorite project—a Natchez mansion rescued from the wrecker's ball, the last of the original pieces uncovered for the restoration of Stonewall Jackson's study at the Virginia Military Institute, funding to combat dry rot along the colonnades at both campuses of the National University. The Vice President was far better at this than his superior: adept at the telling mumble, quick with the small, precise questions that proved his engagement.

Meanwhile, the President's mind wandered to the farm, his youth, to his mother and Waddell, best friends from childhood, sitting on the veranda, rocking. The two of them seemed always to be sitting and rocking, glasses of sweetened iced tea by their sides. At their feet, Alice, not yet out of diapers, played with a set of hardwood blocks that her four older brothers had nearly worn out in their time.

"Ya'all slow down," Spencer could hear his mother yelling. "Someone's going to break something bad."

They always said, "Yes, ma'am," but none of the boys ever seemed to slow at all, and no one ever broke anything worse than a collarbone. Waddell was right: He and his brothers had lived like wild animals; they'd had to raise themselves. Davey and Billy, the two oldest boys, had taught Spencer to jump from the barn loft spread-eagle into a hay pile when he was only five. Banks, just two years older than Spencer and never to see his own nineteenth birthday, made sure his younger brother did his homework and helped him with his chores. Spencer was only six when Alice, the last of the children, was born, but he had had to change her diaper himself more often than not, or else she would have dripped her way from room to room, from hall to porch, a whimper her strongest complaint.

"Mama, Mama," he could hear himself saying, "Alice is real wet."

"Lord, boy, you don't know what wet is. Go tell your daddy."

Which meant a trip to his father's study, which meant in its own way pure terror. The room seemed dark as pitch at midday—heavy curtains were drawn across the windows, and a fog of pipe smoke hung from the ceiling—and it had a sweet smell that Spencer now knew was bourbon but then thought was simply what a father smelled like.

"Daddy?"

"Yes, boy?"

"It's Alice, sir. She needs changing."

"Take her to your mama, boy. I'm waiting for a call."

Finally, it just seemed easier to change her himself.

"Spencer!"

He'd drifted away. Waddell was standing by the south windows, summoning him to her side.

"Don't you do it!" she told him in a fierce whisper when he drew up beside her.

"Do what, Waddell?"

"Don't you let them tear down the remains of that glorious building." She was gesturing with her head toward the old Capitol—its walls shored and buttressed, the roof still bearing the marks of the fire that had nearly reduced the whole structure to ashes one hundred thirty-five years before.

"Waddell—"

"I know you, Spencer. I've known you all your life. You'll say you won't do it; then you'll try to please the greatest number of people you can. And if the greatest number of people want it torn to the ground and carried away, you'll do it. That's why everyone loves you."

"It keeps old wounds alive, Waddell. It divides."

"It unites, Spencer. It doesn't divide. Your grandfather Davis began this nation in that building. *Began* it. And when he was done and the building was beyond ever being used again, your grandfather Lee finished the work that your grandfather Davis had begun."

Kay was signaling him from the alcove. The photographer had

arrived. Spencer glanced at his watch. The press briefing would be starting in fifteen minutes, and he needed ten minutes alone with Sheila Redmond, his press secretary, before it began. He placed a hand on Waddell's back and began to steer her gently toward the group.

"That's not just an old building," she said as they turned away from the window. "That's the heart and soul of Richmond, the heart and soul of this nation. You can't escape family, Spencer. If you're not true to family, you're not true to anything."

They were his great-great-grandfathers, actually, but Spencer Jefferson Lee was willing to forgive his mother's old friend a few generations. He thought, too, that Waddell might finally be slipping. She had forgotten to mention that his great-great-uncle Madison—James Madison's own grandson; we are so close in this country to the beginning of things—had come up with the Great Compromise that had made the whole improbable package of the Confederate States of America work.

REDMOND SLIPPED IN just as the Vice President was leading the preservationists out. A worry crease seemed to cut her brow almost in half.

"Trouble?"

"Always, Mr. President. Interior just sent over the new environmental data. Sulfur dioxide levels at critical in Boston and Cleveland. Soil lead nearing critical from Cleveland through Detroit and into central Michigan. Carbon monoxide beyond acceptable criteria in Hartford, New Haven, and New York. Visibility above Pittsburgh down to less than a quarter of a mile, due to suspended particulates."

Redmond always delivered bad news telegraphically, the President had long noted. When her sentences started to dip and roll along, the tide had turned.

"The territorial press will be asking. The Canadians too."

"And what will we tell them, Miss Redmond?"

"I don't have the least idea, sir."

3

STATE OF VIRGINIA
BISCHOOL COMPLEX NO. 94,
CHARLOTTESVILLE

FROM THE WINDOW of this seventh-story apartment overlooking the high-school complex, the scene below suggested to Joseph a great river running in reverse—the Nile flowing backward out of the Mediterranean, its water dividing and becoming two rivers as each ran back to its separate source in the dark heart of his dark, dark continent.

As the students left their buses, the rivers were commingled, their waters almost indistinguishable: white, black; black, white. Nearing the triangular projection that separated the two campuses, the waters began to separate: white students to the near side, black ones to the far. Precisely at the projection, they parted completely as the white students veered off to their campus and the black students to theirs.

Beside Joseph, Cara's camera clicked, its autodrive whirring. Joseph scanned with his binoculars to find what she was photographing. There, just before the projection, a black boy, a white girl, sixteen, maybe seventeen, their eyes locked on one another, fingertips just grazing as they split apart to their separate schools. Recruits, maybe. Fodder. They'd match the photos to the yearbooks, get the names, make inquiries. Maybe it was only a passing affection, a curiosity. Teenagers were curious. It was their nature to want what they couldn't have. Maybe it was more. If it was more, it was doomed. If it was doomed, it was an opportunity.

The outcome no longer concerned him. He had become honed to living in the present.

Across from Joseph, Randy sat at a Formica kitchen table, working a crossword puzzle. He was tall, rangy, as purely white as Joseph was purely black. Randy's arms stuck out of his T-shirt like thick ropes. A hawkish nose popped from his face just below his eyes.

"Look."

Cara's hand brushed Joseph's shoulder, a touch as soft as rain. She was pointing with the long lens of her camera. Her skin was a creamy mocha, her lips were almost full, her hair—without the wig—formed tight curls against her scalp.

The boy walked into Joseph's view: a little under six feet tall, he guessed; maybe one hundred sixty pounds. He was wearing baggy khakis, low-cut basketball shoes, a gray sweatshirt with NUS—National University of the South—emblazoned on it in large black letters. The boy slouched under the weight of his full backpack. He must have been on one of the last buses, because the river was thinning now. No one walked with him.

Joseph swept his binoculars for twenty-five yards in all directions around the boy. No security. He'd been gone from his homeland eight years, but it still amazed him how even the most prominent people in America came and went on their own. In bleeding and torn Africa, no one who could afford the protection would think of leaving the house without a squadron of armed guards. That was all that kept Africa unconquered, that and its plagues and its iron-willed viruses and germs: No one wanted it.

"Why not just grab him?" Joseph asked.

"No," Cara said. "No. He must come on his own." There was an edge to her voice, somewhere between anger and longing.

"Now," she said suddenly, and Joseph shifted his binoculars. A white student approached from the boy's side. A smile passed between the two, a hand slap. Joseph could just see the white edge of the paper as it passed from palm to palm. The boy quickly folded it and slipped it into his pants pocket. The camera was clicking again, the autodrive whirring beside his ear.

"The number," Cara said. "He's got it."

Across the room, Randy grunted—an "oh" or an "ah."

At the triangle, the white student hurried to catch up with his classmates. The other boy looked after him for a moment, then turned and began climbing the incline to the black high school. In the distance Joseph could hear a first school bell ring. The boy ran to reach the doors before they were shut.

CARA HAD ALREADY broken down her camera and packed the lenses when Joseph turned from the window. Standing at the counter, barefoot, the sleeves of her light cotton jersey pushed up, she was pouring a cup of coffee.

"Do you want one?" she asked. "I can make more."

Joseph shook his head: No.

At the table, Randy filled in the last boxes on his newspaper puzzle, laid the pencil down, and turned to Joseph.

"So the sunny Caribbean didn't agree with you?"

"Section fourteen," Joseph answered. His ebony head seemed huge, round and glossy as a bowling ball. "Subsection C."

"Fourteens" were behavorial washouts, the most common failures of the Patriation Program.

"C?" Randy asked. His voice had the sort of careful modulation that Joseph still tended to associate with colonial clerks.

"Conduct unbecoming a Level Two worker."

Randy simply raised his eyes in question.

"I hit an acclimation officer."

"Ah," Randy said. "Antisocial tendencies."

A soft laugh passed through the apartment.

"I was two months away from Level Three," Joseph said. "I was already on schedule to be shipped to the mainland."

"Do you want to tell us about it?" Cara's voice was softer now, gentle, coaxing.

Joseph walked around behind her, took a glass from over the sink, and filled it with ice and water.

"It happened on Barbados," he began. Leaning against the sink, he drank deeply. "I'd been moved a year earlier out of the cane fields, into the bottling operation at the giant rum distillery that takes up most of the north side of Bridgetown. A record order had come in from the German interior ministry. Shifts were doubled.

"In the second week, I was riding a bus back to the barracks, drowsing in my seat, when an acclimation officer prodded me awake with his nightstick. The bus was full. An elderly lady was standing in the aisle beside my seat. I was about to rise and offer her my seat, when the officer dug his stick deeper into me, just below my rib cage.

"'Don't,' I told him. 'No, there's no need.' I think I grabbed the stick then. With my left hand."

As he told the story, Joseph could feel the nightstick pushing up against his chest. The acclimation officer had one of those thin, triangular heads Joseph associated with Somalia, Ethiopia, the Horn. He had leaned into Joseph's face. There was rum on his breath.

"'No?' he said to me. But it was a threat, not a question. I was going to be demoted, sent back to Level One—I could tell that already. Who knew what else was going to happen."

"And so?" Cara asked, taking Joseph's glass from his hand and filling it again.

Joseph shrugged. "And so I hit him. The punch drove his face into the metal bar behind the seat. I apologized to the woman who was waiting for my seat, of course. She reminded me of an aunt, one of my father's sisters. At the next stop, I left the bus and ran the rest of the way to my barracks. The driver would soon learn what had happened. He would radio ahead. There was very little time.

"I'd managed to hide some money in the bottom of my pallet— odd jobs, some black market business. I took that, went to the docks, and bribed my way onto a freighter that was sailing for Savannah."

"And at Savannah?" It was Randy this time, leaning forward in his chair.

"What was I going to do? I had no papers, and the charges were now more serious than simply striking the officer. If I was caught, I would be repatriated. The freighter docked a little after seven in the morning. I got off and started walking away from the sun, west, through the port, through the city, into the marshes and swamps, where not even dogs would follow me. I think it was two days before I came to dry land. I don't know how long it was after that when I was found."

Again, he stopped, remembered: He had built a little tent of palmetto leaves to shade him from the sun and had simply lain there and waited to be discovered—by whom, by what, he didn't care, finally. He could still feel his cracked lips, his body swollen by mosquito bites.

"I was lucky," Joseph said. "I was passed along." His throat was dry, raspy; he hadn't talked this long in months, maybe years.

"And you?" Joseph asked Randy. "How did you come to be a nonperson? You seem to have been born to higher things."

"Ah." Randy leaned back in his chair, smiled, cupped his hands behind his head, and stretched out his long legs in front of him. "Love. I was done in by love. A fatal combination of idealism, affection, and the pleasures of the flesh. Soon to be cured."

Soon indeed, Joseph thought.

As Randy spoke, a look passed between him and Cara, and as it did, Joseph thought of the song the Christianization matron had taught them on Barbados: "I once was lost, but now am found. I was blind but now I see." I should have noticed it earlier, Joseph told himself: I've fallen out of touch with that too.

"You'll want to be alone," he said now. It was a statement, not a question.

Cara nodded her head, smiled a thanks. She was in her late twenties, maybe thirty, he guessed, a dozen or so years younger than the white man. Age didn't seem to be the issue.

IN THE SMALL bedroom at the back of the apartment, Joseph busied himself packing his valise: a change of clothing, his straight razor and shaving cream, a toothbrush and toothpaste.

He gently pried away the lining at the back and removed a Polaroid photograph of himself, taken the fall before. Behind him was a backdrop of oaks, poplars, chokecherries, beeches, sumacs, all in a riot of reds and oranges, yellows and golds; behind them, a stone outcropping, almost a wall. It was where he had arrived after he was found on the edge of the swamp in South Carolina—where he had first met Cara and first heard of DRAGO. He'd come to love the spot—the breezes that cooled it in summer, the way snow piled up against the cabin door in winter, the colors and smells of the trees and shrubs, even their names. The trees marked the seasons, a concept foreign to his growing up.

Everything ends, he thought; sooner or later, everything ends.

There is no forever. DRAGO had given him a second life. Maybe somewhere a third one waited for him too.

He fished in his pocket for a pen, wrote his name on the back of the photograph and, underneath it, the date he remembered its being taken:

JOSEPH NGUBO
OCTOBER 5, 1999

His last name almost surprised him. It had been so long since he had said it, so long since he had seen it written down.

Now he took an envelope from the bottom of the suitcase, slipped the photograph inside, and wrote another name on the outside and an address in Lagos, Nigeria. From his shirt pocket, he removed a sixty-cent international stamp, licked it, and pressed it onto the envelope. Maybe his mother was still alive, still a government clerk. Maybe she still lived at the address. Maybe—the biggest maybe of all—mail was still delivered and deliverable in Lagos. Too many maybes, but all he could do was try. Before he left, he would ask Cara to mail it.

Cara. He tried not to listen, but from the bedroom at the other end of the apartment he could hear the thin bed rattling, Randy's heavy guttural breathing. There was a long, low roar like building thunder. He could hear Randy—ah, ah, ah—and then Cara began almost to keen: a low animal sound that was half shriek, half cry. And then everything went silent.

"Goddamn," he could hear Randy saying. "Godfuckingdamn!"

Pure chance—short straws—had brought him and Randy together, but he liked him. He'd hold up his end.

There was a knock on his door.

"Fifteen minutes," Cara said.

Joseph snapped the valise shut, slipped the envelope into the breast pocket of his sport coat, and stepped out into the hall.

Randy was dressed now in the costume he had arrived in—blue gabardine pants and jacket, the logo of a plumbing firm prominent across the back of the jacket, a name stitched over the front pocket: Ray.

A toolbox was open on the kitchen counter. Randy unscrewed the top of a can of plumber's caulk, tipped out a small envelope that bulged slightly in the middle, and handed it to Joseph.

"You can't swallow it," Randy explained. "You need to bite down hard."

"I know." Joseph slipped the envelope containing the capsule into the side pocket of his jacket.

Two wallets sat on the counter—black and plain, a cheap leatherette. Cara checked the cards in the first and handed it to Randy; the second she gave to Joseph.

"Quite the likeness," Randy said as he studied the photo on the driver's license. "My doppelgänger." A national work card sat in a plastic sleeve opposite the license. Otherwise, the wallet was filled with stray receipts, business cards, and a photograph of a woman in her late thirties with two children.

"My family!" Randy said, holding the photo up for Cara and Joseph to admire.

Cara smiled. "You always wanted to be a father."

"So I did. So I did. This is all we'll need? Just a photo ID and the work number?"

"For the junior wait staff," Cara said, "that's all. You're not serving the head table."

"And my good friend, my look-alike here—he won't be missing his wallet?"

"No," Cara said. "It's a permanent loan, but guaranteed good for twenty-four hours only. If there's any delay with the dinner or if you can't get inside, destroy the IDs." She could still hear the slight crunch of the bolt cutter, still marveled at how easily it went through flesh and bone. Fingers, she had thought, were more substantial than that.

"How about you?" she asked Joseph. "A good likeness?"

"An improvement, I'd say," he answered. "Time has been kinder to him than to me."

Cara rinsed the glasses and cups, and set them on the drainboard.

"We were fortunate," she said, "after you drew the straws. Fortunate to be able to find two people so physically similar to you both."

"Sometimes," Randy said, "God looks after the fools." He closed his toolbox and put on a baseball-style cap—also emblazoned with the logo of the plumbing firm. At the apartment door, he stopped with his hand on the knob.

"You're sure this will work?" he asked Cara.

"He'll call, baby. I know he'll call. He's got the number now. All he needs is a push. And once he calls, I have him."

"And you're sure this is worth it?"

"We've been over this. New times, baby. New challenges. We drew. It could have been any of us. Nothing stays the same," she answered.

"Not even you."

Cara smiled again and blew Randy a kiss as he tipped his cap to her.

"I'll see you, then," he said, "in heaven or in hell."

Randy turned now to Joseph: "You I'll see sooner. Four o'clock, on the west steps of the old Capitol. We'll walk from there."

Joseph nodded. "You know the way?"

"To the Hotel Richmond?" Randy laughed as he pulled the door open. "I had my sixteenth-birthday party there—fifty of my nearest and dearest. My grandfather owned a one-third interest in the hotel. We'll find it."

"You okay with this?" Cara asked Joseph as the door closed behind Randy.

Joseph shrugged. "We drew." There was nothing more to say.

CARA HAD DARKENED her skin with powder; her wig, medium length this time, was a jumble of loose curls. As she and Joseph stepped out into the hall, she took his arm—he carried his valise in the other—and they made for the elevator.

Out in the sunlight, they could see Randy standing by his plumbing van at the far end of the parking lot, deep in conversation with an electrician. Joseph stowed his valise in the back of a battered sedan and slipped behind the steering wheel. When the engine caught, he cranked his window down.

"What about you?" he asked Cara. "Were you done in by love too?"

She rested a hand on his forearm.

"You've seen my real skin, honey," she said with a soft laugh. "I was done in by someone else's love long ago. This is the Confederacy, sweetheart—we like everyone to come in one of two colors only."

Joseph took a pair of sunglasses from the dashboard and was

putting them on as Cara, still grinning, turned and walked back into the apartment building.

Not exactly an answer, Joseph thought, as he pulled out into traffic. He had already cleared town when he realized that he had forgotten to give Cara the letter to mail. He'd have to take care of it himself when he got to Richmond.

4

THE NATIONAL UNIVERSITY
OF THE SOUTH

LUCINDA WINSTON WAS at work in her study in Pavilion Three when she heard the front door open and close downstairs. John Henry, she thought, and looked at her watch. It was a little past noon—a half day at his high school. After more than two decades on the university faculty, Lucinda couldn't imagine facing such streams of students every day, class after class, twenty-five and more at a time. Unsmiling faces, if John Henry was any guide. Angry faces.

Lucinda felt a shudder begin deep inside her and work its way to her shoulders, her neck. At the same time, a pain shot through her head from back to front, before settling just behind her right eye. She let her reading glasses dangle on their gold chain and softly massaged her temples with the tips of her fingers. Slowly, the pain retreated, back the way it had arrived. Lucinda breathed deeply, in and out, in and out, her eyes closed, her mind drifting over nothing. And slowly, too, the shudders subsided.

Yesterday's argument about the Patriation Program had been one of the worst. Lucinda had almost shouted at John Henry, just as she had let her voice rise this morning when she was telling Nathan about the argument. I've come to a pretty pass, she thought, when my own son can so upset me.

Lucinda heard the radio come on in the kitchen: African chants— what John Henry called "nativist" music—with almost no regard to history. Next, she heard him open the refrigerator door—she had put the remains of the apple pie on the top shelf so he would be sure to see it. Now she heard the scrape of a chair. He would have a book out of his satchel already, or some new magazine he had picked up at one of the shops along University Avenue on his way home. She could see him hunched over the kitchen table, intent as always, absently guiding bites of pie and the glass of milk to his mouth as he read. Who would it be this time? she wondered. What radical theorist of the week, what disappointed tenure seeker, what bomb thrower from the former European nations would John Henry be quoting today? He had gotten all her academic genes. And none of his father's graces.

Lucinda turned in her chair to look down into the garden at the back of the pavilion, bounded by serpentine brick walls. With April more than half completed, the boxwoods that lined the central path were capped by the soft green of new growth. Behind the small fountain and flanked by matching stone benches, a bed of late-blooming daffodils had only recently begun to droop, as had the tulips in the side beds. In compensation, the azaleas that ran along both side walls were just coming alive with color, the spreading dogwood beyond the back wall had broken into a splendid pink, and the lilacs clustered midway along the south wall of the garden were in full glory. Lucinda had moved into this pavilion more than two decades earlier, when she married Nathan Winston—he had just become provost, at age forty-four, and she was a very junior faculty member. In all the years since, she had never failed to marvel at the sheer beauty of it.

Her one o'clock tutorial was with a Cuban doctoral candidate. She checked the title of his dissertation in her day planner: "Caribbean Neo-Colonialism Since the Inclusion Acts." All figures, all data. The technocrats were invading the social sciences, sweeping over the wall with their charts and graphs and matrices. Still, he meant well. She would urge him to step back from the numbers, to search for a context to consider them in. Perhaps he would listen; perhaps he wouldn't. All she could do was try.

Listening to the slight growl of her stomach, Lucinda realized that she hadn't eaten since dinner the night before. Ever since John Henry had been a little boy, she had had juice and cereal with him in the mornings as he was leaving for school, but they had breakfast together less and less of late. Today he had come downstairs with only seconds to spare, grabbed an apple from the bowl on the kitchen table, and barely said good morning as he raced out the door for his school bus. By the time Lucy was up and ready for her usual coffee and toast, Lucinda had already gotten started on the stack of thesis proposals waiting for her commentary. A slice of pie, Lucinda thought, wouldn't be the worst sin. She could put off lunch until after the tutorial, or skip it altogether.

Lucinda saved the file she was working on and put her laptop to sleep. At the top of the stairs, she thought: John Henry is my son. You don't avoid a son; you talk things out with him. Lucinda took another deep breath, closed her eyes, and let it out as slowly as she could. Then she started down.

John Henry was nowhere to be seen when she got to the kitchen. Lucinda turned off the radio—tribal rhythms held no charms for her. Then she put tea water in the microwave and cut herself a piece of the pie, larger than she had intended. When the water was heated, she dropped in a bag of lemon-and-cinnamon-scented English tea and carried pie and cup into the living room.

He was seated in the needlepoint wing chair by the front windows, still in his NUS sweatshirt. One foot was on the floor; the other leg was thrown over the arm of the chair. Lucinda thought about correcting him—it had been her mother's favorite chair, and his posture was already terrible. If it had been Lucy, her firstborn, she wouldn't have hesitated. But Lucy never would sit like that. Lucy understood the importance of gesture, of appearance; decorum came naturally to her.

"Yours?" John Henry asked, looking up as his mother settled opposite him on a Victorian settee. He was holding a manuscript in his hand. Lucinda had left it on the hall table to remind herself that it needed photocopying before she mailed it.

"It is. How was school, John Henry?"

"Half as long as usual."

Lucinda hoped he would lose his tart tongue before he enrolled in the university next fall, but she doubted it. More and more of the undergraduates she met were like him. Language had been courtly, a waltz, when she was their age.

"Who's it for?" He was scanning the last page as he talked.

"The Journal of History and Ethnography." Lucinda had chaired the

review panel for the journal the previous year and still sat on the committee. Publication was set for the fall issue.

"It's very well written."

"Thank you." Lucinda was flattered. John Henry was frugal in all aspects of his personality, but he was never more frugal than with compliments. Lucinda eased back into the settee and felt the tension running out of her shoulders.

"About yesterday, John Henry. I apologize for raising my voice. I think we both—"

"It's also very wrong."

"Wrong?"

"Your article."

John Henry was paging backward now through the stack of papers.

" 'In the great American experiment that emerged from the War of Dissolution, politeness became more than a social lubricant. It became the guarantor of racial harmony.' "

He paged again until he found another passage.

" 'But it is not the principles of confederation, finally, that have allowed this relatively new nation to prosper. It is not any economic construct, though such constructs have served the nation well. It is not the engines of war, though they have assured a peace rarely broken in well more than a century. It is just this: civility, attention to the rules of social behavior. It is civility that bridges the races, civility that allows each to communicate with the other, civility that allows each to prosper equally and each to maintain its own identity.'

"How can you write such things, Mother?"

"I can write them because they are true, John Henry. I can write them—"

"It's not 'civility' that makes everything work, Mother. What you call civility, what you think of as politeness, is just the way we adjust to the fact that we're all expected to be comatose."

"John Henry—"

"We set up a Patriation Program, and we tell ourselves that it's just to make sure that the people who go through it will know how to be Americans by the time they become citizens, and then we close our eyes to the fact that they're made to work in awful conditions, that they're little more than slaves."

"We were over this yesterday, John Henry. Over it and over it."

"We spend an unbelievable amount of money on the waterway project and tell ourselves that it will allow us to grow crops year round and protect our economic leadership around the world. And then we close our eyes to the fact that that unbelievable amount of money has to come from somewhere—and that someone has to do without it so that the waterway people, and the farmers and ranchers who want the water, and the construction companies who won the contracts to build it, can have the money."

"Nothing is free. If it's capitalism you object to—"

"Of course nothing is free, Mother. But why don't we ever ask who has to pay? You don't have to be a raving socialist to ask that."

"And I suppose you know?" Lucinda could feel her headache coming back. She leaned forward and set her pie plate on the small inlaid chest beside the settee, another piece from her mother's family.

"Know?"

"Yes, I suppose you know who pays. I suppose you know what it's like to be in the Patriation Program, what it's like to come from someplace where there is no hope, what it's like to wake up one morning and find that you have what you never thought you'd have: a future. You know all that? You've done that? You've been there?"

"You know the answer to that. Of course I haven't. But I read. I try to find out. I try to learn. I don't intend to go through my whole life denying that there's a price for this supposed paradise we live in. It's not the fact that we're a civil nation that allows us to prosper. It's the fact that we're a nation of sleepwalkers."

Lucinda was holding her cup in both hands now, sipping at the tea as it cooled.

"And which one is that?" she said.

"Which one?"

"Which one of your radicals are you quoting today, John Henry? Which one is the expert on sleepwalking? That's what I was asking."

"Why does it have to be someone else all the time? Why can't it just be me I'm quoting? Why can't you ever believe that I have ideas?" John Henry searched his memory as he defended himself, afraid that his mother had been right. Sometimes he worried that he had no ideas of his own, that he was borrowing life from the books and magazines he read.

"I didn't mean it that way, dear—"

"Look out the window, Mother." John Henry was drawing the thin linen curtain back with his hand. "What do you see?"

"You know what I see. We've been over this before too. We've been over everything before."

"No, look! Really look! What do you see, Mother? I want you to tell me."

She set the tea down beside her pie plate on the small chest and leaned forward. From her pavilion halfway down the West Lawn, Lucinda could see the uneven spacing of the similar structures on the east side. Both sides had been designed so that their pavilions would appear equidistant from one another when viewed from the perspective of the great rotunda at the north end. Between the two sets of colonnades, the Lawn spilled terrace by terrace to the south, toward the cluster of academic buildings at its far end.

"I see, John Henry, a campus designed by one of the greatest minds Western civilization has ever produced."

"You don't, Mother! You see a campus *copied* after the one Thomas Jefferson designed. Jefferson's campus is a quarter of a mile that way." He was pointing east, across the sunken highway that split the university in two.

"I see a campus training the best young minds in the country to answer the highest callings—"

"Dammit, Mother—"

"I won't have that, John Henry. You know that."

"I'm sorry, but look at those students, Mother. Look at them. Do you notice anything about them?"

They were passing by the window now in twos and threes, headed from classes to the library, fraternity houses, dormitories—for lunch, to study, maybe for nothing in particular. Lucinda had been among them thirty years earlier, and Nathan more than forty years earlier. She could see herself passing by this very window—her plaid skirt held together by an oversized brass safety pin, a soft cashmere sweater thrown around her shoulders. Everybody seemed to know everybody else then. The university was smaller; cohesion came more easily.

"Yes, I notice something about them. They're young and bright, just like you, John Henry. They question, just as you do. They're—"

"How else are they like me, Mother? How else? Why can't you say it?"

"All right. I will if you need to hear it. The students that are passing by our window are black and they're brown. Just like you. Just like me. Just like your father and your sister. They're Negroes, John Henry. This is the Negro campus. That is the white campus." She gestured with her head to the original campus, to the east, the one that had been known as the University of Virginia before the Great Compromise was reached. "Is that what you wanted to hear?"

John Henry looked less triumphant than pained—his face mirroring the pinch in his mother's voice.

"Are you satisfied now? Have I been honest with you?"

"Mother—"

"No, I've heard enough of your polemics." Her voice was rising, heightening in pitch as she tried to rein it in. "I've heard enough. Sit up. Get both feet on the floor, John Henry. You're going to listen to me now."

He dropped the curtain, shifting the room to a softer light.

"You look out on this campus where you have lived your whole life, and you see a symbol of the failure of our society. I know that. I even understand why you do. I was seventeen once. But I look out on this same campus—and I've lived here for nearly my whole life too, it seems—and I see a symbol of our society's success. I see a university where black and brown people have exposure to the best minds of their race, just as the white students on the East Campus have exposure to the best minds of their race. I see a university where we—Negroes and Caucasians together—have disproved the horrible myths of racial inferiority that bedevil every other society in the world.

"Do you think that the students who are walking out there are less able than the white students at this university?"

"Of course not."

"Do you think the men and women who teach them are less able than their white colleagues? Do you think that the person who is teaching my classes over there is more intelligent than I am? Better able to communicate with his students? Do you think they have better equipment than we do—finer labs, more advanced computing systems?"

"You know I don't, Mother."

"You asked me what I see when I look out that window, and I'll

tell you what I see every time I open the door of this pavilion. I see
the most perfect example of biequality the world has ever achieved.
I see a nation where your father, John Henry, your *father* can be
Vice President. I see a nation so structured that every black man and
black woman has as good a chance of becoming a lawyer, a doctor,
a judge, a scientist—or, yes, a bum—as every white man and every
white woman. I see the only nation on earth, John Henry, where
two races have learned to live together in complete harmony, complete civility, complete opportunity. I see the only nation on earth
where black people and white people rise or fall on their own merits,
the exercise of their own responsibility—not the color of their skin.
Do you have any idea how rare that is, John Henry? Do you have
any idea how rare it is for two races to even tolerate each other,
much less exist side by side as coequals?"

Lucinda had exhausted herself. She laid her head on the back of
the settee and closed her eyes. John Henry was sitting upright in his
chair, his feet on the floor, the manuscript on his lap.

"There is a price, I grant, for this," she said without opening her
eyes. "Our equality is a separate equality. As you're well aware, we
are trying an experiment in coordination in the history department—
over my objection, I should add."

"It's a budget move, Mother. A controlled experiment. Lucy and
Jason Lee and eight other perfect students. It's got almost nothing
to do with the real world."

"I'm still talking." She was sitting forward again. "There is a
price, as I said, but what is purchased for it is beyond value. I look
out that window, John Henry, and I see the most perfectly balanced
society the world has ever achieved. I see a world held together by
a common civility, a common respect. That is what I was trying to
get at in that little article of mine."

Again, she laid her head back. It was a quarter to one. She would
have to leave for her tutorial in ten minutes.

"Are you through?"

Lucinda nodded her head.

"You love Dad, don't you?"

"Of course I do, John Henry. You know that perfectly well, although I don't see what this can possibly have to do—"

"What if he were white?"

"What?"

"Dad ... what if he were exactly the same person, the same in every regard, except that his skin was white?"

"John Henry, if all this is about some infatuation you have with a white girl, I assure you that you'll get over it."

"Why won't you ever take me seriously? I'm not talking about me. I'm talking about you and Dad. What if he were white? Would you still love him? Would you still want to live with him?"

"I'm not going to answer that. Your theorists can deal in absurd hypotheticals if they want to, but I'm afraid they don't interest me. Your father is what he is, and I'm what I am—for all the world to see. Besides, I have a tutorial to get to."

Lucinda took a last sip of her tea and used her fork to gather up the final crumbs of pie.

"Or Lucy?"

"What?" Lucinda stopped the fork halfway to her mouth and put it back on the plate.

"What if Lucy were to fall in love with a white man?"

"No."

"What if she were to have a baby by a white man?"

"John Henry!"

"Would we all just sleepwalk our way through that one too? Would we just close our eyes when they came to get her and her baby? Would we just stand at the train station and wave while they were shipped off to the territories? Because there's not a lot of choice, Mother, not a lot of choice if we're going to keep the races distinct."

"No!"

"Would we just shake our heads and say, 'Well, that's the price we pay for this beautifully civil world we live in. Bye-bye, Lucy. Bye-bye, little baby.' Is that what we'd do?"

"I won't have this!"

John Henry felt as if he'd been pushed back in his chair. He'd never heard his mother so loud.

"Do you hear me? I won't have this! You can take that some-where else. Somewhere else entirely, young man. This is my house, John Henry. This is my house and your father's house, and as long as you intend to live here with us, you will not talk like that again! Do you understand? Do you understand! Goddammit, do you un-derstand?"

Lucinda felt as if something had detonated randomly inside her skull—pressure seemed to be building against it, from all directions.

"I'm sorry, Mother. I don't mean to get you so angry, but when I look out that window, I see the most complete segregation the world has ever known."

IN THEIR MUTUAL silence, John Henry and Lucinda heard the front door opening. Lucy burst into the room, a high flush on her cheek.

"Well, who died in here?" There was nervous laughter in her voice. She was used to the tension John Henry brought to every conversation with their mother. Her role in life, Lucy sometimes thought, was to mediate it.

"How was the coordinate class, dear?"

"Oh, wonderful, Mommy. Absolutely wonderful."

She wore an ecru linen blazer over a white oxford cloth shirt that seemed to deepen the dense chocolate of her skin. Her black hair, long and wavy, fell to her shoulders. John Henry, Lucinda thought, could be just as handsome as Lucy is beautiful if only he would make some effort.

"Scrabble, Germ?" Lucy said to her brother. "I've got about half an hour." The two of them had been playing a nonstop, self-renewing version of the old board spelling game for almost ten years. John Henry had been narrowing the scoring gap steadily over the last three years.

"Not today." He was unable to scowl at his sister. "I've got a paper due tomorrow. 'Mitosis in the—' "

" 'Robertson fruit fly.' Is he still assigning that thing?"

"The sun couldn't set if he didn't." John Henry rose and handed his mother her manuscript just as she was standing up from the settee.

"I'll take these out to the kitchen," he said, picking up her plate and teacup.

"Thank you, dear." Lucinda tried to bring herself to look at him, tried to force herself to smile, and found to her sorrow that she could do neither. "That's very thoughtful of you."

Lucinda stopped at the hall closet for her Burberry raincoat. Her briefcase and day planner were waiting at the base of the stairs.

"Will you need the car, Lucy? It's got very little gas in it."

"Oh, no. I'm meeting Jason at the graduate library—the East Campus." Standing in the arched entrance to the living room, Lucy could see her mother's shoulders freeze.

"Lucy, I don't think that's a very good—"

"It's Dr. Cuthbert's idea, Mommy, not mine. He's paired off the coordinate class into five teams. Jason and I are going to do a presentation on transmigration in the Pacific Northwest."

"And Dr. Cuthbert has . . . prepared for this?"

"He's made arrangements for the teams at the library. We'll be able to use the stacks, and a space has been set aside for us to work in."

"Well, then." Lucinda let out a long breath before giving her daughter a kiss on the cheek and hurrying toward the door. "I'll be late. Please be sure to give Jason my very best."

Lucinda had just shut the front door when it popped back open again.

"Lucy, John Henry," she called inside. "I forgot to tell you. Your father's office called. He'll be spending the night here. We'll eat late. And John Henry, it will be a pleasant meal. There will be no arguing." In spite of herself, Lucinda could feel her voice rising. "Your father gets more than his share of that in Richmond."

In the kitchen, John Henry had just placed his mother's cup and plate in the dishwasher. As she spoke, he fingered the scrap of paper in his pants pocket. He had already memorized the phone number written on it.

"You and Jason Lee?" he said as Lucy stuck her head into the kitchen. A rare grin played across his face. "The Dream Team?"

Lucy smiled. "Or Overachievers Anonymous. We'll find out. You and Mom were at it again, weren't you?"

"Tooth and nail."

"You're wearing her out. You don't realize how much these things hurt her. Her eyes were swollen this morning when I went up to say goodbye. I think she'd been crying."

"But it's not just me! She—"

"You've got to give her a break. Just a break, Germ. That's all."

Lucy winked and turned for the stairs.

"I don't know if I can, Luce," John Henry said to the spot where his sister had been. "Some days, I feel like I'm going to explode."

5

ROUTE 2,
MASSACHUSETTS TERRITORY

"DANIEL, WHAT IS this?"

Daniel Brewster felt a hand on his arm, a slight push. Beneath him he could feel the bus struggling up an incline, rattling as it labored. He opened his eyes and looked out the window, and he knew exactly where he was.

"It's a river, Jorge." Daniel had to struggle to put a trace of Flemish into his voice. Just awakened, he had to fight to remember who he was and what had brought him to this spot.

"Not an aqueduct?"

"It's a river without banks. It runs through a concrete culvert so they can control its flow."

"They?"

"The water engineers. That's all I know. Maybe we'll learn more."

"Yes, maybe," Jorge said. He stole a sidelong glance at the man seated just behind the driver. A three-ring binder with what looked like typed notes lay open on his lap. The information officer was in his mid-forties, brownish blond and square-jawed.

Jorge was leaning forward now, eyeing something above the bus. Daniel didn't have to bend over to know what his seatmate was looking at.

"High-voltage wires." As a child, Daniel had imagined he could see the current running along those wires. At night, he used to lie in his bed and think he could see the wires glowing.

Daniel talked more slowly now, more carefully. Jorge had owned a small orange grove near Valencia before Greater Germany nation-alized the citrus holdings across the entire Iberian peninsula. In New York, in the first phase of the Patriation Program, he had worked on the docks, unloading raw materials for the factories that filled the shores of the Hudson River in an almost unbroken line to well above Poughkeepsie. Daniel had no idea what Jorge might know about nuclear power.

"This river . . . ," he said. "I'm told there are power plants along it all the way north to Canada. Nuclear reactors."

"Ah."

From the top of the arched bridge that spanned the culvert, Daniel watched the Connecticut River run south into what seemed an im-penetrable wall of smoke, tinged at its edges with sulfurous yellow. Beyond that, he knew, lay the smokestacks of Deerfield, Northamp-ton, Holyoke, Chicopee, Springfield, Hartford, finally New Haven. He thought of it as he always did, as a landscape painted with the devil's palette—ash gray, the sulfurous yellow, charcoal. When I go to hell, he thought, I'll have an advantage: I'll have been there al-ready.

"This is so different from Valencia, so different," Jorge said. "Is it so different from Antwerp?"

Daniel patted his seatmate on his arm and smiled at him. "It's like another world," he said. Not that he'd ever been to Antwerp. Not that he really had the least idea how it looked—all his stories, all his memories of life in the Old World, were his mother's, and she had fled Europe sixty years before.

DANIEL BREWSTER HAD grown up breathing the redolences of the smokestacks they were looking at. As a college student, he had helped to stoke their furnaces. At day's end, exhausted and needing to study, he had returned to his parents' house down streets so filled with industrial dust that his shoes left footprints as he walked. This was his home, Daniel wanted to tell his new friend, and as fright-ening as it might look, there were places far worse, and not all that far away.

At Buffalo, below the tamed and harnessed Niagara Falls, the sky was blackened for miles by high-voltage lines; to drive underneath the grid at high noon was like experiencing a total eclipse of the sun.

And Buffalo was only one of many wonders of this Northeast Industrial Zone. In southern Pennsylvania Territory, Daniel had once seen the Susquehanna River turn green, red, yellow, and brown all in a single afternoon, just before the waters were captured and purged of their effluents and sent, sparkling blue, to join the Chesapeake Bay and beyond. At Pittsburgh, the Allegheny and Monongahela rivers crashed into the Ohio beneath an industrial din that could be heard on a still day as far west as Wheeling and Steubenville, a din so loud that the noise seemed to climb inside you and shake your organs.

Daniel was only a decade older than Jorge, and in all likelihood he would never see him after this trip. Still, he felt protective, almost fatherly. There was so much he could tell him, but as the bus crept down the far side of the bridge—its brakes squealing, the transmission laboring dangerously—he said nothing at all. There are sins of omission and sins of commission, Daniel thought to himself; someone in my line of work has to know which ones are worse.

LIKE HIS FATHER and his grandfather and all his ancestors in a seamless procession that ran straight back to the eighteenth century, Daniel Brewster was a Congregational minister. The church had grown up in colonial New England, and it had prospered in the years after independence as the industrial revolution set up shop along the roaring rivers and streams of the Upper Northeast. Then came the war—Congregationalists had been in the forefront of the abolitionist movement—and like New England, like the whole Northeast, the church had been virtually stamped out of existence.

Daniel's grandfather and father had both tried to keep alive a parish church of sorts in Springfield, but in the end, it was only nostalgia. Few people came on Sundays; fewer still sought pastoral care. Congregationalism's reputation lingered: It was suspect—half denomination, half cult. The new citizens who filled the territories had come to fit into America, not stand out in it. Finally, on the advice of one of his teachers at the seminary, Daniel had simplified his ministry. He'd sold the church building and kept the parish house—his grandmother's money had bought both—and he'd become a circuit rider, a spiritual counselor to those for whom church membership was not a practical option.

Six weeks before, Daniel had been making one of his regular circuit stops—a group house on the south side of North Adams, in the Upper Berkshire Valley—when a woman named Cara took him to the basement and showed him documents being made: documents that could reinstate a worker who had washed out of the Patriation Program, documents that could create a history that might lead to citizenship, documents that could make paperless people exist, at least temporarily.

"We want to thank you for caring about the people who live here," Cara had said. "We want to thank you for helping us. What document would you like?"

Brewster had thought only a few minutes before asking for one that would identify him as a Level Two Patriation worker—halfway up the ladder to citizenship. He asked that it be made up in the name of Daniel Arny—his mother's maiden name. Then he reported to Boston, where a month-long orientation session for Level Two workers was just getting under way. If he was going to bring his ministry closer to the Patriation workers, Daniel believed, he had to know what they went through. He had to walk in their shoes. The orientation program was far from hard labor, but it was a start. Every journey had to begin somewhere.

IN BOSTON, DANIEL had been paired up by chance with Jorge, and the two of them had been assigned, along with four others, to a dormitory room—three sets of bunk beds, ten rooms to the hall, a group toilet at the end of it. Daniel had been surprised to find that the roof of his dormitory room leaked at the corner; he'd been surprised, too, that half of the eight toilets the sixty men on the floor shared couldn't be flushed. The Patriation Program was stern, he knew, but he hadn't thought it was seedy. The other men in his room, though, barely blinked at the conditions. When it rained, they pushed the bunk bed from the wet corner into the center of the room. When it was dry, they pushed the bed back into the corner. In the bathroom, the men simply waited to use the toilets that worked. By the standards of what they had just been through, they said, this was paradise.

As Level One workers—the stage from which they were now hoping to move on—the men had put in twelve-hour shifts on the

docks of Boston, New York, Philadelphia; in the red-hot steel mills
and sheet-metal factories of Allentown, Pittsburgh, Cleveland; in the
chemical-processing plants of Trenton and the Susquehanna Valley
and Akron. As payment for their labor, they said—in the soft whispers they used to talk about such things at night—they had been
fed, though only enough to keep their strength up for work; sheltered, though only enough to keep them from falling ill; tended to,
though only when necessity demanded.

"The man who supervised us on the docks in New York called
it 'tough love,' " Jorge explained one night as they lay in their beds.
Softer love was earned. Brewster took the bottom bunk. His paunch
made it hard for him to climb into the top one, and a quarter century
of cigarettes left him winded when he tried.

As Level Two workers, they would serve ten-hour shifts, the men
had been told. The plates would be heaped higher at mealtime, the
beds be less lumpy. Level Two workers had ceiling fans in their
dormitories. Level Threes had air-conditioning and, if they agreed
to a Christian marriage, conjugal visits. The Christianization matron
would tell them more about that later. Beyond Level Three, the wide
world was waiting: citizenship, inclusion, a new existence. Life
moved by stages in the Confederate States of America. Conform and
you progress, the men were told time and again; rebel and you egress.
The choice was simple: Here in the C.S.A., you made your own
destiny.

"Soon," Jorge said, "everything will be better. Even the love."

To ENTER THE Patriation Program was the essence of simplicity.
You arrived at your point of debarkation—Boston for those coming
from Europe; Kingston, Jamaica, and the Caribbean Corporation for
Africans; Seattle and the Pacific Northwest for those out of ruined
Asia—and had your name entered on the Patriation Registry. From
there, you were asked to submit your blood to the registry nurses to
assure that you did not harbor epidemic or potentially fatal diseases
and that you were at least seventy-seven percent racially pure—
seventy-seven percent having been determined to be the exact per-
centage beneath which recessive genes could play havoc with racial
typing. ("I gave them my blood," Jorge had told Daniel with a smile.
"It was all I had left to give, Daniel! The Germans had taken every-

thing else.") Next, you surrendered what personal history you could to the Patriation interviewers. "Could" or "would"—the difference was not great; history lay before you in the Confederate States of America, not behind. And that was it. Ahead lay work, mountains of it.

To graduate from Patriation was almost as easy. You simply had to prove that you were ready for citizenship in the Confederate States of America—that you had learned its civics, its history, its theology. The work you had done in the program, what you had endured to get to this point, proved everything else about you.

In between entry and exit—in between wanting and becoming—lay this midstream orientation program, a tour through the stations of the American cross. And it was this that fascinated Daniel Brewster. Little by little, Jorge and his coworkers were taught to shed whatever coarseness and eccentricities of behavior they might have brought with them from their place of origin. Little by little they learned to stand when a lady entered the room, to say "please" and "thank you" and say them in English. Little by little they were purged of whatever bizarre religious beliefs they had brought with them, whatever antediluvian attitudes they might have had about the Negroid and Caucasian races.

They learned, too, in this critical tour through the stations, to worship not just any god but the American God; to speak not just any English but American English, filled with the rich vernacular of a growing land. Most important, they learned that biequality was full equality and that biequality meant just that—two peoples living in equal opportunity side by side. Side by side. As one, but not one.

They learned all this because they wanted to learn it. They learned because, like Jorge, they had no choice, no place to return to. It had been fifty years since Greater Germany swept from the Baltic to the Mediterranean, from the Atlantic to the Urals, and each year seemed to bring some new repression, some larger desperation. Africa was simply gone, unviable, perhaps irredeemably so. Since the mid-1930s, the rivers of Asia had run more with blood, it seemed, than with water. Only America had escaped untrammeled the century of warfare—America and its precious little protectorate England. The workers learned the stations of the American cross because they led away from where they had been, what they had been and known.

They learned them in order that they could become citizens and send for their children, so their spouses could begin the same long journey. Or they failed to learn them, and really, it didn't matter. Washouts were not uncommon; there were always five people waiting to take every failure's place.

Brewster had been almost asleep one night when a terrible fight broke out in the hallway between one of their roommates, a Serbian in his mid-thirties with an angry scar across his cheek, and one of the few blacks in their orientation group, a Sudanese who had been raised by a Franco-German couple. Racial epithets were shouted— awful words that left the other men cowering in their beds. By the time Daniel opened the door to peer out, maybe five minutes after the fight had begun, blood splattered the walls. The Serbian was sent back the next morning, put on a freighter to be off-loaded somewhere on the Adriatic coast. Maybe he would stay on board; maybe he would jump. The choice was his. The Sudanese had simply disappeared. That, too, happened. America was a very big place.

AT THE BOTTOM of the bridge, the bus turned right into a parking lot that overlooked the river. As it drew to a stop, the information officer rose and unsnapped the microphone from its holder above him.

"Gentlemen," he began, "please take a moment and have a look at the power lines running above us."

The men craned their heads in absolute silence.

"Those wires, gentlemen, are part of the greatest electrical power network the world has ever known."

The power, he said, ran the factories of the Northeast Industrial Zone, and the NIZ was part of the Economic Triangle of America. The factories here turned out the tractors and combines that tilled and planted the soil from Maryland and Virginia, south through Florida and Old Dixie, and west to the Pacific and the far reaches of Mexico—and reaped its harvests when the growing season was done, which these days was never. Two-thirds of the world's wheat was produced in fields worked by machinery turned out here. Nearly half of its produce, a third of its corn. The figures went on. America feeds the world.

"Now that you've looked up, gentlemen, have a look down," the information officer continued. "What you're seeing is not just a river but a miracle of engineering."

The river, he explained, had been culverted as part of the InterAmerican Waterway project, and now that the project was complete, water could be sent anywhere. One engineer sitting at a computer screen in central Nebraska could enter the commands that would send the flow of the Penobscot River in Maine Territory southwest through canals and tunnels into the Kennebec and from the Kennebec into the Merrimack, and those waters southwest and west through more canals and tunnels into this river, the Connecticut, and from the Connecticut to the Hudson, the Susquehanna, the Ohio, the Mississippi, the Arkansas—onward and onward until what began as rainfall in the scarred pine stands of far New England came rushing out onto the vast irrigated vegetable fields of Texas and New Mexico. Snowfall in the American Rockies watered grazing land in Sonora, Chihuahua, and Durango provinces of Mexico Territory. Rainfall in Yucatán and Quintana Roo was channeled across the peninsula to the year-round wheat fields of Campeche. In a pinch— poor snowfall, drought, the odd caprices of El Niño, disruptions of the jet stream, "unforeseen circumstances"—water could even be carried over the Rockies now. East meets west. West meets east.

" 'Now that the Waterway is done,' " the information officer read aloud from his notebook, " 'the Continental Divide does not necessarily divide anything.' " He laughed as he said it and paused to let the men on the bus know it was a joke. Daniel guessed that the reference was lost on nearly all of them—continental what?—but they laughed in response. Politeness, after all, was a station of the cross they had mastered, and to get here, they had done it well.

The waterway, the officer said, was the second corner of the American Economic Triangle: America feeds the world. The world pays to be fed.

"And the third part of the triangle?" he asked, still smiling. "Gentlemen, the third part of the triangle is you!"

Nearly half the world's sugar was processed by Patriation workers in the Caribbean Corporation; almost a third of the paper the world printed its books and newspapers on came out of mills manned by Patriation workers in the far Northwest. The information officer's voice was swelling with pride now. Soon, he said, America and its interests—its associates, its protectorates, its wholly owned subsidiaries—would stretch from the Bering Strait more than five thousand miles south to the Guatemalan border, just as on the East Coast it now stretched thirty-five hundred miles from the crown of Maine Territory to the southern tip of the Lesser Antilles. And every one of those associates, every one of those protectorates, every one of those wholly owned subsidiaries, would make use of the Patriation Program.

"America feeds the world its food, its trees, its greenery," the information officer said. "The world feeds America its workers, and the best of those workers—the best!—become Americans. Our job, gentlemen, is to make sure you are among those workers."

There was a trace of something to his voice. Czech, Hungarian . . . Daniel couldn't tell.

"Daniel," Jorge said as the information officer sat down and the bus started up again, "have you ever smelled an orange grove in bloom? Have you ever walked through the trees at sunrise when there's dew on the blossoms? Walked through and just smelled it all?"

"No," Daniel said. "I've never even seen an orange tree."

"It's the sweetest smell there is. Someday, you can walk through my orange grove and smell the blossoms. Right here in America."

AT THE END of the parking lot, the bus turned right and continued due west. Half of this group of Patriation workers was headed out to the textile mills, the piecing shops, and the specialty manufacturers of the Berkshire Valley. The other half, Jorge among them, was going on to a huge sheet-metal factory in Albany. Daniel planned simply to walk away in North Adams, where he'd left his car.

He was dreaming of orange blossoms, forests of them, when he was awakened by a high-pitched sound. He, Jorge, and most of the passengers had been dozing. Now the Christianization matron who had been riding on one of the rear seats was standing in front of them. She blew once again on her pitch pipe to wake the men. Her generous proportions and blue-rinsed permed hair reminded Daniel of a widowed neighbor who had come to Thanksgiving dinners when he was young. Every time she hugged him, Daniel was afraid he would suffocate in her bosom.

The matron blew a third time on her pitch pipe, drew her vast breasts up so that the "C.S.A." embroidered on her pocket seemed to leap forward, and began to sing as she half walked, half marched toward the rear of the bus: "Rock of ages cleft for me . . ."

The workers joined in immediately, their voices a babel of accented English:

> *Let me hide myself in Thee.*
> *Let the water and the blood*
> *From Thy wounded side which flowed*
> *Be of sin the double cure,*
> *Save from wrath and make me pure.*

And so it would be, Daniel thought. Like the polluted waters of this Northeast Industrial Zone, these workers with whom he had lived a month would themselves wash out over America, and as they washed out, they would be made pure or, if not pure, at least American. At the moment, it seemed to be everything Jorge, for one, wanted.

He felt Jorge's hand on his arm, his arm being shaken.

"Daniel! Daniel! Look. What is this?"

Daniel Brewster bent to the window, and there, painted in a black scrawl on the side of an electrical substation, was a single word:

DRAGO

That would be Cara, he thought, or more likely Sean. Sean worked at an NIZ electrical transfer station only twenty minutes up the road.

"DRAGO is for the people who don't make it, Jorge," he said. "It's for the people who don't fit. I think DRAGO is something you will never have to know about."

Daniel could hear the driver radioing the coordinates of the substation. Within the quarter hour, the graffiti would doubtless be gone.

Jorge leaned back in his seat and relaxed.

"Do you know what I'm going to be doing in Albany, Daniel?"

Brewster shook his head.

"I'm going to be a punch-press operator, whatever that is, and I'm going to become the best punch-press operator the Confederate States of America has ever known. And then, Daniel—then I'll become a citizen."

Jorge's dark-brown eyes were shining, like polished wood.

"I'll start as a picker in Florida. That's all, just a picker. Anyone can do that. But I'll work harder than anyone else. I'll work day and night until I can afford to buy a tree. One tree, Daniel. And I'll make that tree the best orange tree there ever was—in Florida, in the C.S.A., in the whole world. If there's a frost coming on, I'll cover the tree with a blanket. I'll blow on each orange, each blossom, to keep it warm. Then I'll buy another tree, and another. By the time I'm an old man, Daniel, all my cousins, all my friends from Valencia, will be living in Florida with me. And we'll all be rich. And we'll all be Americans."

Jorge's voice was like a Spanish guitar, full of inflection, rich with overtones. He stopped for a moment, looked at Daniel Brewster, and smiled even more broadly.

"After my grandfather died, Daniel, my grandmother remarried—a man she had met while he was vacationing near our house. Afterward, they moved to his home in Antwerp." Jorge was speaking softly. His black hair fell across his forehead. "You've never been near Antwerp, have you?"

Daniel smiled back, enormously relieved. He felt better than he had in weeks.

"Not much closer than I am right now. When did you figure me out?"

"Oh, the first night we were in the dormitory room together. You said your prayers in English—A-mer-i-can English." Jorge drew the word out, the way their language instructor had. "I think you were praying in your sleep."

"I'll include you in them from now on. I'm a minister, Jorge. I got a chance to see the Patriation Program from the inside. I didn't want you to know too much. Knowing too much can get you in trouble."

Jorge had closed his eyes. He was ready to drift off again. "That would be nice, to be on your prayer list. When I'm an old man and ready for my grave, you can come and give me last rites."

When you're an old man, Daniel thought, I'll be ancient. Maybe I could be buried in your orange grove instead.

"One more thing." Jorge once again put his hand on Daniel's arm and whispered softly. "I've been wondering, if America is so wealthy, why did the roof leak in our dormitory room? And why are we riding in a bus that's so old it could barely make it over the bridge we just crossed? I know this tough love is good for us, but wouldn't we be able to work harder if we got just a little more food?"

"I don't know, Jorge. I don't know."

Daniel had just been wondering much the same thing. The Christianization matron's uniform looked almost tattered, as if a strong wind would simply blow it all to pieces.

6

THE NATIONAL MALL

JOGGING WAS NEVER fun for Spencer Lee. He did it to escape, to think, to keep the demons at bay, as much as he did it for his health. But jogging after lunch was the least fun of all. There had been domestic lamb, inevitably, for the New Zealand agricultural minister: butterflied and grilled, and served with a garlic sauce that Spencer still could taste. There was wine too, a shiraz brought from New Zealand—he had taken only enough for a ceremonial toast—and pecan pie that someone's mother had made and sent over to the White House: It was the South; people sent over pies and cakes all the time, whatever their purpose. Kay would have the name; she'd get the thank-you note ready for him to sign. Now he felt sluggish, pasty-skinned in his jogging shorts, on public display.

He was stretching his legs as he always did at the beginning of his run, leaning into one of the four granite monoliths at the far north of the Mall, just in front of the White House. Installed in the first year after the war, the monoliths each memorialized a general who had given his life for the Confederate cause: Albert Sidney Johnston, Thomas "Stonewall" Jackson, James Ewell Brown Stuart, John Bell Hood. Today Spencer was leaning into Hood, sturdy as always—until he had been shot in his saddle while leading his army into Washington from the east. Around the President the Secret Service had cordoned off a semicircle to keep the gawkers away. Beyond the semicircle, agents had stationed themselves every eighth of a mile along the President's jogging route, a sinuous line of broad-shouldered men in government-blue suits, chattering into their lapel microphones, extending from the White House down the length of the Mall to the James River. For the Secret Service detail assigned to the President, it was business as usual.

Despite the semicircle, despite the security, Spencer was far from alone.

"Mr. President!" the calls came.

"Hey, jog over here."

"Hell, Spencer," came one voice he recognized. "Don't you ever stop running, boy?"

It was Tommy Lee Vassar, the head of the National Agricultural Association, working his way slowly back to his office from the luncheon Spencer had left half an hour ago. A cigar the size of a small baseball bat was clutched in his hand.

"I'm going to see you tonight at the dinner, aren't I, Tommy?" Spencer called over. The NAA was a major donor to the President's Freedom Party and a major beneficiary of the InterAmerican Waterway.

"You are unless you're gonna be running your mouth then too."

Spencer laughed and went back to his stretching. He was working on getting into what he called the Zone—a place he'd learned to head for long ago when he first entered seriously into politics, somewhere he could be alone with his thoughts and still work a crowd. He pressed harder into the monolith, stretched his leg behind him until he could feel the tendons straining, and felt the words being called to him turn into a kind of ambient background hum. Then he looked up at the master bedroom of the White House, the room he had shared with his wife and now slept in alone—most nights— and he could have sworn that Frannie was in the window, lying in the hospital bed they had moved there near the end. What's more, he could have sworn that he was sitting in one of the easy chairs pulled up beside her bed, holding her hand.

HE REMEMBERED THE day, the moment, exactly. Frannie had come home from the hospital a week earlier, through with surgery, through with chemotherapy, through with radiation, ready to see things to an end. It was six in the evening when Leo Manzini finally stopped fussing with the bedroom, convinced at last that he had everything right. He'd left a plate of cold sliced roast beef—rare, the way Frannie liked her beef—along with a little saucer of horseradish, a bowl of potato salad made with capers and new red-skins, and a basket of biscuits prepared in the White House kitchen. A bottle of champagne sat in a bucket next to Spencer's chair; the bed tray was set with china, silver, linen, and a single yellow rose in a bud vase, waiting for Frannie to be hungry. Jason was a junior in high school then, playing soccer that season only because his mother had insisted on it. She wasn't going to have her son sitting vigil for her. Leo Manzini had been devoted to Jason his whole life. He and his wife, Helena, were going to see Jason's team play that evening. Afterward, they would take him to their house, where he'd spend the night. Over in the official wing of the White House, Kay was in her office, ready to direct any calls short of nuclear attack elsewhere. Nathan Winston was waiting in his office too, in the Executive Office Building next door. Spencer would find out the next morning that Nathan had arranged the evening and that he'd left word up and down the White House staff that he would personally kill anyone who tried to get through to the President that evening. The shock value alone seemed to do the trick: Nathan had never been known to get really angry, much less murderously mad.

Spencer had poured Frannie a small flute of champagne. It was the first time in months that she had been able to hold down anything alcoholic. She was sipping at it like a bird, pecking the bubbles.

"Leave that champagne alone," she told Spencer. "Go pour yourself a bourbon, a big one. Leo means well, but he's still a European at heart. He's never understood about Southern men and their whiskey."

By the time Spencer got back from the bar in the alcove, Frannie had repropped her pillows and used the motor to raise the head of her bed. She was looking out over the Mall as the sun was just beginning to dust it with pink.

"We're going to play a game, Spencer Lee," she said to him. "We're going to play Clear the Mall."

"I don't believe I know that one." He sat down again, covered Frannie's hand with his own, and took a deep sip from his glass.

"Oh, it's easy," Frannie said. "You take away a monument, then

I take away one, then you take away one, and we keep going until this damn place is empty enough to plow up and turn into something useful."

"Who starts?"

"You do."

"Okay," Spencer said. "I'm taking away Varina Banks Howell Davis."

"You'd yank your own great-great-grandmother, just like that? Right from the center of the Lower Mall. You're an awful man."

"Never could stand that monument," Spencer said. "The pedestal's ugly. She's too big by half, and if you stop and take a good long gander, she looks like a cross between a milk cow and a nutria."

"The sculptor was probably working from a bad likeness." It seemed to Spencer the first time in months that Frannie had laughed out loud.

"Undoubtedly. And your first choice?"

"Thomas Jefferson. There's something fishy about the way he looks up at that old Capitol of his, like he thinks there might be a family of rats living in the basement."

It took them only a few more minutes to get rid of the statuary on the Lower Mall. The Upper Mall was another matter.

For the next fifteen minutes, the two of them traded generals for humanitarians and educators. Spencer gave up the monoliths near the White House, beginning first with Jeb Stuart, "a hothead," and ending with Albert Sidney Johnston for sentimental reasons: He was the one his great-great-grandfather Lee seemed to have most deeply missed. Frannie meanwhile sacrificed the grouping to the right of the White House piece by piece: the great educator Booker T. Washington, second president of the National University; the great inventor George Washington Carver; Mary McLeod Bethune last and with the most reluctance. Frannie admired the dogged way Bethune had finally won the franchise for the women of the Confederacy.

Spencer chucked Jefferson Davis next. The whole hulk of an old Capitol was all the testimony needed to Jefferson Davis. Frannie followed with the Lee obelisk.

"The Lees always were a no-account family," Frannie said. Spencer had poured her a second half glass of champagne.

"Well, George Washington never amounted to a hill of beans either," Spencer answered, dismissing the equestrian statue of the First Founder that sat to the west of the old Capitol.

Spencer knew which monument Frannie would choose next, not because she wanted to but because there was no other choice.

"Bye-bye, Judah," she said with a flick of her wrist. "I'll miss you."

Spencer and Frannie were going beyond history, he thought. They were getting into the vitals of the Confederacy: Judah Benjamin shouldn't be dismissed with a flick of anything.

"You'll miss him with good cause," Spencer added. "He put everything on the line."

Judah Benjamin had been the first Jewish cabinet member in America, attorney general and later secretary of war and state under Jefferson Davis. On the morning after Davis's death, Benjamin had sailed secretly for England under horrible conditions—the boat was too small, the seas were too high, and he'd left a host of anti-Semitic enemies behind. Remarkably, he'd made it. More remarkably, he had finally persuaded the English to choose for the South in the New World. Jefferson Davis's self-immolation had given the Confederacy a mythic figure and helped Benjamin's argument; more than that, the British textile barons were using the last of the bumper crop of Southern cotton they had been warehousing since 1860.

Within two weeks of Benjamin's arrival, London had released the two powerful ironclads built for the Confederacy but held in English waters almost for the duration of the war. Within four weeks, British warships themselves were racing across the Atlantic. Four years earlier, they would have been no match for the federal Navy and Yankee privateers, but the Navy and the privateers were as spent and worn as everything else, everyone else, everyplace else. Before long, the coastal blockades that had choked the South were broken. Cotton could begin to flow freely once again to English and European mills, and capital could flow freely back across the ocean to fill empty Confederate coffers. It was as if a dehydrated man had been led to a pure mountain spring: Suddenly, the South couldn't stop drinking. By the time Judah Benjamin returned from England, he was a national hero, and the blood guilt of Jews was never again to be raised in official circles.

Frannie pushed herself over to the side of her bed and looked down to her left. She seemed to be almost hovering over Judah Benjamin's statue.

"Truth is," she said, "I'll miss his monument more."

Benjamin was seated in a grove of azaleas on the east side of the Upper Mall, not far from the White House—his face wrenched in grief for Davis. A British flag and a Confederate one were draped across the back of his chair. Between them, carved into the top of the chair, was a Star of David. The statue was generally taken to be the master work of the nineteenth-century American sculptor Augustus Saint-Gaudens. Now Frannie dismissed Saint-Gaudens, too, with another flick of her hand.

"Your turn," Frannie said, once Benjamin was rubble. "We've got to get this Mall plowed, and there are still two stumbling blocks out there."

"Frannie, you can't ask me to—"

"Spencer, sweetheart, you have to learn to let go of things. If you don't let go of things, you get stuck inside them."

My God, Spencer remembered thinking as he stared out the window at the old Capitol and the statue of Madison Tompkins that flanked it to its east. How could anyone possibly make such a choice? He had begun to pace in front of the windows that overlooked the Mall, and as he did so, he found himself reciting for Frannie the words carved in the base of Tompkins's statue—the words Madison Tompkins had shouted out from the well of the newly opened Capitol, the words every schoolchild, every Patriation candidate, every aspirant to America and Americanism, had been made to learn by heart:

" 'Together, white and black, Negro and Caucasian, let us work to create a new social order, that we may share, each with our own, the fruits of this great and bounteous land.' "

The year had been 1871, a half decade after the war was brought to an end, and the new nation built on the prewar social inequities was proving itself as inadequate to the times as the Old South had become.

" 'What did we fight for, upon what principle did we ask our men to sacrifice their lives?' " Spencer pounded his fist into his palm for emphasis as he paced, surprised that he remembered so much of that famous address. " 'Was the principle the subjugation of one half of our peoples? If so, my friends, then we have fought a very evil battle, and God shall judge us a devil's work. If so, then we shall never move forward, for every hour we spend in oppression is an hour not spent in opportunity. But if that principle was, as I believe it to have been, solely the right to determine our own destinies, then let us be about that business. Let us be about finding a way that all our peoples may live together, that all our peoples may profit from the mutual application of our wits and talents, that all our peoples may step into the sunshine of God's great grace.' "

It was from that speech that the Great Compromise had flowed and a history had been born. The South had won, at terrible cost. Now it had to make winning mean something. And what were the South's blacks going to do? Say no? They were given the House— half of Congress—as the Confederacy's token of earnestness. More important, they were shown a world in which with hard work and education they could aspire to the highest professional ranks, and they were provided with the means to attain that education. The South's African descendants were being let in on the boldest creation of human civilization. It was the deal of a lifetime.

Spencer strained to see some hint of Tompkins's statue in the dying light. He'd been a planter and slaveholder himself—that's what made his argument so compelling. And he'd been a warrior as well. He'd lost a foot at Sharpsburg and an ear at Ball's Bluff, although the sculptor had kindly given both back when he captured him in bronze for eternity.

"We can't tear old Madison down, Frannie. We've got to pay honor."

"We don't 'gotta' do anything, sweetheart. All we've got to do is breathe and look both ways before we cross the street, and you don't even have to do the second of those. You're the President, Spencer Lee. Someone will look both ways for you."

Madison Tompkins had predicted it would take a century to fully realize the biequality he had envisioned. It took less than half that time. By 1910, the Negro division of the National University had outgrown the replica of Thomas Jefferson's "academical village" that had been constructed for it. By 1920, demand for black education at the university for the first time equaled the demand for white education, and by then the new nation had the money to match its vision. Across the ocean, weaponry manufactured in the Confederate States of America had helped England, France, and others to thwart German ambition. On this side of the ocean, pounds sterling, francs, guldens, and more grew by stacks, by piles, by huge full vaults. And thus finally was delivered the promise of equality that had been made a century and a half earlier, on July 4, 1776: the "self-evident" truth that all men are created equal. Would it ever have happened if the North had won the war? Spencer doubted it. Nothing imposed ever really takes hold. Like every other battle, the ancient battle of race had to be resolved on its own battleground.

One more thing had been implicit in Madison's famous speech: All societies hate someone—the English, the French; the French, the Germans; the Hausas, the Ibos; the Koreans, the Japanese; and on and on and on. For the Confederacy to survive, for its people to prosper, for the holy experiment Tompkins foresaw to take root and grow, the hatred contained within the society must be directed else-where—toward a common foe. Happily, there was a vanquished enemy just to the north, waiting to be hated.

Spencer stopped his pacing now and refilled his drink at the small alcove bar. How do you possibly lay Madison Tompkins off against the old Capitol, against Jefferson Davis? Without Davis there would have been no Tompkins. Without Tompkins, Jefferson Davis might have died in vain.

"Well," Frannie said when he returned. "Which one is it to be? That team of mules is itching to get plowing."

"I can't do it, Frannie. It's too hard, too much."

"You'll learn," she'd said. "You'll learn, Spencer, because finally you'll have no choice. Now we're going to play an easier game—Clear the White House."

It took them only a few minutes to chuck out the official Davis Wing and the reception areas of the old central part of the White House, and only a few minutes more to reduce the private Lee Wing to the room they were in. Even the famous monumental portraits that stood at the entrance to each of the wings went in a hurry: Jefferson Davis with fire blazing at his feet as cherubim and sera-phim reach down to welcome him to the Kingdom of God; and the simpler one of Robert E. Lee with blood-soaked sword raised high above his head. Soon Spencer and Frannie were tossing out the fur-niture around them—dressers, chests, armoires as old as the nation.

This time it was her turn to go last.

"You better climb aboard," she said as she folded the sheet open beside her. She was wearing a gown that Spencer had bought her years before. Now it engulfed her. "I'm all that's gonna be left once I get rid of the plug-ugly chair you're sitting in."

Within minutes of Spencer's joining her in the bed, Frannie fell asleep, done in by the champagne, by sheer fatigue, by life. He held her three hours by his watch, until ten. Then he got up and fixed himself a light dinner of roast beef on biscuits, spread with horseradish, before undressing and climbing back in bed with her again. Frannie didn't wake until morning. Two weeks later, she was dead.

As SPENCER TURNED now toward the Mall, ready at last to jog, he could see that learning to let go had been the whole point of the game. Frannie had tried to teach him with her last breaths. He wondered if he had learned a thing.

Spencer wound his way now along the gravel path, feeling his muscles loosen, his energy return. "Mr. Whittaker," he said as he cleared the obelisks. "The old Capitol. I'd like to visit it after I come back up the hill. Could you please have someone open the private entrance. Just ten minutes."

Spencer could hear Agent Whittaker speaking into his lapel mike before he had even had a chance to jog away. The visit would take a few minutes to prepare. Tourists in the ruin would have to be shooed out; those waiting in line would have to wait a little longer.

"Hey, bird-legs," someone shouted from Twelfth Street as the President veered to the east side of the Mall to skirt Madison Tompkins. The President smiled and waved. The same man had been calling him bird-legs during these runs for the better part of four years, and whoever he was, he was a potential voter.

As the path fell from the Upper to the Lower Mall, Spencer simply let himself fly. For a moment, poised halfway between the White House and the river—between duty and escape, as he thought of it—he felt almost free of the effects of gravity.

WHEN SPENCER FINALLY labored back up the hill fifteen minutes later, the private east entrance of the old Capitol was waiting open. He didn't know why he felt such a powerful need to be there. Maybe

it was remembering the game he and Frannie had played that evening four years earlier. Maybe it was the way the game had plunged
him into the mythic vitals of the nation. Maybe it was simply that
Spencer couldn't resist reliving a great story.

He'd heard it himself the first time not out of any textbook, not
through any of the hundreds of dramas, television shows, or movies,
but from his paternal grandmother, Alice Bathurst, who had gotten
the story from her own father, who had himself been a ten-year-old
boy sitting on his own father's shoulders, pressed hard against these
walls, when history was made and the course of mankind forever
altered.

Standing in his jogging shorts, the sweat cooling on his back,
Spencer recalled the sheer thrill he felt at that first telling. He was
only ten himself then. Covered in liver spots and hobbled by rheu-
matism, Grandmother Alice had seemed ancient, but Lord, could
she tell a story! Spencer remembered her gesturing with her cane to
the destroyed meeting rooms at the front and the back of the building—long unsafe for anything but looking at—and then beginning:

"It was in these chambers, Spencer, that the Confederate War
Congress had sat, contentious, bickering over conscription and other
fine points of states' rights while the country that it had sought to
create was slowly being eaten away. Your great-great-granddaddy
Jefferson had sent the members to Danville, Virginia, on March 31,
1865, promising to join them two days thence. It was a promise he
never meant to keep."

More than forty years later—over half a lifetime—Spencer still
heard her voice and felt the hair rising on his neck as she talked on.

"It was on April first that Mr. Davis sent word to Ulysses Grant:
He wished to receive him and as many of his fellow officers as were
free to attend in the rotunda of the Capitol at noon of the following
day. Although Mr. Davis did not say for what purpose, Grant and
the others assumed it was to surrender the Confederacy. On the
second, three dozen of Grant's most senior officers gathered as requested. High above them on this balcony"—his grandmother had
waved her cane over her head—"waited such members of the Confederate cabinet and Congress as had chosen not to leave town, as
well as still more of Grant's staff, so many men that my father swore
he could hear the whole building groan under their weight. Still
others—the curious, the bold, latecomers, those who wanted to be

present at the creation of history—stood waiting in the two chambers that flanked the rotunda north and south, out of sight of Davis but not out of hearing, or so they hoped. An assortment of local dignitaries and invited guests watched from along the wall over there"—waving her cane again, at the south wall. "That's where my daddy was, sitting on his own daddy.

"Mr. Davis waited in a simple suit at the center of the rotunda, with a candle lit on a small table beside him even though the sky that Sabbath day was cloudless and the rotunda brightly lit by the skylight that crowned its upper dome.

"Anyone familar with the Capitol would have noticed instantly that Mr. Davis stood on the exact spot where Houdon's life-sized statue of George Washington had stood undisturbed for sixty-nine years, but they wouldn't have been surprised. We Richmonders were burying our treasures wherever we could in expectation of the Federals' despoiling our city. Armageddon was upon us, Spencer. Armageddon!

" 'Hold there if you will please, sir,' your great-great-granddaddy asked of General Grant as he finally entered the rotunda, in full-dress uniform, and advanced toward the lectern. 'I have but a few sentences I would like to say.'

" 'As you will, sir.' "

And here Grandmother Alice's voice suddenly dropped an octave. She was a natural mimic, Spencer had come to realize in the years since—an actress with this single show to star in.

" 'War, gentlemen, is a ghastly undertaking,' Mr. Davis began. His face had suffered from neuralgia and tics ever since the attack of pneumonia in the early 1830s. Added to that now was recurring malaria, partial blindness, a foot that had never healed from an injury suffered in the Mexican War, dyspepsia—a whole medical book full of problems, Spencer. He'd virtually abandoned his official office down on Bank Street; there were days when he couldn't leave home at all. And there was the weight of despair too, despair not just for the Confederate cause. The Davises were short-lived—you're lucky you've got that Lee blood and our Bathurst blood to cross with it—and they were star-crossed as well. One son, little Samuel Emery, had died before his second birthday; another, Joseph, only five, had been killed less than a year earlier when he fell off the White House's east portico. And Mr. Davis's beloved Varina—your great-great-grandmother—had fled to Danville, two weeks ahead of Congress, taking the four surviving children, including the infant Varina Anne. Mr. Davis was alone, son, as alone as a man could be.

"'As all soldiers know and too few politicians do,'"—again, Grandmother Alice let her voice drop an octave, to words Spencer had long ago committed to memory—'to undertake war lightly is the worst of sins. I undertook the duties of commander in chief with no such lightness in mind. Rather, I undertook this office because I deeply believe in the cause for which so many men have given their lives, their fortunes, their futures. And as President Lincoln refuses to recognize what I consider the intent of the American Founding Fathers—that states shall be free to pursue their destinies, individually or collectively, within or without the federal union—I find myself incapable of surrendering to his authority.'

"There was now a gasp from the crowd," Grandmother Alice said, her eyes darting wildly around the rotunda.

"'I know not what course my nation might choose, but as for myself, I choose to die a free man, a Southerner, a Confederate.'

"And with that, Spencer, with that Mr. Davis picked up the candle"—and here she reached over and raised an imaginary candle—"and he put the flame to the plank floor of the rotunda"—bending down painfully to simulate that as well—"and the plank floor having previously been treated with an incendiary, it burst into flames!

"'Please, General,' your great-great-granddaddy's last words had been as Grant stepped forward to rescue him, 'my conscience is heavy laden enough without adding you to it.'

"And there Mr. Jefferson Davis stood in a perfect calm while the flames spread quickly across the floor to the walls, quickly up the walls almost two dozen feet to the balcony above, and quickly across the balcony to the dome, its peak almost sixty feet above where your great-great-granddaddy waited for his Maker. General Grant, my daddy told me, was the last to leave, the last to see Jefferson Davis alive. He drank for years afterward to escape the image, the smell, the sound of *sizzling* flesh."

Lord, Spencer thought, how that word "sizzling" had burned its way into his imagination. In the years since, he had never fried an egg, never grilled a steak, without thinking of his great-great-grandfather—without wondering about the limits of what a man can do, of what can be expected of humankind.

The rest of the story was the common history of Spencer Lee's people. Jefferson Davis had done more than immolate himself: He had let loose a tectonic shift, when the plates of historic destiny grind against one another and something new is born. Even then, as a ten-year-old, Spencer had known the details almost by heart:

The smoke from the Capitol, visible nearly everywhere in town, seemed at first proof of the city's worst fears: The Federals had seized the building; the pillage of Richmond was only in its infancy. Within the half hour, true word had spread, and the people of Richmond, electrified once again by possibility, had begun to torch their own houses, shops, buildings. The fires started in the bottomland, along the wharves and in the business district, in Shockoe Slip and Shockoe Bottom. Soon flames were lapping at the foot of the burning Capitol itself, consuming whatever dared to lie in their path. High up on Shockoe Hill, wealthy home owners looked at the spectacle first with horror, then with mounting apprehension, finally with inevitability, as they took what treasures they could, set their own mansions on fire in many cases, and tried to beat a path northwest out of town before the powder magazines exploded. In the great conflagration that followed, some thirty-five thousand people were killed—half of them civilians, half soldiers, most of the latter Union troops who had moved into the city in expectation of surrender. The loss to the Union officer corps alone was catastrophic. Grant himself narrowly escaped, by following the river back to his headquarters.

Within the week, the torpor that had settled over the South vanished. Desertions had been running into the tens of thousands, maybe more. Now fresh fighting men—more often boys—came forward, fresh funds that had been hoarded in expectation of flight. Lee again was poring over his maps. A warrior people had become warriors once more.

In Washington, Lincoln and his henchmen had been preparing for the military occupation of the South; there was talk of seizing the great planter estates and dividing them up among the freedmen, talk of turning the governance of the South over to the slaves. Now all that was put on hold, as were the congratulatory luncheons, the celebratory speeches, further vindictive schemes, Lincoln's beloved evenings at the theater.

Two weeks after Davis's death, John Bell Hood crossed the Chesapeake. The day after that—pure inspiration—Nathan Bedford Forrest slipped across the Pennsylvania border into Chambersburg and seized, of all things, a button factory. For months the Army of Northern Virginia had been holding its pants up with fraying pieces of string, bent green twigs, vines, rusted lengths of wire. Now Forrest dispatched riders with saddlebags full of buttons—wooden, metal, mother-of-pearl; buttons for suits and dresses and fine winter coats. It didn't matter. For weeks after the raid, soldiers could be seen sewing by the flickering light of their campfires—it was so much easier to charge a gun emplacement when you knew your pants wouldn't fall down on the way.

Soon rebel yells were echoing off the dairy barns of eastern Pennsylvania, the rocky palisades of New York City, where they were met by the cannon fire of British warships. At the depth of its fortunes, the South had claimed its future.

"You see, Spencer," Grandmother Alice had ended her tale, tears streaming down her face, "those Federals had nothing to match our mythology: no Jeff Davis being borne to Kingdom Come on clouds of fire, no Avenging Angel to match the pure rage of Robert E. Lee. It's mythology that counts, Spencer, son. You've got to have something larger than life to believe in."

SPENCER HAD TOLD Grandmother Alice's story to Jason on *his* tenth birthday. More and more now that Jason was away, Spencer had come to look forward to telling the story to his grandchildren as well. He could see himself stooped and balding, mottled with liver spots, as he held his grandson's hand, waved his own cane at the old meeting rooms, and began: "It was in these chambers..."

Well, maybe he would, and maybe he wouldn't. Grandchildren were up to God and Jason, not him. And maybe, he thought as he stretched his legs and got ready to resume his run, maybe this story is something else I need to let go of. Maybe I'm stuck inside it, and maybe I've tried to stick Jason inside it too. But my God, I've spent a lifetime on it. What if this story is all I am?

A gold disk—six feet in diameter, of the purest metal—now marked the spot where Jefferson Davis had stood. Dressed in his jogging shorts and a T-shirt, Spencer Lee did as he always did when he visited the site. He looked carefully over both shoulders to make sure he was alone; then he quickly squatted down and placed his hand on the golden circle.

"Great-great-grandfather, give me strength to know what is right."

He had been praying to Jefferson Davis, he suddenly realized, for most of the last five decades.

7

CHARLOTTESVILLE

RANDY HAD LEFT two letters with Cara to mail. She took them now and tore them in half. Then she took those pieces and tore them in half, and in half again. Cara was standing at the sink. The window on this side of the seventh-floor apartment overlooked the black campus at the bischool complex. Four boys were playing basketball on the court behind the school, using up the last of the daylight. A boy and a girl had walked away from the court a little while before, headed into the trees that shielded the school complex from the highway behind it. Cara could just see the glow of their cigarettes.

She tore the pieces once more and this time let them fall into the sink. When she was finished, she opened the kitchen window and turned on the exhaust fan over the stove, and then she touched a match to the tiny pieces of paper in the sink, stirring them with a chopstick to keep the flames going. When the letters were nothing but ashes, she washed the ashes down the drain and ran them through the garbage disposal. Next, she poured baking soda on the scorch mark where the fire had been and rubbed the mark away with a dish brush. Then she threw the brush, the charred chopstick, and the remaining baking soda into the trash can below the sink.

One of the letters had been addressed to Randy's mother and father, now in their early eighties and still living in the family home just off the golf course at the Country Club of the James, on the west side of Richmond. The other letter was to have been sent to a post office box in a small town in northern Alabama—the last

known address of the black girl Randy had fallen in love with when
they were both in high school. Whether it was still her address,
Randy had had no idea. The girl—now a woman of almost forty—
had answered only one of Randy's letters over the last decade, and
that was more than five years ago.

Cara had thought about reading the letters before she destroyed
them. She didn't want to, she finally decided. The letters would be
mawkish and sentimental, Randy's way of saying goodbye without
saying goodbye. Sentimentality was Randy's problem.

She'd thought, too, about not destroying the letters, about mailing
them, letting them get where they were supposed to go. But she
didn't want Randy hanging around in some dusty corner of the
C.S.A. postal system; she didn't want his letters marked "Return to
Sender" or "Customer Will Not Accept." Cara could still feel Randy
inside her; she wanted him gone when he was gone.

Randy wanted to run DRAGO like an orphanage, someplace for
life's miserable people to wash up, find warmth, be comforted, maybe
even healed. An orphanage wasn't enough, she had argued. Nor were
the sort of street-theater demonstrations Randy so adored—well-
crafted interruptions of major events, which amounted to nothing
and never went anywhere. People were suffering all over the territories. The waterway had sucked up money; it had turned the Patriation Program mean. Cara had dared to dream. She had dared to
dream that the Greater Confederacy's miserable people—its exiles,
its Patriation washouts, the ones who could never get papers in the
first place—could all be bound together. Together they could demand what would never be granted to them as individuals: that they
be allowed to exist. First, though, DRAGO needed an entrée to
power; first, the group needed to make the world take notice. Cara
had dared to dream about that too.

Nothing stays the same—"not even you," Randy had said. So be
it. She was tired of just being herself.

CARA CHECKED THE drawers in the kitchen, both bedrooms, the
bathroom medicine cabinet, the cheap desk that the television sat on.
Nothing. She took her suitcase from the sofa and placed it by the
front door. The refrigerator was empty. All the dishes from the
drainboard had been put away. She reached up now, pulled out two

bobby pins, slipped her wig off—its jumble of loose curls—and carefully laid it in her oversized pocketbook. Next, she took a dish towel
and held it under the kitchen faucet. With the wet towel, she wiped
the dark powder off her face, her neck, the arms, whatever had been
exposed. Night was far enough along now for Cara to see her reflection in the kitchen window. As she worked, as she dabbed and
scrubbed, she saw herself emerge from the person she had been: her
mocha skin, the tiny curls tight against her scalp.

When she was finished, she dropped the dish towel in the trash,
took the plastic bag that lined the can, sealed it with a wire tie, and
set it beside her suitcase. She would drop it down the chute later,
when she left.

There was no need to wipe the apartment for fingerprints. Randy's
were on file somewhere, but Randy's fingerprints were no longer the
issue. Nor were Joseph's, if they even existed anywhere. As for Cara,
she had never been fingerprinted, never been booked, never even
been born, if birth requires some sort of proof committed to paper.
To steal the fingertips from people who have no identity would be
malicious, Cara thought. To steal them from people who exist is
simply being cautious.

Cara switched off all the lights in the apartment. Then she turned
on the television to the government affairs channel, punched the
Mute button, and settled into the same kitchen chair where Randy
had been working his crossword puzzle that morning. Some sort of
taped debate in the House of Representatives; a sea of black faces
seemed to be listening attentively. Soon the image dissolved and was
replaced by one of a hotel ballroom. The camera panned the famous
faces at the head table—President, politicians, captains of commerce
and industry. Then it pulled away for an overhead shot as type rolled
across the screen to inform viewers that for the next fifteen minutes
the network would be leaving the House debate to cover the opening
festivities of the dinner honoring completion of the InterAmerican
Waterway. The debate, viewers were assured, would be shown in its
entirety when coverage resumed.

Cara leaned close to the screen and studied the two rows of waiters
standing at attention in the middle of the ballroom floor. Joseph's
huge round head was clearly visible on the right side.

"I'm sorry, Joseph," she whispered to the screen. "You just looked
too much like someone not to use."

Cara ran her eye over the white waiters on the left. Randy was almost directly opposite Joseph: perfect placement.

"You could have dreamed with me," Cara said to him just as the camera shifted again and Spencer Lee, at the center of the head table, rose to his feet.

Cara reached to her right, picked the phone off the desk, and brought it over to the kitchen table beside her.

"Now call, baby," she almost cooed at the phone. "Call your Cara. Don't be afraid. Cara's going to take good care of you."

8

BALLROOM,
HOTEL RICHMOND

HE HAD MANAGED a bourbon while he showered and dressed—a double, on the rocks. Now, as Spencer sat listening to Margaret Barnes make small talk, he regretted he hadn't had another.

"It's rather nice, isn't it?"

Margaret was holding up a glass of water, turning it for inspection as if it were a fine wine. Type rolling across the giant screen at the far end of the room was informing the ballroom crowd just then that this particular water had been brought from Indiana by means of the canals, tunnels, channels, and charcoal-filter sluices that made up the infrastructure of the InterAmerican Waterway. Margaret had claimed to find a certain limestone sweetness to this Indiana vintage. To Spencer Lee, water was pretty much water. He just wanted to be sure there was enough of it. Everywhere.

Margaret and his sister, Alice, had been suitemates for three years at Saint Catherine's before college. Afterward, Alice had gone off to Sophie Newcombe in New Orleans—even when it was a smaller institution, the National University had been too big for her—while Margaret followed her father's internationalist tendencies and enrolled at Oxford. Alice was married before she ever graduated. Having grown up with four protective older brothers, she had a faith in the goodness of men that it took Harry Spalding almost fifteen years to cure her of. At least she was rid of him now, Spencer thought, and childless in the bargain—proof that good can come from infertility; proof, too, that good blood could grow thin, become fallible: Harry Spalding was a direct descendant of the great George Mason.

Margaret meanwhile had become something of a professional hostess for her father as he shuttled between ambassadorships and the State Department. Now that he was dead, she was looking for somewhere new to ply her hostessing skills—alongside a widowed President, for example. Spencer had no doubt that her talents for planning a dinner party were exemplary, but he knew that if he had to wake up every morning to hear her drawing out the "ah" on her "rathers," he'd be tempted to leap from the third-story bedroom window of the Lee Wing. Margaret had never quite gotten over her four years at Oxford.

"Alice is in England," he was explaining over the din of the ballroom, "although I have to confess that I don't have the least idea where."

The fact that he had lost track of his sister seemed to confound Margaret. He suspected that she had never lost track of so much as a hairpin.

"It's not that big an island," he blundered on. "And Alice is tall. I'm sure they'll be able to find her."

"Rah-ther."

SPENCER AND MARGARET were sitting at the center of the head table, raised on a dais some five feet over the ballroom floor. To her left was a Baptist minister, head of Richmond's largest black congregation, here to officially bless the waterway once Spencer had completed his remarks. Beyond him sat Tommy Lee Vassar, representing the agricultural interests that had been so influential in promoting the waterway. As Spencer leaned toward him to say hello, Vassar smiled and pulled back the lapel of his London-tailored blue pin-striped suit, to show the President an envelope sitting in his breast pocket. Whatever was inside—and it appeared to be precisely the right length for a contribution to Spencer's Freedom Party—it would be up to Sheila Redmond, the President's press secretary, to collect it. Redmond had worked for Vassar at the National Agricultural Association before signing on with Spencer at the start of his second term. Beyond Vassar sat Garnett Washington, the youngest grandson of Booker T. himself, representing the cement industry, whose trucks had helped culvert the rivers that fed the sluices and canals. Beyond Garnett was an array of other association heads and corporate CEOs. The waterway had cost trillions of dollars, but it had secured harvests, protected farmers against drought, and opened up new grazing lands through irrigation. Hardly an industry group hadn't been helped—either in the construction of the waterway or in its newly available benefits. Hardly a Confederate worker hadn't seen at least a tiny portion of the trillions of dollars show up in his paycheck. Spencer waved vaguely in the direction of the guests at that end of the head table. Without his glasses, he couldn't make out their faces, and he tried never to wear glasses when the television cameras were coming on. The glare from the lenses made him look too academic, almost sickly.

"Mr. Vassar," Spencer heard Margaret saying beside him, "I believe I had the pleasure of meeting your father some years ago, aboard the *Queen Elizabeth*."

"Was he drunk?"

God bless Tommy Lee, Spencer thought.

To Spencer's right sat Toby Burke, the barrel-chested Speaker of the House of Representatives. Toby had been the most prominent black surgeon in America when he decided to run for office two decades before, and although he was now gray-haired and nearing seventy, he still practiced his profession out of an office in Jackson, Mississippi, during the four months Congress was not in session. Beyond him was Willard Wilson. It was Spencer's opinion that Willard Wilson had invested the position of Senate Majority Leader with so much fulmination and pretentiousness that the slot had been redefined for at least a generation, perhaps more. Willard's face was a kind of magic screen that shaded from milky white to a fire-engine red when he was angered by an issue, and angered he frequently was. But unlike Toby Burke, Willard was of Spencer's own party, and thus they were obliged to be allies, if not friends.

Beyond Willard Wilson, the House and Senate leadership alternated seats—black and white, white and black. It was the way head tables were always set for such official events. America was a confederacy not just of states but of the black and white races as well—one people, yet not one; one nation, yet two; a perfect harmony in two keys.

To Spencer's right on the main floor of the ballroom, the black guests—more congressmen, builders, engineers, entertainers, academicians, statesmen—were just beginning to take their seats at the long table that stretched perpendicular to the end of the head table. To his left, the white guests—more congressmen, builders, engineers, entertainers, academicians, statesmen—were starting to do the same. A long lineup of white waiters stood on either side of the white table; black waiters stood ready at the black table. Behind the head table, the waiters were like the guests—black and white, white and black.

A COLD LOBSTER bisque and a garden salad were waiting for the guests. The Hotel Richmond was noted for its smothered chicken, and Spencer was guessing that was coming up next, when he heard a voice saying, "Quid pro quo." It took him a second to realize that it was Toby Burke speaking.

"Politics, Spencer, is built on quid pro quo. This for that. We've had the 'this,' Spencer." Toby waved his hand at the crowd, the dinner, the pending celebration. "You've got your waterway. It's time we moved on to the 'that.' "

Toby's Independence Party had supported the project, but only tepidly. Toby himself had wanted it built over twenty-five years, instead of merely a dozen. Spencer had been determined to see it finished before his term was up, and his will had prevailed. But Toby was right: In politics, absolutely nothing came free, and there was no ducking the Speaker of the House forever.

"May I ask what 'that' you have in mind, Toby?"

"Indeed you may. Mexico. Kill this statehood initiative. Quash it. Cut it out at its root." Toby drummed his fingers on the table as he talked. As always, Spencer marveled that hands so muscular could do the delicate work of a surgeon.

"Mr. President, I really must object." Willard Wilson had leaned in from the other side to join the conversation. "This is hardly the time or the place." Willard's face had shaded already to a mild rose.

The President held up a hand to stop him.

"We're listening, Willard. We're giving Toby the courtesy of a hearing before the festivities get under way."

"So long as we're *only* listening." So, Spencer thought, I've been warned.

"I have sympathy with the aspirations of the Mexicans who seek statehood, of course," the Speaker went on, "but I am conscious as well of the history of that tumultuous land—of the way in which Spanish and Indian and even African bloods have been freely intermingled in the populace. And when one consults that history, one can arrive at only a single conclusion as to this matter of statehood."

"And what, Toby, would that be?"

"That no good can come of union with a mongrel people."

"We've been over this before," Willard Wilson broke in, redder now. "The economic advantages of statehood are obvious. Genetic testing can be used to determine racial predominance, and the populace will vote accordingly. This is the same red herring—"

"Mongrel not just in blood but mongrel in *attitude,* sir!" Toby started to slam his fist into the table, saw the lobster bisque sitting in his soup bowl, and thought better of it. Instead, he slammed his fist into his own open palm for emphasis. "Mongrel in attitude. Mongrel in outlook. Mongrel in thought and action. Open up Mexico to statehood, sir, and you will have opened up Pandora's box!"

On Spencer's other side, he could hear a desperation in Tommy Lee Vassar's voice. Margaret had buttonholed him on some subject—crop subsidies, Amish stencil painting, he couldn't tell what—and there would be a debt to pay off there too. For the moment, though, Toby Burke was not to be ignored. What's more, Spencer knew that because Toby had brought up Mexico first, it was the payback possibility he cared least about.

"May I assume, Toby," the President said now, "that the 'this' of your 'this for that' is not limited to a single option?"

"You may. There is another choice."

"And it is?"

"The old Capitol—get rid of the thing. We've lived with it long enough."

"But why, Toby? Why? It's our fountainhead, the seed from which this great nation sprang."

"No, it's where the South that used to be ended. It's the last relic of a place where to be dark-skinned meant the assumption of inferiority. The South didn't begin in the well of that old Capitol, Spencer. It began in the well of the new one, when Madison Tompkins rose to speak. Turn that into a shrine if you need another one."

Spencer turned to greet a small lineup of guests who had been standing patiently behind him. When he turned back, Toby was sitting with his arms crossed on his chest.

"You don't change the past by ripping out its artifacts," the President countered. "Even if your point were a valid one—and I certainly don't concede it—the old Capitol would still tell us less about what we used to be than how far we have come in the years since."

There was another hand on the President's shoulder, more people waiting to shake his hand, to greet him, to congratulate him on the waterway.

"I'm a surgeon, Spencer, not a historian." Toby Burke didn't seem to have moved a muscle while the President's attention was diverted. "You don't leave a diseased organ in the body so that the patient will remember where his illness began. You take it out so he won't die of the disease the organ harbors. The irony, Spencer, is that if the North had succeeded in its war of aggression, we would have torn the ugly old hulk to the ground ourselves."

"If the North had won, Toby, we would today be the craziest damn bunch of drunks, poets, and suicides the world had ever seen."

From Toby's other side, Spencer heard a sputtering that sounded like a geyser about to erupt. A blood vessel had begun to bulge dangerously across the center of Willard Wilson's forehead, cutting it vertically in half. As his color rose through red to a violent crimson, the Senate Majority Leader spread the fingers of both hands wide, laid his palms slowly on the table in front of him, and fixed a glowering stare on the House Speaker.

"Unthinkable, sir. What you propose is a slander on this President and his ancestry, on this nation, and on history itself. Need I remind you, sir, that it was Jefferson—Thomas Jefferson himself!—who designed that magnificent building? Are we to tear down Monticello next? Bulldoze his rotunda for the National University? Pave over the Lawn? Root Mr. Jefferson out of the history books? Where will it end? Unthinkable. Good gracious, unspeakable. Un—"

"Gentlemen?"

It was one of the technicians from the government affairs network—sallow-faced and chicken-chested, as if he had never been outdoors. He was wearing a headset with earphones and small microphone.

"You're up next, Mr. President. Thirty seconds. The camera with the red light. Twenty-nine, twenty-eight . . ."

By the time Spencer got to his feet, Willard Wilson's face was already fading toward white. As the technician finished his countdown—"six, five, four . . ."—the Senate Majority Leader and the House Speaker appeared to be sharing a joke. That, too, was part of the code of politics, part of the code of the Confederacy, part of what made it all work: nothing untoward in public, especially between black and white.

Spencer tried to imagine a world without the old Capitol, without a gold disk he could pray to. He found that he couldn't.

"Two, one," the technician was saying, "and, Mr. President, we're live."

"LADIES AND GENTLEMEN, distinguished guests"—Spencer nodded to his right and left along the head table and saw Tommy Lee Vassar looking darts at him—"my esteemed colleagues in the Senate and House, everyone: We'll get to something a little more suitable for adult consumption in a minute." Spencer was holding his water glass aloft as he spoke. "And we'll get to praying over this feast as soon as I shut my yap." He winked now to the Baptist minister, as a general wave of amusement ran through the crowd. "But before we do, I'd like to ask you to join me in a toast to the star of this evening's festivities. Don't bother to rise yourselves, but hold those water glasses high."

As he spoke, Spencer noticed that two of the waiters, one from the black cordon and one from the white, had broken ranks and were meeting in the center of the ballroom. Why, he hadn't the least idea.

"We have completed, ladies and gentlemen, the most massive public works project in the history of this nation, perhaps the most massive and costly in the history of the world. And we have completed it on time! We have completed it on cost! And we have done it *right*!"

"Hear! Hear!" echoed through the crowd. "Bravo!"

"This glass of water," Spencer said, peering into it, "is not just any water, my friends. This glass of water is the fruit of the most advanced engineering system—"

It was just then that the protest began:

"Rivers of death . . . polluter," delivered in an amazingly loud, flat monotone.

Spencer went on, but somehow the two waiters in the center of the ballroom had tapped into the same public-address system he was using, so that their voices and his formed together an amplified strophe and antistrophe.

"It is a glass of water," Spencer was saying, "that is not just any water but the envy of the world!"

And in counterbalance: "Real equality, not biequality. Real freedom, not half freedoms."

"Raise your glasses high, my friends. Toast the engineers who designed the waterway . . ."

"Children are dying. The land is dying."

". . . the workers who built it. Toast yourselves for having the vision to support it, and most of all toast this glorious, glorious water!"

With the glare of the TV cameras now turned on them, the two waiters separated, and a banner unfurled between them. Spencer Lee had already guessed what would be on it. It was not the first time DRAGO had found its way into these functions.

"Dray-go," the two waiters were saying now, in the same flat monotone. Between them, "DRAGO" was written out in a stylized scrawl.

Spencer could see security agents advancing on them. It was just a matter of letting the ritual play itself out now. The waiters would extend their hands, palms up, to show they were people of peace. The banner would be confiscated, they would be led away chanting, and then the evening could resume. Protest was as old as the nation, and in the early days, back when "Little Phil" Sheridan was leading his guerrilla raiders out of the hills of Pennsylvania and New York, it had often been a bloody, bloody business. There were still some violent groups holed up in the NIZ and particularly in the Caribbean Corporation—there would always be rooting out to be done. By comparison, DRAGO was mild as talcum powder. Spencer could even admire the stagecraft: How *had* they gotten into the public-address system? His own Secret Service contingent had barely budged; better to let the hotel security people handle it.

But as the security force went to corral the black waiter, he lashed out with his feet instead of offering his hands, palms up. Then, with a beef of a fist, he swung high and wildly at a barrel-chested guard in a gray uniform, who ducked inside his swing and hit him once with a chop on his windpipe. As the blow landed, Spencer felt two hands on his shoulders, pushing him down. Instinctively, he resisted, and then he realized it was one of his own agents, forcing him back into his seat, talking to him in a coaxing voice.

"It's for your protection, Mr. President, just until the demonstration is over."

Spencer took his seat just as the black waiter crumpled to the floor. The strange thing, he thought—and this would be replayed on television time and again in the night ahead—was that the waiter seemed to be falling before the blow landed.

At the other end of the banner, the white waiter—rangier than his colleague and taller by a head—had cleared a circle around himself with a knife he held in his hand. As the other waiter crumpled to the floor, the white one left his back uncovered, and a bold guest, who would later be identified as one of the chief engineers on the waterway project, brought his chair crashing down on the waiter's head. Almost before he hit the floor, his arms had been pinioned and cuffed behind him. Like the other waiter, he lay motionless where he had fallen.

"DRAGO has raised the stakes," Spencer said to Margaret as the protest finally was brought to a close. "They've changed the rules of engagement. I wonder why."

She seemed not to have the least idea what he was talking about.

9

WASHINGTON, D.C.

DETECTIVE LIEUTENANT CLARK Haddon had spent the hour before he had come on duty sitting in a freezing morgue, teeth chattering, waiting to hear from the two corpses whose removal from the City Canal he had supervised not much more than half a day earlier. Now he was in high denial that this was odd behavior. Yes, he may have caught his death of a cold—he could feel something beginning to clot up his sinuses—but the dead *do* have something to say. That was one of the lessons insomnia had taught him: The dead talk all the time; you simply have to be awake to hear them.

The lieutenant had helped the morgue assistant transfer the bodies from the cold-storage drawers they had been lying in to the marble slabs where autopsies were performed. A body in a drawer was garbage, human trash, something waiting to be dug under. A body on a slab was potential—narrative, character, and plot all rolled into one. That's what the lieutenant was after: the potential. He wanted the corpses to tell him their story. He wanted to find himself inside what they had to say, be there when their ankles were bound, hear the bullet rip out their throat, explode through their brain. He wanted to feel the crunch of the bolt cutter as it methodically worked its way up and down their hands. (And which had come first, Haddon wondered: chicken or egg? bullet or bolt cutter? The former, he hoped, but it was the second possibility that helped keep him awake.)

Instead, the two bodies had lain there stiff as boards, mute as rocks, their mutilated hands frozen in silent repose. After an hour by his watch, Haddon gave up. Now he was sitting at a bar on Twelfth Street, down by the bus station, with the tips of his fingers and his thumbs bent in so far they were useless, trying to pick up his beer mug. He could almost do it, the lieutenant found, if he squeezed the mug as hard as he could and ignored the pain. If only the mug hadn't been stored like the bodies themselves had been, in an ice chest: Two-thirds of the way to his mouth, the frost-covered mug slipped out of his grip. Haddon steadied it just as it hit the counter, but not before a third of the beer had sloshed on his shirt and pants.

"Fuck" was all he could think to say. "Even if they had lived, they would have had to drink beer through a straw the rest of their lives."

How hard would it have been for the goddamn stiffs just to have told him something—anything? Where were they ever going to find a better listener?

AT THE LIEUTENANT'S left elbow, Jenkins saw the mug working loose from Haddon's grip and jumped off his stool just as it was covered with a slop of beer. Jenkins was mopping it off now, using water from a glass that had been left on one of the tables behind them. The lieutenant was plainclothes: If he wanted to look like a bum, it was his business. But Jenkins loved his uniform—loved its crispness, the way it seemed to grab hold of him every time he put it on, the way it kept him in place when he was wearing it. You start getting sloppy with your uniform, Jenkins figured, and pretty soon you're going to get sloppy with your life. Jenkins was a family man—unlike Haddon, unlike Flannerty. He intended to retire wearing his uniform, not be buried in it.

"Hot tea," he said now as he gave the stool a final inspection and slid back on it.

"Hot tea?" the lieutenant asked.

"With honey. And a spoonful of bourbon. That's what my mother always gave us when we had a cold coming on. Works like a charm." Jenkins had seen the blue of the lieutenant's lips when he showed up at headquarters, the shake of his hand as he drove them to Paulie's place. Drinking wasn't the lieutenant's problem. Jenkins had known him too long to think that. Morgues were the problem, and he never wore a winter coat. "Christ," he once told Jenkins when he'd asked about it, "they're buck naked. You think they're going to talk to me if I'm dressed up like a goddamn Eskimo?" You worked with some odd ones in this business, Jenkins figured, and the lieutenant was better than most, smarter than almost all of them, even if he was one step away from the loony bin.

"Have some tea now," he said, "and another one before you go to bed," knowing how rare that was.

On Haddon's other side, Flannerty leaned his head forward so he could see Jenkins and almost managed to stick his ear in his own beer mug.

"Hey, Jenkins, wasn't your mother like a camel or a humpback whale? Nothing human could produce something as ugly as you."

Jesus, Haddon thought, one beer made him almost tolerable; two turned him into a moron. They'd throw Flannerty into the back of the car and pray that nothing bad happened. That was something else Clark Haddon was in denial about: that it was likely nothing would happen. The radio in his car outside was almost certainly crackling with unanswered directives, and sooner or later somebody was bound to figure out that Haddon had driven his crew straight to Paulie's, where he'd been coming since he was sixteen years old.

"Hey, Paulie, you got any tea?" The lieutenant was grateful for Jenkins's suggestion; he just didn't like being mothered by someone five years younger than he was and way down the food chain.

"You want tea, go to China," Paulie answered from behind the bar.

"Any honey?"

"Last time I introduced you to one you married her and almost ruined her life."

"Bourbon?"

"How much?"

"A spoonful now and one at bedtime."

"You're a miserable son of a bitch, Haddon," Paulie said as he handed him a glass. "And you're going to die of pneumonia if you keep this up. Jenkins's mother had the wrong formula."

The lieutenant threw the drink down in one long swallow—half bourbon, it tasted like, and half bitters, lemon, and sugar. Suddenly, he felt much, much better.

. . .

A TELEVISION HUNG suspended from the ceiling near the back of the bar. It was week two of the baseball season—someone against someone else. Haddon couldn't care less. He'd gone to the games when there was a minor league team in Washington, but the team was as sorry as everything else: last in the American Association, just as its city was last in the heart of Americans. Still, the lieutenant wandered to the back now, to air his beer-soaked crotch, to move, to forget for a little while about those blue sheared knuckles—it was all he could do to straighten his own fingers.

Loyal or without imagination—sometimes, Haddon thought, it amounted to the same thing—Flannerty and Jenkins wandered back with him. And thus the three of them were standing there when the game was interrupted and the footage of the demonstration at the Hotel Richmond was replayed for what must have been the thousandth time that evening.

"Dead," Flannerty said as the black waiter took the chop to his neck and crumpled to the floor. And "Dead" again, just as the chair came crashing down on the back of the white waiter.

"Dead?" Haddon asked.

"It's like bad action movies, Lieutenant. You know, made in Japan. The punch and the sound don't quite connect. Look." They were replaying the protest in slow motion. "There! He's started to fall before the chop ever gets to his windpipe. And there again! The waiter is on his way down when the chair hits him. See?"

Haddon didn't, but he was willing to take Flannerty's word for it. Maybe the fact that Flannerty had never read a book in his life was useful. Maybe the fact that he'd pissed away one marriage and most of his life watching movies with titles like *Revenge of the Big-Breasted Teenage Ninjas* had its advantages. Maybe Flannerty wasn't a moron—just an idiot savant. Besides, the lieutenant couldn't be happier. The hour of shivering in the morgue had been worth it after all. So was the wet crotch and even the company he was keeping. As soon as the slow motion began, he knew that bowling-ball-shaped head, those ropy arms, the hooked nose. The two corpses hadn't merely talked to him. They'd come alive!

The lieutenant searched his pockets for a quarter. When he couldn't find one, he went back and grabbed a quarter off the tip pile he'd left for Paulie, just before Paulie could gather up the pile himself.

Back by the toilets, Haddon squinted in the dim light at his pocket address book, then fed the quarter in and dialed the assistant medical examiner at his office.

"Call off the dogs," Haddon said when the M.E. finally answered.

"Sit, Fang. Heel, Rover. Why?"

"The two canal stiffs—"

"Ah, yes, John Doe number one and two from last night. I really haven't had time—"

"Their identical twins were on the government affairs channel."

"Chatting up El Presidente? Bathing in the refreshing waters of the world's most impressive waterway?"

"None of the above. Dead. I'll be the most surprised detective in Christendom if they weren't using our John Does' IDs."

"And you won't rest until you've wormed your way to the bottom of this little mystery, I suppose."

"I'm off to Richmond in the morning," Haddon said.

"Give it my best."

10

CHARLOTTESVILLE

THE PHONE RINGING in Jason Lee's apartment, just off the East Campus, summoned him back from the sleep of the lost, the dead. He had had his television tuned to the government affairs network the night before, but instead of paying attention to the dinner at the Hotel Richmond, he had been sprawled on an oversized easy chair, making notes for the report on transmigration in the Pacific Northwest that he was working on with Lucy Winston. A legal pad had been balanced on one thigh, a monograph on Asian immigrants on the other. Beside Jason, within reach on the floor, had been a large tumbler of Pepsi-Cola and a half-eaten jumbo bag of potato chips. Blond like his father and with the same blue-gray eyes, Jason, who was thinner and two inches taller, could snack from sunup to sundown and never gain a pound.

He remembered hearing his father's voice just at the edge of his consciousness: "toast to the star . . . not just any water. . . ." The sound had been like a gentle shower to him: Even at age twenty, he was happy to admit that he missed his father's company. Slowly, though, he had become aware of other, eerily flat voices intermingling with the familiar one: "polluter . . . real equality . . . biequality . . . dying. . . ." Jason had paper-clipped his spot on the monograph and looked up just in time to see the white waiter whirling in a circle with a knife in his hand. He remembered looking irrationally around his own small apartment to see if his father was safe. Then he had seen the chair come crashing down on the waiter's head. From there, the camera had cut to his father sitting at the head table, leaning to his side as he talked with a woman Jason recognized as Miss Barnes. His father had looked drained, surprised.

Afterward, Jason had worked two more hours on the transmigration report and another three hours on a military history course he was taking to please his father. By two-thirty, even the cola couldn't keep him awake. Now, only four and a half hours later, he was being asked to resume consciousness. Had he not known with an absolute certainty who was calling, he might have resisted.

"Hello?" The scales falling off his voice.

"It's oh-seven-hundred hours, soldier. Rise and shine."

"Don't you have a nation to run?"

"That's why I'm calling. Do you think I should fire Kay?"

"Kay? What for?"

"Insubordination. Lying. Subverting the will of the President. She told me you couldn't come to the dinner with me last night because you were in the middle of midterms."

"And?"

"And usually reliable sources tell me that midterms were three weeks ago. I've got a whole Secret Service waiting on line two. I've got domestic intelligence operatives on every street corner. How dumb can you people get?"

"I made her lie for me," Jason said, rising sleepily to the moment.

"How?"

"I have photographs of her."

"Photographs? Good ones?"

"With Hitler. Kay was his mistress. There's lots of leather—"

"Enough! How are you?"

"Tired. Awake. Awakened. I saw some of what happened last night. You were sitting with Miss Barnes."

"That's your fault."

"You looked—I don't know—spent, surprised. I'd missed the start of your toast."

"Missed it?"

"Not really missed it, just not paying attention. I was researching a paper that Lucy Winston and I are doing for the coordinate class."

"I'm delivering a toast to the most ambitious public works project since the Great Wall of China, and you're not paying attention? You should have been on your feet, saluting! You should have been—"

"I think it's going to be a good paper, Dad—a really good paper. Lucy and I work well together. It's really strange. Her mother's this famous academic and her brother seems to be such a brain, but Lucy's as smart as they are. She just doesn't show it. She's got this way of reducing everything instantaneously, so anyone can understand it. You know I can't do that. I keep beating every subject to death. . . ."

Spencer Lee let his son ramble on. Jason had been twelve when his mother's cancer was first diagnosed, sixteen when she died; he'd gone from boyhood to manhood while she traveled from womanhood to nothingness. He had dealt well with it all—said all the right things and shown all the right emotions. He'd been strong and loving too, to his mother and his father, and he'd done well on public display, of which there was much too much at the end. No father could have asked more of a son, but a spark was gone; Jason had grieved so long inwardly that he had less now to show the outside world. Instead of entering into the life of the university—fraternities, debating societies, even keeping up with the soccer he had starred at in high school—Jason had retreated into his studies. Spencer could hear his son coming out of it now. There was life in his voice.

"You sound good."

"I am, Dad; I really am. How about you? You seemed pretty unsettled last night."

"I was. What was that about? DRAGO's always followed the rules before."

"Maybe the rules have changed."

Lucy's father had come home last night, Jason remembered. She would have been watching the speech with him.

NATHAN WINSTON HAD awakened, as he always did, with the sun. Now, wrapped in his old bathrobe, a cup of thin decaffeinated coffee by his side, he was sitting in his den, talking on the speakerphone with his office. The Richmond coroner had confirmed what the chief agent at the hotel had surmised. The bitter-almond smell on the breath of both protesters had been cyanide. Death had come not from the blow on the windpipe or the chair over the head but from massive cyanide poisoning in both instances. Remains of the gel capsules they had used were found lodged in their teeth. Thus far, fingerprints and dental records had failed to reveal any identity, although police thought they might be close to a make on the white protester.

Nathan wondered how John Henry would react. His son had been almost impossible to read the night before.

They had watched the speech—all four of them—in Nathan's office. Nathan and Lucy had been sitting on the old leather sofa, facing the television; she was leaning against him, as she always did when they sat together, her feet drawn up beneath her. John Henry and Lucinda had been opposite each other, in flanking easy chairs. At first, Nathan thought, his son and his wife had seemed as if they occupied warring camps, but as the evening went on, the tension softened. Nathan and Lucinda were drinking chardonnay—or rather he was drinking and Lucinda was sipping. Lucy had some wine as well, in one of Lucinda's thimble-sized crystal glasses.

As they waited for the President to make his remarks, Nathan, who had no head for engineering, tried to explain the fine points of the waterway construction to his children.

"I think the engineers refer to them as 'prophylactic sluices,'" he was saying.

"That's because only the sterile water gets through," Lucinda explained.

"Safe sluicing?" John Henry asked.

"Responsible waterways?" Lucy added. Even Lucinda laughed.

Nathan remembered marveling at the close-up of Willard Wilson's head, just before Spencer rose to give his remarks. My God, he thought, what has Toby said this time? Then, of course, the demonstration had come, and all that followed. Tensed forward in his seat, John Henry seemed to take the chop to the windpipe, the chair crashing down on the white waiter's head, personally. Watching him from the corner of his eye, Nathan remembered sitting the same way, flinching with each blow, when he watched boxing matches during the early days of television. Maybe a lust for blood sports was built into the male anatomy.

John Henry stayed on at the television while Lucy and his mother finished preparing dinner and setting the table and his father went upstairs to change, and thus it was John Henry, as the family was sitting down to dinner, who delivered the news on the demonstrators:

"Dead."

"Dead?" Lucy asked.

"The DRAGO demonstrators. They're both dead."

"But it didn't look as though—" Lucinda started to say, but she found herself with nowhere to go.

Nathan remembered now: His son's eyes had looked red-rimmed.

Lucinda clearly had braced herself for the worst. Nathan could see the tension in her neck; he knew from long experience what it meant when she closed her eyes and took those long breaths in and out, in and out. But over a dinner of fresh shad, grits, and asparagus, there was surprisingly little discussion of the incident. John Henry asked about Nathan's father, who had been a surgeon, and his grandfather, one of the first general practitioners to graduate from the National University Medical School. When the meal was over, he and Lucy cleared the table and filled the dishwasher, while their parents lingered over a last glass of wine. At ten, John Henry gave his mother a good-night kiss and his father a hug, as he hadn't done in over a year. Nathan could still feel his arms around him—he had thought he might never feel them again.

"Scrabble?" John Henry asked his sister.

They were still playing at the board set up in her room when Lucinda and Nathan went to bed.

DIRECTLY ABOVE NATHAN'S office, Lucy Winston awoke with a start. The people in her dreams were always black. For the first time that she could remember, she had dreamed of a white person.

The setting had been practically her first lesson in American history: the rotunda of the old Capitol, the fire igniting and lapping at the feet of the man who stood there. But instead of Jefferson Davis, it was Jason Lee who was being consumed by the flames. What surprised Lucy, though, wasn't the fire or the crack of glass as the skylight above gave way. What surprised her was Jason's perfect composure. There was almost a grin on his face.

As she slipped on her bathrobe, Lucy pulled the curtain back slightly from her front window. The day was just beginning to brighten. Below her, in the den, she could hear the low murmur of her father's voice. Two square-jawed black men in government-blue suits were standing on the Lawn, directly in front of Pavilion Three. Secret Service, she thought, and wondered why. It had been a point of honor with her father: No one, not even the Vice President, needed extra protection at the National University of the South.

In her bathroom, Lucy brushed her teeth, rinsed her face with a cleansing lotion, and rubbed in moisturizer before brushing her hair. She found her slippers on the floor of her closet and was turning to go downstairs to start a pot of coffee—real coffee, not her father's— when she stopped by the Scrabble board set up on a card table by her side window. John Henry had left the score pad open. They had played until midnight. Finally, he'd thrown up his hands in submission. He'd lost more than a hundred points to her last night, a tiny reverse in his march to the lifetime championship. She remembered hearing John Henry pick the portable phone off its cradle on the chest at the top of the stairs. Who, she had wondered, would he be calling at that hour?

Lucy's last word the night before, the word that broke John Henry's back, had been "gizmo," descending from the *g* over a triple word score. She looked at it now. While she slept, someone had slipped into her room and added his own letters to her floating *o* to create a new word: "DRAGO." Lucy's first thought was that proper names were not admissible. Then she raced across the upstairs hall to John Henry's room. His bed had not been slept in.

11

RICHMOND

SO NOW THERE were two mysteries. Spencer Lee was sitting by himself in the formal Morning Room, where he and Frannie had taken breakfast before she fell sick, before she had to be hospitalized, before she had to die. He had mostly avoided the room since then—Manzini was almost shocked to find him there when he brought up his fresh-squeezed orange juice, a bowl of cereal topped with strawberries, and his first pot of coffee—but the room crowned the east portico and was flooded by sun in the morning, so situated that the city and the surrounding countryside seemed to be bowing in honor. Its position atop the private Lee Wing—and at its most remote reach—also made the Morning Room the quietest place in the very unquiet residential quarters of the very unremote White House. One of the more profound fictions of government was that the president of the most powerful nation in the world could live in a white "house." "White OpCen," Spencer called it: No "house" should have to deal with such endless comings and goings.

He was wearing the T-shirt and boxer shorts he had slept in—his habit, his comfort, since Frannie had been gone from his bed—covered by a light summer robe. On the table in front of him, his breakfast tray was pushed to the side, replaced by a yellow legal pad. If four years at the Citadel had failed to teach Spencer Lee much about poetry or music, it had managed to make him a ruthless logician when problems arose. At the top right of the pad he had

written "John Henry"; at the top left, "DRAGO." With the edge of
a book, he had drawn two exact lines the length of the pad to create
a middle column, with no heading. Under "DRAGO," he now wrote
"Hotel Richmond" and, under that, "unconnected?" with a horizontal arrow pointing away from the center column, and "connected?"
with a second arrow pointing toward the middle of the page.

Under "John Henry," he wrote "temporarily missing?" and, in
smaller letters under that, "girlfriend?" and "lark?" and "mad at
parents?"—the latter twice underlined. Arrows beside all the entries
pointed to the outside of the page, but none seemed likely with a
boy as serious as John Henry. And so the President created a second
subcategory: "gone?" and, below it, "run away?" and "to
DRAGO?"—this spelled out in block letters like Scrabble tiles and
underlined as well, with a heavy arrow pointing toward the middle
column. Finally, below all that, he wrote "voluntary?" and "involuntary?" and below both an arrow that pointed in both directions.

He stopped now, poured a tepid second cup of coffee, and sat
back to look at his notes.

Nathan had been in his home office when he called to say that
John Henry was missing and had not slept in his bed. Spencer could
hear Lucinda in the background, talking about abduction, about the
violation of her home. There was panic to her voice, as there should
be, Spencer thought, but abduction seemed to him by far the less
likely scenario. The two Secret Service agents hadn't taken up their
posts outside the Vice President's home until almost daybreak, after
it was determined for certain that the DRAGO demonstrators had
caused their own deaths. Until then the Winstons' pavilion at the
university had been unguarded, unsecured, as it always was at Nathan's insistence—this was the Confederate States of America, not
fascist Germany, not warlord-riven China. Not only that, it was the
National University of the South, Thomas Jefferson's university: Respect must be paid. Still, there would have been a struggle if John
Henry had been taken involuntarily. He was willful and young; the
pavilion was old and creaky; and no one slept that soundly.

Nonetheless, Spencer dialed Kay's office and had her patch him
through to John Stanley, the head of Secret Service. It was an administration, a government, unused to crisis, unused to the unusual.
Everyone—Kay, Wormley, secretaries and cabinet members, key

staffers and even minor ones—had arrived at work an hour or more earlier than usual, sent to battle stations by the DRAGO demonstration, unsure of where to point their guns.

"I want someone on Lucy Winston and on Jason," he said. Stanley had slept in his office. Spencer had heard it in his voice an hour earlier when he had the White House operator bring him in on the conference call with Nathan. But Stanley was glad, too, for coordinates, for a place to begin fighting back. "Loose, Mr. Stanley. Very loose. I'd rather they didn't know they're being watched." Still, the President cared more about their safety than their comfort; if the security became apparent and offended them, so be it. Hadn't Jason said something about working on a paper with Lucy? Where did they work on it? he wondered. How?

"And Alice too, Mr. Stanley, when she gets back from England."

Maybe that's another fiction, Spencer told himself when he had hung up: that we're not like the rest of the world, that in a nation built on civility, the security of even the most prominent citizenry is assured. Maybe beneath the veneer of our politesse we're just as ready to spill blood as the Germans and Chinese, as the Russians and Koreans and all the other barbarians of all the other barbarian states that spread their gore daily through the far reaches of the planet.

Dear God—dark thoughts. Spencer buzzed Manzini and asked him to bring up a croissant, fresh jam, and a new pot of coffee. He would not be joining the Vice President for coffee in the Oval Office, as was their custom; the Vice President was unavoidably detained in Charlottesville.

He went back to his pad, this time to the middle column, where he began simply to list the players. "Demonstrators" at the top, in tiny print. Below that, slightly larger, "John Henry." Farther down, larger still, "Lucy," "Jason," "Alice." Next, "Lucinda." Then, almost filling the column: "Nathan." And below that, in big capitals: "ME."

Spencer was half studying the list, half daydreaming of the family beach house at Pawley's Island, in South Carolina, now owned by his brother Davis, when Manzini arrived with the new tray. The son of a mixed Italian-Portuguese marriage, Manzini was an almost perfect product of the Patriation Program. He'd fled Genoa in the early 1960s as a sixteen-year-old when the remains of the German National Socialist Party had turned on the remains of their former Italian comrades. Heads fell. Bodies fell. By the time the Italian nationalists were begging to suckle at the breast of Mother Germany, Manzini was in Buffalo, learning English by night and maintaining turbines by day. He'd come to the Lee family as a Level Three worker, assigned to tend the family patriarch as he drank himself into his grave. By the time the latter had been accomplished, Manzini was a full citizen. Spencer and his brothers had offered to set him up in business, any business, but the Lees, and Spencer especially—the same age as Manzini, some said his double—had become Manzini's habit, *his* custom.

Manzini had knocked once and a second time before entering with the breakfast tray. He was preparing a space for it when his eyes fell on Spencer's legal pad and its lists.

"Chum, Mr. President," he said, nodding toward the center list.

"Chum, Mr. Manzini?"

"Chum, Spencer." It was a game, their daily descent into familiarity.

"Chum, Leo. Chum what?"

"My father was a fisherman."

"I know, I know."

"Here's the chum," Manzini said, his hand tracing the tiny letters at the top of the center column.

"And here's the small fish that it attracts." John Henry.

"And the large fish that chase the smaller fish." Lucy. Jason. Alice.

"And the larger fish that chase the large fish." Lucinda. Nathan.

"And the largest fish of all." ME.

"Was your father a successful fisherman, Leo?"

"Oh, very successful, sir. We had mermaids for dinner every night."

MANZINI WAS NOT yet out the door when Spencer Lee asked to be put through to John Stanley again.

"It's not your province, I know, Mr. Stanley, but I would be very grateful if you could find a way to seal the DRAGO investigation and the inquiry into John Henry Winston's disappearance."

More targets. More coordinates. John Stanley was thrilled.

"Consider it done, sir."

"I do."

Mr. Stanley had been inherited from the previous administration. He was one of those people heard but rarely seen. Spencer tried for a moment to remember if he was tall or short, fat or thin, black or white. For the life of him, he could conjure up no picture.

Redmond would take care of the press. Better still, the press would take care of itself. Officially, John Henry would never have disappeared, because while the press was officially free to pursue the truth and print whatever it might find, it was in the official interest of the nation that some truths be less pursued and less publicized than others. It was all a matter of taste, of timing, of sacrificing individual exigency to the common good.

"There's such a thing as too much truth," Spencer's predecessor had told him on Inauguration Day more than seven years before, as they rode together to the swearing-in ceremony in a horse-drawn carriage that had once belonged to Madison Tompkins.

"People don't want to know everything, Spencer, and don't make it your job to tell them. People want to know just enough to feel good about things. Sketch a broad picture, son."

NINE BLOCKS AWAY and three stories underground, Detective Lieutenant Clark Haddon of the District of Columbia police force was waiting for a Richmond police clerk to photocopy the national work cards and other papers found in the wallets of the two waiters who had died on nationwide television the previous night.

The lieutenant hadn't been able to see the bodies. The Richmond coroner had them under lock and key while they were being prepped for autopsy. But the coroner's office would be sending up morgue portraits tomorrow morning. In the meantime, Haddon hoped that the national work cards would tell him who his own John Does were and put an end to at least that part of the case.

While he waited, Haddon was studying an envelope and a photograph that had been sealed inside it. Both had been found in the jacket of the black waiter after his death, and both now were sealed in a glassine sleeve, having been dusted for prints and checked for stray gene-bearing particles. Clark Haddon was certain that the evidence was rife with prints, both finger and DNA. He had no doubt that both would trace back to the Patriation Registry and beyond that to an African point of embarkation and beyond that to . . . nothing—a vast, recordless continent. The gleaming Metropolitan Richmond Department of Public Safety routinely ran DNA tests and Patriation Registry matches because it could, not because the tests and matches might yield something. His own police department, housed in a third of the space, yet faced with three times the serious crime, routinely did not run such tests and matches, because they couldn't with any ease and within any budget, not because they might not yield something. On the whole, it seemed to the lieutenant pretty much of a draw.

The photo was only partially visible through the translucent sleeve, so Haddon slit the seal with his thumbnail, then laid the photo and the envelope under a reading lamp so he could study them in decent light. He kept a thin magnifying strip in his wallet—tribute to his weakening eyes, his passion for detail. He pulled that out now, and as he did so, another photo fell from his wallet onto the desk.

Now Haddon could see: The black man was in a clearing, the trees wrapped in autumnal colors. Where was it? The Blue Ridge, the Alleghenies, the Catoctins or Berkshires? The Great Smokies, Ozarks, or Appalachians? The Rockies or the Andes or the Urals? Someone could look at the mixture of trees and tell Haddon—he himself didn't know an oak from a maple. Behind the man and to his right was a rock escarpment, a natural stone wall almost, streaked laterally near its top with white.

Quartz? The lieutenant hadn't paid much attention in that class either. On the back, a name—Joseph Ngubo—and a date. Real or not? The lieutenant guessed yes to both, and yes to the address on the envelope. A last message home. A letter meant to say, "Hi, I'm alive," when he would by then be dead. Who was the patron saint of futile gestures?

"It'll only be a minute more, Lieutenant," the clerk called from his cubicle. "I just want to find something to put these copies in for you."

Richmond, the lieutenant thought: where they kill you with kindness. He'd left his apartment in the District of Columbia at six that morning and been in Richmond by eight. It was past nine now. Hunger was worming its way into him. Biscuits. Red-eye gravy. The lieutenant's imagination was tearing into a mountain of side meat when he noticed a supervisor come out from behind his frosted panel and take the clerk aside. Behind him he sensed, though he didn't see, more movement.

"A good likeness, Lieutenant?" the supervisor asked, advancing on Haddon and gesturing to the photo of the black waiter. "The spitting image of your John Doe up there in Washington?"

Haddon took his magnifying strip and studied the head in the photo.

"Almost," he answered. "Certainly, close enough so that an ID card would fool most people. But the shape of the head isn't quite right. This one ..." He flipped the photo over and looked again at the name on the back. "Joseph Ngubo's head is rounder; the eyes are slightly closer together. I'll send down a photo of the John Doe for you to—"

"Not necessary." Something in the supervisor's voice made Haddon look up from the photo.

"Not?"

"Lieutenant, I'm afraid I'll have to ask for that photo back. If you'll forget you saw it, I'll forget you opened a sealed envelope and tampered with evidence. Professional courtesy," he added, winking conspiratorially. "The feds are taking over the case, as of this moment."

"Consider it forgotten." The lieutenant held the glassine sleeve open, swept a photo and the envelope back into it, and tore off a small piece of tape to reseal the package. Then he pocketed the magnifier and the other photo. "I've got a memory like a seining net. If I could just have those ID copies, I'll forget I've ever been here."

This time the supervisor simply shook his head.

"Professional courtesy?" the lieutenant asked. He turned now and saw that uniformed officers had stationed themselves at each door. "I don't suppose there's a cafeteria here where I could get some breakfast."

"I think you'd be a lot happier, Lieutenant, taking your breakfast down the street. Miss Bessie makes a shit on a shingle that's not to be believed."

Half an hour later, Lieutenant Haddon was inclined to agree. If creamed chipped beef on toast ever could be said to be transporting, this one was. Spread on the counter in front of him were the two books he had picked up at a store around the corner: *Trees of Eastern America* and *Geology for Dummies*. He had been a poor student, the lieutenant was willing to admit, but not an incurious one.

The lieutenant didn't mind so much that he hadn't been able to secure the identifications of his John Does one and two. Police work was police work, and in his experience, when information was sequestered, there was often a good reason. Besides, a day and a half had passed and no one appeared to have missed either John Doe. But he couldn't get the bolt cutter out of his mind. People, he thought, ought to be allowed to take their fingertips with them when they die. What kind of person could do that to dead men—not once, not twice, but twenty times? And feed them, for God's sake, to *rats*? He looked over his shoulder, checked his neighbor at the lunch counter—a retiree lost in coffee and thought—and pulled the photo of Joseph Ngubo out of his shirt pocket. What did this black man with the huge head have to teach him? How was he going to place this photograph, give it a home? How could he make Joseph Ngubo talk to him?

12

CHARLOTTESVILLE TO
PENNSYLVANIA TERRITORY

THIS IS WHAT it's like, then, to walk out of a life: You wait and wait and wait until you think you can't wait any longer. You wait until all the lights are out, wait until the last toilet has flushed, wait until all the snuffling and wheezing and sighing of a household going to sleep has blended into one harmonious note. You wait until you are sure hours and hours have passed and sunrise is just over the horizon, and then you check the clock by your bed and it is less than an hour since you said good night to your sister. And then you listen, and it is your snuffling and wheezing and sighing you have been listening to these last twenty minutes.

You wait and you wonder if this is the most wrong thing you have ever thought of doing in your entire seventeen years, and then because you have already left in your head, have already taken that trip out the back door, through the garden, have already leapt the serpentine wall exactly where you know to so you will hit the soft shredded bark on the other side and not the noisy gravel—because you have already done all these things in your head, you rise noiselessly off your bed, an inch at a time, and begin to do them.

Crammed in your closet now, way in the back behind your clothes, you take out the piece of paper that has been burning a hole in your pocket since the morning and dial the number written on it. You read the number carefully as you go, even though you have memorized it and tested your memory time and time again. It is a number you don't want to get wrong. You dial it, the little *beep* of each number muffled by your Sunday suit, your winter parka, and it rings once, and suddenly there's a voice, a soft woman's voice, and it says one word: "Ready." Not quite a question. Not quite a statement. A voice—this you will think about much later—that seems to have no purpose except to have waited for you to call it. And you say, so softly you can barely hear it yourself, "Yes." And she tells you where you are to go and when—*when* being right now—and that is all there is to it. And now what you have done in your head you have to start doing in your heart.

In the upstairs hallway you lean against your parents' door—his regular *humph, humph* as if there were always a wad of gauze stuck somewhere in his nose; her very proper in and out, almost a whistle. You listen for a minute, and you kiss the doorjamb, once, twice, because that is all you can do. You can't wake them up and explain that if you stay, you'll explode. And then you turn toward your sister's room, where the door is cracked slightly open, and you slip inside because you have to do that as well. For a moment, you just look at her, unable to look away—an angel's face awake, an angel's face asleep—and then because you can't bear the thought of just leaving, of evaporating, of suddenly *not being*, you sift silently through the Scrabble tiles in the full moonlight and add your word, assert your being, your existence: This is what I was; this is who I will be; I'm doing this for you, for Mom and Dad, for black people and white people, for the whole delusional mess we call the Confederate States of America. D-R-A-G-O. Shift the letters around, Lucy, hold them upside down, look at them through the magic glasses we used to pretend we had. They read "I love you." You'll see. You'll see. And then even her angel face is gone, and you are on the stairs, in the kitchen, out the back door, over the wall (exactly on the soft shredded bark, exactly as you had planned it so the back gate wouldn't creak), and at the appointed place—two blocks away—and the appointed time—now—a car is waiting, black on the outside, no dome light inside, and you get in, and the door closes, and that is how you leave a life.

Nothing to it, really.

Nothing.

. . .

JOHN HENRY WAS jumping the serpentine wall of the rear garden when he remembered: "Delusional mess" had come from a radical French academician who sought refuge in Montreal after displeasing the German education ministry. His mother was right, John Henry thought. He had been seeing the world with other people's eyes. Now he was going to see it with his own. For the first time since he called the number, John Henry could feel the pain lifting off him.

There were two people in the car in addition to the driver: a man in the front seat and someone in the back on the far side, turned away from him; someone he couldn't see. It was the man in the front passenger seat who opened the door for him; the man in the front passenger seat who fit the two soft adhesive pads over his eyes and the dark glasses over them so it was now darker inside his head than it was outside; the man in the front passenger seat who said to him, "Leave a note?" And John Henry said, "No," because strictly speaking he hadn't, because he was afraid to say what he had left, because he was still John Henry and stubborn, even if he was slipping out of one life and slipping into another.

And then: silence. Miles of it.

The car climbed for a while, its engine straining slightly, headed into the hills, but whether north or south or west, John Henry had no idea. Once, he heard a plastic lid being removed and the flip-tops being opened on two carbonated beverages, and then the man from the front seat was fitting an ice-cold can of cola into his hand. Another time there was a crinkling of cellophane, and three peanut-butter Nabs were given to him. The road was slower, more twisting now. Someone rolled down a window, and he could smell the pine, the buds, spring in the air. Very slowly, the adhesive on the soft pads that covered his eyes began to loosen, just at the edge, and he could see daylight starting to appear. Very slowly, too, John Henry's tiredness turned to weariness, his weariness to exhaustion.

He nodded, he slumped, he snored more or less sitting up, and then there was a hand on his shoulder and a woman's voice: "Tired, baby." And John Henry knew it was the same voice that he had first heard saying "Ready"—neither statement nor question. And he nodded; yes, tired, very tired.

Very gently now, the woman pulled him down so he was lying across the back seat, his head in her lap. Very gently, the first sun of morning lit the back seat, and through the edges of his eye pads,

John Henry could see her arm, her mocha skin, as she stroked his head, his neck, his shoulders.

"Sleep, baby," she said to him. "Sleep, baby. Your Cara's going to take good care of you. Sleep."

And as the car drove on into the rising morning, John Henry did.

PART II

MAY—JUNE

13

NATIONAL UNIVERSITY
OF THE SOUTH

LIKE THE GRADUATE library on the West Campus, the one on the east side had its upper floors given over to study carrels and small rooms for seminars and tutorials. One of the smallest of the tutorial rooms had been set aside for Jason and Lucy to prepare their transmigration project: a room no more than six feet by eight, with a thin rack of shelves at one end, a table that took up a good two-thirds of the floor space, four aluminum chairs with black vinyl cushions, and barely enough room for two people to turn around in. There were no windows—rooms with a view were reserved for doctoral students and the highest-level tutorials—but a glass pane, crisscrossed with safety wires, had been built into the door. A small black shade had been drawn down over it, perhaps by a previous occupant anxious not to be disturbed in her studies, perhaps by a library staff assistant, sensitive to the precedent that was being broken, to the presence within the room of students from both campuses.

Jason was sitting at the far end of the room, staring at the black shade as he waited for Lucy to come back from what she had called "the facilities."

Maybe, Jason thought, the shade hadn't been drawn by a student or a library staffer. Maybe it had been drawn by a Secret Service operative. He had no idea how watched he was, largely because he didn't want to know and his father had never mentioned it. No agents tracked him from class to class, but did someone wait in the shadows outside his apartment building while he slept? Was the path from his apartment to the campus checked for bombs each morning before he had even risen? Were the overhead lights in his kitchen, his bathroom, his bedroom, wired for sight and sound? If Jason knew he was being watched, he was certain he would be paralyzed— that's why he'd never asked. He couldn't imagine himself getting up in the morning and brushing his teeth, much less leaving for class. Still, he doubted such surveillance was being undertaken. That kind of supersecurity was for other parts of the world, rife with revolt, sick with court intrigues. America was different: "Peace through strength, Strength through peace" had been one of the slogans of the Freedom Party in the last election. And what could be truer? America was strong, beyond all reckoning. America was also at peace, and one condition clearly served the other.

Nevertheless, Jason thought because he couldn't avoid it, somewhere in the protective services someone was bound to have noticed that the President's son and the Vice President's daughter were taking a class together. A call would have been made, a breakfast meeting arranged: *Just keep an eye out*. What exactly did that mean? Draw the shade? Find an agent who might pass for a student, dress him in chinos and loafers, and station him at the end of the hall or in the carrel next door, with a stack of books and a backpack full of legal pads? Perhaps Jason would have a look when he went for water or needed "the facilities" himself.

Jason knew he was too self-conscious, far too much so, but being his father's son, the heir to his father's history, meant never being entirely unaware of his own body and blood.

HE'D MET LUCY by prearrangement on the steps outside the library—met her with that hearty handshake that was the troth and bond of biequality and an open smile that had deepened since their coordinate course began. He had offered to come to the gate where the two campuses joined, but Lucy was known, her mission approved. It was a gate used mostly by administrators and department heads—joint meetings of this and that, the joint dedication of so-and-so—but it was nonetheless a well-marked course. And the time, after all, was broad daylight.

"I think, Jason," she had told him, "I can walk the two hundred yards to the graduate library all by myself. You're not having a crime wave over there, are you?"

Eternally prompt—or neurotically early, as his father would contend—Jason had arrived at the library steps a full fifteen minutes before the appointed time. This was only the second time they had met at the library. Jason had thought Lucy might still feel some discomfort about coming to the East Campus. Coordinate programs between the two campuses were rare; coordinate courses unheard of until this one. But if Lucy was nervous, she showed no sign of it when she appeared, ten minutes after they had agreed to meet. Her hair fell loose on her shoulders, over a blue oxford cloth shirt, and her smile when she finally saw Jason was enough, he thought, to light a small city. As Jason rose to greet her, he could see students stopping, turning, wondering. One—Jason recognized him as the teaching assistant from a sociology course he had taken his first year—actually dropped the stack of books he was carrying.

Well, Jason thought, Lucy glowed. She was one of those people who carried a light inside them, one of those people who warmed you. He was remembering the first time he met her—almost eight years ago, at the national convention, after her father had been nominated for the vice presidency—when the door of the tutorial room swung open.

Jason leapt to his feet. "Lucy!" It was too loud, he could tell, much too loud. He'd been almost dreaming.

"This is a study group, not dancing class, Jason. You don't have to stand up every time I walk into the room." Lucy had tied her hair back and rolled up the sleeves of her shirt. Her smile warmed the walls. "Hadn't we better get back to work?"

Spread across the table was a hodgepodge of statistical tables, notes, fine-bore treatises, and general historical overviews. Jason looked at them now, rearranged them in piles to his right, away from where Lucy sat, and rolled up his own sleeves.

"It's like I was saying," he began. "The subject's too large. 'Transmigration in the Pacific Northwest' isn't just a seminar report, Lucy, or a senior thesis. It's not even a dissertation or a book. It's a whole field of study; it's a lifetime of reading. Every time I pull on one thread of evidence, it leads to something else, and that leads to something else, and that leads to something else still. And before I know it, I've got these stacks and stacks and stacks of *things*—all this paper, all these words—and I haven't gotten us any further than we were when we began."

"Maybe I should be looking too." Lucy took her pen and started to make a note on a legal pad.

"No," Jason said. "No. That's not the arrangement. I'm not going to have you do my work, Lucy. I find the the raw material; then you dig into it and tell us what's important. That's what we agreed upon."

"But—"

"Listen, it's just that every time I think I've got the raw material pinned down, something explodes out the side, and I have to chase that."

Jason reached across the table and slid one of the piles in front of him.

"Here, for example. Korean transmigration soared in 1942. Why? Because Korean migration spiked dramatically in 1938. And why was that? Because boatloads of refugees had fled the peninsula both before and after the May twenty-eighth Japanese invasion."

Jason dug through the stack, found a monograph, opened it to a page marked with a paper clip, and began to read:

" 'The Korean refugees had been willing to face the terrible risks of sea travel—storms, Japanese Zeros, capture by the Japanese Navy—on the thin hope of arriving safely at the Confederate States of America and its Patriation Program.' I mean, there's a whole dissertation here about the sea travel alone—how many made it, how many were captured, how many died at sea, why they left, what they found when they got here."

He dug into the stack again, found a thick collection of tables, and began paraphrasing them.

"Koreans working in the timber industry in the Northwest Pacific states—logging, pulp and paper mills—grew thirteen percent in 1939, eighteen percent the following year, another fifteen percent in 1940, and ten percent in 1941. And then comes 1942, and the bottom drops out on Koreans in both industrial sectors. Why?"

Jason grabbed another book and held it in the air. "Because by 1942, the Japanese were being driven into the sea by the Chinese, just as the Koreans had been driven into the sea by the Japanese. All of a sudden, there's a new influx of Japanese into Patriation."

Jason turned to still more tables. As he talked, he could see Lucy begin to drift. She was sitting now with her chin on her hands, staring at a spot on the wall directly opposite her. Scared he was losing her, he talked more and faster.

"So, Lucy, what's the issue? That's what I've been trying to figure out. Where do we focus? Do we write about the precipitating events that drive people to seek Patriation? Because, really, that's what forces transmigration once people are here—you have all these new waves of people coming into the Northwest, and each new wave drives an older one forward. But if we do that, how do we keep from getting bogged down in thousands and thousands of years of Far Eastern history? And for that matter, do the precipitating events really matter? I mean, it doesn't really matter why people come."

"Doesn't matter?"

"Not really. Patriation's about learning to become an American. It's not about whatever war drove people to leave their homes. If you think about it, the wars, the uprisings, the revolts, whatever they are, don't really count."

"So long as they send their money?" Lucy seemed to be trying to crawl into the spot on the wall she had been staring at. The light had gone out of her eyes. She was twisting the cap on her pen back and forth, back and forth.

"Their money?"

"The wars don't matter as long as they fight them with American-made parts? As long as whatever weapons they use are made in the C.S.A. and purchased with hard cash? Is that what you're saying, Jason?"

"Lucy, that's not at all—"

"Who cares if someone's home gets destroyed, if the children are blown to smithereens, so long as it's one more person for good old American Patriation, one more dollar for good old American industry? Is that it?"

"Lucy?"

"I mean, you seem to have followed every other line of inquiry, every other stray thought you might have had, so maybe we should follow this one too. Maybe our transmigration report should be about how cold-blooded American foreign policy is. Or maybe if you look long and hard enough and let your brain wander far enough, you'll find a space alien who transmigrated through the Pacific Northwest, and we can do a report on that too."

"I don't know what you're saying, Lucy."

She threw her pen down on the table then and watched it bounce off into the far wall.

"Listen, Jason. I don't give a damn what subject you choose. I don't care. Just pick something, for God's sake. Pick something, anything, and we'll write about it. Just get on with it."

Jason fell back in his chair. He felt as if he'd been kicked in the ribs.

"Christ, Lucy," he said when he could talk again. "I'll go to Dr. Cuthbert tomorrow. I'll tell him I've screwed everything up. I mean, I have. You shouldn't have to be tied down with me. It's late, but if I talk with him, I'm sure he'll let you finish up a smaller project on your own."

Lucy raised her eyes to his with what seemed a question.

"It's not like I'm going to flunk out." Jason laughed slightly, desperately trying to decipher her gaze. "He might let me try something smaller too, something I could handle. I might rescue a C. Who knows, with an experimental course like this, they might not even count it on the GPA. I mean—"

Then, as Jason started to restack the books he had once again scattered all over the library table, Lucy's face simply broke apart, crumpled, dissolved.

"John Henry's gone. He's been gone for two weeks, Jason. We're not supposed to talk about it, not supposed to tell anyone."

And so she did.

"HE DISAPPEARED IN the middle of the night," Lucy was saying. "I knew he was gone before I looked out my window and saw the two Secret Service agents on the Lawn. I knew it before I looked on the Scrabble board and saw the word DRAGO. We were so close, Jason, so close. I ran over to his room. It was so neat, just like it always was. I remember thinking that it looked like a museum room—one that should have a blue velvet rope over the doorway so you can just peer in and a brass plaque that reads: 'In this room John Henry Winston . . .'

"Do you have any idea what it feels like?" Lucy asked, not so much of Jason as of some invisible audience that included him. "Do you have any idea? It's like having something ripped out of you—

an organ, a joint. You were whole, complete, and then all of a sudden there's this *thing* missing, this gaping hole."

Jason knew just what it felt like: There was a gaping hole where his mother had been. He wanted to stop Lucy now, to tell her that—had wanted to tell someone for such a long time—but it was Lucy's grief, her show. He would sound like all those hearty men and well-dressed women who had wrapped their arms around him after his mother's funeral or held his cheeks in their gloved and scented hands: "I know what you're feeling, Jason. I've been there too." "You'll get over it, son; life will go on." Bullshit. Bullshit. Jesus, it felt good even to think it.

Tears were splashing down on the table now. Jason slid a copy of the *American Demographics Journal* out of their way. His pockets were a jumble of saved paper napkins. He handed the cleanest of them to Lucy and used the worst to blot the tabletop.

"I know," he said. Only: "I know."

Lucy stopped then and looked at him. They were so much the negative mirror images of each other. They'd sat so often on the same platform at the same events, public children arranged at either end of a long stage while someone praised their fathers, or their fathers praised someone else or cut a ribbon or exhorted the faithful, the true believers, to part with their votes, their time and energy, their hard-earned cash. God alone could count how many times their photographs had appeared in the same frame: Spencer Lee and Nathan Winston with their arms around each other's shoulders; their wives at either side; Jason and Lucy and John Henry arranged along with them. You could watch the children growing from the first campaign, when all three could stand in front of their fathers; you could see the professional arrangers shifting first Jason, then John Henry and Lucy, out to the sides as they grew tall enough to obscure their vaunted sires. As Frannie Lee faded slowly from the frames—became thinner, less substantial, until finally she disappeared altogether—you could see Jason's eyes grow deeper, darker, with each new proof of his mother's insubstantiality. This is the thing about being famous: There's a record, always a record.

Jason and Lucy both knew without being told that their families had done better than almost all the others—had given them a semblance of private lives, had protected them when they could from the prying television cameras, the treacly "human interest" reporters.

Still, they were the human furniture of the political spectacle of the Confederate States of America, expected to sit still, look interested, stow their pain away for a place and a time where it wouldn't "embarrass," become "part of the debate," give "aid and comfort" to the opposition.

For Lucy, that place and time had become this small study room, this May afternoon. In Jason, she had found the perfect listener. The two of them had known each other without really knowing the first thing about each other for so much of their lives. They had much to learn, and John Henry's disappearance was providing a crash course.

"MOTHER BLAMED EVERYONE at first . . . ," Lucy was saying, "your father, the Secret Service, my dad maybe most of all. 'This is a boy, Nathan, our boy, *your* boy. How could you have failed to protect such a perfect human thing?' "

Lucy's imitation of her mother's careful diction and precise pronunciation was uncanny.

"Eventually, she stopped that," Lucy went on. "It was maybe five days after John Henry disappeared. I came home from class late that afternoon and found her sitting at the kitchen table with no lights on, nothing in front of her. 'Blame isn't going to bring your brother back,' she said to me. 'I'm through blaming. We've got to bring him home now.' But, Jason, the pain that's still in her face. I can't stand to look at it. I come home now and go straight up to my room. I look *beside* her when we talk, because I can't stand to look at her. She knows it."

And there was this too, Lucy went on: Her mother may have stopped blaming, but she had adopted a single version of events: In the still of the night, on the sacred Lawn of the National University of the South, on April 20 of the year 2000, a boy aged seventeen had been abducted from his home by hostile forces—soundlessly, with no disruption, by abductors so careful that they tidied John Henry's bedroom after they had secured him.

"Do you know how hard that is?" Lucy said. "Do you know how hard it is to live in a house where only one truth is allowed? A truth that doesn't make sense?"

"No sense at all," Jason agreed. "I mean, even space aliens leave *some* kind of calling card: a little scorching in the garden where the

phasers first touched down, one of those ectoplasmic streaks on the
wall. Lucy ..." Like his father, Jason wanted to please. He wanted
everyone to be happy, but Lucy didn't have happiness in her at the
moment. She was already moving on. She had more to say, and she
was going to say it all the way through, now that she had started.
There was a smell of something in the room: jasmine, a spring field,
flowers just in bloom. Even with her hair tied back and her eyes
swollen from crying, Lucy seemed to Jason to have stepped out of
the pages of a magazine. He had lived too little in the company of
women—had no idea what it took to smell the way Lucy smelled,
to look as she looked. Dressed in wrinkled chinos and an unpressed
white button-down shirt, he could have passed, he supposed, for half
the male students walking around the East Campus right now. His
father was right: Camouflage had become his habit. Jason sat back,
tried to lose himself in the black vinyl of his chair. If Lucy wouldn't
be humored, then he was willing to listen until she had said everything she had to say, until her voice was raw and her tongue bleeding
and there wasn't a word left in her.

"Dad," she went on now, "Dad's been just the opposite. He's
dragged John Henry's disappearance into his heart. You look at him,
Jason, and you can just see it eating away at him day by day. You
can just see him chewing over everything Mom threw at him in
those first days." Again, her mother's perfect imitation: " 'A man's
first obligation, Nathan, is to protect his family.'

"They used to have a drink together before dinner whenever Dad
was home, just the two of them most nights, even if John Henry
and I were there. Ever since I can remember. Now Mom puts something in the oven—anything, almost—and goes to her study, and
Dad pours his own drink and sits in his study. They're almost right
on top of each other, and there's not a sound between them. Sometimes I can't stand that either. I went in the last time Dad was home
and poured myself a glass of wine to have with him. He was blaming
himself again—he hadn't paid enough attention to John Henry,
hadn't really listened to him." Lucy's voice became deeper as she
talked; Jason could hear her father's rolling cadences. " 'Your brother
was wrong about so many things,' he said, 'but he was eloquent, he
had passion. God, Lucy, how could I have failed to respect that? It
would have been so easy to have spent more time with him.' How
am I supposed to answer that, Jason? How?"

Meanwhile, Lucy said, all of them jumped at the ring of the phone. They passed by the mail slot in the front door a hundred times daily, looking for a scrap of paper quickly shoved inside. They walked slowly to their classes, their offices, through the grocery stores and malls, so that someone could overtake them from behind, whisper stealthily in their ear: "If you want to see your brother again, . . ." "Your son wants you to know he's okay."

"You wouldn't believe what listeners we've all become, Jason. My God, the things we think we hear."

Meanwhile, too, a story had been concocted, cover—politics, more politics—put out: John Henry was visiting a sick uncle in California, completing an oral history project before the uncle died. The uncle did exist—a noted if eccentric agronomist, Lucinda's oldest brother. He was indeed sick, although far from his deathbed. Most to the point, he lived in splendid isolation a dozen miles outside Marysville in the Sacramento Valley, down a road you could see forever along. A bag had been packed with some of John Henry's favorite clothes and sent by government courier to Marysville. Assignments were collected from school; perhaps they were sent to the uncle, perhaps not. Lucy had no idea. Enough of John Henry's voice was on tape that an audio engineer sitting at a console could fabricate a limited phone conversation if need be—John Henry calling a classmate to ask about an assignment, John Henry returning a reporter's call to squelch rumors of his disappearance. The result would be slow, halting, but the uncle had no hard-wired phone at his house, in any event. He communicated by a primitive satellite uplink of his own devising.

"There's a virtual John Henry out there," Lucy said, "a virtual brother for me. The problem is: Where's the real one?"

"There's been nothing?" Jason asked. "No word at all? No contact?"

"Nothing," Lucy said. "John Henry has always been good about keeping quiet."

LUCY SAT QUIETLY now. She looked up as Jason stripped the cellophane from a pack of Nabs—a gross violation of library policy—but shook her head when he extended the package to her.

"What makes it even harder on Dad," she resumed, "is that if

John Henry didn't just tiptoe away on his own—if he was lured away, taken away—then the target has got to be Dad. Let's face it, Mom and I don't count for much in the larger scheme of things."

"No," Jason said, stronger now, his mouth almost choked with a peanut-butter cracker. "You can't say that about yourself, Lucy."

She laughed now, sweet relief.

"Uh, Jason, do you suppose my brother is being held until I spill the beans on what I'm wearing to the spring formal? Or until Mom improves the kidnapper's grade from a C to a B? Or agrees to publish his article on 'Articulation and the Social Code in Turn-of-the-Century Discourse' in *The Journal of History and Ethnography?*"

Suddenly, Jason could feel some of Lucy's lightness returning and, with it, his own. Spring formal? He'd forgotten such things existed.

"What about you?" he asked now.

"Me."

"You've told me how your mother and father have taken it. How about you? How are you taking it?"

"I don't know," Lucy answered. "I never paid a dime's worth of attention to DRAGO in my life. What is it? What's the goddamn name even mean?"

Lucy's anger came in a flash, snuffing out her smile and making her eyes water.

"I see that word every day on the Scrabble board in my room. I see DRAGO, and I ask myself how can a word mean more to John Henry than I do?"

"All I know is what I've read in the papers, Lucy. DRAGO takes in washouts from the Patriation Program; it seems to draw its recruits from undocumented workers and exiles sent to the territories. The only time anyone ever heard about it was when it staged some kind of protest about environmental conditions in the NIZ or the miscegenation laws or something like that. A lot of its members, I guess, are people who have failed the racial purity tests. Everything was always peaceful until that demonstration at the Hotel Richmond—"

"And John Henry walked away, walked out of our lives over a single goddamn word."

"But, Lucy, I think it's more than that. I mean, DRAGO's been around for more than a decade. It's not just a—"

"It's a word, Jason! It's one word." Lucy slammed both palms down hard on the table, made the books and monographs jump. "What's a word against what we had, for God's sake?"

Lucy dabbed at her eyes again and refused another of Jason's Nabs. The crinkle of the cellophane seemed to make her jump this time, as if it had startled her out of her thoughts.

"John Henry was nine when Dad campaigned for the first time. You and I were twelve. It was okay for us, even exciting sometimes. You remember? We'd walk into school and see our photograph on the bulletin board, from some newspaper or newsmagazine."

It was a different school, a different bulletin board, but Jason did remember. When he was twelve, the world seemed almost to bow down to him. When he was twelve, his mother hadn't yet started to dematerialize.

"John Henry," Lucy went on, "never made friends easily. Even then he was too hard on everyone, too hard mostly on himself. That's when we started playing Scrabble—in our hotel room when we had to go on the campaign trail with Mom and Dad. Those events scared him, terrified him, really. He was afraid he'd have to say something or that he'd make an ugly face when photographers were around. He was terrified he'd embarrass Dad. Most of all, he was afraid Dad would win. John Henry was convinced that Dad would go off to Richmond and we'd never see him again. We would spend hours in the room, play game after game, anything to avoid his going out in public.

"We kept the games going when we got back home—until ten or so if Mom was home, much later if we were being taken care of by one of the students she would hire. Some nights, we would play so late that John Henry would take a pillow off my bed and a blanket from the closet and sleep on the floor by my door. Then some nights became most nights, and most nights became every night. It made him feel safer, he said. He couldn't sleep in his own room. What was I going to do? Mom said he'd grow out of it. Dad had other things to think about. They were both gone a lot that first term in office. Mom was away with Dad or she was off chairing some conference. She was already well known in her field. Once she became the Second Lady of the Confederacy, invitations poured in.

"In some ways, it was easier to have him there, curled up on the floor like a dog. It was like I was raising John Henry—at least I

knew where he was. And I had someone to say good night to, someone to talk to sleep, to talk me to sleep. Sometimes we'd play telepathy games when we were lying there in the dark. It was amazing
how good we got at it. John Henry would think of a color; I'd think
of a number. You'd have to scribble it down in the dark on a piece
of paper to make sure no one cheated. When we were having trouble
sleeping, we'd make our breath match; I'd tell him to imagine that
we had one heartbeat.

"It ended when he was thirteen. One day, Mother noticed that
John Henry wasn't a baby anymore. 'He's becoming a man, Lucy.'"
The imitation perfect again. "The next day, she told him he had to
sleep in his own bedroom. It had to happen sometime—we both
knew that. But for two years I had to go into his room whenever I
got home and kiss him on the forehead. If he couldn't sleep, we'd
match our breathing. Even after that, I'd keep a night-light on just
by my bedroom door so he could see the glow under his own. John
Henry said the light connected us. That's what he walked away
from, Jason. That's what he walked away from for one goddamn
word!"

"But, Lucy, you're not even sure he left on his own. I know it
doesn't seem that likely, but he could have been—"

"For Christ's sake," she said, her anger back in a flash. "John
Henry wasn't stolen from our home. There's no such thing as an
immaculate abduction, is there? You know, I was followed for a
week, tailed wherever I went by these two government thugs. You
probably were too."

She looked at Jason, but all he could do was shake his head. He
didn't know, was so oblivious, so out to lunch, he thought.

"Finally," Lucy said, "I screamed at them, at Dad, at Mom. I
wasn't going to be abducted; nobody was. And I wasn't going to
walk away unless they made me. At any rate, it worked. I was
Superbitch, and the Secret Service went away."

Again, she paused to get control of herself, only to lose it again.

"Don't you see, Jason? John Henry must have known how much
pain he was going to cause, and yet he did this. He walked out of
our lives with no note, nothing, just that single word. What about
me, Jason? What about me? Am I just supposed to get over it?"

The tears were back. Jason found a fresh paper napkin in his
pocket. The ones he'd given Lucy earlier were shredded and soaked.

"I had longer to get accustomed to it." Jason's voice sounded to him like it was coming from the bottom of a cavern.

"Longer?"

"To the loss. When my mother died. She'd been dying for so long. I'd had time to prepare myself, but I still wasn't ready. You know, you're supposed to think, 'Oh, what a relief for her. She's out of her suffering. She's gone to a better place.' But it's all crap. And then every time you turn around, there's some photographer or some reporter. And you've got to 'be brave,' 'be a man,' 'put on a good show.' Still, at least I had time to think about it. I think with John Henry the thing is that it's so sudden, so—"

Her tears turned into sobs then—aching, bone-rattling convulsions that would have scared Jason if he hadn't suddenly become convinced that he had said absolutely the wrong thing.

"Dead? John Henry's not dead! How can you even—"

Jason's first instinct was to cover his face. If he could have, he would have crawled into the corner of the study room and pulled the cheap green carpet over him. There was no end to his ineptitude.

"My God, Lucy, I'm sorry, I'm so sorry. I never meant to—I mean, Jesus, what am I thinking? What am I saying? John Henry's fine. He just needs to figure things out. Or maybe he is being held captive somewhere—it's not his fault. Oh, Christ. Christ."

He wanted to put his arm around her shoulders, hold her tight, smother her sorrow against his shoulder, still her chest with his own, but his arm wouldn't move. He looked down, puzzled, and saw their fingers were lapped over each other like black-and-white stitchwork. He felt the warmth of his fingers on hers, the warmth of her fingers winding through his, and then he realized: Ever since he had sorted through his pocket and handed Lucy the last paper napkin—five minutes ago, maybe—they had been sitting with their hands joined. Lucy must have realized it at the same moment; climbed out of her anger, grief, confusion, just long enough to see that at the end of her left arm, her hand was intertwined with Jason's right hand, a white hand, the hand of a white man, and that he and she were standing on a precipice, for that is exactly what it was. Behind them lay safe ground. Hands meet, they join in the emotion of a moment, in comfort, in friendship. And then if they are black and white hands they separate. They go the way of their separate arms, bodies, lives, because that is the way life is led, always has been, always will be.

There was no penalty in it—protocols get stressed in the heat of the moment, traditions violated. Everyone knew that; everyone respected the possibility. Such events are wholly understandable, wholly excusable. But for a black hand and a white hand there was a time— not a time on the clock, but a time that was really a measure of intensity—when each must let go, when nothing but free fall and the immutable laws of nature and the terrible laws of gravity lie ahead. And although they were young, although they both had led privileged and sheltered lives, Jason and Lucy knew about that time. They knew they had come to the edge and that ahead lay an abyss they could spend a lifetime trying to climb out of. Their knowing was evident in their eyes as they stared at each other; it was evident in the jolt of electricity that passed from finger to finger, hand to hand, brain to brain.

Jason loosened his grip first, perhaps; or maybe it was Lucy who first unlaced a finger. Slowly, inch by inch, their grip came undone. Finger parted from finger, palm from palm, heavily pigmented cell from lightly pigmented one, until finally there was just the moisture of their hands that joined them, a shared surface tension of sweat. And then that, too, was broken, with a kind of liquid *pop,* and order was restored to the world. The sun would rise again in the east, set in the west; tides would ebb and flow according to the usual tables. Lucy's crying was now of the normal variety of sorrow—not for a brother lost forever but for the possibility that things had come apart for her, for her family. Jason looked at her, trying to measure her mental state. And then in what he would think of forever as the most impulsive act of a measured life, he slid his chair around the end of the table until it was next to Lucy's, put his lips on her cheek, tasted the salt of her skin, and held her with both arms until her tears stopped and she held him back.

IT WAS NEARLY dusk by the time Jason and Lucy left the library. She'd brought with her a sheaf of what seemed the most pertinent documents; he had a list of further materials to gather. Most of what Jason had lugged to the library carrel was stacked and labeled on the shelves there. Lucy had found a thread they could pull on, tweak, bend around—just as he'd hoped she would, just as he knew she would.

He walked her to the gate this time, without asking, without opposition. The gate was really just an architectural fancy midway across the bridge spanning the sunken highway that ran between the two campuses: a guess at what Thomas Jefferson might have done with the same space at the same spot for the same purpose, although perhaps it was a purpose even the great Jefferson never could have imagined.

Lucy and Jason walked closer together as they mounted the slight bow to the bridge's crest, wrists brushing, shoulders touching once, twice, a third time—tiny bursts of electricity that seemed to Jason like the very essence of existence. The guard waved Lucy through. He, too, was merely a formality, someone to fill the space that had been created to fill a space. At the crest of the bridge on the east side of the gate, Jason watched Lucy disappear into a mirror image of his own campus, his own life. He felt a release that nothing in the moment could explain. The kiss, the embrace, were only small emblems of a larger sexual world that he had been late to explore; but it wasn't just the feel of Lucy, the taste of her, the touch of her. Something deeper than sex had been let loose inside him. At the same time, Jason wondered if he and Lucy hadn't just signed something very much like their own death warrants.

14

NORTH ADAMS,
MASSACHUSETTS TERRITORY

TO LIE IN his narrow bed beneath his threadbare sheet merely feeling normal seemed to John Henry a kind of conquest. They'd driven for two nights and a day from Charlottesville. After he woke from his first sleep along the way, John Henry had been left alone in the car for twenty minutes, maybe half an hour. He could hear water flowing nearby. Only an occasional car worked its way past them, always—it seemed to John Henry—at a low speed. When he didn't bolt, when he didn't pull his eye pads off, didn't sit blind in his seat and cry out for his mother and his father, beg to be taken back to everything he had left behind, curl up on the seat and suck his thumb—when none of that happened, the eye pads had been pulled off and he had been helped out of the car to stretch his legs: a first token of trust, of acceptance, too easily earned. The eye pads were falling off, in any event. As John Henry's eyes adjusted to the light, he could see that the car was parked in a clearing, maybe fifty yards upstream from a two-lane drawbridge. The two halves of the bridge were lowering, falling together.

"This is Pennsylvania Territory," the woman said as they climbed back into the car, "and that's New Jersey." She gestured across the river that lay in front of them. "We're on our way to North Adams, in Massachusetts Territory. And I'm your Cara."

Cara he had already glimpsed, felt, been touched by. She was older than his sister by eight or ten years, he guessed; younger than his mother by twice that much. Her skin tone seemed to John Henry to be on the absolute dividing line between black and white, as if God Himself had set out to find what a single race would look like if opposite pigmentations were mixed in perfect proportion. Now that his vision had been restored, John Henry had trouble keeping his eyes off her.

James, older than Cara, and Randall, younger, were introduced, as Cara had been, by first names only. They alternated driving. Cara said little other than to note geographical landmarks: "These are the Taconic Mountains, baby. . . . Now we're coming into the Berkshires." The others said nothing. Afraid that whatever he might say would be the wrong thing, John Henry was quiet as a tomb.

Wherever possible, they traveled off the beaten path as they worked their way northeast from the Delaware River. The roads were country ones, two lanes at best, rutted gravel-and-dirt trails at worst. Still, John Henry saw the tar-paper shacks they stopped at to check on this person or that, take on food, find water; the soft green of the few budding trees muted by a gray dust, washed by a gray light that seeped through the thick, leaden sky; streams so choked with sludge that the water could barely push itself along; in the distance, smokestacks, power grids, the grind of gears as truckers on the interterritorial highways hauled in raw goods, hauled out finished products.

This is it, John Henry thought. This is real experience. My life is just beginning.

And then, finally, they'd gotten to North Adams.

The large frame house, across a brook and up a narrow drive about a mile from the edge of town, was set in a small forest of ragged, tenacious maples. Just behind the house, the hills climbed sharply to the west. John Henry's room was one of two side by side on the third floor, each tucked into a dormer, with a bathroom to share in the rear.

The bathroom turned out to be critical, that and the fact that the other room was vacant and thus there was no one to share the bathroom with. On day one at the house, John Henry rested, went downstairs and briefly met a few of the others—the "inmates," Cara called them, not without cause—and rested some more. On day two, he felt queasy and weak, and left his room only rarely. On day three, all hell broke loose. John Henry had sweats and chills. He lay covered with every spare blanket in the house, or almost naked on his bed. Fluids seemed to pour out of him from every available exit. How could the human body become so vast a reservoir?

The next two weeks passed largely in a blur as John Henry fought his way out of illness and fever. Cara seemed to be there almost always in the first days—at least when John Henry was awake and aware of his surroundings. He remembered her mopping his forehead, his chest, his arms and legs, with a damp washcloth. Her soft voice: "It's all right, baby. Everyone gets it. It's the water. It's just like you moved to a foreign country. Think of it that way. You won't die. Your body has to adjust. Nothing is as clean up here as you're used to." Cara was dripping sugar water from her own fingers onto his lips, his tongue, as she talked.

For a time, the "won't die" promise seemed problematic. When John Henry was again able to tend to himself and knew that Cara had been right, he saw a scarecrow staring back at him from the bathroom mirror. How much weight had he lost? How much of himself had just run out of him, leaked away? Cara starting bringing him soups then, soft drinks, ice creams, puddings, gelatins, eggs, fruit concoctions, stews—anything soft, anything heavy in protein, anything he could hold down. Slowly the scarecrow began to fill out and again become John Henry.

And books. Cara brought those, too, after John Henry was well enough to read them—book after book on social justice, environmental justice, racial justice. Some were smuggled in from abroad; many simply had been carried across the border from Canada, where publishers did a brisk business in anti-American diatribes. Some titles John Henry knew; some he had read; a few he had read to the end. He'd always been a quick and voracious reader, and he lived, after all, on the grounds of a great academic institution. "For here we are not afraid to follow truth wherever it may lead . . ." The words were from Thomas Jefferson himself, much quoted at university functions. John Henry had paid attention: He'd followed truth, followed it right off campus, followed it right out of town.

Sitting on his hard plank chair or lying propped up in bed, reading by the light of his dormer window or by the weak, naked bulb of his bedside lamp, John Henry devoured the tracts Cara brought him. Once, he winced, almost cried, when he saw his mother's scholarship ridiculed in print—her theses pinned and wriggling on the page.

The author struck John Henry as an idiot. Other books shocked him
with the speciousness of their arguments. The academic gene ran
deep in John Henry, a critical faculty that hated the intellectually
cheap. He took to marking the margins of the books with a pencil
stub: "Who says?" "What proof?" Collectively, though, the library
Cara forced on John Henry did its job. Slowly, John Henry opened
up. Slowly, what had been for him just a philosophical viewpoint—a
theoretical way of seeing the world—assumed mass and substance.
Slowly, most important, his theoretical world gained real people:
Cara's "inmates," the menagerie of this DRAGO holding tank.

"JOHNNY?"

IT WAS the name Cara had given John Henry, the one he was
known by in the house. John Henry looked up from his bed—he
was propped against the pillows, reading again—and saw nothing.

"Johnny!" More urgent this time, the accent unmistakably Caribbean.

John Henry shifted his gaze, looked down, and there in his doorway was a man with coal-black skin, less than five feet tall, thin as
a stick, an elf with dreadlocks and eyes that seemed to be darting
everywhere.

"I've come to read your fortune, Johnny." His teeth were stained
a deep yellow and brown—colors John Henry had never seen teeth
be—but the man's smile ran all the way across his face.

"I've got the magic, Johnny! Jonah has the mojo!" He held a
Ziploc plastic bag as high up as his arm would reach. As he shook
it, John Henry could see large brown pellets dancing inside.

"What are they?" John Henry was laughing, unable to resist. He'd
swung his feet over the side of his bed and was sitting on the edge.

"The mojo, Johnny! The mojo! The truth! Here, come on."

The man squatted down on the floor and motioned that John
Henry was to join him. He was just opening the bag, getting ready
to roll its contents onto the floor, when Cara showed up at the door
with yet another small stack of books.

"Out," she said. Only one word, but not angry—she was laughing
herself.

The man looked up at her, smiled his ear-to-ear smile again.

"Oh, no, Cara, no. The boy needs to know his future. We're going to roll the mojo!"

"No, Jonah. Not your future. I'm Johnny's future."

Cara smiled at John Henry as Jonah zipped his bag, rose, and disappeared down the hall. John Henry could hear him chortling on the steps as Cara set the books on the table beside his bed.

"What was in the bag?" he asked.

"Turds, baby. Bassett hound turds. That's what he tells the future with. Jonah says they're the best because bassett hounds do their business close to the ground. 'Da turds drop true,' he says. He's a forger, honey. Jonah can make the prettiest papers you ever saw. Be a good boy, and maybe he'll make some papers for you."

Two hours later, John Henry was sitting in the chair beside his bed, staring out the window at the rocky hillside behind the house, when a man wearing a burnoose showed up at his door.

"Allah is great," he said. He was John Henry's height at least, with olive skin and sandals on his feet.

John Henry had no idea what to say back.

"Flee the house, Johnny. Flee. It's filled with Christian pigs."

And then he, too, was gone. John Henry recognized his voice. He occupied the bedroom directly below. John Henry could hear his repeated prayers to Allah.

THE EVENING MEAL downstairs was a communal one—for everyone, it seemed, but John Henry. He would sit in the stairwell and hear people gathering. Next, the smells would begin to drift up to him—boiled meat, maybe; steamed vegetables; sometimes fresh-baked bread. Always a pall of cigarette smoke came along with it. After the smells came the voices. A single person might be holding forth—there was an Irishman who could dominate conversation, John Henry noticed. Once John Henry knew who Jonah was, he could hear his high-pitched voice dancing over the others. Sometimes the house seemed to rock with laughter as the people downstairs ate; other times, there would be arguments, angry words, shouts, the thud of a fist or the smack of a body flying against a wall. John Henry longed to join them. The louder the roar from downstairs, the more his room felt like a cell. Time and again during the third week, he asked Cara to let him out, allow him to eat downstairs with everyone else, but Cara wouldn't permit it. He had to wait, needed to regain strength. Dinner with the "inmates" wasn't for "the weak of body, the faint of heart."

"You think you know so much, baby, and you know so little," Cara told him one evening as she sat with John Henry, the two of them eating their meals off trays. "You think you've seen the world because you've traveled with your daddy and your mama, because you've been on the plane and traveled in the motorcade and when you got out of that limo there was someone waiting who would have let you pee in his pocket if you'd wanted to. Where have you been? Tell Cara what you've seen of this world dark and wide."

"Berlin," John Henry answered. "New Zealand—Auckland and Wellington. Buenos Aires." He felt tiny, petulant, as he ticked off the stops: the grand tour of South America; the grand tour of the German regional capitals—Amsterdam, Paris, Madrid, Rome, Vienna—as well as Berlin itself; London, of course; always with the motorcade, always with the person just waiting to have his pocket pissed in if that was what John Henry so chose. He knew who Cara was talking about; he could picture him at almost every stop along the way.

"Truth is, honey, that's just a tiny little bit of the world," Cara said when he was through. "Those are just the places you see in picture books, and picture books are just the way you saw them. Truth is, honey, you don't know jack shit."

A few minutes later, the two of them were sitting quietly when there was a sudden roar downstairs. The Arab who had come to John Henry's door two afternoons earlier was screaming.

"Jesus be damned!

"Mary be damned!

"Joseph be damned!

"Fuck the Holy Ghost!"

His voice pounded the walls—it was as if there had been an earthquake; the house seemed to be shaking. John Henry almost jumped back when he heard the screams.

Cara reached over, put a hand on John Henry's knee, and patted it. "It's just Ibrahim," she said. "He's caught in no-man's-land. Sometimes he has to let it out."

"No-man's-land?"

"He can't go back to where he came from, baby. He's got a wife there and a little boy with a hole in his heart. If that boy doesn't get an operation before he's fourteen, he's going to die, and the only place you can get that operation is in the good old Confederate States of America. Ibrahim needs to become a citizen so his boy can be operated on. He's been trying for six years."

"Why . . . ?"

"He just can't do it. He went through the Patriation Program once on his own and a second time with papers we made up for him, and both times it was the same thing. He sailed through—he works like a dog. But the last thing you've got to do, baby, the very last thing of all before they let you through those pearly gates, is renounce all other gods, all other prophets, and accept the Christian God as your own. Ibrahim can't do that. He can't renounce Muhammad, he can't defile his faith—and he can't save his son until he does. We're just giving him a place to live until he can figure it out."

"Isn't there anything that can be done?"

"Nothing. Nothing so long as everyone can just sleepwalk right past Ibrahim, right past all of us, because we're all in no-man's-land, baby. We all have nowhere to go."

It was uncanny, John Henry thought, how often Cara took words out of his mouth, out of his mind. "Sleepwalk" was what he had said to his mother that last afternoon. He could see the living room; he could feel the tension in his mother's neck and shoulders.

"We've got to make people take notice," Cara was saying.

"How?"

"Oh, your Cara has a plan. And, baby, you're a big part of it—a big part. But first we've got to get you well."

Cara took her fork, lifted the piece of apple pie off her own tray, slid it onto John Henry's, and then took a pinch of his cheek, his arm, his stomach just above his beltline.

"You're getting some meat back on you. You're going to live."

WHILE JOHN HENRY waited to be allowed downstairs for dinner, he worked on doing what for him was maybe the hardest thing: making what acquaintances he could, being social. "Hello" came out of his mouth like something indigestible he was spitting back out. "Hi" was easier, or "Hey." That much he found he could handle.

Small talk was harder, both because Cara had told him to give away nothing about himself and because small talk simply wasn't in him, especially with strangers.

Still, John Henry made inroads. During the third week of his stay, Cara allowed him to come downstairs from midmorning to mid-afternoon—after the morning-shift workers had left, before they returned.

He met the two Marys, lesbians who lived downstairs and worked as cook and housekeeper. One of the Marys, Cara told him, had been a professional photographer, the other a college professor, before they decided to live publicly as they had so long lived privately—as a couple, as lovers. Soon thereafter they had been exiled to the territories; not many weeks later, they had washed up at the house in North Adams. John Henry could barely tell them apart, and then he realized there was no need to. Mary and Mary came together and went together. Together they were raising a Chinese-looking baby that for all John Henry knew had dropped out of the sky into their laps.

One day, a Mary took John Henry down to her photographic studio in the basement—nothing more than a plywood enclosure that leaned against the stacked-stone foundation of the house.

"Sit here," she said.

When John Henry was properly positioned on the high stool, she adjusted two lights and slipped behind her camera.

"I used to specialize in portraits," she was saying as the flash went off. "Magazine covers, corporate reports, that kind of thing."

John Henry could hear her camera whirring. Something was coming out the side of it.

"Now," Mary said, "I specialize in these."

She handed John Henry a one-inch-by-one-inch black-and-white photo of himself. On the way back upstairs, they stopped at another plywood enclosure and watched Jonah laminating a similar one-inch-by-one-inch photo to a national work permit. That, Mary told him, was for paying customers.

The photo she had taken was lying on John Henry's bedside table that evening when Cara poked her head into his room.

"No, baby," she said as she took the photo and slipped it into her pocket. "We don't want this getting loose."

John Henry didn't know why, but when Cara left with the photograph, he felt devastated. Maybe, he thought, it was proof that I am.

Two afternoons later, a little before it was time for him to go back upstairs, John Henry was sitting on the steps of the front porch, staring off into the maples that surrounded the house, when the other Mary came out, holding the baby who John Henry thought was Chinese.

"Ever hear the phrase 'smoked Yankee'?" she asked him. The voices were the only, slight difference John Henry had been able to discover between the two Marys. This Mary cut off her words more sharply.

"Sure," he said, grateful for the company. He could hear his mother's father saying it clear as a bell: "That boy's dumber than a smoked Yankee." But he'd never given the phrase two thoughts in his life.

"It was born right over there," Mary said, pointing due east through the woods, "just a few miles away."

She sat down beside John Henry on the steps, handed him the baby, and lit a cigarette.

"It was the fall of 1865," she said, "and Nathan Bedford Forrest was driving the last remnants of a Massachusetts regiment in front of him, up this narrow river valley. Not far from here, Forrest's men managed to flank the Massachusetts boys to the west and come back at them from above, and so the Yankees took refuge in the Hoosac Tunnel. The tunnel—you'll see it one of these days—is nearly five miles long; it was one of the great engineering marvels of the mid-nineteenth century. But what's good for railroads and commerce is not necessarily good for soldiers.

"Forrest had been forewarned that the Federals might make for the tunnel—farmers up and down the valley were singing like canaries, hoping to save their fields and homes and barns—and so he'd sent a dozen riflemen around to the other end. Now he sent word to the Union soldiers trapped inside: 'Surrender; your position is hopeless.' 'Not until hell freezes over,' word came back out. So Forrest camped by the marble natural bridge on the northeast edge of town that night. By morning, a strong breeze was blowing in from the west, so Forrest wandered down to town, had a fire lit by the tunnel mouth and green boughs thrown on once it was roaring. What happened to the Yankees at the other end was their problem. No one could say he hadn't tried.

"Thus, smoked Yankees."

The baby in his arms was impossibly small, John Henry thought, as delicate as porcelain. He rose and carefully handed the baby to Mary, as if he were handing over dynamite or vials of plague virus.

"Thanks for the story. I've got to get inside. Cara doesn't—"

"She's not going to break," Mary said as she took the baby from him.

"I don't want to find out."

My God, he thought as he started upstairs. Small talk!

AND THE TWO Marys were only part of the wonder. One night, two men had shared the vacant bedroom next door to John Henry. He heard them cooing to each other through the paper-thin walls, heard the grunting, the huffing, the wet sounds of what had to be lovemaking, or sex-making, or climax-making, whatever it was— culminating in long sighs of ecstatic relief. John Henry lay in his bed amazed. Another time, a man he never saw had slept in the same room. John Henry had awakened in the middle of the night to hear the man talking with Ibrahim, in fierce whispers, in a language John Henry had never heard before, a language that seemed to be nothing but sibilants. In the morning, his ears were still filled with the hissing sounds, but the room next door was completely empty.

Black men slept with white women, black women with white men. Or so John Henry imagined. Like Mary and Mary, they sat together, ate together, held hands together, went off to bedrooms together, and together closed their doors. Whites with flat noses and flared nostrils and tightly curled hair came and went. Escapees from the Patriation Program passed through day after day. By the end of the third week, John Henry had decided that he was ready to agree with Cara, agree with her absolutely and forever and beg her for-giveness for ever doubting her: He had been so many places and seen so little; he had seen all the picture-book cities and none of the real picture. He had constructed a whole universe of theoreticals without ever getting down on his hands and knees and studying the details.

This is what John Henry had thought: He had thought that he had the world down pat, that at the tender, protected age of seventeen he had come to know all the permutations and combinations of human possibility. This is what he now knew about himself: He didn't know jack shit. John Henry could round any corner in this house, he thought, and run headlong into a circus hermaphrodite, a woman with three breasts, a fishboy who breathed with gills, a cyclops, Tom Thumb riding a rat. He'd fallen out of what he thought was the real world and ended up in Petronius's *Satyricon*, and a Satyricon was just what the real world was. John Henry got healthier and healthier, and every day the world he inhabited was rich with revelation.

Time and again, John Henry found himself trying to frame the scene for Lucy, thinking how he would tell it, thinking where he would tell it: in her bedroom, over the Scrabble game. She'd be too shocked to say a thing. His joy was to have fallen so lightly—sickness aside, but it was the water and, Cara said, it happened to everyone—into such a human carnival. His sorrow was to have no one he loved to share it with, but maybe that would come. Maybe it would come.

Midway through his fourth week at the house in North Adams, John Henry woke up late in his narrow bed feeling more normal than he had felt in a month, went downstairs after the day shift had left, and learned that Cara had gone. Where, no one seemed to know, or for how long. John Henry was on his own.

He found a scrub brush and disinfectant under the sink, a pail in a pantry closet off the kitchen. He warmed water on the stove so as not to deplete the small hot-water tank in the basement. While he waited for the water to heat, he poured a cup of coffee from an urn that always seemed to be on and full, toasted bread over the gas burner on the stove, and slathered it with margarine and honey. The coffee, his first stimulant in so long, nearly took the top of his head off. Meanwhile, his stomach cried out for more toast, more honey. Go slow, he told himself; take one step at a time.

Upstairs in the third-floor bathroom, he scoured the toilet bowl, the sink, the shower stall; scrubbed the floor; found a rag and washed down the walls, the taps, the top and sides of the toilet tank. His lungs filled with disinfectant, and it seemed as if the lye, the antibacterials, whatever it was that went into such products, was disinfecting him as well. Forty-five minutes later, all carefully wiped down with fresh warm water, the bathroom glowed. What a swamp it had been, John Henry thought, what a cesspool. He set about next on the two second-floor bathrooms. Night-shift workers were still asleep, and Patriation dropouts and other escapees, even when they did stay overnight, kept to the shadows while the sun was out. John Henry had the second floor almost wholly to himself. He'd mopped the first bathroom with a disinfectant and was backing out to let it dry when he felt himself bump into something.

"What the fuck?" a man's voice said.

It was one of the night-shift workers, John Henry guessed. His eyes were thick with sleep, his brain was barely functioning, as he stood in the hallway, naked except for his underpants, his white skin covered from neck to feet with large tufts of black hair.

John Henry looked at the bathroom floor—it was soaking wet— and then led the man by his arm to the bathroom at the other end of the hall. As he walked down the hallway, the man held his penis, engorged with urine.

"I gotta. I can't," he was saying.

"Just a few more steps," John Henry encouraged him, "just a few more."

Finally, they reached the other bathroom, and John Henry could hear a long stream of urine splashing into the bowl. When the man was finished, John Henry led him back down the hallway to an open door. One side of the bedcovers had been thrown back. A black woman was lying in the other half of the bed. John Henry gave the man a gentle push into the room, closed the door, and hoped he'd delivered the right person to the right place.

By two o'clock that afternoon, the second-floor bathrooms were done, and the downstairs powder room, and the sink and countertop and stovetop in the kitchen. Ravenous, John Henry fixed himself a stacked peanut-butter sandwich—four slices of bread separated by thick layers of margarine and peanut butter—took it outside to the front porch, and sat down on the same step where Mary the professor had told him the smoked Yankee story. It was late May in New England, a place John Henry had only read about in history books: the staging ground for American colonization, the graveyard of Yankee greed, pride, hegemony, vaulting ambition, so the books said.

John Henry tried to imagine this town, this space in the continent, this tiny dot in the universe, in the years before the War of Dissolution. Massachusetts had been a colony first, later a state, and only finally a territory. It seemed to have peaked in some earlier life form and been moving steadily backward in evolution since. By the end of the eighteenth century, Massachusetts had fashioned itself as the cradle of patriots, the birthplace of the American Revolution, although clearly it was Virginia—cradle of Washington, Jefferson, Mason, Madison, Monroe, etc.—that had earned both honors. This land would have been beautiful back then, John Henry supposed, the trees lush and thick, rivers and streams full of fish, bear and deer in all the woods.

But that was before: before the war, before Lee's army had scoured New England in flames, before the mill owners and industrial barons and railroad lords had seen the end coming and made common cause with the South, before the Northeast Industrial Zone had been born and the Yankees had begun to learn to pay not just with their lives and their fortunes but with their very land, the air they breathed, the water they drank—the water, John Henry thought, that had made him sicker than he had ever known he could be.

He left his sandwich plate and milk glass on the front step and walked down the drive, through the scraggly forest toward the road. Squirrels chased each other in front of him. They were thinner than the squirrels that filled the university grounds; their coats seemed slighter and filled with battle scars, as if each acorn had to be won, not found. In front of him, the brook, surprisingly full and clean with last night's hard rain, ran downhill toward the town.

As he walked, John Henry kept to the side of the driveway, hidden as best he could be from the small parade of cars that worked its way into and out of North Adams. He had no idea if his photograph was plastered over territorial police offices, whether he was the subject of an all-points bulletin, and he had no desire to find out. John Henry turned around now, found himself a good two hundred yards from the house, almost out of sight of the front porch, and instinctively started to hurry back. But "hurry" was the wrong word. Just as he turned around, John Henry felt as tired as he had ever felt before. His legs were lead as he trudged up the front steps, up the two flights to his bedroom, past the open door of the bathroom that seemed to glow as if from some inner light. Hard work, he told himself. Good work. He was asleep almost before his head hit the pillow.

John Henry dreamed that afternoon of, of all improbable things, tennis. He and his father were both dressed in impeccable whites, playing on the clay courts that sat beside the old gymnasium. Lucy and his mother sat at courtside watching them, a pitcher of hand-squeezed lemonade on the table between them. Wide-brimmed hats cast their faces into deep shadow. The sun was brilliant, blinding.

When he woke, it was dark outside. A roar was coming from the dining table downstairs, and John Henry felt as if he hadn't eaten in months.

"AH, OUR FAIRY godson. My God, boy, the bathroom was so clean I had to do my business out the back door!"

John Henry stood on the stairs a moment, unsure whether to go back up or keep coming down. Cara was nowhere to be seen.

"C'mon, Johnny boy. C'mon. We won't bite you hard, and it's payday. We've got all the trimmings tonight. I'm Sean. I'll let the rest of our merry band make your acquaintance on their own."

Sean was sitting at the head of the table, a six-pack of Guinness at his side. John Henry had no eye for ages, but something about Sean's thinning reddish-brown hair and the lines around the mouth of his square head said that he was in his mid-thirties, neither young nor old. As he talked to John Henry, Sean's voice fell into a heavy brogue.

"A wee meal wouldn't be the worst thing for you, laddie. Not after what you've been through."

There was a general murmur of agreement, a round of light applause for his cleaning efforts. As John Henry took the last few steps, a chair appeared at the far side of the table, bodies squeezed together left and right to create a space. No one at the table was within seven or eight years of John Henry's age; nor was anyone anywhere near his father's age, as best as he could tell. Other than that, he thought, there was not a single thing in common shared by the people sitting there. At Sean's right, Jonah bobbed up and down, waving at John Henry, seemingly thrilled by his company; next to him was a woman in a flowered housedress whose weight must have been three times Jonah's. Her head seemed to rest on her shoulders—John Henry could discern no neck in the flickering candlelight. One small shift in her seat now that they were all cramming together, and she might crush Jonah. Directly across from John Henry as he sat down was a man with the largest Adam's apple he'd ever seen. To the left of the man, the two Marys, hand in hand, smiled at John Henry. Not even the seats around the table matched—half seemed to be folding chairs, the others looked as if they were held together with tape.

A plate was put in front of him, a jelly-jar glass, enough utensils for the purpose. Then came the communal plates, stacked high with food: fried chicken, rice, green beans, gravy. *Gravy!* John Henry had visions of his grandmother's rambling Victorian house in Raleigh— his mother's brothers and sisters, his cousins, all bent to grace at Thanksgiving as the gravy bubbled in its boat. Here, there were jugs of wine at either end as well, red and white. John Henry's glass disappeared from in front of him; when it returned, it had been filled to the top with red: another badge of acceptance. The first swallow burned in his throat; the second felt better. Heretofore he had been served wine in the thimble-sized crystal glasses passed down through his mother's family, glasses so delicate that John Henry trembled even to touch them. And then only one glass. And then only on state occasions. The glass he held in his hand now looked as if it could be punched through a wall, and the wine supply seemed endless.

After the first few minutes, attention faded from John Henry. The huge woman in the flowered housedress had begun reading aloud—a long, long poem about prisons and convicts and the injustice of justice, perhaps her own composition. By the time she ended, John Henry was tucking into a second helping of chicken, more rice, more gravy. Sean lurched to his feet, carried the empty six-pack to the kitchen, and came back with a fresh six. He didn't seem to be sharing. There was an argument about dessert—now? later? only for those who had paid extra into the kitty? Later won, eaten in the living room and for everyone. The woman who had been reading the long, long poem was now singing nursery rhymes, as if they were opera arias: *Jack Spra-a-at could eat no fa-a-at*—the *a*'s trilled and held for what seemed minutes at a time. Sean hit the woman with a piece of balled-up white bread before she could launch into Mrs. Sprat and the fact that she could eat no lean. John Henry was assailing a third piece of chicken when everyone seemed to rise more or less simultaneously and carry the debris into the kitchen. He carried his own in just as the dishwashers for the night were finishing up the pile.

"Keep your glass, Johnny boy," someone said to him, picking up Sean's rendering of Cara's version of his name and carrying him still further away from who he had been, what he had been, where he had been that person.

By the time John Henry had washed and dried his own dishes, put them away, and topped off his glass, amateur hour was under way in the living room. Quiet as a church mouse, as invisible as he could make himself, John Henry slipped into the room and found a seat at the end of a long, worn sofa. He knew where Cara would want him. Cara was entitled to her opinion, but Cara didn't know how badly he wanted human company. He'd stay for a while, he'd listen, he'd leave. No harm would come of it. None.

The woman with the Jack Sprat arias had just been warming up at the table, John Henry learned. As he settled into the sofa, she broke into a tearful version of "Shenandoah." She was coming to the end—"Away, I'm bound away! 'Cross the wide Missouri"— when she tried a bound herself and crashed toward the corner of the coffee table. No one cared—the wine jug was rescued before she came down. Mary and Mary did a surprisingly graceful tango—one with a rose in her mouth, the other with a thin black cigar—while Sean balanced the Chinese-looking baby on his knee, threw her into the air, caught her just before she hit the floor. Then Sean and Jonah excused themselves, were gone for a few minutes, and came back in costume—Sean in a white shirt and red-white-and-blue tie, his hair slicked back; Jonah dressed more smartly, a suit coat over a dark-blue shirt, a deep-purple tie matched with a purple dish towel that spilled out of his breast pocket, and a huge pillow stuffed inside his waist. Something in their costumes snapped John Henry to attention. Then he realized what it was: They were dressed as Spencer Lee and his own father. Almost instantly, they broke into an old Alphonse and Gaston routine:

"After you, Spencer."

"Why, no, Nathan, after you."

"But I insist."

"But I insist *aussi*."

Time and again, they started through the doorway from the den together. Time and again, they collided—Spencer's shoulders were too big, Nathan's belly was too wide. Soon they fell on each other, trying to push one another through the door first. Nathan grabbed Spencer's tie and tried to choke him with it; Spencer grabbed Nathan's belly, reached inside his shirt, and started to tear huge chunks out of the pillow. Before long they were rolling on the floor, pretending to pummel each other. For John Henry, it was impossible not to laugh, impossible not to be scared, impossible not to wonder if this was meant for him and him alone. And then the finale—double somersaults through the door, a leap to their feet, riotous applause—and the show moved on. Jonah settled in with his pipe and some kind of tobacco, sweeter than John Henry had ever smelled. Sean disappeared into the kitchen and came back with more Guinness. A ventriloquist sipped water from a glass, threw her voice across the room, and worked a dummy's head; a musician plucked his guitar and sang of a mixed-race baby left to die by the railroad tracks; a monologist told a very funny story about the night grandfather fell out of bed. And then, before John Henry knew it, there was no one else—there was only himself.

"What about you, Johnny boy?" It was Sean, crouching in front of him. Behind Sean, John Henry could see the two Marys rise, hand in hand, and leave the room. Jonah bounced beside them, headed it seemed wherever they were going.

"I don't really have any talents. I don't sing or dance—" John Henry's voice was soft, his eyes averted.

"No, no, I don't mean that. Just tell us about yourself. Tell us who you are. That'll be entertainment enough."

"Me? I'm just me. I'm nobody."

"Oh, no, you're not just nobody." It was the woman he was sitting next to. John Henry had felt safe with her. She was among the oldest women in the room, with her graying hair pulled back in the kind of twin buns John Henry's grandmother had worn. Beneath her ashen skin her body had started to go heavy and soft—the sort of body a grandmother should have, a body for leaning into. Now she leaned forward and turned to him. "You're one of Cara's. Cara doesn't do nobodies."

"You're somebody, Johnny." Sean was cooing to him now, closing in. John Henry smelled the stout on his breath. "Everybody's somebody. We're just all different somebodies."

The woman next to John Henry poked him on the arm. "A thoroughbred. Look at that skin—he's a real thoroughbred. No white man's gotten over that family wall in generations."

Laughter.

"And young. What are you, Johnny? Sixteen? Seventeen? Eighteen?" from across the room. "Why would someone so young be one of Cara's specials?"

"Maybe he's famous." Another voice.

Yet another one: "Maybe he's somebody famous's boy."

John Henry tried to sit still, to not hear, to be somewhere else in his head. But his head was here all the same. He heard. Inches now from his face, Sean saw it.

"Famous daddy? Famous mommy? Which will it be?" John Henry could see the dental work in Sean's mouth, the stray pieces of food trapped in his teeth. "Which will it be, Johnny boy? Mommy or Daddy? Dear Dad or Dear Mom? Tell us a story."

"No."

"Johnny boy—"

"No. Please. Leave me alone."

John Henry saw Sean's right hand move, a flick, a glint. He felt the blade pressed flat against his neck, felt it turning over slowly, slowly, felt a tiny rivulet of warm blood slip over his collarbone and run down his chest.

Sean's mouth was pressed hard against his ear now, whispering, imploring, warning: "One thing about the company you're keeping these days, Johnny boy. We've none of us got anything to lose."

John Henry could feel his own sweat now, parallel rivulets to the tiny stream of blood. He was awash; his body was turning to liquid again.

"You've cost me big, Johnny boy. Cost me big. Someone has to pay."

John Henry heard a click, a slam. He felt Sean draw back and the woman next to him settle deeper into her seat. Cara was standing at the front door.

"Oh, baby," she said. "Oh, baby, what have they been doing to you?"

She pulled John Henry up by the hand, put her arm around his waist, found some tissues in her pocket, and pressed them against his neck as she led him up the stairs. "Cara told you, honey, didn't she? You don't know jack shit." And again, John Henry agreed.

She cleaned the cut in the third-floor bathroom, then put some alcohol and a Band-Aid on it. It was nothing, a nick. In the bedroom, Cara laid John Henry on his mattress, pulled off his shoes and socks, helped him out of his jeans, and covered him with his sheet.

"We got to teach you, baby. We got to show you the world," she said as she turned out the light by his bed and closed the door. In the morning, Sean was gone, along with every evidence of his existence.

15

WASHINGTON, D.C.

"HEY, HADDON. TOO bad about your stiffs." It was Andes, in a cubicle a few units down from the lieutenant's. "I mean, after you'd spent so much time getting to know them and all."

So, Haddon thought, everyone's heard. He'd been out almost a week with the cold he picked up in the morgue—a deep, dry hack that he felt all the way through his rib cage. Nothing seemed to work on it, not Jenkins's mother's tea and bourbon, not even Paulie's bourbon, bitters, and God knows what else. Finally, Haddon had used his badge to bully his way into the only decent health club in the city and settled into the steam room, determined not to leave until the cold was gone. Four hours later, puckered like old fruit, he'd had to crawl to the steam-room door and pull himself up by its handle, but it had worked. The next day, he'd shown up at work, to learn that his two John Does had gone *poof* in the night—requisitioned by the federal coroner in Richmond and delivered promptly to his care.

"Condolences accepted," Haddon called back, "in the spirit in which they were meant. And your vacation, Lieutenant Andes?"

"Warm, Haddon. Very warm. Not a frozen body for miles around."

"Sounds like heaven."

For months now, a poster had been stapled to the wall above Lieutenant Andes's desk. It showed a beautiful Hawaiian beach. The sand was snow white; the water a remarkable aqua. Two scantily

clad women lounged on the beach in the foreground. One of them
was covered with blood, thanks to a suspect in a grand larceny case
who had taken it into his mind, as he was being questioned, to try
to drive a stapler through his interviewer's ear. The interviewer, who
had been using Lieutenant Andes's cubicle in his absence, was still
in the hospital.

OFFICIALLY, THE CASE of the two bodies in the Washington City
Canal no longer belonged to Lieutenant Haddon. The feds had
moved in, seized his stiffs, and elbowed him out of the way. There
would be a coroner's report—undoubtedly there already was one—
but Haddon would never see it, unless the case suddenly became
unimportant enough for the feds to dump back in his lap.

Officially, too, Haddon didn't really care. The crime itself didn't
interest him all that much. The feds could run the tests, make what
matches they could, find whatever links there were to be found between the two bodies and the two men—their virtual twins—who
had shown up live that same day at the dinner honoring the
InterAmerican Waterway. Resemblances like that didn't happen by
chance, especially when so much blood was involved.

But Haddon couldn't let go of the way the crime had been ac-
cessorized. The fingertips still rattled around in his mind a month
later. Were the two men dead when the bolt cutter came out? Or
still alive? The coroner might actually be able to tell that. What he
wouldn't be able to tell was what had been going on in their heads
if they had been alive. Did they wonder what might come next, after
the ends of their fingers? What did you think about when your
fingertips were being sheared off one by one? Or did you try not to
think at all? To an insomniac like Clark Haddon, such questions
had a way of coming alive at inopportune moments. They haunted—
fingertips dancing across the floor, fingertips with smiley faces
painted on them, fingertips packed into little tins marked "for export
only." The haunting could be exorcised only with answers.

But there was more to it than that. Professional pride, for one
thing. More than four weeks had passed with no inquiry that might
be linked to the two dead men. No missing person report had been
filed for anyone remotely resembling either of them; no all-stations
bulletins concerning the two had come clattering over the wire from

Richmond's Central Bureau. The two men had come from dust and returned to dust with seemingly no one noting their passage in between. Yet their lives didn't begin with them dead in the Washington City Canal, centerpieces for a rat banquet. And, of course, someone *had* noticed them. Someone had paid attention to the two men at least long enough to see that they bore an uncanny physical resemblance to two other people, who themselves would turn up dead less than twenty-four hours later on national television. Someone wanted to borrow that resemblance, short term, just for the day. Someone wanted the resemblance enough to bring a bolt cutter along—sorry about the fingertips, that ugly little crunch of bone.

That was the connection that fascinated the lieutenant: Who would that someone be? The dead were dead. It was the living that held his interest. Until he'd seen the faces of the two waiters close up on the government affairs channel, so much like the two frozen bodies he had just been chatting up in the D.C. morgue—until that moment, DRAGO had been barely a blip on the lieutenant's radar screen: a nuisance, yes; a pest, sure, but someone else's pest. And who, at any rate, would have noticed DRAGO's presence in Washington? Washington was the world capital of outcasts, a Calcutta of despairing souls. Half the population spent its waking hours in static-free shoes, gliding from computer console to computer console to produce and manage and count and collate the forms that kept the bureaucracy of the Confederate States of America humming. (Genius, the lieutenant thought. Genius to keep that away from Richmond, to leave it here! Who thought of it? Or did it just happen? More grist for his insomnia.) The other half of Washington came out at night, slithered along the shadows of the great diagonal avenues, waited in the scabrous parks that dotted the downtown, found its way to the brambly privacy of the Mall or to clubs with spyholes cut in their front doors. Maybe, in fact, it was the same half of the population day and night—spirits broken daily, daily seeking repair. The lieutenant could never tell; maybe he didn't want to know. In any event, it didn't matter.

Now, though, two bodies had been left in the City Canal. On Detective Lieutenant Clark Haddon's turf, his territory. There was answering to be done for that, and DRAGO, whatever it really was, seemed to have at least part of the answering to do. At the least, Haddon's professional pride needed to be satisfied—you couldn't just leave two murdered and maimed people where he could find them and expect to walk away.

Besides, a case like this was perfect for a man whose brain had trouble slowing down. What was the lieutenant going to do otherwise? Play charades with Jenkins and Flannerty? Discuss Locke with them? Work the Sunday crossword puzzle with his two loyal patrolmen?

"Hey, Lieutenant, what's a nine-letter word for dumb fuck?"

"F-l-a-n-n-e-r-t-y?"

Also, there was this: The lieutenant had been high-hatted in Richmond. He understood, of course, the need for controlling the investigation, for security. The President of the Confederacy had been at the banquet where the two waiters died, and the President wasn't a pork salesman from Nebraska. Security was critical; most investigations leaked like old buckets precisely because too many people got involved, too many jurisdictions, too many bruised egos and waggy tongues. Fine, close the investigation. Call him off. Tell the District police to get lost. Take the bodies. What was the lieutenant going to do with them? Thaw them out and throw them in the Crock-Pot? But do it right! Don't send some supervisor mincing out from behind his smoked-glass partition to pull the files right out of the lieutenant's hand.

Maybe that's why he had palmed the photo of the black man standing in the clearing, Haddon thought. Because of that conspiratorial wink the supervisor had given him in Richmond, that crap about "professional courtesy." Maybe he had done it because everything about that headquarters building had been so sparkling—no cracked glass such as enclosed his own cubicle, no flaking paint, no blood-splattered posters. There'd even been carpeting on the floors, for God's sake, soft music piped from the ceiling. Maybe, the lieutenant thought, he'd palmed the photo simply because he could do so, because if you finish high school in a combination pool hall and bar instead of a classroom, there are certain skills you learn that prove surprisingly useful in the real world. Maybe he'd palmed it because for all their glittering trappings and advanced criminology degrees, the Richmond police hadn't seemed all that bright.

Jesus, the photo he'd left in its place—the one he'd pulled from his wallet along with the magnifier—was a fifteen-year-old snapshot of his sister, blank-eyed and wide as a whale, in a bathing suit at the Maryland shore. Had anyone looked at the evidence envelope since? Didn't they think it a little odd to find that there? Or were the feds going to run Doris to ground, shove a .45 up her nostril, and get her to confess to being the DRAGO mastermind? Hell, she'd probably be proud. Thirty-year-old women with Down's syndrome don't get much chance for celebrity. The lieutenant just hoped they didn't shoot his mother before his sister fessed up.

And, of course, if the photo had not been the point then, if it was incidental to the getting of it, it was very much the point now. The photo was what the lieutenant had to go on—nothing else. There were no bodies in the morgue anymore, no bodies waiting to spill their secrets. If the lieutenant was going to get to the bottom of things, the photo would have to speak to him now. If it wouldn't speak to him, he'd have to make it.

"Ve have our vays!" he screamed at the black man, the trees beside him, the rocks behind him. "Ya, ve have dem!"

Jenkins and Flannerty didn't even turn from their lockers. This had been going on for days.

"WHAT AM I looking for, Captain Haddon?"

"It's lieutenant, Dr. Ridley, and it's not him," Haddon answered, pointing to the black man in the foreground. "Forget him. Who he is doesn't matter. It's the place. Where was this photo taken?"

The photo had been digitized, thrown on a computer screen. Robert Ridley was chairman of the geology division at the Johns Hopkins Unified Laboratories in Baltimore. A hand-printed sign over his office door read: "Geology Is Destiny."

"Above a thousand feet, below five thousand feet, on an east-facing slope. The trees, the lighting, tell you that. You don't need a geologist."

Ridley had been notably unenthusiastic when Haddon called him, two days earlier. He would meet with the lieutenant only in his own lab, Ridley had said, and only at his own time and only for a very little of it. Haddon had expected to find a burly man, hardened by the elements, capable of surviving for weeks with nothing but a pickax and a canteen. Ridley seemed to be a laboratory geologist instead, slightly built, with a neatly trimmed salt-and-pepper beard and small, soft hands. On the desktop beside the computer, a piece of reddish rock the size of a silver dollar sat embedded in a square of lucite.

"Mars, Lieutenant," Ridley said as he picked up the lucite and handed it to Haddon. "I had a hand in the last probe."

While the lieutenant studied the rock, Ridley turned his monitor off, spun in his chair, and started to rise, ready to dismiss his company. Haddon was out of his jurisdiction, off the reservation—he hadn't found a Washington geologist worth the effort. Ridley had every right to ask him to leave.

"Try harder, Dr. Ridley," the lieutenant said, leaning across him and turning the monitor back on. "It's a puzzle. People died. Fingertips were cut off and fed to rats. Let yourself be engaged by the subject. Thus far, you've managed to limit the spot to—what?—ten percent of the earth's surface?"

"Less than that, Lieutenant. We're mostly water and lowlands, and not all the foothills face east."

Oh, the tone of that. The disdain. The lieutenant could feel himself being measured for the kill. Still, Ridley had liked the fingertips part, liked the rats. The lieutenant could tell.

"Sheared off one at a time, Dr. Ridley, with a bolt cutter. What more do the trees say?"

"Middle latitudes. That's obvious. Were they alive or dead? The people? When the bolt cutter was used?"

"A question that keeps me up at night. A question that won't let me sleep. That's why I'm here. What are we down to? Seven percent?"

"Less."

"How about the rocks?"

Ridley sectioned the screen, selected a frame, blew it up; sectioned that, selected another frame, and blew it up again. The photograph lost definition, became individual pixels. Again and again. Whatever it was that he was seeing was lost to the lieutenant, a professional mystery. Now Ridley reversed the process, brought the photo back to life. The cursor was sitting on the frame he had started with.

"Do you see that, Lieutenant? Do you see where the rock seems to flow right there?"

The lieutenant didn't, but he'd take Ridley's word.

"It's volcanic."

"Volcanic?"

"That's dried lava."

"I was an indifferent student, Doc. Help me here. What are we learning?"

"What kind of mountain range we're dealing with. Look, most of the mountains you're familiar with were created by what's called orogeny. Continents collide; the underlying tectonic plates grind together; the earth's crust gets folded; and all of a sudden you've got the Appalachian Mountains, bluegrass music, and families living six to a trailer between a bunch of hogback ridges. All sorts of strange things can occur when orogeny happens. Just north of here there's a huge deposit of chromite that got kicked off the ocean floor hundreds of millions of years ago and churned up to the surface. It was thought to be the largest one in the world until even bigger ones were found churned up to the surface of South Africa."

"So what we've got here is an orogenous mountain?"—a beautiful word, at least; wonderfully suggestive even if the lieutenant still had no real idea what it meant. As far as he was concerned, the chromite was just showing off.

"Quite the opposite. That's what I've been trying to tell you. The mountain range in this photograph was created by volcanic action, like Indonesia, the Hawaiian islands. It exploded through the surface of the sea."

The lieutenant's heart sank—Joseph Ngubo was standing on some island archipelago with astoundingly familiar vegetation.

"New Zealand?" The name just popped into his head—an upside-down eastern America, he'd once heard it called.

"Could be, but I suspect it's much closer by."

"Something just offshore of, say, New Jersey?"

"I said *most* of the mountain ranges you were familiar with were created by orogeny, not all of them. One of them formed as an offshore island arc—a volcanic eruption—and then got rammed onto North America as the continental plates were colliding, pushed up, and laminated onto the East Coast. Five hundred million years ago, Lieutenant—a tenth of the life of the planet."

The lieutenant waited this time. Like most academics he'd encountered, Ridley loved to parade his knowledge but was loath to give away the punch line. Haddon hated to give him the satisfaction of asking. On the other hand, life was short, the drive back to Washington would be hard, and he really didn't like Robert Ridley very much.

"And what mountain range might that be, Doc?"

"The Blue Ridge, right next door."

"Practically in my own backyard. Anything else to go on? People who use a bolt cutter on other people tend to be repeat performers. And sometimes they don't stop with fingertips."

Ridley turned back to the screen once more, studied the image, selected another frame, and blew it up once, twice. This time the lieutenant could still see what was being displayed.

"This dark spot here: I can't be sure, but it looks like the entrance to a cave to me. The Blue Ridge is dotted with them. You've got a clearing," he said, using his cursor as a pointer, "a pronounced horizontal streak of quartz at about seven feet up this steep wall, and quite possibly the entrance to a cave just at the back right. Try spelunkers' clubs. Get the Geological Survey maps—they're quite good. A little of that shoe leather you police people are so famous for, and the whole thing should be solved."

As the lieutenant rose, ready to go, Ridley reached in his shirt pocket and handed him a card. His upper lip was beaded with sweat, his brow covered with it. A son-of-a-bitch geologist who got off on body parts. Lieutenant Haddon would make a notation, start a file. There was never an unuseful piece of information about anyone.

"I'd be glad to be called as a witness, Lieutenant Haddon, but I don't testify for free."

Make that a greedy son-of-a-bitch geologist who got off on body parts—life never ceased to amaze the lieutenant. He waited until the office door had closed behind him, then wrote a note on the back of Ridley's card and slipped it under his door.

"No need to testify," the note read. "We'll just kill them when we catch them."

16

NATIONAL UNIVERSITY
OF THE SOUTH,
WEST CAMPUS

"THE COORDINATE COURSE Jason and Lucy are taking is a small experiment," Spencer was saying. "There's no hidden agenda, Lucinda. The course is nothing more than what it is. The trustees' meeting made that quite obvious. Everything is out on the table."

"Still—"

"But we have to look to new possibilities, new ways of doing things. We can't be afraid of change."

At the far end of the Winstons' living room, away from the windows, Nathan was silent as a stone. He and Lucinda seemed to be avoiding each other, Spencer thought, giving one another elaborate space for passing, each going to the most distant point in the room whenever the other sat down. Behind Nathan, in the kitchen, Spencer could hear Wormley on his walkie-talkie, worrying about the fine points of the stroll the President and the Vice President were scheduled to take across the Lawn in twenty-five minutes, screwing down the last details of the reception that was to be held on the steps of the rotunda. Upstairs, Redmond had taken over Lucinda's office. Spencer had seen her pull out what seemed like dozens and dozens of pink call-back slips before she headed up the stairs. Thank God, he thought, it was her, not me. Beyond the drawn curtains of the front windows, Spencer could see two burly shapes—agents, he assumed, keeping the sightseers away.

"And the budget pressures *are* real, Lucinda," he went on. "They're very real. It's not just the waterway, although I'll admit the waterway has meant less money for everything else. It's deeper problems, more long-term ones. This university can't lead the way if it can't lead in the sciences, and the sciences get more and more expensive. Supercomputers, high-speed computer networks"—Spencer searched in his breast pocket and found a printed list—"bioprocessing labs, low-background neutron beams, research reactors, equipment for biological and medical imaging, for supercritical extraction and nondestructive sensing, for nanofabrication, artificial intelligence, magnetic-field fusion . . . You name it, you've got to have them all these days. If we didn't have to provide separate facilities for the two campuses, if we could establish a tradition of dual education—just at the highest academic levels—it would be a lot easier for the university to maintain its leadership. That's a large part of what Lucy and Jason's course is about. Dr. Cuthbert is going to report to us at the next board meeting on how successfully the students from both campuses worked together. He expects, we're told, to deliver a very favorable report, but we'll see. We'll take some measurements and proceed carefully."

"I'm well aware of the budget pressures, Spencer. We feel them even in the low-cost humanities."

"Low cost, high gain—a politician's dream!"

"You're changing the subject, Mr. President."

"I hope so. I deeply do."

Spencer Lee never felt so large, so oafish, as when he sat in the front parlor of the Winstons' pavilion on the Lawn. He'd been raised with furniture built to withstand a male-dominated household—heavy pieces that even a hurricane couldn't blow away. Lucinda's antiques—the parlor pieces had passed down almost exclusively through her side of the family—were just as old and well wrought as the family pieces of the Davis and Lee clans, but they all seemed built for sprites and fairies: delicate, fine-boned people like Lucinda herself. Spencer wondered how they had withstood Nathan's heft all these years. He also wondered what he might say that would move this whole get-together into Nathan's home office: a battered leather sofa, stuffed club chairs, a place where you could take your shoes off and throw a leg over the chair arm; a glass of whiskey instead of the cup of thin tea he was now balancing on his knee. He could see himself at age fourteen, wearing his scratchy blue suit, a punch bowl cup perched where the teacup was now, as he tried to find some

hint of approval in the withering attention of his dancing-class chap-
erone, Miss Escott. We never grow up, Spencer thought; we just get
more like we've always been.

Spencer wondered, too, if he really had succeeded in changing the
subject, and if he truly wanted to. There were subjects far more
delicate than dual education, subjects far more explosive. John
Henry, for example: a name that had not been spoken in the twenty
minutes since Spencer had arrived, a subject he had no intention of
raising first. Spencer avoided conflict whenever he could—he was
not only a politician; he was a politician suitable for high office.

THE NATIONAL UNIVERSITY was just that: national. As President
of the Confederacy, Spencer was an ex officio member of the university's board of trustees. But he also was an alumnus—he'd attended law school here, after the Citadel, and stayed on for a fourth
year to finish JAG school, the judge advocate general course for
military attorneys—and he tried to take his responsibilities seriously.
That's what had brought him to the university today and to Lucinda
Winston's parlor: a breath of air between the monthly trustees' meeting and a dash back to Richmond for a dinner with the party faithful;
a chance to see and be seen among the next generation's best and
brightest; in truth, an elaborate photo opportunity. Spencer was never
again to run for anything, had done that, been there. But there was
the party to think of. Besides, there was time in his schedule for
trustees' meetings, time occasionally even for golf, tennis, fishing—
time even for the week at Pawley's Island he was scheduled to take
in early June, at the Low Country family cottage that had passed
down to his oldest brother.

This had been the biggest surprise of his seven years in the Oval
Office: Being President of the Confederate States of America wasn't
nearly as hard as he had thought it would be. The War of Dissolution hadn't been fought for nothing. The national government existed at the sufferance of the states, not the other way around. It
taxed at the states' sufferance, and legislated that way too. States
made the tough calls; governors were put on the griddle. All Spencer
had to do was walk the middle line, keep everyone more or less
happy, cut a ribbon or a deal. He thought of himself sometimes as
the emcee of the most successful national show in history. It came

to him naturally, like shooting quail or riding a bike. It was something at which he was good.

"THERE ARE OTHER ways."

Spencer wondered for just a second where the voice had come from; then he realized it was Lucinda and that Lucinda had no intention of letting the subject drop. Maybe, like Spencer, she was afraid of where the conversation might go next. He bent his ear toward her and stared off into the middle distance, his way of saying: continue.

"You could move the most technology-dependent sciences, the ones with the most costly equipment, off the university campus altogether. Set up national research centers where the exploration will be dual, the lab teams mixed, just as they are in industry. Let the university do what it does best—teach the humanities, teach character."

"But you wouldn't want this great institution to relinquish its lead in the sciences, would you?" Spencer appealed with his eyes to Nathan, but Nathan was pacing back and forth now at the end of the living room, out of contact with them both.

"We'd train them for the research centers," Lucinda was saying, "just as we train them now for doctoral work. Our role would be the same in that regard. And you know as well as I do that if dual education gets a foothold in the doctoral programs here, it will sink down slowly—and maybe not even slowly—into master's programs, then the undergraduate majors. There will be more meetings like the one you had today. Everyone will say how well this test program went, how well that one is working. The budget officials will beam at the savings, the trustees will beam at the budget officials, and no one will remember why bieducation was so successful in the first place. No one will remember how bieducation created equal opportunity; how it assured each race its dignity; how it freed up young men and women to learn, to be the best they can be; how it fostered decorum. You can't measure something like that against cost. You can't justify it on a balance sheet."

Lucinda sat crisply at the edge of her chair, her legs crossed precisely beneath a dark-green pleated skirt. Each word was chosen carefully, pronounced correctly, cut off at exactly the right place. A white silk collar climbed halfway up her neck. It, too, seemed crisp, correct, perfect for the moment. His mother, Spencer realized, would have said that Lucinda was "a woman all of a piece," a great compliment in her book, something she herself had never been. Spencer bent his ear still more in Lucinda's direction, trying even harder to concentrate on what she was saying.

"These children are too young for dual classes, Spencer. You know that—you must know that. They're just learning to be adults. It's not fair to throw that on them. They're children, really, just children. This works," she said, throwing her hand out to take in the Lawn, the West Campus, the east one, the National University of the South, bieducation, biequality, the entire holy experiment of the Confederate States of America. "It has worked for one hundred thirty years."

"I'll mention it at the next trustees' meeting, Lucinda. I'll present the case exactly as you have. You really ought to come to one of our meetings."

"And, Spencer, you and the rest of the trustees have to stop thinking of these children—Lucy, Jason, the *children* in this coordinate course everyone is so high on—as lab rats." Lucinda's voice seemed suddenly a half pitch higher. "You can predict what lab rats will do—lab rats have a limited repertoire. But these are human beings. Do you understand? Human beings. You don't know what you might be planting, Spencer. You don't know."

Upstairs, a door opened. They were listening to footsteps, heels clicking on the wide plank flooring of the upstairs hallways, when the phone in Lucinda's office rang. She nearly jumped out of her chair and was racing for the stairs when Nathan stepped forward, put his hands on her shoulders, and stopped her in her tracks.

"Dear, it's Miss Redmond. Her media calls. She'll get it. If it's anyone else, anything else—"

Nathan had turned his wife and was walking her back to her chair when she held up a hand and cut him off in midsentence.

"Spencer," she said as she seated herself again. There was a new tone in her voice, something that hadn't been there seconds earlier, a soft tremor that seemed to spread through the room. The President felt his teacup slip on his knee, caught it up with both hands, and held it stiffly in front of him like a mannequin.

"Why isn't more being done?"

"Done?"

"To find my boy. To find my John Henry."

"Oh, Lucinda."

"To *find* him, Spencer. Nathan tells me we have one of the finest domestic intelligence services in the world—as good as Germany, better than Palestine—"

"Fortunately, we don't need it as much as Germany." Nathan was speaking. "And we don't have Palestine's problems."

"I'm aware of that, dear, of course. But the point isn't *why* we need it. The point is that we *do* have such a service. It's staffed. It exists. Why can't it be set to finding John Henry? This was a boy who was abducted from our house, the house of the Vice President of his nation—stolen from us while we slept."

"There are practical considerations," Spencer said, "statutory restrictions on the domestic services. They simply can't go around spying on anyone."

"I'm aware of those. I'm aware also that if you declared DRAGO a terrorist organization, the statutory restrictions would disappear. It's not that hard, Spencer. It's been done. It's just a matter of signing a presidential directive."

"Even then, Lucinda. Even then. There's more to it than signing a piece of paper. You don't want to compromise agents. You have to be very careful about closing down communication channels. This is very delicate. Of course, I've . . . we've"—here he gestured to Nathan, standing stock-still, back once again to the far end of the room—"we've talked with the proper people. They have feelers out; they're listening; inquiries are being made. No one has forgotten about John Henry, Lucinda. Far from it. But we're not even certain of the details. We're not even certain that DRAGO is responsible for John Henry's disappearance."

"Spencer." It was Nathan this time, trying to interrupt the President, maybe. Maybe trying to raise a point of order. Maybe trying to deflect him from the route he was headed in, the slippery slope he had just chosen. Whichever the reason, Spencer Lee wasn't yielding the floor.

"Not certain beyond a reasonable doubt. One word on a Scrabble board doesn't meet the statutory requirement even if DRAGO were declared a terrorist group. I don't mean to be harsh, Lucinda, but it doesn't meet logical requirements either, if you think about it. The domestic services can't go rolling up entire networks of contacts based on a single word, based on one solitary, ambiguous clue. There have been no contacts since that time, no follow-up."

"You don't have to tell me that, Spencer. I'm well aware that there's been no 'follow-up,' as you put it. I'm aware of it every minute of every day." Lucinda's voice had gone flat, cold.

"Lucinda, you know I would never do anything to hurt you. But it's important you understand the conditions we're working under. We also have to be very careful not to confer undue celebrity on DRAGO, to give the group more authority than it merits. The whole purpose of this may be precisely that. If we give them exactly what they want, we have no bargaining position left."

"I've heard all that before, Spencer—heard it all from Nathan. And I want you to know that I don't care a fig, a whit, a damn about any of it. This is my boy, Spencer, *my* boy. My God, you've known him for half of his life. I want him home. I want him home. Now. Here."

Lucinda rose as she spoke, picked up the silver tray with the china teapot—yellow and purple, with inlaid gold—and the matching sugar bowl and creamer, and started for the kitchen.

"Don't we have to consider one more possibility, Lucinda?" Spencer said to her retreating back.

"One more?" Lucinda stopped, stood rigid. Spencer was looking into the teacup in his hand.

"Don't we have to at least consider the possibility that John Henry doesn't want to come home quite yet? It's very hard to find someone who doesn't want to be found."

The tea tray hit the floor just as Spencer was finishing. The sugar bowl and creamer spilled their contents but somehow managed to survive the mishap, their fall cushioned by the plush Oriental carpet underfoot. The pot itself broke into three pieces. Lucinda had placed them carefully back on the tray by the time Nathan returned with a sponge and towels, and both he and Spencer bent down to attack the debris.

"I'm so sorry, Lucinda," Spencer said. On his knees beside her, he mopped her hands with a towel, made sure there were no shards from the pot that could dig into her flesh. "I had no right."

"My grandmother bought it in Dresden. In 1931. You could buy anything in Germany back then for almost nothing." She was staring into the remains of the teapot as if she had some kind of special mending vision, as if her eyes alone could repair what was irreparable.

"It's beautiful."

"Lucy will be so sorry to have missed you, Spencer. She spends all her time in the library these days. I hardly ever see her anymore."

And then suddenly, still without looking at Spencer, Lucinda simply rose, left the room, and began climbing the stairs. Nathan and Spencer had just finished cleaning the rug when they heard the bedroom door close.

"FORGIVE ME, NATHAN," Spencer said. "I didn't know."

They'd settled in the Vice President's office—Spencer sprawled on the sofa; Nathan half standing, half sitting on the edge of his desk. A Brahms piano concerto was playing: Nathan's idea, to "soothe the savage soul," he had said. While Nathan got the compact disk going, Spencer went to the built-in bar and poured them both two fingers of bourbon, neat. He was holding his glass in his palm, swirling the amber liquid, staring into it.

"Didn't know?"

"That Lucinda . . . that there were things I shouldn't talk about . . . that—" Spencer waved his hand toward the ceiling. He'd run out of words.

"That Lucinda seems to be having a nervous breakdown? That she has concocted this fiction that allows of only one explanation for John Henry's disappearance? That she's put her teaching assistants in charge of her classes and won't even leave the house anymore for fear that she'll miss a phone call, a messenger, some kind of sign, human or divine? Is that what you didn't know, Spencer? You didn't know that this has broken her? Sorry. There never seemed to be a good time to mention it."

It was the closest the President had ever known Nathan to come to open bitterness, to pure anger.

"Oh, God." Nathan passed his hand over his face now, seemed to be trying to wipe away the memory of what he had just said, the conversation in the parlor, the cracked teapot. "We try, Spencer. We try. Lucinda tries so hard. But he's our son, and he's gone."

Nathan had started pacing again as he talked, glass in hand. Now he settled heavily into one of the club chairs.

"What do you want, Nathan? What can I do for you?"

"I want you to make Lucinda well again. I want her to be able to wake up again and feel as if the world is manageable. I want the world to not be this crushing weight for my wife. I want to hear her laugh."

"I'm not talking about Lucinda now. I'm talking about you. What do *you* want?"

"I want five minutes with my son, Spencer. That's all I ask. Five minutes to tell John Henry I'm sorry that I spent so little time with him, five minutes to tell him I love him. Can you arrange that?"

Nathan had left his drink untouched. He downed it now in one long swallow.

The President was staring into the bottom of his glass when there was a knock on the office door. Wormley edged it open before either man could say come in.

"The photographers, Mr. President, Mr. Vice President—they're getting frantic. We'll have trouble making the evening news as it is."

Wormley shot a cuff and looked at his gold watch, beautifully inlaid with silver. He tapped a woven leather loafer on the Vice President's rug, then looked up and studied the ceiling through the most handsome pair of tortoiseshell glasses Spencer Lee had ever seen. It was almost worth it, Spencer thought, to drive Wormley to the edge of scheduling despair, because he was so damn amusing when he got there.

"And I'm afraid, Mr. President, that we'll need to head straight to dinner once we get to Richmond. I've got a freshly pressed shirt in the limousine."

"But, Mr. Wormley, surely a half hour here or there won't make any difference?"

"Aargh!" Wormley slowly closed his eyes; he seemed to be fighting to control himself. Perfect, Spencer thought. Perfect. His scheduler was almost as tall as he was, practically the same weight, but worrying over the tiny time grids of the President's life had seemed to compress him, to make him shorter than he was.

Wormley looked at the two empty glasses now, wrinkled his nose, furrowed his brow. "We really do have to get you gentlemen moving," he said, "and, of course, you'll both be needing time to freshen up."

One of the great mysteries of Spencer Lee's life was how suit coats as impeccably tailored as Wormley's could contain such a variety of breath mints, pungent herbs, astringent gargles, palm-sized aerosols with the power of tiny nuclear antihalitosis bombs.

Wormley reached in his side pocket, removed a small plastic dispenser, shook out two tablets, and handed one to each man.

"You might want to chew on these before we meet the press." Wormley could cover up the smell of whole bulbs of garlic. Two fingers of bourbon were nothing for his portable pharmacy.

"THE INTERVENTIONISTS IN Congress will be howling. They'll want to make sure the right man succeeds him," Nathan was saying as he and Spencer crossed the Lawn, heading for the rotunda and the waiting limousine.

"Yes," the President said, "but the isolationists will win. We always do, Nathan, and thank God for that."

"Amen."

Nathan was briefing Spencer on the funeral service he had attended only four days earlier: the president-elect of Colombia—a natural death, yet tragic and sudden. He'd been a close ally, and Colombia was practically a part of the Greater Confederacy.

Lucinda hadn't gone. Nor had she gone with Nathan to last Tuesday's gala dinner dance in Chicago, part of a round of regional affairs celebrating the opening of the InterAmerican Waterway. Lucinda also hadn't accompanied Nathan on his quick goodwill mission to Mexico, where the foundering statehood initiative was stirring up local resentment.

"Speaking of which," Nathan said, "I had lunch with Toby Burke yesterday, in his office. He's not letting up on the old Capitol, Spencer. He's determined to see it blown to bits, leveled."

"How determined?"

Nathan pounded his fist on an imaginary table. " 'An insult, sir. A blight.' The usual from Toby, but he means it, Spencer. He's not going to let up." Nathan's own voice was flat, impassive: a voice intent on giving nothing away.

"There's so much of me in that building," Spencer said as they walked along. "My blood. My family."

Nathan turned his palms up, kept his eyes straight ahead. Not for the first time, Spencer wished that he had a time machine, could crank it ahead ten months, be out of office, feted, honored, retired. But then what? he wondered. What then?

IT WAS A sight made for television and long-distance news-photo lenses—the President and Vice President of the world's most powerful nation walking side by side in deep conversation, a sun-swept day, the terraced and colonnaded great lawn of the nation's premier university, Thomas Jefferson's own majestic rotunda waiting for the two men in the near distance, and absolutely nothing and no one to disturb them. It was too beautiful a day and too late in the afternoon for many students to be around, but the students on the East Campus of the National University couldn't have gotten close enough to the President and Vice President to shout a question or stage a protest even had they wanted to. The Secret Service had cordoned off the Lawn at either end and warned the students and faculty members who lived there to stay indoors until the walk was over. Like many politicians, Spencer Lee spent much of his life on stage sets carefully designed to look like real life; he wondered sometimes if he could still tell the difference between the two.

"You'll want to be home more," Spencer said, gesturing with his eyes toward the Winstons' pavilion, Lucinda, her "troubles." It was half a question, half a statement, almost imperative. "You can back off from some of your duties, Nathan. We'll spread them around the administration. It's not like you have to—" Spencer found himself short of words.

"Not really." As he often did when he walked along the Lawn, Nathan wondered why he had ever allowed himself to answer the call to politics in the first place. Was it vanity? Had he been bored? Probably more of the latter, although the vice presidency was in many ways the provost's job writ larger: mediating disputes, welcoming visitors, soothing fragile egos. Richmond, where he worked now for the most part, was the city of his birth, his growing up, but there was not a spot on earth he loved nearly so much as where he was standing now. How do you get back? he wondered. How do you reverse what is?

"We'd talked about it, Spencer, talked about my spending more time at home, before Lucinda became—" Nathan shrugged. What exactly had his wife become? Distraught? Gaga? Loopy? A stranger to reason? A kind of self-committed invalid? Unglued? He didn't know.

"We discussed my setting up shop at the home office, bringing some staff out to Charlottesville, maybe even moving someone into the pavilion full time. Lucinda was willing, of course. No one's more willing than Lucinda. But where would people stay? The pavilion isn't big enough. There's no extra space—only John Henry's room. And that's—" Nathan paused, fought for the word: "Unthinkable. The room will wait for him, Spencer. He'll be coming home."

The President put his arm over his friend's shoulder, squeezed it, and thought again about Jason, his own son, so close by.

"Besides, I have my duties," Nathan said, his eyes going wide, a grin breaking across his face. "And who, Spencer, who in this world could possibly want to fulfill them other than me?"

"We could get an intern from the undertaking school for half of them, probably."

"Probably indeed, but there's this too, Spencer." Nathan's voice turned somber. "I think I might be in grave physical danger if I stayed home. You surely noticed that Lucinda and I keep a respectful distance from each other these days. It's easier for us both. But it's not a very big house, really. If I stayed at home more, we'd be bound to get tangled up eventually. When that happened, she'd start pounding me on the head with a frying pan—she's a terrible fright with a skillet. Large welts would rise up on my noggin. Finally, the press—even the *friendly* press—would have to notice. There would be a congressional inquiry. We'd both be forced to resign in disgrace, not to mention the trouble I'd have finding a hat."

Nathan was near laughter, near tears. "Lucinda's sister is coming. She'll be with her for at least a week. We'll cope, Spencer. We'll get through."

It amazed the President that Nathan had any sense of humor left. Spencer tried to imagine himself in such a situation—Jason missing, abducted, run away; himself waiting for some word, some hint of his only child's fate. He decided he would be as nearly broken as Lucinda. Perhaps Nathan had already gotten there. Perhaps he was coming out the other side, if there was another side to despair.

"Still," Spencer said, "we could slow your schedule down."

Nathan flicked his hand—an impatient gesture, a dismissal. During his tenure as university provost, he had gained the nickname "The Buddha." His patience in the face of the usual faculty nonsense was legendary. Now Nathan's jaws were working, weighing which words to let out.

"Don't you understand, Spencer? I need to be in motion. All I think about when I have the time to think is John Henry. Lucinda has her needs, her ways of meeting them; I have mine. Don't put me on ice, Spencer. Don't."

They were nearing the steps of the rotunda, getting ready to plunge into the "interaction opportunity" Wormley and the advance people had set up to conclude the NUS visit. The chancellor of the university was waiting, along with provosts from both campuses (one of them Nathan's successor). Arranged behind them were deans from both schools, the sort of students (big men on campus, earnest political science majors, editors of both campus newspapers) for whom a President and Vice President are both an event and an opportunity; and, of course, camera crews and the press. Nathan was just waving up at his successor, preparing to put on his crowd face, when Spencer pulled him around into private conference.

"Fine, Nathan. Fine. If you want to be in action, let's put you in action. A one-day fact-finding mission to the NIZ. One day, one site. We'll figure out where later. Or better yet, let Wormley figure it out; he'll have to get you there. But if John Henry is in DRAGO's hands"—the "if" hanging heavily in the air between them—"this will send a message: We're not afraid to stare reality in the face, and we're not afraid to go look at reality hard where people seem to like us least.

"We'll shake the trees a little bit, see what falls out. If DRAGO has something they want to say to us, this might be the incentive. But we don't want to hand them a golden public relations opportunity, a chance for some street-theater protest. There'll be no advance publicity. Work with Redmond to figure out what reporters and commentators you want to take along. 'Friendlies,' of course, but not all. Have them show up an hour before flight time—destination to be announced. It will put some suspense into the trip, guarantee a good turnout.

"We want this inquiry to be pure, Nathan. There will be some security, of course; you'll need camera crews in place so you can make the evening news. You can't have laboratory conditions, but this will be close, 'close enough for government work.'" The old joke, still accurate. "What do you think?"

"Think? My God, Spencer, of course, of course." Movement, Nathan thought, action, and maybe . . . maybe . . .

Wormley meanwhile was beside himself, shifting from foot to foot, shooting cuffs left and right, studying the sky, the rotunda dome, anything, as he waited for his two luminaries to break off their tête-à-tête and approach the restraining rope. There was an order of greeting to be observed, a protocol; the limousine cortege was lined up and ready to go; events already were being backed up in Richmond, God knows, probably into the next day.

"One bottleneck," he was explaining to the provost of the West Campus as they waited, "one stall, sir, one uncooperative President and Vice President, and—well—miseries pass all up and down the pipeline, and for weeks to come. They have other things to think about, of course. That's why there are people like me, but when it comes to scheduling, politicians are—"

Even Wormley was at a loss. How to describe them? Infants? Obstructionists? Merely naive? Now the President was signaling him, calling him to join them. What next?

Quickly, Spencer outlined the plan to his scheduler: a week from today, no later, minimal advance work. He and the Vice President would need to choose the right place. Could he do it?

"Can I?"

Wormley frowned, puzzled, finally beamed with sublime confidence. He hated disorder and delays—hated a schedule that had slipped out of whack—but he hated much more to be on the outside, looking in. Wormley was making notes in his pocket organizer when the two men broke free of him, broached the restraining rope, and waded into the crowd, Spencer in the lead.

"Hey, how are you? It's great to see you again."

"My gosh, I knew your father way back when. Give him my best, you hear?"

The President was working on getting in his private zone again. He could feel himself dipping and rolling with the wave of the crowd. Behind him, Nathan was doing his own version of the same:

"Absolutely, Dean Witherspoon, absolutely," Spencer could hear him saying. "I'll have my people take that under immediate advisement."

"How do you people get anything done around here? I've been away too long. I've forgotten how beautiful spring is here."

With the still photographers and television cameras preserving the moment for a very small piece of eternity, Spencer and Nathan stepped to a makeshift bank of microphones.

"Mr. President," came the first question, "is it true that the university is going to have to cut its budget by twenty percent to help pay for the waterway?"

"Absolutely not," Spencer answered, wondering which dean, which college head, which department chairman, had planted the question. "Nothing's free, ladies and gentlemen. We're all going to have to help. But twenty percent, I should think, sounds far too draconian."

"What about political stability in Colombia?"

"You'll have to ask the Vice President about that," Spencer answered. "He's been there within the week, not me."

"How about it, Mr. Vice President. And how's Mrs. Winston? She missed the Mexico trip, and now we're told that she's had to cancel the last week of classes. Is her health okay?"

Nathan stepped forward to the microphones as Spencer dropped a half step back.

"Mrs. Winston is fine, fine, and thank you for asking," he said with a full smile. "It's just the usual parade of springtime viruses. You ladies and gentlemen be sure to take your vitamin C, and a wedge of lime floating in rum is *not* a vitamin supplement, Mr. Farley."

Nathan was staring directly at the popular Atlanta correspondent. Farley laughed as he said it, knowing that he could dine out for months on the anecdote, vitamin supplement close at hand.

Last, far from least, came the White House photographers:

Mr. Provost, Ms. Editor, Madam Department Chairman, if you'll just step over here, I'm sure we can get a shot of you with the President. That's it. Right there. Mr. President? Mr. Vice President? Click. Click. Click.

My God, Spencer thought, as the last of the photographs were being taken and the press was being led away to its waiting van, how good we are at this, how very, very good.

At the door of his limousine, Spencer shook Nathan's hand a last time, gripped him on his beefy arm, looked him hard in the eye.

"It's going to work, old friend. John Henry is coming home, safe and sound. Have faith." Whether Nathan did or not, Spencer Lee couldn't tell: Seven years in the vice presidency had made him a politician too, deft at giving away just what he wanted to give.

BEHIND THE TINTED glass of the limousine, Spencer loosened his tie, took off his jacket, and slipped out of his tasseled loafers.

"We'll leave town by University Avenue, Mr. Jarvis," he said to the driver. "Take her due east. You're pointing in the wrong direction."

"Sir." Wormley spun around in the front seat. "There's the traffic. We're running dangerously late. If we go west, we can catch the bypass and swing back around east in no time. Everyone"—gesturing hopelessly to the lineup of security vehicles and vans that cradled the presidential limousine in its midst—"is pointed that way."

"Then everyone, Mr. Wormley, is wrong."

Horns blared as the cortege laboriously reversed itself—a short-term political disaster. People didn't remember the health care funding that cured their mother's lumbago, but they did remember being kept waiting at rush hour by a presidential limousine that seemed to take forever to make a U-turn. Wormley made yet another note, this one for Redmond: "Explain." He'd let her worry about damage control. In the back seat, Spencer Lee took the cell phone from its cradle, clicked it off the secure channel, punched in a local number, and waited until a familiar voice answered at the other end.

"The commander in chief of the Free World is about to roll beneath your window, soldier. Be prepared to stand at attention and render salutations."

Spencer Lee missed his son immensely.

17

CHARLOTTESVILLE

JASON HAD BEEN sitting on the sofa when the phone rang. He took the receiver now, walked to the window, and pulled the curtain all the way back. A makeshift window screen stood between his apartment and the rich and varied flying-insect community of greater Charlottesville—Jason had made it himself of one-by-ones and plastic mesh. He popped that out now, clearing his view. Jason's window faced southeast; University Avenue ran below it, due east, at an angle.

"Keep your eyes at ten-thirty, Corporal. We'll be passing underneath any second."

His father had been in this apartment just once, near the start of the school year. It amazed Jason that he could remember the window's orientation, much less the location. The Citadel, he told himself—that's the military man in him, the army DNA, genetic memory passed down from the Great Avenger, the Great Martyr. Jason thought that perhaps the military gene had died out of the family altogether with himself: He could get lost walking from his bedroom to the bathroom, and his father had long ago despaired of getting him to snap off a crisp salute.

"Slower, Mr. Jarvis."

Jason stood by the window in his jeans and T-shirt, barefoot, listening to his father bark instructions inside the limousine, hearing the chaos grow. It was the sort of scene his father loved, the sort of scene he loved about his father ... the kind of moment that made his father's aides and escorts and security details stark crazy.

"Slower, dammit, Mr. Jarvis! Mr. Wormley, sir, if you make an attempt to crawl into this back seat, I'll have you court-martialed. Do you hear me? Court-martialed! They'll break your sword, paint a yellow stripe down your back, and send you barefoot into Indian territory! You won't survive it, Wormley—you'll be buzzard meat! Buried to your neck, covered with honey! Son, are you still there?"

"Yes, sir."

"The first car should be heaving into view."

And just then it did—a plain black van, packed to the gills with God knew what firepower, creeping along at a walking pace. As the second car arrived below his window, Jason could see the windows rolling down, the heads popping. The security men were talking rapidly into their lapels. Maybe a weapon was flashed; Jason wasn't sure. For a moment, he was seized by blind panic—DRAGO; the whole creepy universe of psychopaths spilling out of blood-red foreign shores. Maybe John Henry's disappearance had preyed on his mind more than he realized. Maybe it was just that he couldn't imagine life without his father.

Then came the presidential limousine, and Jason saw what all the commotion was about. Spencer Lee was halfway out of the car, sitting on the ledge of the window, cell phone in hand, as he waved up to his son. Waving back, Jason thought that perhaps he could see Mr. Wormley lying on the floor below his father, desperately grasping his commander in chief's feet. If so, he wondered what Mr. Wormley could see of him. If not, he wondered precisely what was keeping his father from flipping backward, headfirst onto the pavement.

"I hate not having time to see you, Jason—hate it. Come see me next weekend. Stay at the damn White House with me. We'll get drunk as skunks and drive golf balls off the roof into the river."

"Can I borrow your clubs?"

"Never! Never! Those are your President's clubs! *Slower, goddammit, Jarvis!*"

"Can I use your golf balls?"

"Do you know the price of golf balls, son? We're in a budget crisis, for God's sake. Not to mention the fact that the river would be one hell of a drive. Do you think anyone can hit a golf ball that far?"

"I wish you had time to stop, Dad. I really do." Meaning it without thinking, as he always did.

"Soon, Jase. Very soon." The sheer weariness of it shocked Jason. He'd thought of his father always as inexhaustible.

The limousine was half a block down the street now. From Jason's perch at the window, his father was beginning to look merely life-size. It occurred to Jason that if a press car was tailing the cortege, it would have a photo by now and enough footage to lead the evening news. If that was the case, someone would want the who, what, why, when, and where, and want them in short order. Questions would be asked at the university, around the neighborhood. Very soon, the questions would lead to him as the proximate cause of such presidential shenanigans. There would be a call to confirm, or a knock on the door. In either event, such cover as he'd been able to provide himself would be blown. Jason had decided that he no longer could control his luck. His life had become unbound from everything it had been.

"Listen, Jase, it's a beautiful day." His father's voice was softer now as he slid back into the limousine. "The sap's rising. Flowers are in bloom. Baseball games are being played. The rich bounty of Southern womanhood is just waiting to be plucked by a good-looking fellow such as yourself, and it's in the nature of good-looking fellows to do a little plucking once spring has come. Close your book, son. Go outside. You've got the rest of your life to study. Give yourself a shot at life."

"I've got a life, Dad. I really do. Dad, listen, I need to tell you—"

Jason stopped then—a single black finger laid across his lips to close them. A single word whispered in his ear, soft as an ocean breeze: "No."

Lucy stood behind him, in the shadow, half hidden by the pulled-back curtain, in jeans as well, the tail of her white linen blouse waving gently in the breeze. Instinctively, Jason grabbed the window screen, popped it back in place. No one was looking. No one could have noticed. Still. Still. The finger softer now, softer, releasing him.

"Son?"

Jason grabbed a book from the counter behind him, opened it

wide, held the phone receiver near at hand, and slammed the book closed.

"Hear that, Dad? I'm shutting up the old books."

Jason pounded the book now with his fist. *Boom. Boom. Boom.*

"I'm nailing the covers down, Dad. Bye-bye, bookworms!"

Jason signaled to Lucy, pointed to the kitchen cabinet, waved his hand back and forth until she understood, held the receiver toward her as she opened the wooden cabinet door and slammed it shut with a roar.

"That's it! I'm out the door! Watch out, Southern womanhood!"

"Son?"

"Sir?"

"It was just a little paternal advice. You're overreacting."

"I know. I know. I'm sorry. I'll explain it—" Lucy shooting him a glance, her eyes saying what her mouth had said only a little while ago: No. "I'll explain it someday. Dad, listen, I'm happy, really happy."

"That's all I've ever wanted. Nothing more."

LUCY SHOWED UP one day as the pizza delivery girl, the next day with two bags from Groceries To Go, a third day in a Chicken Pix hat, with a roaster, fries, and slaw on the side. She came, she delivered. She didn't leave until it was time to go home for dinner, time to go home for bed. It was the paper, they kept telling themselves. There was so little time, so much to do. The library study room was impossible—too stuffy, too close. They couldn't think there; they couldn't breathe there. They felt they were on display every time they met on the library steps. Jason and Lucy needed space to spread out their books and papers, space to walk around the material and think things through. Jason's apartment was hardly large, but at least it had a floor, a table, a sofa, a countertop—flat usable spaces. By now they were having to tiptoe their way through the piles. Before long there would be no space at all—they'd have to eat off the windowsill, use a hoist and tackle to get from the living room to the kitchen, the kitchen to the bathroom. By the time they were through—soon, soon, it had to be soon—there would be nothing left to say on the subject of "The Patriation Program, Fishery Employment, and Korean Transmigration in the Northwest Pacific States: 1941–1943." Nothing. This would be it—the final word. For that was another part of it: They weren't going simply for a good grade; good grades were a dime a dozen. They weren't working to produce merely the best paper of their experimental coordinate course; their classmates were hardly competition.

"Lucy," Jason had said as they sat on his floor one afternoon, poring over employment tables. "You know what we're doing? We're going for *perfection*!"

That such perfection required extra time; that it caused Lucy to fabricate stories about library trips to satisfy her mother's curiosity (admittedly waning, given her preoccupation with John Henry); that pursuing perfection caused Lucy to become a habitué of hamburger joints, pizza parlors, and other carryout establishments, such as she had never been in or heard of or indeed had any previous desire to enter; that she and Jason were required to spend hours and hours together in the pursuit of such perfection; that they thought best when they were touching, brushing up against each other, sitting back-to-back on the sofa, engrossed in their individual reading, the ions of their skin snapping against each other—that perfection demanded all this was the price they paid. Paid gladly. Sometimes they even laughed at the lie. Sometimes they even let it out to run around the room:

"Oh, no, these figures for June 1943 don't match with the Patriation count. I'll have to come back tomorrow."

"We can't afford a single mistake, Luce; can't afford to have one *i* undotted, one *t* uncrossed. How about Chinese, from that place by Barracks Road?"

And so it went. They were puppies, babies at love. They couldn't stop touching.

There was this too: They were going to get caught. Jason calculated the odds at one hundred percent. The Confederate States of America wasn't a hotbed of spies, snitches, little government eyes and ears at every chink in the wall, every keyhole. Privacy was respected in the C.S.A.; self-reliance was glorified. Every man, every woman, was given his or her due, and there were no false idols. Some of Jason's family chromosomes may have been muted; some may have gone underground; but he was after all the genetic repository of the Second Founders, and not a few odd genes from the

First Founders too—a prince if the nation had believed in such nonsense. Yet no one in his apartment building had ever mentioned such a matter to him. No one had bowed and scraped as he walked up the steps or even asked him for appointments or favor. The one time his father had visited the apartment, he had sneaked in and out without retinue. So far as Jason knew, he was to his neighbors simply what the small card on his mailbox proclaimed him to be: "J. Lee, 3-B." A student, one of thousands, not the First Offspring. Nosey Parkers were impolite, and in the C.S.A., politeness was the test that almost everything ultimately came down to. Jason and Lucy had even shown a surprising talent for deception, although that was perhaps their age and their cause.

Still, some things were obvious—the same delivery woman day after day, delivering the food of a different provider, arriving and not leaving, leaving long after she arrived. It was like two plus two: If it equaled three, bells went off. If bells went off, someone had to look into it. If, when, someone looked into this—this omnipresent, all-purpose delivery girl and this omnivorous, mild-mannered student; this perfection-striving dual-race academic team—if, when, that happened, well, Jason fully expected that holy hell would break loose. An abyss would open up. It would swallow them. It was that simple. Privacy was respected, of course—until you abused it. Then you forfeited your right to any privacy at all. Nor was there any question what form the abyss that Jason and Lucy were headed for would take, because that also was clear, written in granite, as old as the nation itself: exile, that special noncitizen citizenship reserved for all those whose loves dared not speak their name—cross-race, same sex, it didn't matter. Once the love was out in public, once it couldn't be ignored, the abyss was inevitable.

In theory, of course, exile was an opportunity: Start a new life! See the world! Cross-racial couples could go to whatever place would have them, and there were said to be exile communities along the La Plata River in Argentina, an hour or so upstream from Buenos Aires, at Guayaquil on the coast of Ecuador, elsewhere in South America, and spotted sporadically around the globe. In practice— because of wildly fluctuating currencies, rapacious dictators, frequent changes of government and subsequently of policy and compassion— exile meant mostly the territories of the Confederacy. More exactly, it meant mostly the Northeast Industrial Zone. The Caribbean Cor-

poration was hard duty for anyone, and jobs were too scarce. Mexicans aspired to statehood for the economic advantages; Americans—
miscegenists, homosexuals, or otherwise—they could do without.
Utah Territory was its own world. And to the far north, Canadian
border guards had license to shoot to kill. The NIZ at least had jobs.
Even if you had no standing, no papers anymore, no rights, no claim
to territorial services, in the NIZ you could—in theory—exist.

Sometimes when he lay in bed at night by himself, Jason would
close his eyes and see the two of them, hand in hand, part of a vast
human stream being herded out of the C.S.A., north into Pennsylvania Territory and thence he knew not where. In the vision, he
would look back and see his father and Lucy's parents standing at
the Maryland border, waving a last time, diminishing, finally fading
from sight. The dream, the vision, whatever it was, reminded him
of the stories he had read in his history books about the defeated
Federals trudging home after the war, heading into the dead of
winter toward their ransacked homes, their burned fields, their
slaughtered cities.

My God, the risk, the risk, he and Lucy would say to themselves
as they lingered over a sentence, a pronoun, a comma, a touch. And
such a certainty of a bad end. Why throw everything away for what
you would never be able to have? It was madness, by definition.
Their only hope was what the young always believe: that the two of
them could change everything, that they could create a world in
which they would be possible.

"Why couldn't it happen?" Jason had said one evening as Lucy
was getting ready to leave, her Chicken Pix hat perched carefully on
her head. "Why not? If not us, Luce—I mean, if not us, who?"

Lucy had simply started to cry then, standing by the front door.
Someone had to be a realist for them.

AND THEN THERE was this: Jason's inexhaustible appetite for junk
food had never been better catered to. There was no fried-fat-
craving, sugar-loving, carbohydrate-guzzling molecule of his elon-
gated, slightly scrawny body that wasn't overflowing with
satisfaction. And he himself had never been happier. He meant what
he said to his father: Happiness was his. A tissue of mistruths masked
the why of such joy from his father, which was a sadness to him

and eventually would have to be atoned for. He may have been bereft of the family military gene, but the family honor chromosomes ran deep and true. Yet feeling Lucy behind him as he stared out the window, feeling her hands resting gently on his hips, the warmth of her breath on his neck, his shoulder—these things more than made up for his shame, were a kind of honor all their own. Everyone, Jason told himself, had to leave home sometime.

"NOT THAT THERE'S anything wrong with hard work and good grades. Don't misunderstand me."

Jason had nearly forgotten the phone in his hand, his father at the other end of it. The presidential cortege was picking up speed now, breaking free of traffic as it got ready for the rush to Richmond. From Jason's window, the limousine and its escorts formed a snake of flashing red lights, nothing more, moving between two rows of pink and white fringed in green. This was almost the end of dogwood season, flowers and leaves commingled on the trees—University Avenue was lined with them as far as the eye could see. It was one reason Jason had wanted the apartment so much, for just this brief interval in the year.

"You're getting faint, Dad. Fading to black. Your eyelids are heavy, very heavy. Sweet dreams. Good night."

"The President of the Free World never sleeps, Jase. Never sleeps."

But Jason could imagine Wormley laying out the pillow. He could almost hear his father's head hitting it as Wormley draped him with the navy-blue wool blanket with the great seal of the Confederacy at its middle. The presidential helicopter was easier on everyone, and certainly faster, but the noise of the thing! The roar inside! In a very few moments, Jason knew, his father would sleep. In the far distance, the cortege had been reduced to a single red point of light. As Jason watched, it disappeared, and his father with it.

18

REGIONAL AIR FACILITY NIZ-27, NORTHWESTERN MASSACHUSETTS TERRITORY

"LADIES AND GENTLEMEN," Nathan was saying, "we're going to be in the air for less than two hours and on the ground, once we reach our destination, for eight to nine hours at the most. Those of you who have early deadlines will be able to file your stories from the plane, of course." Nathan gestured toward the bank of modems built into the wall of the main cabin. "Most important, no one's going to miss his or her beauty sleep tonight. You'll all wake up tomorrow bright-eyed and bushy-tailed."

A raspy voice called out from among the general groans: "Mr. Vice President, you haven't told us where we're going."

"Patience, Mr. Reidy. Patience," Nathan said. "Sit back and enjoy the lovely view."

In this early light of the morning, the view was not much. Maury Field, Richmond's government airport, had been named for the great nineteenth-century hydrologist and meteorologist Matthew Fontaine Maury, but the name was more evocative than the locale—scrubby flatland a dozen miles southeast of the capital. As Nathan talked, the plane taxied out to the far end of the short runway, turned 180 degrees, and raced into the rising sun for takeoff.

"And our destination today, good citizens," Nathan said, feeling the wheels lift off the tarmac and then that quick, heavy sinking in the stomach that he had never managed to get over, for all the millions of miles he had spent in the air, "our destination is . . ."

"We're airborne, Mr. Vice President," the same raspy voice said. "We can crash, but we're not going to turn back. Tell us."

"Regional Air Facility NIZ-27," Nathan answered. "North Adams, ladies and gentlemen, in northwestern Massachusetts Territory, the upper Berkshire Valley."

"I vote for crash," Reidy said, snapping his notebook shut to a chorus of hoots.

"I trust, Mr. Reidy, that you'll feel different by the end of the day," Nathan said once decorum was more or less restored. "This trip is a chance for all of us to see the Northeast Industrial Zone and the Patriation Program at ground level, through the eyes of the workers. We're going to tour several factories and have a good look at the town itself, and we've tried to keep everything as unrehearsed as possible: minimal notice, just enough advance work for everyone's safety. I don't have to tell any of you, I'm sure, that territorial workers are the backbone of America and that the Patriation Program is America's stepping-stone to the future.

"This administration, President Lee and I—and you can quote me on this—we are committed to—"

"Mr. Vice President?"

It was Farley, the Atlanta correspondent, suddenly awake.

"Yes, Mr. Farley."

"Sir, would there be any coffee aboard this aircraft?"

"A long evening, Mr. Farley?"

"It's the vitamin supplements, Mr. Vice President."

"I told you, Mr. Farley. I told you that you could overdo a good thing. But"—Nathan felt a growl in his own stomach—"perhaps this would be a good time."

He pushed the buzzer on the seat beside him. Soon a steward and a stewardess were taking orders: fresh fruit, hot biscuits, side meat, and coffee. The Vice President was using the small official aircraft for this trip, the one the press had dubbed Air Force One Half—a corporate jet that had been customized for the purpose. Six television displays were built into the bulkhead that separated the cabin from the cockpit, so that a breaking story could be followed on any network that mattered. The cabin itself was outfitted with a two-seater sofa that converted to a double bed and six leather-covered club chairs on swivels, so that occupants of the cabin could face one another, as was now the case. Seven reporters and commentators split between print and television were along on this trip—a full load. Beneath their feet lay a thick carpet in a muted gray-blue. The walls and ceiling of the cabin, wherever electronics didn't intervene, were covered with cherry veneer.

Seated in one of the swiveling club chairs, the Vice President was dressed in a dark suit, a starched shirt, deeply colored—almost magenta this time—and a matching tie and pocket foulard. His only concession to the occasion: walking shoes. He'd sprained an arch a few days earlier when getting out of the shower and had not fully recovered.

Between bites, the questioning went on, unevenly: environmental reports issued by the government, others leaked to the press, a congressional dustup over territorial status generally, Patriation funding levels, public-private partnerships, and on and on. DRAGO was mentioned, but only as one of several groups protesting conditions in the NIZ. The bizarre incident at the Hotel Richmond back in April—two dead on national television, the President's speech interrupted, the banquet thrown into disarray—had dropped off the public's radar screen weeks before, replaced by turmoil in grief-stricken Colombia, a fungus that was beginning to affect the corn crop in the Midwest, and week eight of the baseball season. The Birmingham Barons, last year's Series champs, had stumbled into the second division in the black league. In the white league, the seemingly invincible Raleigh Rebs were off to their usual earth-shaking start. As always, there were calls for a superseries between the two divisions.

"What do you think, Mr. Vice President?" one reporter wanted to know. "Are you backing a superseries?"

"I understand attendance is high for both leagues and nearly all the teams," Nathan answered. "Why rock the boat?" He hadn't been to a game in years.

Beneath him, Nathan could feel the plane dropping into North Adams. He looked out the window and saw a mean strip of tarmac and a control tower thrown down in what seemed one of the few flat stretches available. North Adams was remote, but it was an important territorial manufacturing center and a common stop on Patriation workers' journey to citizenship and Americanhood. It had seemed a good place to take a pulse—Nathan and Wormley had pored over the possibilities, maps and maps of them. In fact, Nathan thought, as the plane thumped into the landing strip, he had no idea what to expect.

THE CAR WAS waiting when they arrived—a plain black government sedan, just what Nathan had ordered up. Behind it, a van waited for the media contingent. In front, a single police car, just in case traffic needed clearing. Camera crews—government issue, government paid—were already in place in North Adams. Standing next to the car, waiting for Nathan, was Curtis Widmeyer.

"What a pleasure, Mr. Vice President! What a treat! Allow me to welcome you to the NIZ." Widmeyer couldn't have been more than forty years old, a regional administrator for the industrial zone.

"You've hurt your foot, sir? Your ankle?" He was looking at Nathan's walking shoes, studying his slight limp as the Vice President approached the car and shook hands.

"A slip, Mr. Widmeyer. And age. Nothing ever *fully* recovers anymore." Both of them were laughing as they settled into the back seat of the sedan.

"In your good shape, Mr. Vice President, I can't believe full recovery would be any problem at all. It just takes a little longer." Widmeyer seemed confident that Nathan could recover in a mere few hours from massive brain surgery or multiple amputations if need be. The younger man looked as if he'd never been sick or injured a day in his life.

Half Widmeyer's salary was paid by the national government, half by the coalition of manufacturers that was the government's financial partner in the enterprise. It was an arrangement as old as the zone itself: The world provided the raw goods, the Patriation Program the workers, the coalition the factories. Everyone came out ahead. If the Patriation workers chose to and if jobs were available for them, they could remain in the zone after they had achieved citizenship and move seamlessly from one employer to the other—government to private industry—without ever having to leave their little corner of the world. It was surprising how many did: Better the known evil than the unknown. Life in the NIZ was like all territorial life— harder, looser. Laws were less surely enforced, customs less surely honored, due process less surely afforded. You did what you did in the NIZ to get through the day, put bread on your table and a roof over your head. Survival skills mattered, sometimes even were rewarded. And then there were the tax advantages—some compensation for living where so few wanted to live. In any event, it all fit together, all worked.

Nathan imagined that he and Curtis Widmeyer were cousins somewhere back down the line, if only by marriage. Lucinda would know. *Lucinda*.

A watery sun greeted them as they headed up the highway into North Adams. The police car in front kicked up flakes of soot, a tiny storm of dust.

"It rained hard a little more than a week ago, Mr. Vice President," Widmeyer was saying. "But it's been a dry spring, unusually so. The trees have been slow to leaf out, the flowers late to bloom. My own lawn looks like the Gobi Desert, not that I've been there, of course. But you're a good harbinger, sir—just what we need. And the Weather Service seems to agree. More rains are ahead."

Widmeyer nodded out both sides of the car at the hills that lined the valley.

"And we're blessed here, in any event," he said. "The Berkshires—one of the natural wonders of the world."

"And the soot?" Nathan asked, gesturing at the flakes flying lazily by the car window.

"A foundry on the north side of town, sir. It had to clean its furnace stack yesterday. The zone's environmental managers had asked the foundry to wait until a breeze was blowing out of the northeast. You never know how far the wind will carry a little soot, and better to soil our own backyard than to risk angering the hair triggers in Ottawa."

Widmeyer shook his head as he talked. My God, he seemed to be saying, the things that upset them north of the border!

"Amen," Nathan added. "Amen." It took so little to get Canada angry.

"And if we'd known you were coming, sir; if we'd had any advance warning . . ." Widmeyer let the sentence hang—his silence implying a world of possibility. Perhaps they could have persuaded the foundry to wait another few days before cleaning its stack. Perhaps they could have seeded the clouds to perk up this dull spring green. For the Vice President of the Confederacy, the sky was the limit.

Widmeyer stared out the window for a minute. He was dressed as impeccably as Nathan, in pinstriped blue suit and starched white shirt.

"Not, of course, that we don't understand," Widmeyer said suddenly, as if it had just occurred to him that he might have given offense. "Mr. Wormley explained when he called, sir, that you had a last-minute opening. We're always pleased when anyone expresses an interest in our work, but in your case, well"—Widmeyer smiled and held his palms up—"what can we say? It's a flattery just to be thought of. And we have been able to cobble together a little schedule."

"Schedule?" Nathan asked. They were nearing North Adams now, he assumed. On his right, a narrow floodplain trailed off into what Widmeyer had identified as the Hoosic River. The houses on his left were widely spaced but near enough to the road to be seen. A parade of driveways—little country lanes, really—climbed into a spare stand of pines and maples. At the end of the driveways, large frame houses seemed to huddle for warmth against a steep stony hill, the start of the Taconic range. Nathan had spent exactly one winter north of the Virginia border—in Minnesota, as a tutor in a Chippewa school during the second and last year of his compulsory national service. He had promised himself never to be that cold again. Now, of course, he carried extra insulation—perhaps thirty pounds of it; then, he'd been as lean as John Henry. We change. We change. Or maybe we just misremember.

"You said a schedule, Mr. Widmeyer?"

"Oh, primitive, primitive. Just to make sure you get a chance to stick your head in everywhere. A textile mill first—mostly Level Two Patriation workers. The foundry I was just mentioning after that. We'll get you on the floor—quite a show, I hear. Lunch at the NIZ housing complex—local dignitaries. The new Spencer Lee Elementary School." Mr. Widmeyer winked at that: wonderful footage for the evening news. "Some recitations. The school chorus. We'll have you back at the air facility by four sharp."

As they entered the city limits of North Adams—left a ledge of rock behind to the west and crossed a channeled river—the streetscape improved dramatically. Planters along either side of the street were bursting with pansies, petunias, and geraniums. Bricks had been sandblasted; the white marble foundations of the churches—the stone cut from a local quarry, Widmeyer said—had been scrubbed nearly to a shine. On the side streets, row houses seemed to trail off into the distance, but even there Nathan could see signs of effort: fresh paint, hanging plants, an occasional plot of green enclosed by a whitewashed picket fence that picked up the pale light of the sun and somehow made it brighter. Nathan had expected worse. If nothing else, he had been prepared for a stench—a huge paper mill sat just to the west of the city. But the mill was closed for the day while the head box was being upgraded, Widmeyer said. Nathan had no idea what he was talking about, but it didn't matter. North Adams glowed.

"The city fathers do what their resources allow them to do," Widmeyer said, reading his guest's mind. "We in the Manufacturers' Coalition try to help out wherever we can." A shrug of his shoulders, his eyes cast down: Give the credit to someone else; I'm a simple man. A line from some play, some movie came back to Nathan: *God protect us from plain, simple men.* He'd gotten up too early, Nathan told himself. He should have eaten less on the plane, and he should exercise more, or at least occasionally. He disliked himself most when he succumbed to dark thoughts, to pessimism. Nathan had a naturally cheerful nature.

Widmeyer was explaining that the North Branch of the Hoosic River had been tunneled in recent years and now ran underneath the street they were driving along.

"The Hoosic was bad enough in the spring runoff, sir," he was saying, "particularly when the snows backed up against a quick thaw and hard spring rains. But when it met the North Branch—right about here, almost exactly where we are—the results could be devastating."

The two rivers, he said, had wiped out whole sections of North Adams and whole sectors of its industry. Worse, the floods had killed workers and ruined the savings of a lifetime, and they'd done so far too many times.

"The Hoosic?" Nathan asked. "Is it tunneled underneath us too?" He'd barely been listening. Every time he turned around for the last seven years, someone seemed to be talking about hydrology projects.

Widmeyer smiled, stretched out his legs.

"That's the beauty of it, Mr. Vice President," he said. "We

brought the Hoosic to the mills and factories instead of making them come to the river."

The Manufacturers' Coalition, he said, had paid for the channeling, the sluices, and the spillways that carried the Hoosic safely around town these days. In the process, they'd maximized the Hoosic's use for power generation at the mills. The work had been hideously expensive—Widmeyer rolled his eyes, suggesting unimaginable figures—but it was unavoidable. Now the reengineered Hoosic hugged the town to the west before it turned ninety degrees and ran on to Williamstown, while the North Branch ran underground through the center of North Adams, powering turbines as it flowed. The coalition, Widmeyer implied, took the long view on its balance sheets.

"OUR FIRST STOP." Widmeyer tapped the driver on the shoulder and had him pull around the police car to just in front of the textile mill's shipping yard.

"The mill workforce is entirely Patriation workers, sir—with the exception of supervisory personnel, of course."

The trucks had been moved out of the shipping yard; the freight railroad siding was empty. Instead, the yard was filled with workers, the loading docks were set up with government camera crews. As Nathan stepped out of the car, the workers broke into polite applause. He held up his hands to thank them before wading into the crowd alone. As best they could, the press contingent tried to wade in behind him.

"How are you being treated?" It was a woman, somewhere in her thirties or forties, her hair held in a snood. She stood unevenly, as if one leg was shorter than the other. Her thin hand was lost in Nathan's meaty paws as they talked.

"Fine, sir. Fine."

"You're getting enough to eat? Not working too long a shift?"

What was she? Norwegian? Swedish? Nathan guessed the latter. Wrong.

"Danish, sir. Two years now. Fine, fine." All a kind of shorthand. She'd entered the Patriation Program two years back, left her home—what?—maybe six months before that. The timing would be right, Nathan thought: driven out by the German resettlement of Jutland. The choice the Germans presented was simple: emigrate—to the Scandinavia Federation across the Skagerrak and Kattegat, to jolly old England across the North Sea, to jolly old Finland across the Baltic Sea, or to America; it didn't matter—or learn to live in the sea itself, to breathe water, to catch fish with your teeth and bare hands. Not surprisingly, most chose to emigrate. Now everything was "fine, fine." As they talked, her eyes flicked right, flicked right again. A supervisor was standing perhaps eight feet away, beaming.

Nathan stopped to speak with a startlingly tall black man standing in solitary splendor; a woman—Russian, he guessed—who looked as if she could lift up the back end of a truck; a cluster of young men, almost alike enough to be quintuplets. Were their sleeping conditions satisfactory? Were their health needs being seen to? What route had brought them here?

The cluster of men all answered, *"Ja, ja,"* when he asked about their medical care—perfect German. Why? he asked himself. Why? And then he realized: Of course, Jewish. The racial purification programs had been tempered—even Führers had to eat, and America fed the world—but purges went on. The men would do well, Nathan thought. They would work hard and be interning in Savannah or New Orleans within five years. The black man had played basketball on one European national championship team after another. Now he was nearing forty, with bad knees and a shoulder that slipped out of joint whenever he raised his arm too far over his head.

"Why come here?" Nathan asked him. "Why choose the Patriation Program?" He had to crane his neck to look the man in the eye.

"What was I going to do, sir?" the man answered. "Return to Uganda? Remain in Greater Germany? I learned to shoot a fallaway jumper with my left hand after this right shoulder first went bad," he said. "I'll learn how to dye fabric now." His voice was deep, his English fluid and flawless, his laugh gentle.

Nathan shook his hand and reached up to grip the man on the shoulder as he did so. This, he thought, is what Patriation is about, what it should be about. This is the Confederate States of America.

The broad-shouldered woman, maybe Russian, could tell Nathan nothing at all.

"Why have you come here?" Nathan asked.

"Yes," she said.

"Are you being treated well?"

"Yes."

"Do you like your work?"

"Yes." Yes to every question, painfully articulated and accented. The woman seemed to fear that if she said "yes" wrong, jumbled it with her own tongue, she would be cast back into whatever void she had come from.

Well, Nathan thought, she was right. Eventually, she'd have to learn the language. If she couldn't, if she wouldn't . . . no one entered Patriation without knowing the pitfalls. To be meaningful, citizenship had to be earned, not given.

He shook her hand now and spoke softly into her ear: "You must work on your language, your English."

"Yes," she said, smiling back. All her lower teeth were missing. Her grip was like steel.

As Nathan moved through the crowd, no one seemed to shrink from him, nor did anyone surge forward to take his hand. With the exception of the tall Ugandan, the faces appeared to be entirely white. Behind him, Nathan could hear the press contingent slipping into his wake: tape recorders clicked on, pads and pens high and at the ready. *Your name? I'll need your name. In English! What did the Vice President ask you? What did you say?* He suspected the press were far more terrifying to the workers than he had been. Behind the press, he could see the overseers, the supervisors, slipping into place too: to help with the questions, to help with the answers. Whatever they might have said was lost in the babel of displaced tongues—the lost languages of the lost tribes of Europe. Soon there would be only two languages that mattered: English and German. Everything else would just be war cries, blood oaths, tiny gasps of civilizations on the verge of extinction.

Nathan was working his way back toward the edge of the crowd when Curtis Widmeyer caught his eye and raised his wrist high as he pointed to his watch. There were other stops to make, a schedule to keep to, however primitive. Handlers were the same the world around. Nathan turned and shook hands along the edge of the crowd.

"Good luck," he kept saying as he made for the sedan. "Good luck." As he talked, he watched the workers' eyes flick right, left,

wherever the next person up on the personnel chart was standing—
or so he surmised. The millworkers would be afraid, Nathan
thought. So much was at stake for these Patriation workers: their
whole future.

In the car, Nathan stretched his legs out as best he could, caught
his breath, and asked for water. The driver had a cooler full of small
bottles on the seat beside him; Nathan's throat was scratchy from
the air, the myriad small conversations. A block later, as he drank
deeply from the bottle, his head thrown back, Nathan thought he
saw a scarecrow woman standing at a third-floor window, rags hanging from her shoulders, a scarecrow baby at her breast. He decided
it was an apparition, nothing more—the product of a fevered imagination. A block later, the sedan turned right into a small executive
parking lot. The walls of the building in front of him seemed to
throb; he could see a flash of light coming out of the windows on
the south side. More fevered imagination—he felt his forehead with
the back of his hand and took a quick, private read of his pulse.
Then Mr. Widmeyer explained: They'd arrived at the foundry.

"IT WAS BUILT before the war," Widmeyer said—the only war, the
only one. "As best we can tell in the Manufacturers' Coalition, the
building was abandoned about the turn of the century."

The coalition, Widmeyer went on, had spent ten years restoring
the foundry and another two years finding experienced personnel to
operate it. It had been open now for five years, making specialty
castings for factories and mills the length and breadth of the Northeast Industrial Zone.

"Why such an effort, Mr. Widmeyer?" Nathan asked. "It sounds
like an enormous expense for the coalition to have undertaken."

They were walking down a long hallway, having been joined by
the foundry manager and the shift foreman. The foreman appeared
to be covered in calluses from head to toe. Empty offices stood along
either side. Heat pulsed from a large central room not far in front
of them.

"Short-term costs, long-term gains, sir." Widmeyer had to talk
louder as they neared the end of the hall. "We've been able to wean
our members from a dependence on foreign foundries to provide

specialty castings. Germany was beginning to turn the screws on us, sir; the Japanese too. Now we can tell them to get lost."

Everyone wins; no one loses—in the NIZ, it passed for a mantra.

At the end of the hall, Nathan was fitted with a fire-retardant jacket, surgically white, a white hard hat, and white safety goggles with tinted lenses. Then he was led out on the foundry floor, looking like a charcoal-faced snowman. Nothing stopped this time; no one suspended work to greet him.

"They're heating a magnesium alloy in this crucible," the manager explained. "They're going to be pouring it into sand castings." He stopped briefly along the way to show Nathan the castings. "Heat's critical to the success of the casting, sir." The manager mentioned temperatures in the thousands of degrees Fahrenheit. "There's a time to pour, a time not to, Mr. Vice President, and you've arrived at just the right time."

The manager walked Nathan up to within a half dozen feet of the furnace and showed him the boiling metal inside. Then the two of them backed away a good twenty feet, to join a ring of men who had assembled to watch the castings being poured. The heat seemed to come right through Nathan's jacket. My God, he thought, I'm going to melt.

At the center of the room, a ladle, suspended by chains from an overhead cable, was dipped into the crucible, hoisted up, and guided over the castings. When the ladle was in position, a worker—Nathan couldn't tell if it was a man or a woman beneath the protective gear—reached up with a long iron pole to tip the ladle over. There was a brilliant flash of light as the molten metal poured out, spilled into the castings, and bounced where it missed along the floor. The noise suddenly was deafening. How, Nathan wondered, could pouring metal be so loud? Or was it just the men in the room, roaring their approval, as the ladle was hauled a little farther down the cable and tipped again over a new set of castings?

On Nathan's right, the foundry manager was shouting something about how the alloy that splashed out of the castings would be recycled and the castings broken down and re-formed. Behind Nathan, there was bumping, a slight jostling, as the crowd craned forward to watch the last of the alloy being poured. Nathan felt a tug on the left side of his fire jacket. He looked over, and there was a man with half the side of his face burned away; scar tissue stretched from above his hairline to below his chin. The man's mangled mouth seemed to be trying to form a word, trying to tell Nathan something. Nathan shut his eyes, shook his head to clear it—what am I seeing? why? When he opened them again, the light in the room was dying, the throb ebbing, and the burned man was gone, displaced, disappeared. Or maybe, Nathan thought, maybe he never was.

Nathan looked down the line of men to his left and saw Widmeyer pantomiming a fork—into the plate, up to the mouth. Mealtime. Nathan nodded. Let's go. Vamoose.

NATHAN WAS SWEATING. He took off his jacket, rolled up his sleeves, and asked the driver to open the trunk. He checked it carefully for oily rags, grimy jacks, general vile debris, and then laid his suit coat carefully in the well. Discomfort was one thing; ruining a six-hundred-dollar suit was another. Nathan had his vanities. The media contingent was lounging in the van next to the Vice President; most of them hadn't bothered to go into the foundry.

The sedan was passing back through the center of town on its way to the Patriation Housing Complex and lunch. The shops and businesses on either side were the usual commercial furniture of any half-dead downtown in the greater embrace of the Confederate States of America: last-gasp variety stores, hair salons, a hardware store, the Dew Drop Inn. Above them, clearly, floors of apartments; offices for attorneys who could find no place more profitable to practice; a depilatory clinic ("Hair Today, Gone Tomorrow"); doctors' offices that looked like places only the dying would seek out.

"We run our own medical clinics, of course, Mr. Vice President," Widmeyer said when he noticed Nathan eyeing a row of second-story offices that offered everything form wart removal to spinal realignment. "The coalition takes its responsibilities to its workers very seriously."

"Who, then?" Nathan said, waving a hand at the line of dust-caked windows. "Who would use these doctors?"

"I suppose undocumented workers, sir."

"Undocumented?"

"People without national work cards, sir. You know, exiles, people who want to disappear. We get our share of those in the NIZ, a disproportionate share, if I may be allowed to say so."

People like John Henry, Nathan suddenly conjectured. My God, what if he became sick, broke a bone, needed some other kind of attention? Would he have to go to one of these people? The possibility horrified him. His own father had kept his medical office antiseptically clean, even though most of his professional life was spent in the surgery wing at the hospital. Nathan pushed the thought aside, sat on it, and returned his attention to the street they were driving along. Soot flakes aside, dust storms and tired offices notwithstanding, the downtown looked clean and swept. There were few people on the street for a noon hour, but maybe that was the factory shifts, local custom. And they seemed presentable, certainly, and friendly. A group of men and women waited at the entrance to a side street, behind a yellow police rope. Some held miniature flags; others carried placards with a photograph of Nathan and Spencer Lee mounted on them. Mr. Widmeyer apparently hadn't stopped to breathe since Wormley alerted him to the Vice President's visit. The sun had broken through. Clouds were scattering.

"Slower, please," Nathan said.

As the car braked to a snail's pace, Nathan rolled down his window, smiled at the well-wishers, and waved.

"Hey, hey, how are you?" he called to them.

"Welcome to North Adams, Mr. Vice President," one man called. He was wearing denim overalls on top of a white T-shirt. A broad smile played across his face.

"Nice tie!" a woman standing next to the man called out.

Nathan laughed now, his first good laugh since he'd arrived in North Adams. He could hear Farley shouting from the van behind his sedan: "Give her the tie! Give her the tie!" Nathan was reaching up to unknot his tie and hand it to the woman when he looked past the clot of well-wishers, past the restraining rope and the flags and placards. Behind them, the side street teemed. At the back, silhouetted near the end of the block, he glimpsed a familiar shape— maybe, maybe not: six-footish, stooped slightly at the shoulders like the beginning of a question mark, a gray sweatshirt.

"Stop!" Nathan said suddenly, not quite through with apparitions for the day.

"Sir?" It was Widmeyer.

"Have the driver stop, Mr. Widmeyer! I want to get out. I intend to walk that block on foot. Now."

"The street we just passed, sir?"

"Yes, yes, for God's sake."

"But lunch—"

"Now, Mr. Widmeyer. Now."

Widmeyer leaned forward to the driver: "Would you alert security, please. We're walking Ramsey Street." Then he turned back to the Vice President: "Basic precautions, sir. We'll have to go around the block to get in place. It will just take a minute."

Halfway around the next block, a delivery truck was pulled perpendicular across the street, preparing to discharge its cargo. It took time to find the driver, time for the driver to turn his truck around.

"Mr. Widmeyer, for God's sake. Can't you get us moving?"

Widmeyer held his hands up, shook his head. What could anyone do, under the circumstances? By the time the Vice President's car squeaked by, the one minute had become seven minutes. By the time the car made its way around again to Ramsey Street, the police tape had been removed and the well-wishers who had been standing behind it were waiting to greet the Vice President in person: "Such an honor." "Thank you so much for stopping, sir." "Hope your visit is going well." Behind them, Ramsey Street was empty.

Nathan looked down the block. Where had the people gone? What had become of the question mark in the gray sweatshirt at the end of the block? Or was it all just something he thought he'd seen? God, Nathan thought, his want was so great. Had he merely seen what he wanted to see?

A low, seemingly vacant brick building filled the whole left side of the street. Multipane windows set in lead frames were anchored to the wall. Nathan forced his attention back to where he was, back to why he was here.

What had the building been? he asked Widmeyer. "Some kind of piecing facility?"

"A warehouse, more likely," Widmeyer said. On the other side of the street were commercial shops and small businesses, still more woebegone than those on the main street—some with "out of business" signs, some closed for lunch, all of them looking as if they were hanging on for dear life.

As the press contingent spread out along the block to try to interview someone—anyone—Nathan walked to the nearest warehouse window, tried to peer in, and couldn't see a thing. He took a handkerchief from his pants pocket, and rubbed at the glass; the dirt was on the inside. He looked once more. Futile. Completely futile. For all he knew, people could be flaying deer, performing *Othello,* or having an orgy inside.

There was a booming voice now, just in his ear: "Mr. Vice President!"

When Nathan turned around, most of the city council and half of the Manufacturers' Coalition had materialized as if by magic on the street all around him.

"Sir," Widmeyer was saying. "Mr. Vice President, allow me to introduce . . ."

Dear God, Nathan thought, there'll be no one left to meet at lunch except a few dormitory matrons. Closing in on the new welcoming party from behind, the reporters were thrilled: Live bodies! People who looked as if they could actually speak English! Something to throw quotation marks around! Nathan made a mental note to open the bar early on the plane back—it will have been a long day for everyone. He looked down the street once more, trying to will the apparition back into existence, but nothing was there.

JOHN HENRY HAD been shocked at how clean the town was, at the flower boxes and the swept streets. He'd learned at breakfast that half the workers on some of the shifts at the foundry had been given the day off at full pay. He'd also heard, the night before, the shouts of the textile mill workers who lived at the house, released from their shifts after only four hours, and the louder shouts of the paper workers, their mill closed down for the whole day. At the end of the street he could see the yellow police tape, the crowd gathered. It was a parade, a holiday of some sort. He hadn't thought of North Adams as a place where celebrations took place.

It was John Henry's first trip to town. He'd been lonely at the house since the knife incident, embarrassed by how afraid he had been of Sean. Avoided by the others, John Henry had wondered if they were ashamed of their own behavior—the way so many had turned on him when Sean had. Or maybe they simply were afraid of Cara. Either way, the effect was the same. Gradually, though, détente had been established. Hellos were again exchanged, nods when they passed on the stairs or met in the kitchen. Two nights earlier, John Henry had even taken a quiet corner in the living room, after eating his dinner upstairs. It was like starting all over again, but knowing this time in what dangerous waters it all could end. His antennae were up, quivering.

Finally, he'd asked Cara to let him go into town. He was prepared to plead his case—he felt like a captive; he'd never know if he was never allowed to see; he couldn't stand one more book about the injustice of justice or anything else—but Cara had proved a pushover.

"Just be careful, honey. Stick to the back streets. Don't stay anyplace too long. And wear these shades."

They were hideous—wraparounds from a fashion epoch long gone by. They made him look like a gangster, John Henry argued.

"Nobody's looking for a gangster," Cara answered, "but they might be looking for you."

Point taken. He'd wear them. And at least there was a little sunshine for once. As John Henry was getting ready to leave, Cara handed him a five-dollar bill and gave him a kiss on the cheek.

"Don't be buying presents for any other girl," she said with a laugh that sounded almost like a song.

ONE OF THE Marys gave him a ride the mile or so to a side street near a cluster of churches and pointed toward a diner halfway down the next block.

"It's a good spot for lunch," she said. "I'll pick you up in front at four o'clock. Do what Cara says, Johnny. Stick to the shadows, and keep moving."

Now John Henry was doing just as he'd been told, roaming the side streets just off Main, moving. He'd been cooped up so long in his third-floor bedroom that he felt as if an enormous weight had been lifted off him. He wanted to break into a run, run as far as his legs would carry him, flap his arms, whoop.

"Cool shades," a boy his own age said as they passed on the sidewalk.

John Henry wanted to stop him and ask what was going on in town, wanted—God knows—the company of his own. But what did he know about the boy? What did he know, really, about anyone he passed on the street or saw inside the shops? He'd made his own bed, John Henry told himself. He'd have to lie in it.

He'd just come to Ramsey Street when he saw what all the to-do in North Adams was about. A black sedan was inching along at the other end of the street, a police car in front of it, a van behind. John Henry recognized the configuration immediately. A "visiting fireman"—his father's phrase—was in town, press in tow. Undoubtedly there was someone sitting in the car with the dignitary, just waiting to have his pocket pissed in. The visiting fireman rolled his window down, stuck a black hand out, and waved to the well-wishers at the far end. It was all John Henry could make out. The fireman's car was rolling away now, his small cortege with it. John Henry's sunglasses were scratchy, dark as pitch. When you get right down to it, he thought, I can barely see a damn thing.

From behind John Henry came one shrill whistle, a single blast. He turned and saw a phalanx of policemen bearing down on him. At the far end of the street, the well-wishers had been pushed aside. A line of police was advancing from that end as well. And all John Henry could think was this: It's over. I'm fucked.

"MOVE! MOVE! MOVE! Move!"

There was something at his back, a nightstick, maybe, but pushing gently. John Henry was being herded toward the center of the block; he could see the herd advancing from the other end, thickening as it condensed. In the midst of the crowd now, the nightstick gone from behind him, he was moving along at the herd's volition, not his own. At some point, his sunglasses flew off—he didn't know how. He tried to reach for them, but his arms were almost pinned at his sides. He might have heard them hit the pavement, might even have heard them being crunched and ground underfoot.

At his right, double doors were suddenly opened, midway along a low brick building that ran the length of the block. There was a pressure now from John Henry's left. The policemen were closing in, using their nightsticks, batons, truncheons, whatever they had, to push the herd through the double doors.

"Quick! Quick! Quick!" they were saying. "Move it! Move it! Move it!" But there was no malice to their voices—just a job to be done, nothing more.

The herd turned into a stream, a river now, and began rushing downhill for the opening. As John Henry flowed through the door, a man in plain working clothes was saying, "It's only for a little while. Move to the center, please. It's only for a little while. Move to the center, please." Almost everyone did, as if this had happened to them before, as if it were an everyday occurrence to be turned into sheep, into water; to be herded and channeled and sluiced.

John Henry peeled off to the left and meandered among the abandoned pallets, the long worktables coated by inches of dust, draped with cobwebs. The building was low and vast, a block deep to match its block long. He was completely by himself. He wandered over to the windows on his far right, which fronted Ramsey Street, and saw something on the other side—someone trying to peer in, someone rubbing on the glass. John Henry took the sleeve of his sweatshirt and began to rub too. The dirt was epic, crusted. Little by little, though, it yielded—first a speck, then a hole, of light. John Henry bent and put his eye to the hole. Whoever had been trying to look in was gone, walking away, surrounded by men in suits, and then John Henry saw who it was.

He froze for a moment. What was going on? Then he realized: The visiting fireman was his father! John Henry raced to the next bank of windows, attacked the dirt again with his sweatshirt, wore a speck, wore a dot, a hole. It was too late. His father was moving on, working his way down the street, gesturing as he talked. John Henry knew it well: his official posture. Mr. Vice President. John Henry stepped back and counted: There were three more banks of windows until the end of the building. He looked left and right: The sheep were standing in the middle, as if they had been corralled. Then he took off running to the bank of windows at the end of the building. He used his fingernails first this time, scrabbled at the worst of the dirt, took the bottom of his sweatshirt and rubbed and rubbed, spit on it, and rubbed some more, until there was a hole big enough for a mouth, big enough for the start of a face.

His father was standing in profile, his shirtsleeves rolled up, no more than four feet from John Henry, listening to another black man, who still wore his suit coat.

Turn, Dad! Turn this way!

And then, as if there were such a thing as telepathy, John Henry's father did begin to turn toward him—slowly, slowly. As he turned, John Henry mouthed the words he had never been able to say to his father in real life, words that had been stuck in his throat, his heart, so many times: *Dad, Dad, I love you.* Then, before his father had turned completely, someone else moved, and the back of a blue shirt was pressed against the window. John Henry wanted to reach out through the glass, smash it, grab whoever it was, shake him until his guts spilled out, and throw him aside: *Dad, Dad, I'm here. Listen, this is not about you! Not about Mom! It's me!* And then the blue shirt moved, and John Henry could just see his father's left foot disappearing into the back of the black sedan.

"Johnny!"

Whispered. Intense. Was it coming from inside his head? And who was Johnny?

"Johnny!"

It was Mary, John Henry finally realized, calling him from the shadows of the warehouse, unwilling to risk the daylight herself. And "Johnny" was he, the person he had become. My God, the shock of that!

IT WAS THREE in the afternoon when John Henry found the black sedan again. Half lost, determined not to get wholly lost, he'd walked in ever-widening concentric squares from the center of town. Finally, he had started climbing the hills on the east side, past a small park, a tiny bone-dry pond at its center, and there the sedan was, in the parking lot of a new school complex. The driver leaned against its fender, smoking a cigarette, talking with a policeman who was pulling on a cola can. Half the complex had been finished; half was still under construction. The sign over the completed building read: "Spencer Lee Elementary School." Maybe that's why his father was here, John Henry thought: representing the President at the dedication. Maybe when it was finished, the school next door would have a sign that read: "Nathan Winston Elementary School," the two of them joined in brick and mortar as they had been for eight years in life. Maybe his father was representing himself: rare for a Vice President.

As he watched from the road, a yellow school bus pulled up, stopped near the policeman, and disgorged a small choir: little black boys and girls, in little robes. They had come from the elementary school whose new building was not quite completed, John Henry supposed. As he watched, the children lined up behind the policeman, waited until he was satisfied, then followed as he marched them inside. Even from his distance, John Henry could sense their excitement.

A path led up to some playing fields, in the opposite direction from the parking lot. John Henry followed it to the edge of the school. Then he listened until he could pick up the noise and followed the noise to some open windows: the cafeteria, doubling today as an auditorium. The little black choir stood on the left of a makeshift stage just in front of the railing for the food line; the little white choir stood on the right. Between them was the music teacher. Seated directly in front of her was Nathan Winston.

The music teacher turned to the black choir, played a C on her pitch pipe, then turned to the white choir and did the same. She held her hand up and played one more C, to get both sides in unison. When she dropped her hand, they all began, exactly on time, their little voices—all their inherited eccentricities, all the odd gutturals and strange sibilants their parents had carried to this New World— merging perfectly into one big American sound:

> I wish I was in the land of cotton,
> Old times there are not forgotten—
> Look away! Look away! Look away!
> Dixie Land. . . .

By societal consensus, the "old times" of the song were postbellum, when the entrepreneurial picking of cotton provided an important first rung up the economic ladder for impoverished blacks and whites alike in the Deep South. And in any event, the voices were so pure, the sound so deeply innocent—and it was the last stop of an exhausting day. Nathan Winston was doing all he had within his strength and power to do: He was beaming. John Henry took a last look—his father's face just visible from the side—then turned and retraced his steps. He wasn't sure how long it would take him to get back to the diner where Mary was to pick him up. There would be hell to pay with Cara if he was late.

19

NATIONAL UNIVERSITY
OF THE SOUTH

IN HER HOME office, Lucinda Winston busied herself with paper-work: piles neatly stacked, stacks neatly placed in folders, folders neatly placed in files. One for college-related matters, one labeled "Business—To Do," another "Personal—Hold," still another "Personal—Answer," one "Misc.," one simply "VP." There were the household accounts to add and subtract, the sponsorship form for Olga, who came to clean twice a week and would soon be an American. What then? Would Olga want to stay on once she had completed the Patriation Program? Did she have a relative somewhere to go live with, a base from which to start her new life? They'd never talked about it. Lucinda would cross that bridge when she came to it; she'd see what she could do to help.

On the desk directly in front of her: a stack of essays, a final assignment from her students before they settled in to prepare for their exams. Her teaching assistant had delivered them this morning, already read and marked, already graded, the grades already re-corded. Lucinda lived a five-minute walk from her classroom—five minutes if she took time to admire Jefferson's architecture, chatted a moment with a colleague or a student—but she was teaching these days by long distance.

Lucinda straightened her back, pulled the chair closer to her desk, and moved her teacup just slightly so it would be within easier reach. She found a pair of newly sharpened blue pencils in her top drawer—blue so her comments and corrections would be distinct from those of her teaching assistant, done in red. Her assistant was wonderful on content, a demon on rooting out phony sourcing. She sometimes seemed to Lucinda to have read *everything,* but she had never learned rudimentary grammar—another sign, Lucinda told herself, of diminishing standards, that one so intelligent should be so lacking. She herself despised poor grammar. A dangling participle was, to Lucinda, not just a logical failure; it was bad taste, something to be rooted out and destroyed. She opened the cover of the first essay and turned to the first page. The words blurred and ran. They seemed to have been written in some unstable liquid. Her teaching assistant's summary remarks—"B+: very solid work but maybe too heavy on speculation with not enough support"—looked to Lucinda like a splotch of angry blood, a gash. She closed the cover quickly, pushed her chair back from the desk, and spun around. Goldfinches, two males and a female by their coloring, were perched on the thistle-seed feeder she had asked the grounds crew to suspend from a branch with a nylon cord so that it hung almost in front of her window, squirrel-proof. Wisteria was in bloom. She hadn't sat in the garden for weeks.

Lucinda walked to the bookshelves, aligned the spines, and made sure her own small tome—*Ritual and Rights,* in hardback and a special paperbound "classroom" edition—was only modestly visible on the far left of the bookcase. A photograph—enlarged, framed, and hung on the wall next to the bookcase—was listing to the side: herself, Nathan, Lucy, John Henry, on the rim of the Grand Canyon, taken almost nine years earlier, before politics, before fame, before . . . The thought caught and died. Lucy was already becoming a woman in the photo; John Henry, only eight, was clinging to his father's hand, afraid of the chasm behind him. Lucinda adjusted the frame, stepped back, adjusted it again, and stepped back again. It did what all old family photographs did to her these days; it made a little rip in her heart. Strange that she so sought them out.

When the phone rang, Lucinda practically screamed.

It was Nathan, the call patched through from his plane to Maury Field, from Maury to the White House operator, from the White House to her—she could hear the telltale background click of a secure channel.

"How was your trip, dear?" To where? Someplace in the Northeast. Why? That was beyond her. She could hear ice cubes clinking,

lively chatter. The press. Nathan had opened the bar—the perfect
host. What he had to say about the trip, she had no idea.

No, she told her husband, Clarisse—her sister—wasn't there.
She'd gone to visit an old friend. Did Nathan remember her? From
Norfolk? Clarisse would pick up groceries on the way home. The
two of them would dine in tonight, alone, as if they had dined any
other way since Clarisse arrived almost a week before. Something
light, Lucinda said—code for: My sister is a terrible cook. Not code
for: And I couldn't care less these days what's put in front of me.
In any event, neither had to be said. Nathan always avoided Clarisse's
puny stews and overcooked fish. Lucinda meanwhile had been losing
weight. Not a great deal, but she had little extra weight to give away.
Soon, if she wasn't careful, if she didn't try to eat more, if she didn't
find a way to sleep more regularly, Lucinda would begin to canni-
balize herself.

"You'll have to eat for both of us," she had told Nathan over
dinner a week earlier, just before Clarisse arrived. He'd laughed,
alarmed.

Lucinda carried the phone to the door, stared out into the hall as
she talked, to her left into Lucy's room, across the hall into their
own, to her right at John Henry's closed door.

Yes, she said, Lucy had been home. She'd blown into the house
and was gone again just as quickly. Lucy never seemed to stay more
than two minutes anymore. She and Jason Lee weren't writing a
paper, Nathan; they were writing a book. But, she supposed, if they
had to experiment with dual education, they should make the course
rigorous. Dr. Cuthbert was letting them substitute the paper for an
exam; they'll be working on it to the very end of the semester.
(Thinking, but not saying: This experiment is the beginning of the
end. She'd beaten that horse to death when Spencer was visiting.
Thinking, but not saying: I have no idea where Lucy has been these
last weeks. She's disappeared from my life. Or I have from hers.)

Yes, she assured Nathan, it was a beautiful day in Charlottesville.
Goldfinches were on the feeder; not a squirrel was in sight. She
hoped it had been just as beautiful in—again the name escaped her—
wherever he had been.

He'd be home tomorrow? For dinner? Lucinda roused herself,
strategized. They'd go to the Colonnade Club; she would make res-
ervations as soon as they hung up. The Colonnade Club overcooked

its fish too—Clarisse would be happy—but at least there would be a steak, a chop, a slab of prime rib for Nathan. Lucinda herself would prefer to live on air, like an epiphyte.

In the background she could hear ice chattering, people chattering, the dull roar of turbojets, so astoundingly muted inside the plane.

"You'd better get back to your business, dear." He was ready to hang up; she could hear it in his voice. "It's dangerous to leave the media alone for long, with a bar so close by." An old gag.

"Tomorrow, then," Lucinda said.

And "I love you too."

And finally, "Bye, dear. Bye-bye."

She put the phone back in its cradle, sat on the settee, and studied the engagement ring Nathan had given her on the steps of the rotunda more than two decades before—a diamond that had been his grandmother's, flanked by two sapphires he had chosen himself. Then she cried and cried and cried.

"That wasn't the call I wanted," she said, half aloud. "That wasn't the call I wanted at all."

Between them, they hadn't spoken John Henry's name one time. What was there to say?

LUCINDA NUDGED THE door to John Henry's room open as quietly as she could, as if there were anyone to hear. The blinds were drawn, covered by thin curtains. It was almost night inside. Lucinda opened his closet. He had taken practically nothing with him, but he had seemed to want almost nothing when he lived with them. Maybe, she told herself, her son was a true epiphyte; maybe he *could* live on air.

Lucinda closed the door carefully, walked to John Henry's dresser, and studied its top: his collection of carved wooden animals; a little bronze Eiffel Tower her grandmother had brought back when France was still a nation, not a political division; a jar of change; a jar of pencils and pens. She thought about opening his drawers— imagined herself burying her face in her son's socks, T-shirts, underwear. Then she thought better of it, crossed to his desk, and sat down on his chair.

Lucinda had always been small-boned, dainty—"Bone China" had been one of her father's nicknames for her when she was little. Yet she had never thought of herself as fragile. She had had a constitution of iron. She rarely got sick, even when exotic bugs whirled around the campus, and whenever she did succumb, she almost never missed a class or a faculty meeting. She had stood up to other kinds of gales before too: her father's slow wasting away; the first campaign, always on the go, nowhere to rest, the children to look after. There's no explaining what a campaign is like until you live through it.

That's why she had been so surprised—not by her grief: even brute animals cry, wail, and rip at their own skin when their young are taken from them. But surprised that this had broken her; that she had given in so completely to her sorrow. What happens to mothers whose entire families are wiped out by disease, in airplane accidents, or because some drunk falls asleep at the wheel, crosses the median, and turns the family station wagon into an inferno? How do they go on? How do they keep from throwing themselves into the grave with their loved ones and pulling the dirt down over their own heads?

Lucinda walked across the room and sat on the edge of John Henry's bed. She lay down on it—rested her head on his pillow— and closed her eyes.

"Don't we have to consider one more possibility, Lucinda?"

Spencer Lee's voice suddenly seemed to fill the room, drive the air out of it.

My God, Spencer, of course we do, she had wanted to tell him that afternoon. Of course we do. Lucinda could hear Frannie's voice clear as a bell beneath her husband's: "Facts are facts, Lucinda. I've got to face the facts"—this as she was planning her own death, her own funeral service, her own burial. Of course we have to consider one more possibility. She may have given in to her grief, Lucinda thought, but she wasn't a fool. She could see. She had the gift of reason. No one could have walked into her house and snatched her son as if he were a pocketbook hanging from a chair downstairs. John Henry wasn't especially strong, he wasn't a gifted athlete, but he would have fought like a bulldog. She knew exactly why he had gone. She had known it from the very first: He wanted to turn theory into practice. He was tired of living in books and magazine articles, tired of abstraction. She had given in to her grief; her son had given in to his romantic conception of himself. And she knew something else: John Henry never would have done it if she herself hadn't driven him from the house—if she hadn't argued and argued and argued with him until there was no space for them to live under the same roof. Facts, as Frannie would say, are facts. But, Spencer, we tell ourselves lies all the time! We tell ourselves the lies we have to tell ourselves to keep going. I do. You do. My God, Spencer, you're a *politician*. We all do. We lie to ourselves, and we learn to believe our lies, and if we couldn't do that, who knows what would become of us?

This is my lie, Spencer: *my lie*. Let me believe it.

The phone in the upstairs hallway was ringing—the house line, not her office. For the first time in weeks, Lucinda didn't race to answer it.

20

THE WHITE HOUSE

SPENCER LEE WAS suddenly struck with the rock-hard conviction that he needed to find a new wife, someone to live out his years with. He was in the middle of breakfast: a half grapefruit, sectioned; bran flakes with banana and one-percent milk—all rabbit food, all Wormley's doing. The newspapers were in front of him, the *Richmond Times* on top as always. Above the fold on its front page, a three-column photo of Nathan Winston working his way through a crowd of textile workers. "Vice President makes surprise inspection tour of NIZ," the caption read. "Story: A-6."

Atlanta, at least, had started the story on the front page and given it a very positive spin. God bless Farley—he might be a blowhard, but he delivered. Not surprisingly, the Toronto paper had picked the story off the wire services and turned everything upside down: "Confederate Veep Gets Firsthand Look at Environmental Devastation." What could you do?

Beside the newspapers lay the daily digest of editorials and opinion pieces from the leading regional papers; and beside the digest, a stack of papers Spencer had requested from the congressional liaison office, already marked with talking points for his nine-thirty meeting with the Cattlemen's Association. He'd been through them once. Once was enough.

The President had said no to another stack of papers—far taller, he was certain—that his security adviser wanted him to pore over before the ten A.M. weekly meeting with the Joint Military Command. The JMC meetings mostly bored Spencer to tears. Over in the working wing of the White House, agency heads, department secretaries, and senior aides were lined up three deep, he knew, just waiting for him to arrive so they could pile still more stacks of papers on him: briefing papers, white papers, trial language, an ocean of words.

Oh, well, Spencer thought, he at least had it easier than the German chancellor, followed everywhere—even into the bathroom, it was said—by a hatchet-faced army officer who kept chained to his body a briefcase containing the codes required to launch a nuclear attack. Spencer needed no such angel of death following him, because American policy was crystal clear. The Confederacy was at peace with all the nations of the world, a willing trading partner with each and every one. Should any nation, Greater Germany included, decide that it was not at peace with the Confederacy, should it let a single stone be dropped in anger on the Confederacy or any of its territories or dependencies, then retaliation would be immediate and complete and utter. Peace through strength. Strength through peace.

ON THE TELEVISION built into the sideboard, a morning team for one of the networks was smiling, interviewing celebrities, cutting to the crowd in front of the studio, cutting to ads, cutting back to itself, its smiles, its insistent good cheer. He kept the show on mute until the news, on the half hour.

It was eight-fifteen in the morning, a beautiful sunny morning in the beautiful capital of the most beautiful country on earth. Birds were singing. Lovers were sharing a last kiss at the door, a last touch of hands, before parting for the day, the week, forever. And Spencer Lee was already elbows-high in paper, hip-deep in opinion, suffocating in the forced bonhomie of the TV talking heads. He beeped Manzini on the intercom, reminded him that the Vice President was coming by the private quarters this morning, and asked him to send up something more *appropriate* to the Vice President's appetite. Manzini would know. Then he took the papers from the congressional liaison office, the editorial daily digest, the morning papers, took all that—by now a substantial load—and carried it over to the sideboard. He kicked open one of the doors, shoved the whole pile on top of a stack of place mats, and closed both that door and the doors over the television set. Too much, he said to himself. Too much.

Spencer refreshed his coffee, looked around at the newly barren landscape of the informal White House breakfast room—barren of paper, barren of television, barren of company, a mate, a wife—and thought.

There had, of course, been women in the four years since Frannie's death. Spencer was a man; he was president of the most powerful nation on the planet. There had been nights on international swings in that first year after his involuntary bachelorhood when women had been virtually forced on him: nights when his host—king, president, prime minister for life—would pat him on the arm after dinner, tell him once again how sorry he was about Mrs. Lee, say that he hoped his little gift might offer some consolation. Later, Spencer would return to his official guest residence or to the official guest wing of a seemingly endless palace to find a woman of unimaginable beauty waiting in his bed, a woman of extraordinary imagination as well. Dear God, he ached to think of a few of them, powerless as he was to take the high ground, powerless to say no, thank you.

When Jason was away at college—never when he was living at home, never when he was home on vacation—there had even been women in the private living quarters: women who had lingered after state dinners; women who had mentioned to him over cocktails that they would love to see the scandalous Degas painting of Robert E. Lee on Traveller—the horse and rider almost lovers—that was known to hang in the hallway just outside Spencer's bedroom; women, to be honest, whom he had wanted, whom he had pursued through the fruit and cheese, insisting that they sit at his side for the little musical performance that marked the evening's end. He was a man.

One had been a columnist: a terrible mistake, never repeated. Spencer had seen details of his private life—shaving cream brand, underwear type, knee scar, worse—scattered through her columns for weeks, until he granted the exclusive interview that seemed to have been the point of the whole thing.

His favorite had been the Asian-American wife of the Air Force chief of staff. Had been; still was. She had come to a dinner for a Chinese trade delegation—come alone because her husband was touring bases and because she herself was the sort of shining example of the Patriation Program that Spencer liked to have on hand for such events. Afterward, she had offered to help Spencer clean up, this with a twinkle in her eye: a wonderful joke! A dozen minions scampered this way and that as she said it, whisking away dishes and glasses. They'd walked back up to Spencer's den. She'd driven herself home a little after midnight. Her husband had been two years ahead of Spencer at the Citadel—a brute who had gotten only more brutish with age. She'd worked for him in the final months of her Patriation—as a domestic even though she had trained as a nurse before fleeing Nanking—and married him shortly after attaining citizenship. For her, Spencer was warmth, a port in her little domestic storm; for him, she was warmth as well and also the rarest thing in a president's life—someone who asks for nothing. Manzini alone served them when she visited; Manzini alone took care of the details of getting her out the door. Spencer didn't ask how. Manzini, for his part, would have lied under oath if asked about it—would have allowed himself to be deported, exiled, before he gave up a single detail. She made Spencer Lee happy. Case closed.

Not that it would ever come to anything more. Spencer Lee wasn't merely the prisoner of his high office; he was the prisoner of his blood as well—a Davis, a Lee, lines not to be casually mixed.

Frannie, dying, had told him to remarry, and soon—her incessant clearing of accounts—but she had chosen him, really. How did a man go about choosing a wife for himself? A man who was soon to be unemployed, forced into retirement? And not so luxurious a retirement as all that: enough of a pension to live on, enough not to embarrass the nation, enough so that former Presidents wouldn't be reduced to becoming official greeters at offshore casinos; but no house, no office staff, no driver or limousine or faithful manservant. (All of it Spencer's little fiction, one of the lies he told himself: He had never had to work a day in his life and never would. And Manzini had chosen Spencer too: He wouldn't leave him even if all the trust funds collapsed, the family investments suddenly went belly-up, the real estate proved worthless. Even if Spencer did have to take a job shaking hands at some combination betting parlor and backdoor brothel, Manzini would be standing next to him, fanning him with his shirt, mopping Spencer's brow with his own handkerchief.)

All his life, Spencer had taken the path of least resistance: to Frannie, who wanted him; to politics, which seemed made for him; to the presidency, for which his blood destined him. It was Frannie's ambition that shaped him, not his own—about that Spencer had no illusions—Frannie's astuteness that practically handed him the nomination, Frannie's drive that kept him going through that first, seemingly endless campaign. (The second one so much easier, in part because Frannie was then recently in her grave, and who would dare say a bad thing about a man still grieving?)

Spencer at least knew—or thought he knew—where the path of least resistance was likely to lead him in rematrimony at this late date: the eldest daughter of a plotting billionaire, a professional hostess of background and breeding (Margaret Barnes!), a widow refurbished by a plastic surgeon's scalpel. And what about Jason, he wondered: Was a stepmother what a boy needed at his age? Or would he resent having someone layered on his mother's memory?

SPENCER COULD HEAR Manzini pausing in the hallway, subtly shifting the weight of his tray so he could knock once, twice, on the open door before entering. That, too, was custom. Manzini always refused to appear in person until his name had been spoken. For years, Spencer had wondered precisely what Manzini feared he might catch the President doing. Establishing radio contact with his German spymasters? Touching himself inappropriately? Pocketing the silver?

"Mr. Manzini?" he called now, forcing the question into his voice as always.

"Mr. President." Stepping into the room.

"Leo."

"Spencer."

"Good morning."

"And to you."

Now that Frannie was gone, it was the closest thing the President had to a predictable daily human exchange. For the last three years, he'd taken Leo with him whenever he traveled.

Spencer began to pour from the fresh pot that had just arrived.

"Coffee, Leo?" Knowing the answer. It was his signal to his old friend that he wanted him to sit a moment, that he wanted to talk.

"Just a drop." Knowing that too. "What's on your mind, Mr. President?"

"Girls."

"Ah."

"That's all you have to say on such a fascinating topic? 'Ah'?"

"Maybe, Spencer, if you could be more specific . . ."

"Mrs. Manzini, for instance."

Leo raised an eyebrow, stopped his cup almost to his mouth, and stared over its rim at the President. He had been married twenty years, since the week after Jason was born, the wedding delayed so he could help Spencer cope with his new fatherhood.

"Helena?"

"Helena. How did you meet her?"

"It was a church social, a party for new citizens." Leo relaxed now, put his cup on its saucer, and remembered. "She had the nicest voice, Spencer, and beautiful eyes. The eyes are the window to the soul."

Leo smiled, stood, put his cup and saucer on the tray, then took the covered plate he had brought from the kitchen and placed it in front of Spencer. "Fried potatoes, two pieces of bacon, a slice of toast. For the Vice President."

"He won't be here for another fifteen minutes, Leo. The food will turn cold."

"I thought of that. I'm having another plate prepared. I'll bring it up then."

Spencer had lifted the cover off and was salting the potatoes when Leo turned at the door.

"It that it, Spencer? Is that all you wanted to talk about?"

"How did you know, really know, Leo, that Helena was the right one for you?"

"The heart will tell you when it's right, Spencer. Listen to your heart, and you won't go wrong."

The problem, Spencer thought as Leo closed the door behind him, is just this: The heart can lead you to such lonely territory. The whole time he had known his father, really, that was precisely the land he had lived in.

DAVIS LEE, JR., was the most brilliant man Spencer had ever encountered. Handsome, he had married beauty. Rich, he had married

richer. The two of them—Spencer's parents—had moved into one
of his mother's family farms along the Rappahannock River, and
there his father had waited. Waited for his heart to tell him when
the moment would be right, waited for history to claim him. By
1942, his heart finally seemed to have spoken to him, in a voice that
wouldn't be denied.

Europe was at war again, or rather the war that had raked the
continent for most of the century had re-erupted, ignited this time
by Herr Hitler. The British Isles had been saved. Leaving Britain
alone was the price of America's nonintervention in the war, Germany had been told. It was a price she was glad to pay, and Ireland
was hardly worth the bother. Thus the Confederacy's debt to its great
benefactor was at long last dissolved. Now, though, came word that
a whole race was disappearing in the margins of Chancellor Hitler's
war, and it was to this cause, to the holy rescue of the Jews, that
Spencer's father's heart was to lead him, to this cause that he
would finally attach himself with all his strength, all his soul, all his
being.

Armed with the Freedom Party's presidential nomination—his
name alone declared his pedigree, and who would dare deny him
the banner?—Spencer's father had thundered from one end of the
land to another. Hitler must be warned. The Jewish race must be
preserved. Humanity demanded it. The memory of Judah Benjamin
demanded it. The judgment of God and history and all that was
decent demanded it. His speeches were glorious ones, still studied
for their rhetoric. Unfortunately, they ignored a few things—few
but critical—not easily seen from Davis Lee's study along the Rappahannock River. The speeches failed to notice, for example, that
after the deprivations of the Great Depression, when the global market dried up for American foodstuffs—people ate less, then they ate
nothing—deutsche marks and lire and francs and yen and guldens
and every other form of currency the rest of the world traded in
were once again pouring into the Confederacy. Spencer's father failed
to notice, too, that a factory that produced combines and threshers
and harvesters could just as easily produce tanks and helicopters and
amphibious assault vehicles, and that by now nearly all the weapons
that all the warring peoples were driving and flying and sailing and
firing had stamped on them: "Made in C.S.A." Somehow, holed up
along the Rappahannock River, he missed that Americans were fat

and for the most part happy. While Americans were horrified by the plight of the European Jews, the European Jews were in ravaged Europe, while the horrified Americans were in cozy America. And it would only get cozier, because finally, when the slaughter was over, when all the bodies had been counted and all the borders re-aligned and some new tyrant had installed himself in the national palace and declared himself favored of God—when all that was done, people always wanted one thing more. It was the one thing they were willing to trade their last national reserves for, their last sterling-silver flatware, their last gold fillings and diamond rings, their last anything for; and it was the one thing America had in even greater abundance than it had weapons: food. Something to eat.

The loss in the election that year was a landslide. Not long after, Spencer's father started his serious drinking. Spencer, the youngest of the four boys, was the last of the children to be born while his parents still pretended to anything like a married life. By the time Alice arrived, their parents had long been sleeping in separate bed-rooms—her father would always call her "immaculate Alice." But at least, Spencer thought, his father had tried. His heart might not have led him to happiness, but it steered him to a principle that he stood on until it carried him under, carried him finally—liver pick-led—into the deep, dark ground. Spencer had had it easier. By the time his own turn had come, in 1992, the American people wanted likability, not principle. And Spencer—the youngest boy, the invet-erate pleaser—had been prepared to give them that, by the bucketful.

When does the willingness to stand for something simply peter out in a family? Spencer wondered. And how do you know when you've found something worth standing for?

WHEN MANZINI RETURNED fifteen minutes later, with a new tray of food and the Vice President in tow, Spencer was still picking at the potatoes, by now grown cold on his plate.

"Kay reports unhappiness in the National Security Office," Na-than said as he settled in across from the President and spread a napkin on his lap. "You seem to be ignoring their briefing papers."

"Someone is always unhappy, Nathan. That's the flawed nature of man. And your trip?" The Vice President was tucking into his grits and eggs. "How are things in the NIZ these days?"

"I hit a good day, I'm told. Sunshine for the most part, and the local paper mill was closed down for repairs."

"Providential," Spencer said, wrinkling his nose as he poured them both some more coffee. "Things are generally spick-and-span in North Adams? Considering?"

"Either that or the Manufacturers' Coalition and the town fathers had been working nonstop to make them look that way. Wormley gave the coalition a day to prepare, no more. Flower boxes were planted. The place looked scrubbed, Spencer. Considering, as you say."

"Everything is 'considering' in the territories, Nathan. That's why they're territories. How about the factories you visited? Working conditions? Patriation?"

The President seemed to be reading the questions off a teleprompter that only he could see. Nathan had observed it before: Spencer was fighting to stay engaged, keep his interest level up.

"You have to go sometime, Spencer. I met one man, a Ugandan— he'd been a basketball star in Europe, but his career was over, and he was going through Patriation rather than stay where he was or go back home. Think of what that says!"

Nathan was back in the crowd. He could feel himself reaching up to grab the man's shoulder. As he did so, he saw the rag woman in the window, the man with the mangled face, the boy at the end of the block. It had been almost a day now, and still he couldn't shake the apparitions.

"We only saw two plants, and I only got inside one—a foundry. I didn't see a job I particularly wanted at either one, but things seemed on the up-and-up. The dormitory was clean; the Patriation workers I talked with seemed happy enough. I'm going to have Territorial Affairs take a look at the health records to see how the coalition's medical clinics are performing, but God knows they have to be preferable to the private doctors' offices we passed by."

Nathan paused, sipped at his coffee, and dabbed his lips with a napkin.

"Two elementary-school choirs sang like angels. It was like listening to music from—"

"I saw the footage," the President interrupted. "You were beaming. Bottom line: Nothing horrible? Nothing requiring immediate action? No damage control needed?"

"Not that I saw, no."

"DRAGO?"

Nathan held up his hands. "Nothing."

And that was it—as much as Spencer wanted to hear about the Vice President's inspection trip to the Northeast Industrial Zone. Just as important, Nathan realized, it was what the President wanted to hear. Nathan had shaken the trees, and nothing bad had fallen out— not brutal working conditions, not inhumane living conditions, not a political ax that someone could grind against them. Good. The trip had been the success Spencer had fully expected it to be. Nathan's report had been the good news Spencer fully expected to hear. No son had fallen out of the trees either, Nathan thought, no one's missing boy—but he kept that thought, too, to himself.

When the intercom buzzed, Spencer reached over, punched the red button, and Wormley's voice came on the phone: "The Jefferson Davis Room, gentlemen. Five minutes." It would take them at least that long to walk there.

The President rose, rolled his sleeves down, and tightened his tie. As he slipped on his suit coat, Spencer studied himself quickly in the full-length mirror on the back of the door to the hall. Behind him, Nathan checked his own tie and pocket foulard. Satisfied, both men stepped into the hall, side by side, and made for the opposite side of the White House.

"Still," Nathan said when they were perhaps a minute along, stepping into waters he rarely swam.

"Still?"

"Something was wrong, Spencer. It didn't add up."

"What didn't?"

"The trip, North Adams, the factories, the dormitories. It was too clean, too scrubbed, too antiseptic. I could smell the disinfectant in the dorm rooms I visited. It was like I was walking through a movie set. For God's sake, Spencer, it's not supposed to be a cruise ship— it's the NIZ."

The Vice President could feel his friend stiffen slightly as they started down the escalator for the tunnel that would take them beneath the White House's formal reception halls to the Davis Wing and its public meeting spaces.

"Don't look for trouble, Nathan. Leave well enough alone," Spencer finally said. "You toured, you saw, you conquered."

They were in the tunnel now. The President's voice was bouncing off the sides, magnified. "I looked at the footage last night, all of it—not just the school choirs but everything that any of the networks was carrying. It was great stuff, all terrific. It's the NIZ, just as you said. There's always going to be dirt swept under the rug for a visit like this. There's always going to be extra pressure on everyone to stand up straight and scrape the grime out from under their nails. It's human nature. You can't stop that. People *want* to put on their best face."

"But the fear—the workers seemed so scared, Spencer, so anxious."

"Nerves, Nathan. That's all it was. Nerves."

How to tell him? Nathan wondered. How to tell the President about his apparitions, about the people he had seen or not seen, about whatever might have been on the other side of the warehouse windows. It had all seemed so real at the time, so close to—what?—some kind of truth? But maybe that was all his own nerves. Face it, it was a loaded trip. Besides, Nathan thought, political reality will never be the whole reality—that's the equation you buy into when you buy into politics.

Spencer stopped now, grabbed his friend by the elbow. "Nathan, it works," he said. "It works!" The words bouncing off the walls; Spencer's other hand sweeping around to take in the White House, the Confederacy, Patriation, the Northeast Industrial Zone, territorial government, the balance of payments, the balance of interests, geopolitics . . . Nathan had no idea where the gesture ended. The atmosphere? The ecosystem? Solar rotation? The pulsation of the universe? Caught in the slight echo effect of the tunnel, it seemed a statement that might reverberate forever, grow infinitely outward. It occurred to Nathan, too, that if Spencer Lee had any idea how much he sounded like Lucinda at that moment, he was giving no hint of it.

What works? Nathan wondered. *What?*

OUT OF THE tunnel now, they were on the escalator that led up to the hallway outside the Davis Room. As they came to the top, Nathan could see the men waiting inside, maybe two dozen, decked out in string ties, hand-tooled boots, sport jackets trimmed with leather. Beside him, he could sense Spencer stretching out, becoming more rawboned as he walked—a cowpoke himself, just out of the saddle. By the time they reached the room, Nathan himself was rolling as he walked, hitching up imaginary chaps, scuffing his spurs along the ground behind him.

"Well, howdy, pardners," he heard himself saying, in the deepest baritone he could muster, as he and the President cleared the doors, both of them with their hands held over imaginary six-shooters, ready to draw. The cattlemen's grazing lands were bursting with green; on-the-hoof prices were skyrocketing. They loved the water-way, loved administration trade policy, loved Spencer, loved Nathan. Their laughter was deep, hearty, genuine.

21

NORTH ADAMS

FINALLY, JOHN HENRY could see and feel the poverty. Finally, he could smell the environmental degradation, touch the untouchable people, inhale the injustice he had been reading about ad nauseam. Finally, John Henry was being treated like an adult, like a man, like one of them. Finally, he told himself, he was inside. Finally: life!

Cara had taken him with her down the valley to Pittsfield—an errand boy, someone to lift for her and spell her driving when they wandered onto narrow, winding mountain roads to drop off this package, check on that person. Not long into the trip, at Adams, they'd gone west as far as the road would take them, then followed a brook on foot, finally a stony trail up a steep embankment until they came to a clearing, and there John Henry had seen the most amazing thing he had ever witnessed: a woman living with her four children in a cave! It was almost summer, to be sure; the cave seemed spacious and was lit and vented by a fissure in the roof, with bedrolls and dry straw pallets to sleep on. Still, he had thought caves were for bears, prehistoric peoples, the savages of the Carpathians. He and Cara delivered the package of food and medicines—two of the children had badly scabbed-over rashes and runny eyes—chatted a few minutes, and left. John Henry was too astounded to say more than hello and goodbye. The oldest child, a wild-eyed boy of ten, almost scared him.

They were nearly back to the car before Cara said a word:

"She and her husband met when they were Level Two Patriation workers. You can't fall in love then, baby. You've got to wait until Level Three, until they tell you that you can fall in love. She was about seven months pregnant when they were found out. They lived with us after they ran away from their Patriation dormitories. Then her husband started working at the paper mill, and they moved down to Adams. About two years ago, he died when a roller came loose and crushed him, and she moved into the cave with those boys.

"Even people who don't exist have to live somewhere."

Three days later, Cara had taken him in the car again, for hours this time, nearly all the way to Boston. At Athol, they detoured a half hour out of their way so she could show him the chemical effluent of a plastics processing plant. The effluent appeared to boil as it splashed into the Otter River. Nearby, the rocks were deeply scarred, broken down into tiny bits of gravel. At Leominster, John Henry saw something else he had never seen: darkness at noon, a dense black cloud that grabbed hold of the smokestacks and held on. They drove for ten miles with their lights on; for ten miles the sun was unable to penetrate the cloud, the breeze unable to blow it away.

It was sunrise by the time they got back. John Henry was asleep in the passenger seat when Cara put her hand on his leg and shook him awake. She had pulled off on the side of the road, just as it came through a hairpin turn and started down the back side of the Hoosic Range into North Adams.

"Don't say a thing, baby," she told him as he rubbed the sleep out of his eyes. "Not a thing. Just look."

Below them lay the town and, beyond it, the valley of the Hoosic River, sleeping under a soft blanket of mist, with Mount Greylock rising out of the cloud on the valley's far side. As they watched, the sun cleared the hills to the east and began to burn the mist away. The tortured landscape beneath the blanket slowly materialized—smokestacks sprouting almost endlessly in the distance, electrical lines, power grids. They were too much on top of it to see the railroad bursting out of the Hoosic Tunnel, but they could see the rails disgorging themselves into the freight yard that fronted the river.

"Everything used to be so beautiful," Cara said as she started the car again. "So beautiful. Just like you, baby."

For hours afterward, her words hung in John Henry's ears like an echo.

· · ·

"YOU KNOW WHERE Durham is, down in North Carolina, don't you, honey? Your mama's from right next door, over in Raleigh."

Sometimes it seemed to John Henry as if Cara had studied him, as if she had a Ph.D. in nothing but John Henry. She knew where his mother was born and his sister's name and what class Lucy was in at the university. She also knew that his father had first wanted to go into medicine, surgery like his own father, until he discovered he couldn't stand the smell of blood. The "smell," not the sight; his father was very insistent on that.

He and Cara were walking into North Adams together. She had darkened her skin. The wig with curls that spilled over her forehead was held down by a scarf tied under her chin. A bitter spring wind had blown in from Canada, the Arctic, somewhere John Henry hoped never to be. He was wearing all that he had to wear—jeans, a flannel shirt, his NUS sweatshirt turned inside out over that. Still, he was cold, too scrawny yet from being sick. He had to lean into the breeze to make headway against it.

"Durham is where your Cara was born."

John Henry stopped and looked at her. He'd never thought about it before. Cara had just seemed to appear, to be.

"That's right, baby. Your Cara had a house to go home to, down on the south side of town, just beyond the railroad tracks. I used to wake up every morning to the Silver Queen, southbound from Richmond to New Orleans. My daddy used to set his watch by that train—six-twelve A.M., no matter what time it came through. He was as light-skinned as I am; Mama was almost white. If I ever have any babies, they'll probably come out Irish."

"But—"

"Oh, baby," Cara said for what seemed the thousandth time. "You've been living under a rock. You've seen the whole world and you've seen nothing. There are a thousand Caras living in your Confederacy, ten thousand of us. You see them every day, but you only see what you want to see. That's the rule, John Henry—that's the rule people like you learn in your cradles, the one people like me have to relearn every minute of our lives: We can live among you, but only if we stay invisible.

"Mama took in laundry—washed, ironed, and folded all day long.

Daddy did yard work, odd jobs, for one of the bank presidents—a black man twice as big as a mule. He used to scare me to death. I even went to school, baby, sort of. A Swedish woman who'd come up through the Patriation Program—Mrs. Thullen, her name was, with the bluest eyes I'd ever seen. She had a bunch of us every morning in her basement, taught us reading, writing, math, what she understood of history. It wasn't much, but it got me started, got me hungry to know. Just because you're invisible doesn't mean you don't want to know. Life was almost normal, baby, almost."

"What happened?" John Henry was half afraid to ask. What awful naïveté would he reveal this time? What new ways would he discover to prove that he had spent his life inside a gilded cage?

"That bank president had a son only half as big as he was, but that was still plenty big enough. One day he came roaring home in his car after high school. He was on his way to some game and had forgotten something he wanted to take with him. Daddy was kneeling down beside the driveway, planting a bed, and the boy rolled his car right over his leg and crushed it."

"Jesus—"

"Eight o'clock came, nine o'clock. Mama and I had no idea what had happened; Daddy always came right home. Then about ten o'clock, that bank president drives into our front yard, opens up the back of his big car, and lifts Daddy out like he was a sack of feathers. 'They did the best they could at the hospital,' he says. 'There'll be no bills for that. But it doesn't appear he's going to walk on that leg again. He's going to have to find some other field of endeavor.'

"Daddy was too drugged to tell us what happened that night, in too much pain the next day to say anything either. When he finally could, Mama marched back up to that house and rang the bell. She told the bank president that my daddy had worked for him for twenty years. He couldn't just throw him out. What were we to live on? What was a leg worth—a leg destroyed by a careless boy?

"Two days later, the sheriff came by around five in the afternoon and told us to pack our bags—all three of us. Daddy could barely see, he was hurting so bad. By now there was a raging fever to keep the pain company. An hour later, the sheriff flagged down the north-bound Silver Queen and loaded us on board. At Richmond, we were transferred to the Territorial Flyer. When we got to Pennsylvania Territory, we were put out and told to walk north. Daddy didn't have any walking in him. He died of gangrene a week later. Mama stayed where she buried him. She found work in a chemical plant—a few miles into Pennsylvania, near York. It was as far as we could get with Daddy. I was twelve by then. I kept on going."

"Why would the sheriff—"

"Don't you see, honey? How can someone so smart be so slow? My mama couldn't just walk up there and protest. She had no more standing than my daddy did, than any of us did—no documents, no papers, no nothing. We were okay until we became visible, until we tried to *exist*, and then we weren't okay.

"Somewhere way back, someone on both sides of my family woke up in bed one morning with someone who couldn't be there, carrying seeds that couldn't be carried. And those seeds became my grand-parents, and their seeds became my parents, and their seeds became me. And everything flows from that, baby, everything, because your Cara doesn't exist either. You can pinch me"—taking his fingers and catching a piece of her arm flesh between them. "You can touch me, pat me right here"—taking the back of his hand against her fore-head, her neck, just a graze of her breast, or so it seemed to John Henry. "But that doesn't mean I am, because, baby, your Cara prom-ises you she is not. Once you go off the rails in the C.S.A., there's no going back, honey. Once you're outside, you're outside forever.

"That's what DRAGO is, baby. It's the people who aren't, the people who have ceased to be, the people who never were and have nowhere to go. Where would we go, honey? Germany? There's awful and there's worse.

"DRAGO's the way we look out for each other. Somebody's got to know you exist, baby. Somebody's got to care."

They had rounded the bend. In front of them lay a cityscape of belching smokestacks and electrical pylons.

"Each one of those factories, each of those mills, has three pay-rolls—one for the people who want to be, one for the people who are, and one for us," Cara was saying. "The Patriation workers never see their checks. That money goes straight to the program. They're working for air, water, food, a chance to become. The workers who are—the ones who can open bank accounts, who have histories and records—get paid by check. Taxes get deducted. The companies have to provide retirement benefits, such as they are, and medical benefits, such as you can find around here, and, honey, this is one place you don't want to get real sick. And then there are the people who aren't. We line up each week for cash, nothing taken out so they can pay us less, no benefits added so they can pay us still less, no protections either, no net. That's how people end up living in caves—there's nothing underneath us. When we start to fall, we fall to the ground."

As Cara talked on, John Henry had a vision of the two Marys, Jonah, the wild-eyed ten-year-old, Cara, almost everyone he had met since he left home, even Sean—all of them on tightropes, inching their way across a narrow valley filled with steaming cauldrons of acids, liquid oxygen, molten metals. The only person who wasn't on a tightrope, John Henry suddenly realized, was himself.

"Which workers do you think the factory owners like to hire, baby?" Cara was saying. "That's our only value—the fact that we aren't. It's like Saint Augustine said of evil: We exist only in our negation. Try that on someday, John Henry. Try waking up some morning and finding yourself existing only in your negation."

For days thereafter, John Henry tried just that, tried waking up and pretending he wasn't, tried to will himself into negation. That he couldn't, that he kept finding John Henry there morning after morning—try as he might to negate himself—struck him as his own failure. But John Henry was nothing if not doggedly determined.

"THOSE TWO WAITERS they killed—at that hotel down in Richmond."

John Henry nodded. He knew who she was talking about. He'd replayed the scene innumerable times: the chop to the windpipe, the chair crashing over the head. By the time his father knew that both men had died of self-inflicted poisoning, John Henry was two hours into Pennsylvania Territory, headed for a new life.

"They had names, honey," Cara said. "Those waiters were people. Human beings. They existed."

He and Cara were sitting in a diner two blocks off Main Street a few days later—a different spring morning, this one already stifling hot. The wind had shifted overnight. Now it was funneling all the industrial waftings of the Berkshire Valley straight down the streets of North Adams. John Henry thought he would choke. He was covered with grime and with the sweat of lugging Cara's bags from store to store, block to block: three lengths of rope, duct tape, and a roll of thin wire from the hardware store; food bags from the grocery; two bags of sheets and towels from a yard sale. They were still on the prowl for a cloth bag with a drawstring, which Cara insisted she had to have. Meanwhile, the diner. John Henry had ordered coffee when Cara did; he was loading it with sugar and artificial cream.

"The black waiter's name was Joseph." Cara's voice barely carried to the other side of the table. "That's all we ever knew—that and that he'd come from Africa by way of the Caribbean Corporation. He'd been found in South Carolina, almost dead, sent up the line to us for papers, a fresh start. He worked hard and was quiet."

"And the white one?"

"Randy," Cara said. "Randy, baby. He was born in Richmond. His daddy was a professor, just like your mama. You want to hear about him?"

John Henry nodded as he tore open another packet of sugar and stirred it into his coffee. He wished he'd ordered a soft drink instead.

"Randy's daddy was a professor, honey, but they didn't live on any professor's salary. His mother's daddy had started an insurance company and had more money than God. They spent their summers on the Outer Banks. For Christmas and Easter, they'd go skiing at another house they owned, in the Colorado mountains. Randy went to boarding school over in Lynchburg and had his own convertible. And he was smart, baby, just full of talent. There was a golden highway waiting for him to ride. But Randy made one mistake. Just one."

John Henry sat and waited. Cara was stirring what was left of her coffee as she stared out the window. She seemed to be talking to her own reflection in the glass.

"He fell in love with a black girl. After college, they lived together, right out in the open. His mother cut him off cold, but his daddy would come out to see him and try to talk some sense into him. Randy wasn't having any half measures. It was his mission, his statement. They lasted about two months before someone noticed enough to call the police. She went down to live with some cousins in Alabama—a chance for redemption. He headed north into the territories. It was where they were going to send him, at any rate. That's how we met."

She turned back from the window, back from her reflection, and seemed almost surprised to see John Henry sitting across from her.

"Why was that demonstration—the one at the hotel—why was it different?" John Henry asked.

"Different?"

"The others I've seen, the people just gave up when the police moved in. This time they fought back."

"They were bringing me a present, baby."

She reached across the table and took John Henry's hand in her own.

"They wanted to make sure it got here special delivery."

"What? Me?"

"Didn't seem like you were going to come on your own."

"But how did you even know . . . ?"

"Honey," Cara said, a smile spreading across her face, "I'm not much on those essays your mama cranks out, but you write like the wind, like an angel."

John Henry was puzzled. He had no idea what she was talking about, and then it came to him: "Acirema."

Cara nodded yes and squeezed his hand harder. It had been an assignment the semester before in honors English: Do a paper incorporating the seven principles of argumentation. Mrs. Johnson, their teacher, had suggested they take the pro or con side on some domestic topic of the day: the waterway, Mexican statehood, Patriation quotas. Instead, John Henry had created a fantasy world, "Acirema"—America spelled backward—where everyone was blind and deaf, where the only communication was by touch and no one had a race because no one could see or hear racial differences. Mrs. Johnson had given it a D, John Henry's lowest grade of the semester, maybe his lowest grade ever: There wasn't a clear principle of argumentation to be found anywhere in the piece. She also told him that she loved the essay.

"She sent me a copy, baby. She's helped us when she can. It was like I was living inside your head," Cara said. "You wanted to come to me. I knew you did. You'd even asked that boy about how to get in touch. You just didn't know how to take the next step. We had to help take it for you."

"The waiters—did they know they were going to be . . . ?" John Henry couldn't say it. He didn't know whether to be flattered or terrified. It was as if he were back in his father's vice presidential campaign almost eight years before. He'd had no idea that anyone could make him the center of so much attention.

"Killed, baby?"

"Killed . . ."

"They drew the short straws. They knew what they knew."

Cara put down a dollar for the coffees, stood, and waited for John Henry to gather up all the bags.

"Remember that," she said as they walked out onto the street again, into the rank May air. "Always remember: Your postage wasn't free. Two people died to bring you to Cara."

Cara stood for a moment, studying John Henry.

"We're not playing games anymore, baby. School's out."

John Henry was still as a stone, afraid to move, terrified of what Cara might say next.

HOW LARGE IS DRAGO? John Henry asked another day, as they were making a short drive down to Adams.

"Oh, baby," Cara answered, "maybe it's only me. Or maybe it's me and four other people—D and R and A and G and O. And maybe each of us has five under us, and each of them five under them, and each of them five under them. You're the smart one, honey; you're the student. How long does it take to reach a thousand or ten thousand or a million? How many of us are there who don't exist in your glorious Confederate States of America?"

Cara became expansive, conjured up worlds John Henry had never dreamed existed.

"Are we only the people who pass through these safe houses? Or are we the people who might someday need to? The black woman who wakes up someday in a white man's bed? Her children? The Patriation worker who forgets to stand for the boss man or falls asleep on the assembly line or can't quite bring herself to pray to a God who has ignored her existence for years and years and years? Negation comes easy in your C.S.A., honey—it's hardly even earned."

Cara pulled up in front of a row house as undistinctive as every house in Adams, North Adams, almost every place John Henry had been to up north. It was the land of drab, of dull, of nothing; every color was a variation on gray.

"You know who we're going to see, baby? We're going to see a man who's coughing himself to death because he can't get rid of the flax down in his lungs. You look, baby. You look at that brown-red stuff he coughs up into his handkerchief. That isn't blood; that's lung. He's coughing himself inside out. Pretty soon there'll be nothing left inside to breathe with. And there's nowhere in the world for him to go, because he's another person who isn't.

"We don't want much, baby. We just want someone to see him, to see us. We just want someone to know we *are*.

"Come on, baby," she said. "We've got things to do."

Cara started to open her door. Then she froze in midaction.

"You want to know how big we are?" she said as she turned to John Henry. "When Randy and I and two others started DRAGO fifteen years ago, I was only a teenager, but, honey, I'd *lived* in the five years since I walked away from my mama. Randy was almost twenty-five—a man. He'd taken me in; we'd taken some others in. We all worked then, all supported each other. That's where we got the idea—DRAGO was just going to be that same thing, only bigger, a way to protect each other. The name didn't mean anything; it was just a joke Randy thought up one night. Democratic Revolutionary Army Governing Organization—that was us; that was DRAGO. We laughed about it for days. At first we thought we'd change the name every few years, just for fun, just to see what else we could come up with. Then we started helping Patriation escapees, and one thing led to another.

"We had nothing then. We got our house now—no landlord. It's owned in the name of that nice Swedish teacher I had way back when, Mrs. Thullen, and we got a cabin too, down in Virginia, free and clear. How big does that make us, baby? How big can we be? You tell me. You tell me."

Always, it seemed to John Henry, Cara talked in riddles, answered questions with questions. Always, somewhere, there was a lash to her words, some reservoir of anger and outrage. Sometimes, it seemed, the sting was for him alone. And so he would try harder still—harder to negate himself, harder to absorb Cara's anger, harder to hate the person he once had been, if that's what was needed, if hating that person was the only way to get rid of him.

BACK AT THE house, John Henry knew he had been let inside only at Cara's pleasure, only under her aegis. There were no more raised eyebrows when John Henry walked into a room, no more hushed conversations cut off in midsentence when he suddenly rounded a corner. But there was no connection either. "Johnny" was wallpaper, a wobbly side table—part of the texture of their lives, rarely to be noticed and then only to recall that he was "one of Cara's," dangerous to touch.

Sometimes the loneliness was crushing. If he hadn't convinced himself that it was a necessary step on the road to self-negation, John Henry thought he couldn't have stood it. Through loneliness he would be purified; through loneliness he would destroy the John Henry that had been. Or so he hoped.

He was sitting at the top of the stairs past ten o'clock one hot night—the stairwell acting as a chimney to funnel the heat, the cigarette smoke, the sound directly up to him—when he heard someone arrive and be pointed up the stairs. Soon a man, a minister by his collar, rounded the last landing, nodded at John Henry, and went past him into the vacant room. A few minutes later, the man came back out, his collar off, a T-shirt on now, and sat down beside John Henry.

"I'm Daniel Brewster," he said, throwing out his hand.

"Johnny," John Henry said, marveling at the strangeness of it, the first time he had ever called himself by that name. "You're a minister?"

"Ah, you noticed. The Congregational Church. Ever heard of it?"

John Henry nodded. Heard of it? Who hadn't? The Congregationalists had been the worst of the Yankee Bible thumpers before the War of Dissolution, the most wild-eyed of the lot—like whirling dervishes, the history books said, as they tried to goad the South into secession. After the war, the church had been ground out, although apparently not completely.

"There's a Congregational church here? In North Adams?"

"You're looking at it, Johnny, and only when I'm in town. I've been a circuit preacher ever since I graduated from seminary, just like the Old West."

Brewster paused and turned his face away. When he turned it

back, his tongue was lolling out to the side and his eyes seemed to be rolling in opposite directions. John Henry almost jumped and ran.

"There," Brewster said. "Does that look more like a Congregational minister to you?"

John Henry laughed—a rarity even in normal circumstances. Brewster shook a pack of cigarettes in John Henry's direction. "Want one?" he asked. He was using a small Mason jar he carried with him as an ashtray.

"No. Thank you." It seemed so long since anyone other than Cara had offered John Henry anything.

Brewster inhaled slowly, exhaled even more slowly.

"My ministry, Johnny, is to the outsiders in the Greater Confederacy and particularly here in the NIZ, the people who have fallen between the cracks. Even if I had a church, I suspect most of the people I try to tend to wouldn't dare show their faces at it."

He said it with a chuckle, a twinkle in his eye. Wreathed in smoke, he looked like some sort of discount Santa Claus. John Henry smiled back, stretched his legs, and leaned back on his elbows against the step above him.

"I'm a low-overhead cleric," Brewster went on. Another chuckle. "But you know, God doesn't really care about edifices, documents, official papers, official sanctions. And it's in God's name that I baptize the babies of people whose names will never appear on a birth register. It's in God's name that I marry people whose banns can never be posted. In God's name that I commit to eternity those who will never have a headstone to mark their passage on this earth."

Brewster paused, shook his head, took a last heavy drag on his smoke. "Lordy, listen to me go on."

He reached over, grinning, and poked John Henry in the ribs. "This is where you're supposed to go, 'Hallelujah, brother, I believe! I believe!'"

John Henry tried to form the words while Brewster stubbed out his cigarette in the jar, but he couldn't force them from his mouth. Beyond Cara, he was unsure whom to trust, what to trust. Knives came out of the air; rooms turned upside down.

"You know, I've got a special affinity for North Adams, Johnny." He slipped another cigarette out of the pack, looked at it, then slipped it back in. "It was almost two and a half centuries ago that the Congregationalists tried to establish a permanent settlement here—tried and failed. Now I keep trying, and failing, to establish a permanent settlement for God at this house—which, God knows, needs it." Rolling his eyes, this time both in the same direction, looking more like Santa than ever. "Oh, my heavens, the things that go on here—but, Johnny, you look as if your soul might still be saved."

He stopped now, gave John Henry a sidelong glance, waited for a grin. Finally, it came.

"I'm not sure it's been lost." John Henry had been an Episcopalian all his life. He'd almost never been in another church. The language of lost souls was foreign to him.

"Then I don't think it has. Anything I can do for you before I go downstairs to the Devil's Court?"

It was not lost on Daniel Brewster, as it had not been lost on the permanent residents of the house, that John Henry was not of the usual run of guests. His skin was of the purest color. John Henry was clearly school trained, and he had manners, "thank you"s being rarer than hen's teeth in the Reverend Daniel Brewster's world. What's more, all the usual stigmata of social degeneracy—crooked teeth, missing teeth, no teeth, unmended broken bones and noses, rickets, scurvy, beriberi, hookworm, unchecked acne, etc.—were notably absent in John Henry. Hard cases were common on Brewster's circuit, hard stories more common still. Enigmas, though, came along far too seldom.

Brewster sat quietly to see if this enigma would unfold itself. When it didn't, he hauled himself to his feet, gave John Henry a rub on his shoulder, a tousle of the hair, pulled a card from his pants pocket, slipped it into John Henry's hand, and started downstairs. John Henry felt as if he had been blessed, anointed. He sat for another ten minutes staring at Brewster's name, a phone number in Springfield, nothing more. Nonetheless, the wonder of it! Someone who existed enough to be located, to have a card, to be called, to have not just a first name but a whole one! John Henry rose, stuffed the card in his jeans pocket as if it were some kind of talisman, and started for bed.

John Henry was still lying awake almost two hours later when he heard Brewster working his way up the stairs again, huffing this time. In the room next to him, through the thin wall, John Henry could hear Brewster undressing, pulling the sheet back, finally lying down, his head next to John Henry's. The labor of his breathing slowly eased; as it did, the Lord's Prayer, the Twenty-third Psalm, the Apostles' Creed, began to seep through the wallboard in a thin whisper—prayers for the living, prayers for the dead, prayers for the in-between. If there had been a hole punched in the wall that separated them, John Henry might have put his lips to it and told Daniel Brewster everything.

TWO NIGHTS LATER —it was eleven-ten by the cracked clock on his night table—John Henry looked up from his book to see Cara at the door, a small cardboard box in her hand. A heat wave had settled in. John Henry's pants were folded neatly on the small trunk at the end of his bed. His T-shirt was folded neatly on top of them, his shoes piled neatly at the trunk's edge—the whole of his possessions in this new life amounting to a stack of only a few cubic feet. He was lying in his boxer shorts; instinctively, he reached down and pulled the sheet up to his chest. He had been living at the house for almost seven weeks.

"Baby," she said, "it's time you did something for your Cara."

Later, John Henry would think that he knew what Cara was going to ask him to do before she ever said it, because by then, by later, all the logic would point in only one direction. At the moment, though, he hadn't the faintest notion.

"Sure" is all he said. He marked his book, put it on the table beside him, and sat up straighter in bed.

"I want you to write a letter, honey, just a little note." The box in her hand had stationery in it, a pen. John Henry took a sheet of plain white paper and closed the box so he could use it as a writing surface.

"To whom? What?" Surprised—flattered, really—he was holding the pen in his hand, ready to please.

"It's to your daddy, baby. I want you to write a note to your daddy. Just tell him you're okay, that you want to see him. We'll contact him with the details."

"Cara?" The pen froze just above the surface of the paper.

"Baby?" Cara nudged his knees with her hand and settled on the bed just by John Henry's hips.

"I can't."

"Can't?"

"Can't. I can't. This isn't about my father. This is about *me*. I'm the one who's here, not my father. I'm the one who came."

"Of course, baby."

"That's right, isn't it? This whole thing—all this hasn't been about him, has it?"

"Of course it hasn't, honey—not about your daddy, and not about you, and not even about your Cara. It's about power, power—who has it and who doesn't have it. That's what it's about. Your daddy, honey, he has power. We don't."

"But—"

"We don't want to hurt your daddy, honey. Your Cara would never do that. We just want you to talk with him. We want you to tell him face-to-face what you've seen, what you've learned. That's all. He won't believe it from us, but he'll believe it from you." She was leaning over now, rubbing the back of her hand along John Henry's forehead, brushing her hand along his ear, his shoulder. "That's all, baby. That's all. Don't you want to see your daddy? Don't you want to talk with him and tell him you're okay?"

Later, too, John Henry would think that he had had some choice in the matter. He would think that he could have told Cara then what he hadn't told her before—he had seen his father only a week earlier, through the warehouse window, and he'd told him then, silently, the most important thing he had learned, the most important thing he had to say. Now, though, he held the pen over the stationery, brought it down, wrote the opening line—"Dear Dad"—and stopped again, unable to go on and unable to say no.

"Do it for your Cara, honey. Two men died to bring you here— two people. One letter isn't too much to ask for that. Do it for me and I'll tell you a secret. I'll tell you anything you want to know."

And so as Cara stood and leaned against his bedroom wall, John Henry finally did what she'd asked. She was right: He had come to her at an awful cost. He'd have to start paying back, even if it was this. When he finished, he handed the note to Cara, capping the pen while she read it. Cara folded the sheet once, stuck it in an envelope, and put the envelope back in the stationery box. When she looked at John Henry, he turned his head away.

"How will you . . . ?" John Henry was sitting on the edge of his bed now, sheet draped across his middle, staring at the floor.

"Oh, baby, don't worry. We'll get it to him. Cara will take care of that."

She held his face then in her hands, bent down, kissed him on the forehead and cheek, and pushed him softly on the shoulders. When John Henry was stretched out on his back, Cara reached up and pulled her T-shirt off. Then she unbuckled her jeans and stepped out of them and her underpants, turned off the bedside lamp, and lay down beside John Henry on the narrow bed.

In the dark, John Henry nearly froze. He'd passed seventeen years in life without such a moment. Now he didn't know whether to laugh, cry, or shout. But John Henry was also a male of the species— blood, muscles, hormones—and soon he didn't care whether Cara was a lover or a teacher, didn't care if the skies opened up and poured boiling oil on them or if the floor gave way and they fell into an endless pit. Let me explode, John Henry thought; let me be blown into a billion pieces. Each touch of her skin along his own was like a razor of delight.

IT WAS A little after two in the morning when John Henry was awakened as the bed shifted. He heard steps on the floor. Outside, an owl was hooting; the hot wind was whistling along the ridge behind the house. Cara had put her jeans on and was slipping the T-shirt over her head. John Henry felt as if a ship were about to sail away, as if he would be marooned forever on the island of his bed if she left.

"Why did Sean say I had cost him big? What did he mean by that?"

"Baby?"

"My secret. You promised me a secret."

"It was Randy. Randy was Sean's best friend."

"I don't understand."

"Honey, it was Sean who found the doubles. We needed identification. You can't just walk into something like that waterway dinner. You need papers even if you're not going to work that close to the President. Sean knew a woman who was clerking at a police station down in Washington; she let him page through the mug books until he found the doubles—one for Randy, one for Joseph. That's how we got them their papers."

"You said they had drawn short straws—that's how they ended up being the waiters."

Cara sat down again on John Henry's bed, leaned over, kissed him on the forehead, and rubbed her hand along his chest, the flat of his stomach, the ridge of his hip.

"Baby," she said as she stood up, "they were *all* short straws. Randy and Joseph just chose first."

"But you said Randy took you in. He was one of the founders—"

Cara rose from the bed and fit her feet into the sandals she had been wearing. At the door, she stopped and blew John Henry another kiss.

"Randy never wanted enough, baby. Randy was a drama major; he just liked to put on shows. DRAGO was his way of making up for the fact that he could never go to Atlanta and be on the real stage. The Hotel Richmond was his last performance, and he finally got to play the death scene. He didn't mind too much, really. Sean wants too much; he's too angry at everyone. I don't want to be around when he does his last act. That's why I had to have you, baby. You're my Mr. In-Between."

"Cara?"

"Yes, baby." She had almost closed the door behind her.

"Sean knew who I was, didn't he? He knew who my father is. Why did he do that? Why did he try to make me tell?"

"It doesn't matter, baby. All that matters is that your Cara got to you in time. Cara's never going to let anyone hurt you."

And then the door was shut, and she was gone.

22

THE VICE PRESIDENT'S OFFICE

NATHAN WINSTON LEANED back in his chair and jiggled the brass skeleton key in his hand as he stared out the window. Across Twelfth Street, almost directly in front of him and a story below, sat the statue of Judah Benjamin, a constant source of pleasure to Nathan, even viewed from the rear. The key had been carried over the previous morning by one of the presidential interns. Spencer had had her present it to Nathan on a little satin pillow, as always when the President was going on vacation. Nothing made Spencer love his job more than leaving it.

The intern had been maybe all of twenty-two years old, tall and leggy, blond. "Curvaceous" is the word Nathan's father would have used for her—a "looker." Whatever the proper phrase, Spencer had chosen her himself for this little chore—a harmless gift of physical beauty to complement the loan of the key. Nathan tried to appreciate the gift but couldn't. He had fought against it all his life and tried everything to convince himself otherwise, but he failed every time: White people mostly looked sickly to him. A healthy face should have some color in it—it had been his mother's saying, and Nathan took it literally, then and still.

"It's the original White House key," the intern was saying as she cradled the pillow reverently in her hands. "Nathan Bedford Forrest himself used it!" Her perkiness was almost unbearable.

"And who was Nathan Bedford Forrest?" the Vice President

found himself saying. He'd walked around from behind his desk and was sitting on its edge.

"Why, he was the first President of the Confederacy, sir!" A student's answer, proud in its knowledge of what every grade schooler is taught, the "sir" barked military style. A colonel's daughter, a general's niece. As with most interns, trails of connections spread out behind her.

Your Confederacy, not mine, Nathan found himself wanting to answer. Even thinking it left him unsettled.

Nathan Bedford Forrest had indeed been a brilliant general, second only to the broken Robert E. Lee in the hearts of his countrymen by the time the war had ended, but like the new nation itself, Forrest had been baptized in blood and was unfit for the letting of much of anything else. Policy languished while he fumed at this adviser or that and railed at the foolishness of politicians. His leadership, so brilliant in war, proved almost nonexistent in peace. Mustering congressmen and cabinet members was like trying to corral mercury— they slithered all over the place. Or maybe Forrest, too, was simply tired. Who wasn't after all those years? All that blood? All those deaths and maimings and howling amputations?

Absent direction from the executive branch, old problems rushed in to fill the vacuum, including the oldest: slavery. Where would it all have ended if England had not brought pressure to bear? What might have happened if Madison Tompkins had never risen in the new Capitol, in the final months of Forrest's presidency, to proclaim his vision of a new nation? Nathan had no clue, although he suspected the worst. But England *had* brought pressure to bear. Madison Tompkins *did* rise to denounce slavery, to declare it just as irreparable as murder. He offered a vision of a better Confederacy—one that married the rightness of a cause to the sheer utility of freeing up all the nation's human resources, mobilizing all its strengths— and in the end, sense prevailed. Out of the disaster of that first presidency had come the imperative of change, and out of the imperative of change had come everything. All's well that ends well. Nathan relaxed and smiled.

"Forrest was a better general than president," he told the intern. "Did anyone ever teach you that?"

She looked puzzled, alarmed, as if he had violated some canon of history. "Sir?"

Oh, well, Nathan thought: It was higher education, the canons changed constantly, and he was no spring chicken. He took the key and asked the intern to return the pillow to the President's office— he liked to use it for catnaps on his desktop, Nathan explained— and showed her to the door. As she hurried away, Nathan wondered if she thought he might be insane.

Twenty-four hours later, Nathan was jiggling the key and thinking about the days when a President might have carried it on his person, when someone might actually have used it—back when the White House almost was a house, when the paint smelled new, before the tunnels, the subterranean offices, the rooftop satellite dishes. Back, that is, when people came and went as they did from normal houses, paid calls, left cards, sat for afternoon tea.

"Mr. Vice President?" His secretary, Miss Farnsley, had given up trying to ring him and simply walked in unannounced. "Your phone."

"Phone?"

"Sir, it's been buzzing off the hook for the last ten minutes."

Nathan looked down and saw a bank of red lights blinking at him.

"You'll want to pick up on line one first, sir. It's the President."

"NATHAN?"

Spencer was shouting to make himself heard over some kind of raucous yelling and a dull, undulating roar. And then it came to Nathan: The President was fishing with his brother Davey—Davis Lee III, the oldest of the Lee children. Gulls were screeching overhead; the roar was the motor of Davey's thirty-five-foot Bertram as it plowed through the waves.

"You're not supposed to take a cell phone when you go fishing, Spencer. You're on vacation."

"Did you get it?"

"It?"

"The key? I sent it over by a new advanced delivery system."

"The delivery system worked beautifully, Mr. President." Nathan laughed.

"I'll say. My God, Nathan, if only we were our sons'—"

Spencer caught himself at the last moment, too late.

"Nathan, I'm sorry."

"It's all right, Spencer. But I'm not sure I'm ready to be seventeen again."

There was cussing in the background now—a blue streak of it.

"Nathan, about the key . . ."

"Yes?"

"I want you to use it. Lock the place up. Get out of there."

"A nice thought, Spencer," Nathan said, leaning back in his chair and picking up his schedule for the day, "but I've got the JMC in twenty minutes—"

"Sumner is taking it," Spencer said.

"—followed by the senior staff briefing, the executive staff briefing, the Joint Commission on Urban Revitalization, followed by lunch with . . . Sumner?"

"As in Walter—Walter Sumner, the secretary of state. You've heard of him? Don't worry, Nathan. Everything's covered. I've got your schedule right in front of me. Kay has subbed you out straight through the evening."

"Spencer?"

"Remember that evening you arranged for Frannie and me not long before she died?"

"Of course."

"Well, I've been thinking about that, Nathan. I've been thinking it's time I paid you back. Wormley has Air Force One Half gassed up and waiting for you out at Maury Field. Call Lucinda. Fly there and pick her up. The two of you can go wherever you want for the day, Nathan. I've told Wormley to be prepared to fly you anywhere and provide all the ground support you need. And you don't have a damn thing left to do in Richmond."

Nathan leaned back in his chair, stunned.

"Spencer, I don't know what to say."

"How about 'goodbye'?"

Suddenly, there was a new burst of shouting on the boat, unmistakable profanity this time, decibels louder than before.

"You're hauling lunatics out of the sea, Spencer?"

"Oh, it's just Davey. He's holding a flare gun on me, threatening to shoot if I don't hang up. The gulls are diving. He seems to be under the impression that we're about to catch some fish."

"Do you think he'll actually shoot?"

"There's the problem. Davey agreed to let one Secret Service agent travel with us. He's got a thirty-eight trained on the center of Davey's forehead."

"Spencer, I think I'd better hang up. Goodbye. And thank you."

"Have fun."

Spencer was the social Lee. His brothers were the private ones, and they protected their privacy ferociously.

WHEN NATHAN'S SECRETARY stuck her head in again, he was in a full scowl. "May I assume, Miss Farnsley, that you're an unindicted coconspirator in this nonsense?"

"Unindicted and unindictable, sir. Mr. Wormley's on line three."

Her grin as she closed the door seemed wider than the room.

Nathan put the brass key down on the polished wood desk and studied it before picking up the phone. The key, he knew, represented something beyond just friendship, something beyond the mere fact that he and Spencer Lee had survived seven years in office together. The key was also an index of character, an index of the trust Spencer had placed in him, an index—Nathan thought, not without vanity—of the trust he had made it his lifetime effort to earn. If he was nothing else, Nathan thought, he was an honest broker, a man who would listen to all sides, a man who would assure that all points of view were heard, a man who would never betray a confidence, a man—in short—in whom you could put your total faith.

Nathan pulled out his top desk drawer, placed the key in one of the built-in compartments, and punched line three. As he locked the drawer with a key from his own chain, Nathan found himself regretting that he could not climb into one of the drawer compartments himself.

"MAY I PHONE Mrs. Winston, sir?" Wormley was saying. "I can get a driver to run her out to the airport in Charlottesville. We can be there"—Nathan imagined Wormley shooting a perfect cuff, studying his perfect watch—"oh, I should think, in fifty minutes. I've a limousine waiting in front of your office to take you to Maury Field."

Nathan looked out his window. It was the black stretch with the

presidential seal—Ground One, the Secret Service called it. Wormley
was in seventh heaven, ready to prove he could get anyone anywhere,
and not necessarily within reason.

"I'm afraid Mrs. Winston is still under the weather, Mr. Wormley.
I'll be traveling alone."

"Oh, dear, I'm terribly sorry to hear that. May I ask where to?"

Nathan looked at the wall directly across from his desk. It was
hung with photographs: himself with Spencer Lee at both nominat-
ing conventions; himself, Spencer, Lucinda, and Frannie at the first
inaugural ball; the same group minus Frannie at the muted second
ball; even himself and Spencer standing on the deck of the Lee
family's Low Country beach house on Pawley's Island.

"North Adams, Mr. Wormley," he finally said.

"North Adams, sir? Are you—"

"I'll need a driver, that's all. A reliable one. I'll be traveling alone
otherwise."

There was a silence on the other end. Nathan thought he could
hear Wormley whispering to someone, probably Kay, before his voice
came back on.

"Perhaps, sir, if I were to come with you. Just to lend a helping
hand on the ground. Ease things a bit here and there. My schedule
is lighter than usual too, what with the President away."

"Alone, Mr. Wormley. I'm going alone."

Another pause. Nathan could almost hear the gears mesh in
Wormley's head, the grind of his calculations.

"I could wait on board, sir, watch over things at the regional
facility."

"Mr. Wormley, tell the driver I'll be with him in five minutes. I
want to change my shoes. And Mr. Wormley, remember, you merely
are following orders by sending me on my way to North Adams.
I'm the one who's breaking a trust."

TWO HOURS AND fifteen minutes later, a little after twelve-thirty in
the afternoon, Nathan was touching down once again at NIZ-27.

His driver this go-round was built for hard times—thicker across
the chest and shoulders than Nathan himself, yet shorter by a few
inches and with what seemed like half the Vice President's waist.
His reddish-gold hair was close-cropped, over a freckled face. Irish,

Nathan assumed, the centurions of the Patriation Program. The driver introduced himself simply as Chris, no last name, no service branch given or asked for. Wormley was a true god: He could arrange anything.

"No rain, then?" Nathan asked as they were driving into town, retracing his route of the previous visit. A flaky soot still covered the roadway; a film seemed to have settled on the grass, the bushes, the trees. Nathan felt as if he were looking at nature through gauze.

"Oh, you don't want this rain, sir."

Chris took his right hand off the steering wheel, opened the palm, and motioned to the hood of the car. From his front passenger seat, Nathan could see that the finish looked almost like an impressionist painting, dappled, pointillistic. As he bent to the windshield and looked closer, he could see the tiny gouges in the paint, the surface of the metal—pinpricks rimed with rust, an infinite field of them.

"That's the rain, sir. It'll take the hair right off your head if you stay out in it too long."

And then silence. Another three miles into town. The rock ledge again, the channeled Hoosic to cross. The flowers still sat in the flower boxes as they reached the city limits—unwatered, shriveling, drooping over the sides. The bunting was gone. The coating of dust Nathan had seen outside town sat thicker here. The sandblasted buildings already were streaked with he couldn't guess what. And my God, the stench! The paper mill was back in operation. Ahead of them as they worked their way east down Main Street, the Hoosic Range loomed like some pagan monolith carved magically from solid stone, like a vast malignant tumor.

They came to the textile plant where he had spoken with the workers in the shipping yard—the yard filled today with trucks and forklifts, loading product, unloading raw goods. At the bottom of the yard, two boxcars sat empty on the freight siding, waiting. The fence around the yard was topped with concertina wire. Nathan didn't remember it from before.

"Stop," he said, and Chris pulled over to the curb and backed up to the main gate. By the time he had climbed out to open the passenger door, the Vice President was out and walking. The guard might have been Serbian, low-browed, a face cut from granite. He wore a holster—a revolver jutting from his hip. He stood now, blocking Nathan's path, hand on the revolver butt. Perhaps he recognized the Vice President, perhaps he didn't—it was a face that couldn't be read—but either way, he was unyielding.

"Move." This single word from Chris. Nathan had been in North Adams proper all of ten minutes on this second trip, and already his life had been reduced to monosyllables. Chris flashed a badge, identification, his own heat—more subtle, tucked inside his waistband; still, from what Nathan could see of it, huge. With one hand, Chris stilled the guard's gun; with the other, he drew the guard's ear toward his mouth. What he said, Nathan couldn't hear. Whatever it was, it worked. Inside the mill, a man in white shirt and tie tried to stop them as they moved through a corridor of offices. Nathan brushed him aside; Chris made sure there was no rebound. On the floor of the mill, dust, debris, particulates flew everywhere—literally flew, blown by what seemed to Nathan almost a gale-force wind. He squinted, held his hands over his eyes, and tried to look through his fingers. At the same time, he took the foulard from his breast pocket and held it to his nose and mouth. In front of him, behind him, all around him, workers moved through the storm like ghosts, as if they had been moving through it all their lives. Chris suddenly materialized beside Nathan. He'd somehow managed to acquire safety goggles for them both. The goggles helped, but only slightly. Nothing helped with the noise. On the earlier visit, when Nathan had met the workers here, the hush had been almost funereal. Now there was a pounding and a high-pitched whine, both at incredible volume. Speech seemed impossible. How could you ever draw a deep enough breath for it? Hearing seemed more impossible still.

Together they approached a machine near the center of the mill, where yarn was being made, spun out on large spools. When they were full, the spools were lifted off and replaced by a parade of women in cloth shoes and rough denim dresses tied at the waist with rope. The machine functioned as the eye of the hurricane within the mill, a central refuge where the dust diminished, the sound was somehow muted.

"How long have you been working?" Nathan half yelled at two of the women. Their eyes were sunken and ringed; their skin was pitted with mill debris. "How long are your shifts? How many hours?" The effort—breathing in, breathing out, forming words, making them heard—was almost too much for him.

The women looked at Nathan: His suit, his tie, his shirt told them everything. The strong-arm with him—Chris—told them everything else. They turned and walked away. One of the women was flinching already, as if she expected a fist, a whip, a stick to come crashing down on her back.

Chris put his mouth to Nathan's ear and almost shouted himself: "Notice the shoes?"

Nathan had noticed.

"No one on the floor is allowed to wear any metal. This dust is bone dry. One spark and you can be in the middle of a firestorm."

Were the air to catch fire, Nathan thought, hell itself couldn't be any more frightening.

They retraced their steps—fought their way back into the storm and through it. More white shirts were waiting at the entrance to the corridor that led outside. "Mr. Vice President," one said. Whether it was a question or a statement, an invitation or an admonition, Nathan couldn't tell. He wanted to be out of there.

"How do people learn to breathe in a place like that?" he asked Chris when they were back in the car.

"They don't, sir. They never learn." Spoken, it seemed, from a deep well of experience.

Nathan never asked how he knew. Even with the goggles—or maybe the goggles had come too late—his eyes watered and burned. He was about to say that he would give half a day's pay for a bottle of eyewash, when Chris reached in front of him, popped open the glove compartment, pulled out a bottle of Visine, and handed it to the Vice President.

"You learn to cope, sir. That's all you can do. And once you've learned to cope well enough, you're pretty much dead."

Nathan leaned his head back and filled his eyes with the soothing wash. Then he closed them and rested. When he opened them again, they were passing a Patriation dormitory for Level Two workers, midway up the stream to citizenship, to Americanism.

"Stop," he said again. Chris did, on a dime, and Nathan caught himself against the dashboard with both hands.

The matron was asleep in her cubicle at the entrance, a cup of coffee growing cold by her elbow, the tail end of a cigarette smoldering in the ashtray. Behind her, an arrow pointed right, down a long hall to "Women," one in the opposite direction to "Men." Nathan turned left, stopped at the first door he came to, and knocked.

When there was no answer, he eased the door open. Two single iron beds were pushed against either wall, their mattresses thin as a hand, perched on coiled springs. Between the beds, there was enough room to stand up, nothing more. Nathan sniffed and ran his finger along the wall: mildew. A narrow window at the end of the room opened into an equally narrow ventilation shaft. Nathan tracked the wiring for the fan that hung down from the center of the ceiling and threw the switch. A whir, a flutter, nothing. It was three o'clock by Nathan's watch and almost dark inside.

The bathroom at the end of the hall was communal—stalls without doors, a lineup of urinals against one wall, a large shower room, its walls darkened with grime, the floor splattered with chemical deposits. Nathan turned the spigot at one of the sinks; a thin trickle of brownish water worked its way out, exhausted from the effort. He tried to flush one of the urinals, then another and another. None of them worked. The smell of stale piss, piss as old as time itself, was overpowering. Chris handed the Vice President a menthol rub and told him to put a little under his nose.

Across from the bathroom, the door was cracked on a larger room. Nathan knocked gently, then edged the door open with his foot. The same narrow window, the same ventilation shaft, just the skeleton of a ceiling fan this time—the paddles long since used for something else—the same stale-onion smell of mildew. Four beds were pushed against the walls. A man was sitting propped up in one of them, fast asleep, or so it seemed. Black hair fell across his forehead.

"You've come!" he said as soon as Nathan and Chris had stepped into the room. His right hand was wrapped in a thick bandage that extended halfway up his forearm.

"Come?" It was Nathan who answered him.

"Oh, I'm sorry. I must have been dreaming."

Nathan noticed a blotch of red at the bottom of the bandage.

"Your hand. It's—"

"No," the man said. "That's old. The bandage needs to be changed."

"What happened?"

"I was working a punch press in Albany," the man said. "I wanted to learn to be the best punch-press operator in the Confederate States of America." A Spanish accent colored his words.

"And?" Chris urged him on this time.

"I wasn't. My hand . . ." He held it up and looked at it as if it belonged to someone else's body. "I was careless. My hand got mangled. Now I'm being shipped back to Boston."

"Why?" Nathan asked.

"After the accident, I couldn't fulfill my hours quota. I'm being reassigned, back to Level One. A job a one-handed man can do."

The man yawned. He seemed to be on the verge of sleep again.

"The pills," he said, nodding toward a small bottle that was tucked under the edge of his pillow. "I'm sorry. They make me so drowsy."

"Where did you come from?" Nathan asked as he read the label on the bottle. "What did you do?" The pills were aspirin, laced with codeine.

"My name is Jorge," the man said. "I grew oranges, near Valencia." He looked from Chris to Nathan and back again, uncertain who was in charge, fearful of giving offense. "You don't by any chance know an American minister named Daniel?"

Chris shook his head and looked at the Vice President.

"There are hundreds of ministers named Daniel," Nathan answered, "thousands," but Jorge had fallen asleep again.

Across the room there was a sudden scuttling. Nathan turned in time to see two rats break across the floor and race down the hall he and Chris had just walked up. Nathan almost screamed. Instead, he caught his breath, held it, and let it out slowly. Then he saw what had attracted the rats: a bowl of food, set on the floor at the foot of one of the beds on the far wall—an extra lunch, he guessed, smuggled from the mess hall. Nathan squatted quietly by the bowl. It contained some sort of soup or runny stew. From his breast pocket, Nathan took a ballpoint pen marked "Office of the Vice President," a tiny seal of the Confederacy embossed on it. With the pen, he fished through the soup, found a piece of something, balanced it on the shaft, and lifted it out. Like any good doctor's son, Nathan had become acquainted early in life with the lesser parts of the mammalian body. He knew a section of small intestine when he saw it. What kind of mammal it might have come from, he didn't want to know. Nathan left the pen in the soup bowl, a souvenir for whoever found it. As they turned to leave, Jorge opened his eyes wide and shouted "No!" before falling asleep again.

The matron was awake when Nathan and Chris walked out of

the dormitory. If she was surprised to see such a well-turned-out man leaving her little corner of the planet, she never showed it.

And so it went. At a medical clinic run by the Manufacturers' Coalition, Nathan found fifteen people in line, the chief nurse overwhelmed, and the clinic manager absolutely beside herself.

"Where's the doctor?" he asked the manager.

"The doctor?" Her voice said that the doctor might be drunk or dead, or maybe even on a steamer to Rio. "The doctor is not in."

"When is he expected?"

She looked up at Nathan, looked back down at the account book she was working on, and never acknowledged his presence again.

Outside, Nathan asked an old man near the front of the line how long he had been waiting.

"Since yesterday," the man said.

"Yesterday?"

"What am I going to do? I need more insulin."

Afterward, they stopped at a dye mill on the western edge of town. Behind the mill, they watched emerald-green waste water run into the Hoosic River, the Hoosic run emerald green toward Williamstown. Next, a day care center run by the city. The children were playing musical chairs, but when the music stopped they just stood in place until their teacher reminded them they were supposed to run for a seat. The children seemed limp, like plants that hadn't been watered. From there, he and Chris walked across the street to a diner. Sooty men and women sat at the counter, nursing coffees, cold drinks. A sign above the cash register read "Cola—50¢."

"We'll have two," Nathan said, nodding at the sign. "Two colas, please."

The waitress studied Nathan's clothes and carriage before dispensing the drinks.

"Two dollars," she said when she handed Nathan the glasses. "Two dollars each."

It was as if he were in a foreign country, Nathan thought, at the mercy of exchange rates he didn't know and coins he couldn't understand. He paid, of course.

Always he looked for the apparitions. The man with the burned-away face wasn't to be found, nor was the boy with the slight question mark to his shoulders. Where was he? Nathan wondered. Where? They were driving past a three-story brick building, Chris explaining that it was a warehouse the Manufacturers' Coalition had converted to apartments, when Nathan looked up and saw the scarecrow woman once again at the window. He screamed "Stop!" once again and saw her disappear from view even as he said it.

He was out of the car, counting windows—one, two, three, fourth from the right; third floor—when a large black sedan pulled up between him and the apartment building door and Curtis Widmeyer jumped out.

"Mr. Vice President! What a surprise!"

He had his own security officer with him, a matron as well, borrowed from Patriation. Chris drew the new security man off to have a chat, a leadership conference. In the muscle department, Curtis Widmeyer had come in shorthanded. Meanwhile, Nathan skirted the sedan, used his bulk to split Widmeyer and the matron, and kept walking toward the building entrance.

"If you'll wait just a moment, sir," Widmeyer was saying, "we can prepare things better, give you a first-rate tour. I'm afraid your scheduler didn't get through to me this time."

Nathan had reached the door by now. He used it to brush Widmeyer behind him again. He turned right, found the steps at the end of the hallway, and bounded up the first flight as the regional administrator and the matron scurried to get in front of him. Winded—My God! I'm sixty-five, Nathan thought—he turned and took the second flight more slowly. By now Widmeyer was ahead of him, but he'd given up trying to stop him. Nathan was Vice President of the Confederate States of America.

At the third floor, Nathan figured a window a room from what he had seen at the Patriation dormitory. He counted four doors, knocked, waited, and knocked harder. No answer, not a sound. Nathan stepped back against the far wall of the hall and measured with his right foot before thinking better of it because of his sore arch. With his left foot he battered the door at the handle. It was overkill. The door was barely that at all, half-inch plywood. As it splintered, the handle flew across the room. Inside, the scarecrow woman collapsed in terror to the floor. She was dressed in rags. Bones stuck out all over her body. At her breast was what appeared to be a nearly dead baby, a tiny scarecrow. The woman looked at Nathan—one eye first, then both; a peek, a glance, a stare. And then she began to wail: a high-pitched monotone that bounced off the walls, amplified, drove forward and forward and forward. It was impossible that such a sound could come from such a—what?—thing? And yet it did. Nathan had no wind left. The sound backed them all—Nathan, Widmeyer, the matron—out of the room and flattened them against the far wall of the hall. Then the matron put her head down and shoulder forward and charged her way back into the room. Inside, she bent to the floor, wrapped the woman and baby in her arms, and rocked them both until the sound was merely human and then was not at all.

"How?" Nathan said when his wind finally was back. "How? How in God's name, Mr. Widmeyer, can the coalition allow this? This woman, these conditions"—sweeping his hand across the whole of North Adams—"*this?* These aren't animals. These are human beings, just like you, just like me. How can you live with yourself?"

It was what Nathan had left in him, his last reserve of anger, outrage, strength. He slumped back against the wall, rested his head against it.

"How, Mr. Vice President?" Widmeyer was talking now, himself exhausted, himself at the end of his rope. The placation, the sycophancy, the syrup, was gone from his voice. "How could we not? You wanted your waterway, and you wanted it now, didn't you? Isn't that what the President promised? Isn't that what you and he delivered? Do you think, Mr. Vice President, that these things just happen, that the money just appears, that you wave your magic wand and *presto,* there's a bright new waterway and no one has had to pay? Someone always pays. You take a little away from this person, a little away from that person, but you take the most away from the person you can't see. And who can't you see the most down there in Richmond? Down there in your shining city on the hill? Who the fuck do you think pays?"

Nathan held up a hand, palm out, as if trying to ward off the words. Curtis Widmeyer was shouting now.

"This woman!" He was pointing at the scarecrow, quiet on the floor, maybe asleep, maybe fainted, maybe dead, for all Nathan knew, rid of this world. "The Patriation workers! The people who work in our factories! They're the people you can't see. They're the ones who pay and pay and pay, Mr. Vice President. You take ten percent more from our operating profit to pay for a lock system that will lift water over the Rockies, for Christ sake, and you think nobody feels it? You cut twelve percent from the Patriation support budget, and you think the rats don't start moving into the dormitories? There's a price to be paid, goddammit."

The Patriation matron had scooped up the scarecrow woman and her scarecrow baby in her arms. She was carrying them as if they were nothing more than a bundle of laundry, heading for the stairs and from there Nathan didn't know where—morgue, hospital, trash bin.

Widmeyer stopped her as she went past and pulled back the blanket that the matron had used to wrap the baby.

"Look, Mr. Vice President," he said. "Look. Do you think anyone would take care of this baby even if we had the money to staff clinics?"

Nathan bent over and saw the chalky brown of the baby's skin against the white of its mother's, the broad flat top of its tiny nose.

"Who do you think ends up in places like this?" Widmeyer asked. "Open your eyes, Mr. Vice President. Open your eyes!"

Widmeyer paused to catch his breath. He seemed to think about following the matron, then decided he had one more thing to say, one more demon of his own to exorcise.

"And then what money we have left," he went on, "we have to use to doll up the town so your lordship won't be depressed when he visits—bunting for the buildings, sandblasting, half shifts so the workers won't be sleeping on their feet, the paper mill closed so you won't have to suffer the smell, all of it so you won't have to know what your waterway cost. Really cost. That makes a hell of a lot of sense, doesn't it? That's a well-thought-out directive, for God's sake."

"Directive?" Nathan was stunned by what Curtis Widmeyer was saying. He would have sat on the floor to consider it if he thought there was any chance he could get back up again. "There was a directive?"

"We didn't do it on our own." Widmeyer was spent now too. Like the Vice President, he had used up his last reserves. Calmer now, he imagined himself removed from his job, banished from high councils, forced back on his own, starting over. A price always had to be paid.

The Vice President was talking again. "Mr. Wormley was never told to do that. The advance work was supposed to have been limited to the absolute basics—"

"Mr. Wormley?"

"The President's scheduler. The one who set up my trip."

"It wasn't his doing. With all due respect, sir, we're not going to turn ourselves upside down because some scheduler calls us and tells us to get ready for the Vice President. We do have better things to do with our time. And our money."

"Why, then?" Nathan asked. "Why all the window dressing? Why lay it on so thick? Why didn't you let me see"—Nathan gestured at the hallway, at the room the scarecrow woman, the scarecrow baby, had been in, at everything—"see this?"

"My boss, our director—" Widmeyer stopped, reluctant to go on. "As I'm sure you know, the coalition has been a generous supporter of the Freedom Party."

"Yes?"

"Our director got a call from your boss."

"My boss?"

" 'Make it look good,' we were told. So we did."

And so, Nathan thought, you become someone else, and the people you thought you knew, the ones you trusted as much as they trusted you, become someone else too. It's like a chain reaction. He put a hand on Curtis Widmeyer's shoulder, shook his hand, thanked him, and said he was sorry for . . . He couldn't finish; he was sorry for so much. Then he started toward the stairs, one hand on the wall. He could barely feel his feet on the floor, his fingers scraping along the plaster. He would leave politics, Nathan decided. He would leave it all. He'd go back to the university and beg for his old teaching position.

Just before Nathan reached the stairwell, an extraordinarily small black man, his hair in dreadlocks, emerged from the floor below. When he saw the Vice President, his face broke into a radiant smile, and he thrust his hand out.

"The Vice President! What an honor!" The man's voice danced with a Caribbean lilt.

Instinctively, Nathan smiled back, reached for the hand that was offered him, and felt a small block of paper being pressed into his hand. He thought briefly about looking at it, but he was so tired, so tired. There would be time later. Nathan dropped the paper in his coat pocket, and as he did so, the little man seemed simply to evaporate.

"Mr. Widmeyer," he said from the top step. "There's a Spaniard in the Patriation dormitory. His name is Jorge. He's being sent back to Level One because his hand was injured on the job. It's not fair."

Widmeyer seemed almost to smile. "I'll look into it, Mr. Vice President. Maybe there's something we can do."

Nathan was holding on to the railing for dear life as he started down the stairs.

THERE'S THIS TO be said for pollution, Nathan thought: It makes for a beautiful sunset. He'd lain down for almost two hours on the pull-out sofa in the plane's cabin, sleeping while the crew waited for a valve for the ventilation system to be sent out from Springfield.

When the valve was installed, Nathan roused himself and doused his face with cold water. He was sitting now in his shirtsleeves in one of the club chairs as the plane climbed to twenty thousand feet. To the west, the setting sun was exploding off the billions of particulates floating in the air, each particulate a prism, each prism washed in crimson. It was as if the sky itself were bleeding.

Nathan had asked the steward for a drink before the plane took off: a Scotch on the rocks, no water. The steward brought it with a bowl of cashews, which Nathan waved away. His weight hung heavier on him than it ever had—his age, he thought again. This time his resolve would win out.

And what of his other resolve? The job abdicated? The return to academia? He'd do it, Nathan thought, do it for sure—if not tomorrow, then the next week, before the month was out. He would plead health, his years, fatigue. All that assuming he didn't wake up tomorrow morning to find himself fired—a more likely scenario, now that he thought of it. Either way, the President could appoint one of the bright young House members to take his place for the final half year, a great leg up for someone, the launch of a brilliant career.

At least, Nathan thought, I found one of the apparitions; at least I didn't make that up. And I did, after all, find a kind of truth, didn't I? Nathan thought then of the block of paper he had been handed. Was *that* something he had imagined in his fatigue? He unbuckled himself, walked over to the valet rack, and found the paper in the side pocket of his jacket. The paper had been folded

and refolded and refolded again. Nathan opened it up and flattened
it out facedown. Then he took a long drink on his Scotch, turned
the paper—cheap stationery—over, and began to read:

Dear Dad,

*I had to do this, but I'm sorry for the pain I've caused you and Mom
and Lucy. They want to arrange a meeting between us, just you and me,
so I can tell you everything I've seen and learned. If you'll phone the
number at the bottom of the page, someone will tell you when and where
the meeting will take place.*

Please hug Mom and Lucy for me.
Love,
John Henry

Dear God, he thought, so the boy with the question mark—that
was true too. At last he would have something to give Lucinda: hope.

AT MAURY FIELD, Nathan waved off the air force colonel who was
waiting to escort him and crossed the few yards of tarmac to the
executive terminal himself. His driver, he knew, would be parked
just beyond the door on the other side, pulled up where no other
car could come. Nathan hadn't used a pay phone, he supposed, in
more than seven years. He had no idea where to find one or how
much money to deposit, but he knew he had to use a public phone
for this call. The receptionist was able to come up with two dollars
in change from her purse in exchange for Nathan's paper money.
Nathan put his briefcase on the floor by his feet and spread out his
change on the little lip below the phone, along with his leather-bound
notebook and gold pen. He dialed, then waited what seemed an
unbearable time for someone to pick up. When the phone was answered, he listened carefully to the voice on the other end, made just
enough notes so he wouldn't forget the important points, and hung
up. He wanted to ask so much—how the little man with the note
had found him; how they had found John Henry; most of all, how
his boy, his son, was—but something about the voice told him not
to say a word. Nathan was proceeding on instinct now; he would

have to trust what instinct told him. When he turned around, Wormley was standing behind him, a respectful four or five feet. Still, Nathan was startled.

"The President has cut his vacation short. He'd like to see you in the morning. Nine. The Oval Office." No question in his voice: a command performance.

"Nine o'clock it will be, then, Mr. Wormley. Can I offer you a ride home?"

"Actually, sir, I'm your driver. Just until tomorrow. The President—"

"No need to explain, Mr. Wormley, but we'll need to book you a room, in that event."

"A room, sir?"

"In Charlottesville, unless you intend to sleep in the car. I'm going to spend the night with my wife."

Again, Nathan could see Wormley calculating—an hour and a half to the university, a little longer in the morning, with the rush-hour traffic, the nine o'clock appointment set in granite. Wormley bent now, picked up the Vice President's briefcase, turned on his heel, and looked back over his shoulder.

"Well, sir, in for a dime, in for a dollar."

IT WAS A little after midnight—three days since he had written the note to his father—when John Henry sensed, more than heard, his bedroom door handle turn. Through the slit of one eye, he saw a shape enter, saw the shape was Cara, and was immediately hard as iron. Had she come to him again? So soon? John Henry was learning amazing things about himself in this new life. He was afraid, so afraid.

Cara sat on his bed, put her hand on his shoulder, and gently moved it. "Baby, baby," she whispered softly. She felt John Henry turn, brush against her leg, and try to pull her down to him.

"Oh, no, honey, no. Not that again. It's time to go."

23

WASHINGTON, D.C.

FROM CLARK HADDON'S top-floor apartment on the high ground of Georgetown, he tended to think of Washington less as a necropolis than as a kind of time capsule that had gone bad from neglect; one that was slowly extruding its contents, day by day diminishing into nothingness. The city's parks were littered with pedestals, whatever had once stood upon them long since disappeared. Its "reciprocities of sight"—L'Enfant's phrase—were punctuated these days mostly with mean buildings, not the palaces the French planner had dreamed of. Even the grandiose official name of the place—*District of Columbia*—was like a vestigial tail, a remnant every bit of present evidence worked to deny. There was a Washington that had been, a Washington that is, and year by year it became harder for Haddon to divine their connection.

Georgetown University lay just a little west of him—the lieutenant could look down on its tiny cluster of buildings from his apartment window—and it remained the oldest Catholic college in the Confederacy. But there hadn't been a building raised on the campus in ninety years, students were harder and harder to find, and the Jesuits who ran the university got older and more out of touch by the day. Back when it was a capital, Washington had been a perfect fit with the Jesuits: a place of court intrigues, where it was best to speak in whispers and cover your mouth even then. Richmond was thought to reward a more direct approach. About that the lieutenant had serious doubts.

The university, at least, limped along. It was what it had always been. That was more than could be said of most of the once grand institutions that dated to the prewar days. The "Castle" designed by James Renwick for the Smithsonian Institution had been abandoned when the courts finally awarded James Smithson's bequest to the new American government and construction of a new Smithsonian complex began along the riverfront in Richmond. Two decades later, a little after the turn of the century, the building had been reopened as an insane asylum—Washington needed one badly even then— and so it functioned still. Deep into the morning hours on clear winter nights, when sound traveled best and there was little to compete with it, Haddon would sometimes sit by an open window, shivering, wondering if it was the Castle's inmates whom he heard screaming.

More often than not, the grand artifacts of the past were simply left to decompose on their own. Robert E. Lee had barely ridden out of town with the Articles of Capitulation tucked in his saddlebag before the statue of "Armed Freedom" that had been hoisted to the dome of the Union Capitol in December 1863, in the flush of the Federal victories at Gettysburg and Vicksburg, was attacked by a pair of brothers from the Ozarks of Arkansas. Slavery meant nothing to the boys, and Jeff Davis meant even less. Most of their kin were rooting for Grant and Lincoln, and they would have sat the war out themselves if they hadn't wandered into the company of some good old boys from Pine Bluff, who were forming up a regiment. Freedom, though, the two brothers did feel strongly about. "Freedom for who? Freedom for what?" they had shouted as they stared up at Thomas Crawford's nineteen-and-a-half-foot statue capped with stars, feathers, and an eagle's head. Drunk as lords, the brothers scaled the dome, affixed ropes to the torso of "Freedom," and led the cheers from on high as rebel troops on the ground toppled the monstrosity. Soon, Haddon was convinced, wet rot, dry rot, some kind of rot, would bring the whole Capitol tumbling down. God alone knew who would be inside when it happened.

Haddon had tried to use the story of the Union Capitol to educate a blackmailer he arrested just a week before, in a grand mansion high up on Sixteenth Street. The house the man was so proud of, the cars that brought him such joy, the young and shapely wife who seemed so satisfying to him, were like that old, collapsing Capitol on Jenkins Hill, Haddon had told him, mere vanities that could in a moment be taken away. When the blackmailer demurred, when he failed to see the wisdom of Detective Lieutenant Haddon's metaphor, when he told the lieutenant to commit an anatomically impossible act upon himself, Haddon had kneed him in the groin. The blackmailer preyed upon the sexually weak who prowled Haddon's territory. The lieutenant felt protective of them, and he hated slow learners.

Haddon's eighth-floor apartment would have been ruinously expensive, except that the elevator, even from the first days of the building, generally grew wheezy by the fourth floor and rarely ascended above the sixth. It would have been perilously expensive even then, except that his apartment was a grim little box—a living room the size of a large pantry, a kitchenette the size of a large refrigerator, a bedroom like a closet. Ah, well, he had the two windows, the view, and the elevation sometimes made him feel he was among the stars, useful enough for an insomniac.

And now he had decoration!

Haddon finished stapling the last of the forty-two photographs to his walls—two horizontal rows, twenty-one photos to each row. He had tried the C.S.A. Geological Survey but found it utterly useless for his purposes. Its photos were aerial shots, taken from an angle that bore no relation to his photo.

Ridley's other suggestion—spelunkers' clubs—had proved far more fruitful. It was amazing how organized cave explorers were. One group had a computer file that included photos of the entrances to all the caves its members had explored. Haddon had given them the rough parameters: the quartz streak, a clearing, the location of the cave in relation to the clearing, the estimated height of the entrance itself. The club secretary had come up with forty-two possible matches. The D.C. police photo lab—Haddon had screamed and shouted until they agreed—took the digitized images and blew them up on standard photographic paper. Now Haddon had hung them all and stepped back to admire his work. As he did so, he recalled having done something similar, on a much lesser scale, with the few sheets of his divorce papers shortly after he'd moved into this apartment. On the whole, he preferred this effect.

He took the photo of Joseph Ngubo and began to walk it around the room, holding it up to each of the enlargements. Soon he decided that his method was madness. He would never get a perfect match in every particular. Rather, he needed to match each particular as best he could. So he started again, concentrating solely on the quartz streak. He saw one that seemed to fit, saw another in which the area where the quartz should be located was too shaded to tell much of anything, and by then realized he had forgotten where the first possible match was. So he started yet again, still concentrating on the quartz streak. This time if he saw no possibility of a match, he tore the photo off the wall and threw it on the floor in the middle of the room. Nothing tore neatly. Corners stayed stapled to the wallboard. Tough. By the time he was through, he had fourteen photos still on the wall—fourteen in which quartz could be seen or the area where the quartz was couldn't be adequately perceived.

He started over now, with the entrance to the cave: location only, north end of the clearing. Some photos he saved because he couldn't orient himself in them well enough—where had the photographer been standing? Others he held on to because the location seemed to agree with Joseph Ngubo's snapshot. Next, he moved on to the vegetation in the clearing. The digitized shots from the spelunkers' club were dated right on the image; Joseph Ngubo had written the date on his photograph, and the police lab agreed with it in broad terms. Fine. Brush can grow quickly; trees can't. Haddon concentrated on the trees. He tried to match them image by image, turning the photo in his hand around and around to make sure he wasn't being confused by perspective.

Haddon worked slowly, painstakingly, sweating in the midday heat. The building's owners—a dental association based in Charlotte—had promised air-conditioning. Maybe they had even delivered it, but you couldn't prove it by Clark Haddon's apartment. Or maybe the cool air, like the elevator, simply pooped out at the sixth floor.

By two o'clock, Haddon had two possible matches. Now he focused on the height of the cave entrance: the formation of the shadow in his photo that indicated an entrance, what the entrance that had created that shadow might look like in real life.

Haddon studied the first photo. When he could find nothing, he ripped it off the wall and tossed it on the small round Formica table that served for dining, desk, general storage. He studied the second photo and found the same: nothing. He threw that on the table too.

Angry now, stewing, he pounded his fist into the wall, forgetting that his neighbor labored nights at one of the government file centers where work never stopped, computers always hummed, the lighting was always the same. His neighbor pounded back on the wall. Haddon got a glass of water, breathed deeply, and tried to stay in control.

The problem wasn't the photos, it suddenly occurred to him. The problem was himself: He was forcing the photos to conform to what he wanted to see. He put his glass in the sink and restapled the last two photographs to the wall. If the photos were going to speak to him, he was going to have to step inside them. He would have to make himself part of what he was seeing. Haddon cleared the cat-clawed chair away from the wall beneath the two photos—his wife had kept the cat. And then he simply walked forward, into the image, into the photo itself, until he collided with the wall, until he had almost become part of the wall. His neighbor pounded again, cursed, screamed, but it didn't matter. The photo on the right had allowed Haddon inside it, and there everything suddenly was: the quartz streak, the clearing, the cave entrance, all in perfect alignment. Miracle!

Haddon checked the coordinates of the photo on the master list the spelunkers' club had sent him, found it was in Virginia, and checked those coordinates against a topographical map he had borrowed from the Georgetown University library. It was a stroke of luck, a good omen: Virginia had been the only topographical map in stock. Then he matched those coordinates with his road atlas: about 1.4 miles north of Afton Gap, due west of Charlottesville maybe half an hour. It was going on three o'clock; if he hurried, Haddon could be there by six, with enough light to look around.

He thought about calling the office and telling someone where he was headed. But why? He thought about calling Jenkins and Flannerty, at least, and summoned an even bigger why. They were riding with someone else this evening; the lieutenant had checked out for the day. Haddon was halfway out the door when he wondered if he should pack a small bag in case he ended up spending the night somewhere—a razor, toothpaste and toothbrush. Why? he thought once again. What am I going to do if I find someone? Kiss him?

The lieutenant didn't even wait for the elevator to try an ascent.

PART III

JUNE — OCTOBER

24

THE OVAL OFFICE

"Mr. Vice President."

"Mr. President, suh!"

Spencer Lee reached over to the silver coffee service on the low table to his right and poured a cup of decaffeinated brew. He waited until Nathan Winston had crossed his legs—left over right, pants cuff carefully adjusted—before handing him the cup and saucer. The south-facing windows of the Oval Office gave onto a leaden sky, so low that it seemed almost to be touching the ground. The old Capitol was barely visible; behind it, the dome of the new Capitol was completely obscured.

Spencer checked his watch: 9:01.

"I trust that you had better weather than this at Pawley's Island," Nathan said after his first sip. The words he wanted to say were jammed at the back of his throat, fighting to break free. But this was the Confederacy. Conversation was a dance, and the dance had rules.

"Bright sunshine all day yesterday." Spencer indicated the overcast weather with a sweep of his hand: "This seemed to come on while we slept."

"So it did, apparently. And the fishing? After we hung up?"

"Birds diving everywhere. Spanish mackerel so thick you could have walked on their backs from one side of the inlet to the other. But we couldn't get very many of them interested. We trolled for two or three hours and landed only a half dozen or so. I smoked three of the largest and brought them home. Would Lucinda . . . ?"

"Lucinda's still a bit off her feed"—a world of euphemism implied in that, a world understood. "Why don't you save them for yourself. Maybe for Alice, when she gets back from England—she'll have had her fill of mystery meats and odd puddings by then, I suspect. Smoked mackerel might be just the thing to welcome her home."

Lucinda had been quite specific about Spencer Lee's famous smoked mackerel. She had told Nathan that if he brought any more of it home again, he'd have to dig a hole in the garden and bury it. She wasn't having it inside the pavilion again, *ever*. Nathan was inclined to believe her, and he certainly didn't disagree with the larger sentiment: Mackerel was bad enough however it might be prepared, but Spencer's smoked mackerel—an old family recipe that generations of Lees and Davises had survived just fine—had an especially frightening taste and a smell that took weeks to drive out of the kitchen. Alice at least had a genetic obligation to the delicacy, and perhaps the iron stomach to digest it. Maybe that was why she kept extending her stay in England: She was trying to outwait the mackerel season, maybe outwait the entire species. If so, Nathan applauded the effort.

"Brother Davis?" he asked now. "He doesn't seem to have fired the flare gun at you—or perhaps he just missed. You found him in good health? He's—what?—almost seventy by now?"

"Sixty-eight last week. He wanted to take a grenade launcher out on the Bertram with us, to keep the Secret Service boat at bay. That's when he compromised on the one agent we took aboard. Davey wasn't happy about it."

"Well, then."

"And Lucinda?" Spencer asked as he bent to fill his own coffee cup a second time. "I believe you saw her last night?"

"You're kind to ask, Mr. President. I think she's better. I really do. Time heals all wounds. Or so they say."

"So they do."

Nathan closed his eyes and leaned back into his chair. He was still breathing heavily. Yesterday's flight, the excitement, the long drive to Charlottesville last night and back this morning—it all caught up with you eventually, he thought: every bit of exercise not taken, every elevator ride substituted for stair climbing, every bowl of salad passed over for another pork chop and gravy. The years flew by on the calendar; you were young and then one day you were old. There was at least that advantage to his imminent departure from government: He would talk Lucinda into walking in the mornings, on the track by the field house. For lunch he'd have nothing more than some garden greens, with a light dressing. And perhaps a small baguette. There was a bakery just off campus that he favored. And perhaps some cheese with it, but the dry, crumbly cheeses, not the creamy ones. Wine, he had read, was good for cholesterol—red or white, he couldn't remember which. He would still have that one pleasure, one vice to savor in his dotage.

"Lucy got in after I did last night. She and Jason had been at the graduate library, putting the finishing touches on their magnum opus. They seem to get along well academically."

"Just as we seemed to governmentally," Spencer said.

"We did, didn't we, Spencer? We really did." At last, Nathan thought—we've come to it at last. He fished in the side pocket of his suit coat, found what he was looking for, and jiggled it once in his hand: a last look. Then he laid the brass key on the silver coffee tray.

"Your front door key. I hope you didn't have any trouble getting in the house yesterday."

"Someone was waiting."

"Well, that's one advantage to having staff."

Nathan turned now in his chair, stiffly, uncomfortably, and shifted his legs—right over left now—so he could face Spencer more directly. As he did so, he set his cup and saucer on the tray. More? The President had raised his eyebrows in a question. Nathan shook his head: No, he'd had coffee enough.

"Mr. Wormley?" Nathan finally said, raising his eyebrows in his own question. "Not that I blame him in the least. Just for my own curiosity. He was obliged to let you know."

"Yes, Wormley, of course. And the head of the Manufacturers' Coalition, who had been alerted by a Mr. Widmeyer, I believe. And the chief territorial administrator, who had been alerted by the head of the Manufacturers' Coalition, and—"

"Bad news travels—"

"Oh, very fast, Nathan. You should know that Wormley waited

until you were on the ground in North Adams to tell me where you
had decided to spend your special day. Otherwise, I might have been
inclined to have your plane turned back."

"Or shot down?"

"That would have been brother Davey's solution, but I know the
pilot and the steward."

"Another thing to be grateful for."

"Once you were on the ground, you were beyond my long reach
unless I wanted to create a scene."

"I'll have to thank Wormley for that. On my way out. I was going
to call you myself when I got back last night, but it began to seem,
well, redundant by then. I thought you might enjoy your evening
more if . . ." He waved his hand: If I simply disappeared. If I let us
pretend for another twelve hours that nothing had happened, that
you had helicoptered back from Pawley's Island on a lark.

Nathan turned still further now, slowly, laboriously, until he was
facing the President almost head-on.

"You know what I'm most sorry about, Spencer? I'm most sorry
that you had to cut your vacation short. That was unforgivable of
me, truly unforgivable. If there's one thing I could take back—"

"I keep telling you, Nathan. It's not that hard a job, and Davey
can be a trial."

"Well, at least you were there long enough to get some color in
your face. My mother always said that a healthy face should have
some color in it."

Spencer looked at him then, tried to be stern but couldn't, and
fell into laughter just as Nathan began laughing with him. It seemed
like hours before either of them could speak again.

"Oh, God, Nathan. Oh, God," the President said when he finally
got control of himself. "How did it ever come to this?"

"You know, Mr. President, I've thought a good deal about that
these last twenty-four hours. I had an itch. I had to scratch it. You
kindly gave me the opportunity. One thing led to another."

Nathan reached into his inside jacket pocket, found a sealed envelope there, and laid it on the silver coffee service, beside the key.
He was divesting himself, or so it seemed to him—offering himself
up in small pieces, hoping to find some essential self waiting when
he was through with all the partings. He kept thinking that all this

giving away should be making him lighter. Yet he felt as if he were sinking deeper and deeper into the chair, into himself.

Spencer Lee picked up the envelope, looked at the address—to him, by hand—and laid it back down on the tray.

"What's this?" Knowing precisely what it was—this, too, being part of the ritual, part of the larger game of governance: The Way Things Are Done.

"My resignation, Mr. President." Nathan had thought about the wording of it as he drifted off to sleep last night. He had dreamed of a manifesto of sorts, a document with the ring of history. Instead, he'd risen early this morning and typed it hastily, platitude spilling over platitude, while Wormley waited in the front parlor: "It has been my singular honor . . ." "Thus it is with a heavy heart . . ." More of the same. Nathan's day would be full enough. Like Spencer Lee, he fully expected history to have him for lunch someday. Only a few people could stand its long, withering gaze: Washington, Davis, Madison Tompkins, certainly; Lee, maybe; Varina Davis, maybe; maybe Booker T. Washington and the other George Washington— G. W. Carver. Nathan had no illusion that he was cut of the same stuff. He had behaved disloyally to his President, dishonorably, unable to stop himself. All he could hope to do now was bring it to an honorable end.

"But, Mr. Vice President, I've not requested your resignation."

"Still . . ." Nathan turned his palms up, a submission to the inevitable.

"Not *still*. Nothing is *still,* for God's sake! We all have free will!" Spencer's vehemence surprised them both. "In any event"—calmer now, control coming back—"It's a moot point. I don't accept it. If you want out of here, you'll have to quit, flat and simple."

"Sir?"

"Why, Nathan? Why can't we just go back to where we were?"

"The only way I know how to explain it, Mr. President, is that I opened a door. I stepped through it and saw things—"

"Then turn around, walk back, slam the door behind you, forget what you saw. Seven months, Nathan! For God's sake, that's all we have to get through—a little more than seven months! It's been more than seven years. What's seven more months? A little amnesia. Don't leave me now."

The Vice President dug in his pants pocket and found a white linen handkerchief. He mopped his brow with it and dried his upper lip and his temples before letting his head rest against the wing of the chair. Once more, he closed his eyes, but this time he felt the moment stretching into something longer and gave in to it. Nathan was almost smiling.

"IT'S NOT JUST what I saw, Lucinda. Awful things, unspeakable things happen. I'm sixty-five years old. I've seen enough of the world and I've lived long enough to know that. Things—humans, babies, mothers—things fall between the cracks no matter how hard we try."

"And we do try, Nathan. You try. Spencer tries. We try in our own way here at the university, on the faculty. The whole nation tries."

"I know, I know we do. Listen, Lucinda, that's not my point."

They were seated in Nathan's office, at either end of the worn leather sofa across from his desk. Lucinda had had a bath earlier while she waited for Nathan to arrive from Richmond. She was wearing a robe now over her nightgown; her feet, minus their slippers, were tucked beneath her. A glass of chardonnay sat beside her on the end table, barely touched.

Wormley had dropped Nathan off twenty minutes earlier and walked down the Lawn to spend the night at the Colonnade Club, where Lucinda had found him a last-minute room. Nathan had taken off his jacket, rolled up his shirtsleeves, loosened his tie. His stocking feet were stretched out on the sofa, pressed against Lucinda's knees. Rachmaninoff's Second Symphony was playing softly on the stereo. Nathan was cradling a snifter of cognac in his hands, sorting through his memories, trying to breathe easily. Ever since he'd seen John Henry's handwriting on the plane, his heart had hopped softly in its cage—as if it knew it might finally be released.

"I saw what I saw," Nathan was saying, "but it's not what I saw that I'm talking about. I was on the plane. We were maybe halfway back to Richmond. I'd asked the steward to bring me a second Scotch. 'Just wet the ice,' I said"—Lucinda's eyes had widened— " 'Just wet it.' "

Lucinda smiled, took a small sip of her wine. "You always did hate dry ice, Nathan Winston."

Nathan smiled and tipped his snifter to his wife. Then he swirled the cognac and took a small sip himself.

"I was waiting for the steward to bring the drink," he went on, "when I suddenly realized that what I had seen up there, what I had been witness to in North Adams, didn't just happen. It wasn't some kind of anomaly. All that misery hadn't just dropped out of the sky, Lucinda."

"You can't, Nathan. You can't doubt what we have, what we've created—"

"Let me finish this now, sweetheart. Let me say it now or I'll never be able to say it. This is what I realized: There's no space for gray in our system. You're either black or you're white, and God help you if you're neither. You're either a citizen or you're not, and God help you if you're not. Don't you see, Lucinda? Life isn't just black and white. It's filled with gray areas, *filled* with them! That's what I really saw. North Adams, the Industrial Zone, the Patriation Program—they're all gray; they're all somewhere in between, all filled with people who don't fit our definitions, people who are outside what we're willing to understand, what we're willing to let exist. We have to shut so much out to make this work.

"How could I have missed that? How could I have failed to see that? We don't even have the language to talk about whole realms of existence. We can't even say the words. They would be too—"

Nathan stopped, faltered, swirled his cognac, knowing he had ventured into dangerous ground. His heart hop-hopped again, anxious to be free.

"Too impolite?" Lucinda asked. "Too uncivil?"

"Sweetheart, you know I respect your scholarship, your writings—"

"Oh, Lord, let's not worry about that. I'm barely a scholar at all these days. But whether I'm right or wrong about the role of civility, I know this: We may have missed whole realms of existence, Nathan; our logic might not hold up to microscopic examination. I'm not a logician. But the wonder of this nation, the wonder of the Confederacy, is that the races—the two races, the black race, the white race—have made a separate peace. Think about what that means;

think about the history of mankind, the history of this planet. Nathan, it's unique. There's never been anything like it. This is what I was trying to tell John Henry the afternoon before he—" Lucinda waved her hand. Left? Was abducted? What did it matter anymore? But you had to hold to something, she thought: some version of truth that you could stand.

"Yes," she went on, "people might be left out—I'll own to that. You have to begin somewhere. You have to have some benchmark, some threshold of admission. Otherwise, it's chaos, anarchy. And we begin with seventy-seven-percent racial purity. Maybe the number is arbitrary. Maybe it doesn't make any genetic sense—I'm not a geneticist either—but, Nathan, what we get in return! Look at the Patriation rolls! Look at the streams of people waiting to be admitted, the streams waiting to be put on waiting lists. Humankind votes on the American experience every day. There's no confusion about what their feet are saying. I know it's a cliché, dear. I know our literature department would gasp in horror to hear me say it, but look around, Nathan. Look around the world. The Confederacy is mankind's great hope, the model for what will be. We *are* the shining city on the hill."

"I was on the plane, Lucinda, and I saw this fundamental crack in the nature of things," he said. "That's what I can't turn away from now."

"But maybe this is just what John Henry's abduction is all about." Lucinda was warming to her argument, her voice rising. Sister Clarisse had finally gone, and Lucy was not yet home. "Maybe DRAGO wanted to do this to us, to you. You can't give in, Nathan. You can't!"

"Maybe," he said as gently as he could, "it wasn't an abduction, Lucinda. Maybe John Henry saw that they were right."

He sat up then, slid down to Lucinda's end of the couch, and wrapped his arm around her—his heart still hop-hopping. With his other hand, he reached into his shirt pocket and showed her John Henry's note.

LUCY HAD APPEARED amazed to find her parents together, talking, when she got home. Had it been that long? Nathan wondered as he watched his daughter, and knew the answer immediately: Yes, too long, monstrously long. He'd taken on more than he should have—

planned his life so he would be away from the Lawn as much as possible when Clarisse was there. He'd abandoned his wife when she most needed him. Lucinda had had to struggle back into the world, eyes red-rimmed, all by herself. She'll be okay, though, he thought. She'd always been so tough, and she would be again.

"How's your paper going, dear?" Lucinda asked as she hugged her daughter.

Lucy laughed. She seemed thrilled to be asked. "You wouldn't believe it," she said. "I've never been involved in anything like this before! Dr. Cuthbert's given us two more days, but that's it—the absolute deadline."

Then Nathan hugged and kissed Lucy himself.

"These long absences of mine are almost over," he told her. "Pretty soon you'll both be begging me to go away for a few nights."

Nathan watched as Lucy and Lucinda climbed the steps together.

"You and Jason aren't spending too much time on this paper, are you?" Lucinda was saying. "You both have other courses, you know. And this is just a—"

Lucy laid a hand on her mother's arm. "Don't worry, Mommy. There's nothing left. All our exams are over." She was resting her head on Lucinda's shoulder as the two of them turned at the landing.

Nathan locked the front door, checked the back one, carried his snifter and Lucinda's wineglass to the kitchen, and turned off the downstairs lights. More normality, he told himself. Maybe. Maybe. Maybe it was all for the best—somehow, in some grand plan. He could hear Lucinda moving in her office and wondered how long she would stay there. Lucy was in her bedroom. He could hear that too. She would have turned on the night-light by her bedroom door. Lucy had done so every night since John Henry disappeared, Lucinda had told him—her own little lifeline to her brother.

Lucinda was waiting for him in the bedroom.

"I'm going with you tomorrow, Nathan."

"Sweetheart, no."

"If something were to go wrong, if this is my only chance to see John Henry again"—"alive" hanging in the air between them, unsaid—"I couldn't live with myself."

"There's an agreement, Lucinda. It's no place for—"

"Fine," she said, holding up a hand, ceding the point. "I knew you'd say that. Here."

Lucinda had written out a page full of instructions, all in her spidery script: warning signs for Nathan to look for, questions he was to ask, vitamins and nutritional supplements he was to take with him—"just," she said, "in case."

She was pointing halfway down the page now. "You remember? That asthma he had when he was a boy? That wheezing? I want you to listen, Nathan, listen hard. I won't have him getting respiratory problems, not at his age. Also, his weight. And, Nathan, his posture. He certainly can't afford to get any scrawnier than he is. I want you to look carefully for that—take those nutritional supplements with you, you understand? If he gets too thin, his posture is going to get even worse. And if it's bad now, think what it will be like later—he'll end up a stooped old man. I won't have that."

Nathan put his arms around his wife and smoothed her hair as he bent and put his lips by her ear.

"You know what you've just said? You've said John Henry is going to be an old man, just like me. You've said we're going to get through this."

"Oh, Nathan, of course he is. Of course we are."

Her tears were soft this time, quiet—not a thunderstorm, but a warm summer shower. As Nathan held her tight to him, he felt himself stirring and felt Lucinda stir in return, soften, collapse into his arms. He slipped a pillow under her head as he laid her on their bed, turned the light off, and helped her out of her robe. And then— a *miracle,* he thought—they made love. Nathan finally lumbered awkwardly on top of Lucinda, scared of breaking her bones, feeling a bird fluttering beneath him. His own breath was coming harsher, heavier, while his heart seemed to lift in ecstasy.

Afterward, he had wondered as he often did what Lucy could hear. He was too old to be quiet, too grateful to stifle a moan. It had been so long. The walls were thick, but the floorboards carried sound. Well, he thought, Lucy was almost twenty-one, a woman. She would have children of her own someday, maybe soon—who knew? A grandfather! . . .

THERE WAS A PUSH, a shove on his arm. He felt something heavy stealing across his chest, reaching down his left arm—something settling on him.

"Nathan! Nathan!"

Nathan Winston opened one eye now and saw Spencer Lee standing in front of him, bent to his face. Behind Spencer were the south windows of the Oval Office, the gray sky. Nathan felt the familiar wing chair beneath him and saw the silver coffee service on the table beside him. So that's where he was. Slowly, he struggled back into the present.

"It's like a loose thread in a sweater, Spencer. You begin to pull on it, and everything falls apart. You pull on it, and suddenly you see how every myth we create, every lie we tell ourselves, feeds into the next myth, the next lie."

The President had turned and was walking toward his desk. Nathan saw Spencer pick up the phone and punch a number, heard him ask Manzini to bring up a cola, lots of ice, for the Vice President. He faced Nathan then and started back across the room. The President seemed to be moving in slow motion, speaking as if he were underwater. Nathan kept on talking—throwing out his words as if they were a lifeline for his friend, a way of hauling him to the boat, to shore: "I pulled on the thread, Spencer. I can't just go back from that."

As he talked, the President wavered and seemed to dissolve before assuming normal mass, normal speed. Nathan could see Spencer's concern. Then he realized: The concern was for him.

"You're okay, Nathan?"

"I think so." Nathan reached for his pocket handkerchief, found it still in his hand, and mopped his brow again. The handkerchief was almost dripping. Now he remembered: For a moment, he had felt as if he were being pulled over a ledge by his own distorted gravity. His body had acquired some kind of superweight; a massive density invaded each molecule. It was as if he were being pulled downward against his own volition. Nathan raised his arm now; it offered average resistance, was of average heft. He breathed a sigh of relief and longed for the ice-cold cola. Flu. Whatever. He would be in his bed by tomorrow afternoon, he supposed. Today, tonight, tomorrow morning had to be gotten through. As they said in the military, Nathan had reached "zero option."

THE TWO MEN watched the day unfold as they had from these chairs on so many mornings. A single ray of sunshine tried to pierce the cloud cover. It lit the obelisk to Robert E. Lee, slid off it and lit the obelisk to Jefferson Davis, slid off that, disappeared, then touched down on the charred roof of the old Capitol before disappearing for good. A sign? Spencer wondered. If so, of what?

Spencer was topping off his coffee one last time—a tepid compromise, just better than nothing—when Kay buzzed him on the intercom.

"Mr. President, I'm sorry to interrupt you, but it's Senator Wilson, here for his nine-thirty. You've got Ms. Redmond at ten, sir, to go over the working notes for tomorrow's press briefing."

Spencer hadn't even looked at his schedule for the day—it was still lying beside the creamer on the coffee tray, just where Manzini had put it. But he knew that beyond the Senate Majority Leader and his press secretary waited a whole line of people. Decisions had to be made, causes supported or dropped. Well, Spencer thought, some things can't be helped. Some things are more important than keeping to a schedule.

"Cancel Senator Wilson, Kay. And tell Redmond to stand by."

"Cancel?" It was Willard Wilson. "Cancel!" He's halfway to purple already, Spencer thought, before the intercom went dead.

"Sir." It was Kay back on. "Senator Wilson asks me to remind you that he has put important business aside for—"

"Thank him, Kay, and tell him to have a safe trip back to the Capitol."

Nathan was talking on as if the intercom had never come alive, as if Kay had never buzzed the President about his morning appointments.

"That first trip, Spencer," he was saying. "I saw three wraiths . . . One was a boy, Spencer. At the end of a street. A boy with a sweatshirt on and a kind of hook to his shoulders."

"John Henry?"

Nathan nodded and drew back into himself, then emerged again. "It was the wraiths that were haunting me more than anything else. I couldn't not go back. I'd seen things on that first trip. I had to see them through."

"To govern is to make choices, Nathan. You know that." Spencer was rubbing the back of his neck, trying to knead away a headache before it began. "Sometimes the choices we make work hardships on people; sometimes, God knows, we kill them. But what we work for is the greatest good for the greatest number. Think about it, a waterway that will help feed millions when fields elsewhere are parched with drought—"

"It's not a choice, Spencer, if you don't weigh the options. It's not a choice if you don't recognize what you're choosing between. It's not a choice when you wrap half the equation in window dressing and refuse to see it whole."

Spencer looked at Nathan out of the corner of his eye and found that the Vice President was looking at him in just the same way.

"I should apologize," Spencer said. "I simply wanted your trip to go as well as possible. You were under such strain."

"No apology necessary. I was angry about it yesterday; hell, I was shocked when Widmeyer told me. Then I realized: It's you to a T."

Spencer looked again, uncertain of what was being said.

"Oh, I mean that as a compliment. I really do."

The President stood now and studied the gray Mall. "Leave well enough alone, Nathan. There are problems, of course; there always are. We'll work on them. You could head up a blue-ribbon commission to study the Patriation Program and recommend reforms. You can end up your second term in a blaze of glory. But leave well enough alone. There's still plenty of well to go around."

"I wish I could, Spencer. You have no idea how much I wish I could."

"But?"

Nathan stood, steadying himself on the wing of the chair. He took one step, another, and found himself leaning against the window well beside the President. He felt as if he were learning to walk all over again.

"Think of these monuments, Spencer. Davis, Lee, Madison Tompkins, and George Washington; Booker T. Washington; Jefferson, Madison, Monroe. What would they say if they could talk? 'Leave well enough alone'? 'Do what's convenient'? Your own monument will be out there someday, Mr. President. Maybe mine too. We build monuments to everything, for God's sake, to everybody. What would you like your monument to say? 'Do what's easy'? What would you want Jason to hear you say? That's what I've been asking myself, Spencer. That's the question that won't let me alone: What could I stand to have John Henry hear me say?"

Spencer stood almost at attention. He appeared to be trying to

listen to the monuments. Then he seemed to deflate. His shoulders
went slack. His eyes closed, then slowly opened again.

"The waterway, Nathan. No one got rich off it, at least illegally.
No money was passed under the table. There were no bribes that
I'm aware of. You know the lengths we went to to make sure the
contracts were fairly let—you chaired that working group, for God's
sake. We need the waterway: We all agreed. And we all agreed that
it will pay us back hundreds of times its cost. How were we to know
people were suffering? How were we to know people were going
without? No one told us. No one mentioned it."

"Spencer, don't you understand? They told us all the time. We
just weren't looking. We weren't listening." Nathan put an arm over
the President's shoulder—half for support and half because Spencer
seemed suddenly so tired himself.

"We make people become invisible, Spencer. That's what I realized as I was flying home last evening. If they love someone of a
different race or love someone of the same sex, we tell them not to
make us notice them, and then once we do—and we always do
eventually, it seems—once we do, we exile them, take their papers
away, and make them officially invisible. And why, Spencer?
What's the purpose? That's what I kept wondering. Is it to keep
the races pure? Is it because the Bible tells us that it's wrong?
Or is it just so we won't have to think about it, think about
them, think about anything that would upset this perfect world we
live in?"

"Nathan, I—"

"Wait, please. Listen. I talked with this woman my first time in
North Adams—or I tried to. She was Russian, I think, strong as an
ox. She looked like she was a willing worker, but she didn't seem
to know a single word of English beyond 'yes.' And she was scared,
Spencer. My God, she was scared. I said to myself, Well, that's the
price of citizenship; nothing's free. But on the way back yesterday,
I started to ask myself why we have just this one route to become
an American, just this one way. She might write like Tolstoy, for
all we know. Maybe when she was young, someone thought she'd
be the next Anna Pavlova. But we're going to make her become just
like us, and if she can't, we'll make her invisible too."

Nathan almost lost his footing as the President rolled out from
under his arm. The tips of Spencer's ears had gone red; a flush was

starting across his face. Nathan leaned his back against the wall. Spencer faced him.

"All that's fine, Nathan, if you want to live in a theoretical world. In a theoretical world you can do anything you want. You can break all the rules. You can make sure there's not a poor or unhappy soul anywhere on the planet. But this is the real world. This is politics. And in the real world, Nathan, in the real world—"

Nathan held up a hand. "Don't say it, Spencer. Please don't."

"Why not? All of a sudden you can't stand to hear truth? Dammit, Nathan, in the real world you've got to break some eggs to make an omelet."

"Spencer, don't you see? That's what every two-bit dictator says before he lops a million souls off the census chart. Spencer, the means never justify the end. Never."

Spencer Lee looked as if he'd been slapped. He'd just lost his best friend.

THERE WAS A knock on the door, a second one.

"Mr. Manzini?" the President called, happier than he had ever been for the elaborate ritual of Manzini's entrances.

"Mr. President."

Spencer turned and motioned for his valet to come in.

"Leo."

He was carrying a silver tray, a soft drink in a crystal tumbler balanced in the middle of it.

"Spencer!" Manzini looked past the President, his eyes wide with horror.

Spencer turned again. Nathan was grasping at the air with one hand, at his chest with the other. He made a gurgling sound, a groan or a sigh—Spencer couldn't tell which. He heard words half formed, words that he couldn't make out. The Vice President reached for the curtains, seemed to think better of it—the mess, their flimsiness, their insubstantiality—and looked for something else to grab. Spencer got to him just as he was collapsing and slid to the floor with him, Nathan's head cradled in his arm. My God, the dead weight of the man! The sheer tonnage! Spencer felt something give in himself—an abdominal muscle, something in his hip, his groin. A pain shot up, mellowed, and shot up again.

Manzini had somehow dashed into the bathroom just off the office and moistened a washcloth. Now he slid himself in place beside Spencer, lifted Nathan's head off the crook of the President's arm, and placed it in his own. As Spencer tried to rise, a wave of pain shot through him, and he went back down on one knee. It felt as if a red-hot knife had been slipped into his side. He tried again and this time found a way to right himself so that he could walk. At his desk, he mashed the intercom button and slipped the lock on so the line would stay open:

"Kay, get a doctor in here, now! The Vice President—"

Manzini had stopped mopping Nathan's brow. He was bending over now, putting his ear to the Vice President's nose, holding his palm just above the Vice President's mouth.

"Mr. President!" Kay's voice leapt out of the intercom box. "Dr. Withers is out of the building, sir!"

Who was he? Spencer wondered. Withers? My God, there were so many people! And then the name came back, the face: Raymond Withers had been a private practitioner in Richmond, distinguished, nearing retirement. He was now the black doctor on assignment to the White House, responsible for black personnel, with admitting privileges to all-black hospitals. Manzini stopped listening, checked his palm for moisture, and found none. He put his ear to Nathan's heart this time, listened, then looked up at the President and shook his head.

"Then get Dr. Ashbury!" Spencer yelled back to the intercom, already starting back across the room as his own pain began to localize: lower abdomen, a knife blade just there, where Spencer had always thought the appendix might be, or maybe his spleen.

"Sir?" Kay was uncertain. A white doctor for a black man? Even a black Vice President? Protocols were being bent; rules were breaking down. Medicine in the Confederate States of America was like love and consolation and so much else—an exercise in delicate intimacy. Contact was possible between the races, of course. But there was that fine moment beyond which everything tipped, and nothing on earth could predict when that moment would arrive. How much better to avoid what priests liked to call "the occasion of sin."

"Sir?" she said again, louder this time, the President having gone mute on the other end.

"Now, dammit, Kay. Now!"

Spencer was on his knees beside the Vice President, showing Manzini where to place his hands.

"The heel of the bottom hand goes directly on top of the sternum, Leo. Like this. Then you compress the chest straight down. . . . You'll need to pause after every fifth compression and wait for me."

The door to the central hallway, almost always locked, burst open. It was Middlebrook or Kalinowski—whichever agent had been on guard. Spencer was suddenly at a loss for names.

"Out," he said as the agent hurried toward them. "Out. Go secure the ramp. Make sure it's open for an ambulance."

The order didn't make any sense, Spencer knew. For God's sake, Secret Service agents must be trained in CPR; they had to be. But Nathan deserved to be with friends, and that's what he still was, regardless of what had so recently been said: a friend.

"Find a rhythm," he said, turning back to Manzini. "Find it now, Leo."

No one—class clown, class fool, class dolt—left the Citadel without learning cardiopulmonary resuscitation. And having learned CPR the Citadel way—deep in your bones, where what seemed a million push-ups forced it down and made it stay—no one ever forgot.

As Manzini readied himself to urge the Vice President's heart back to life, Spencer placed his own lips on Nathan Winston's, gently as a kiss, and began trying to breathe for his partner in politics, his—the thought leapt out at him, just as Kay's voice had—his other half.

Breathe, boom, boom, boom, boom.

Breathe, boom, boom, boom, boom.

Nathan's failure to respond did not discourage Spencer. The dummy on which he had learned CPR never breathed back either. Like Manzini beside him, the President had no intention of stopping until Nathan Winston came alive again. What Spencer Lee sometimes feared he lacked in backbone, he tried to make up for in perseverance.

THE EMERGENCY MEDICAL team flew everywhere, shouting instructions, pulling equipment out of midair. Spencer had simply nodded when Kay looked to him for confirmation. When order was restored, Dr. Ashbury had given the President a quick exam—poked him here, prodded him there, until he finally brought forth a gasp, a choked-back scream. The scream was just what the doctor was looking for.

"It seems to be a small tear in the abdominal muscle," he told the President. "You'll need to go easy on the exercise for a month or more. It'll give you a chance to fatten up; you're getting too damn scrawny anyway."

Himself a comfortable two hundred pounds and climbing, Dr. Ashbury reached into his bag, brought out a vial, and tipped a dozen pills into the hand of Manzini, who was hovering by Spencer's side.

"Make sure he takes two every four hours, Leo, no more, no less," the doctor instructed. Then he turned away, back to why he had come: Spencer Lee was not the center of attraction. Far from it.

Framed against the windows where he had fallen, Nathan Winston lay strapped to a gurney. His suit coat had been removed and one of his shirtsleeves cut off. IV tubes ran into Nathan's arm just below his elbow. An elastic band held an oxygen mask in place over his mouth and nose. Nathan's shirt had been ripped away at the buttons; his tie, severed just above its knot, lay on the floor at the foot of the gurney. Sensors suctioned onto Nathan's chest tracked his tenuous purchase on life; a monitor at the head of the gurney recorded it for the medical team to see.

Spencer thought again of the single shaft of sunlight they had been looking at and how it had touched down on the old Capitol. It seemed to have burned brighter at that moment—as if it were drawing light to itself from the gold disk that marked the site of Jefferson Davis's martyrdom. Perhaps it really had been a sign, Spencer thought. How else to explain what had seemed to him a miracle? Nathan—brought back to life.

Like the boy in the nursery rhyme, the Vice President now had one shoe off, one shoe on. It struck Spencer as obscene, something like a final indignity. He approached the foot of the gurney, undid the laces, and slipped off a black wing tip of impeccable pedigree, supple as a glove. As he did so, he saw Nathan open one eye, then the other, saw his mouth moving inside the oxygen mask. Nathan's hand, restrained by his side, was struggling to get free.

"Dr. Ashbury," Spencer said. "I think the Vice President has something he's trying to say."

Spencer picked the other shoe up off the floor, carried the pair over to his desk, and set them side by side in the knee well. Lucinda, he thought vaguely, she'll want the shoes; she needs to be called. My God, what will I say? Then he saw the doctor signaling to him.

"He wants to talk with you, Mr. President. In private. You'll have trouble understanding him, and I've just been informed that the cardiovan has arrived. My professional opinion is that it would be far better for you to wait and talk with the Vice President in the hospital. When he's stabilized. Assuming . . . ." Ashbury let the sentence trail. It didn't need finishing.

"Of course," Spencer said. Then he looked over and saw Nathan still struggling with his hand against the restraint. His mouth was working again inside the mask, his eyes were burning like fire into Spencer's own. "Still, I think I'd better do as he wants. We'll be brief."

"Three minutes, sir, no more. Put your ear close to his mouth. He'll need every bit of energy he can save."

"NATHAN, I'M—"

"No time, Spencer. I didn't tell you everything."

One of the emergency technicians had replaced the oxygen mask with a split tube that fed Nathan oxygen through his nostrils. Spencer could hear its hiss and smell the slight metallic odor of Nathan's breath. He was leaning over the Vice President now, straining against his own pain, his chin almost in Nathan's chest. Everyone else in the room had backed away.

"There was a note." Nathan faltered, slowed.

"A note?"

"From John Henry. In North Adams. It was from him. I could tell. I called, Spencer—"

"Nathan, who? Who did you call?"

"Not now. Listen! Listen!" It was all in a whisper, a fierce whisper. Spencer could feel the strength draining from Nathan.

"Talk" is all the President said. "I'll be quiet."

"There's a meeting. John Henry and me. Just the two of us. Tomorrow morning. Five A.M. on the old Mall in Washington, where the Fourteenth Street Expressway crosses the City Canal. North side. Lucinda knows, Spencer. She'll want to go. She can't. She can't. Too dangerous."

Nathan's voice was growing faint now, the ferocity gone. Across the room, Dr. Ashbury was waving his arm, pointing to his watch, holding three fingers in the air as he made a cutting motion. Stop, for God's sake. Stop. Give him a chance.

Spencer turned his head and put his lips against Nathan's ear. "I'll go. I'll be there. Somehow."

Nathan's lips were moving again. As Spencer pressed his ear against Nathan's mouth, he could feel the moisture of his breath, the texture of each word: "Tell him what I said before, Spencer: Tell him I'm sorry. I love him."

The President was lifting his head now, ready to call Dr. Ashbury and the medical team, when he felt Nathan stir again—one last gasp of strength. Nathan opened one eye, then both eyes. As he did so, he rolled his head toward the window, out beyond it to the symbolic apparel of the nation draped across the rain-soaked Mall—the real one this time.

"And Spencer," he said, "and Spencer, Toby's right. The old Capitol—tear the damn thing down." Nathan's eyes rolled momentarily in their sockets, then snapped back and settled once again on the President.

"Love him," Nathan said, almost more breath than speech.

"Doctor!" Spencer yelled. He grabbed Nathan's hand and held it until the gurney reached the Oval Office door.

IT WAS ALMOST noon by the time Manzini had finished tidying up the Oval Office. He'd thrown the crystal tumbler containing Nathan's soft drink down the small trash chute just off the lavatory. He and the President had stood side by side, listening to it crash two stories below.

"Bad luck," Leo said—explanation enough.

Otherwise, there was the debris of the medical team. It was amazing how much raw trash something as ultramodern as an emergency medical team managed to produce: wastebaskets and wastebaskets of the stuff, it seemed. Leo gathered all that up, sent it down the chute after the crystal tumbler, then folded the shirtsleeve and set it aside to carry back to his own work quarters, along with Nathan's shoes. Those, at least, he could shine and put trees in. He lifted the coffee service, long neglected, and carried it over to the President's desk. Spencer picked up the brass key and slipped it into the top desk drawer. Next, he took the envelope and held it to the light, thinking that he might be able to see what was inside. I don't care, he thought: Either I don't care or I don't want to know. Spencer tore the envelope through once the short way, once the long way, put the pieces back on the coffee tray, and asked Leo to burn them. The letter wasn't. It hadn't happened.

"May I bring you lunch in the private quarters?" Manzini asked,

"No, Leo, no," he said. "I'll just have a sandwich at my desk. Clean around me."

"Then perhaps a nap?" Manzini held his hand over his own stomach—the muscle tear, the pain, more medication.

"We'll see. We'll see." Happy enough with the pills as he was.

Manzini was preparing to leave when Spencer stopped him.

"Leo, may I ask what shoe size you wear?"

"Ten and a half, Mr. President."

"Excellent. And may I ask you one more thing—a favor this time?"

"Of course."

"I'd like to dine with Mrs. Manzini tonight, Leo—dine with Helena alone."

Leo looked at the President a moment, his head tilted to the side as if he were trying to puzzle out an elusive modernist painting.

"Remember, Spencer," he finally said, "I'm Portuguese and Italian, a potentially volatile combination. And I love my wife very much."

"I've always known it, Leo. You're fortunate to have each other."

WHEN MANZINI LEFT, the President had Kay put him through to John Stanley at the Secret Service.

"The Vice President's heart attack, Mr. Stanley?" Stanley had been up to the Oval Office an hour earlier to confer about security precautions at Tompkins Memorial Hospital.

"Yes, sir?"

"Make the story die for twenty-four hours, and I'll try never to ask another favor of you." Years of experience in the protective services had left John Stanley with a jaundiced view of First Amendment rights generally. He had thought Spencer Lee far too obliging where the press was concerned; now he had his second story in almost two months to squelch, to drive from existence.

"I've already dispatched a team to Tompkins Memorial to seal the Vice President's ward, Mr. President, and to make sure the medical teams assigned to him don't talk to anyone." Stanley's voice was high with excitement. "But there's much more that can be done."

Spencer knew precisely what he was talking about: Anyone— White House staffer, Secret Service agent, ambulance driver, emergency medical technician, chief of cardiology—whose loyalty seemed questionable, whose discretion was up in the air, who was suspected of having an itchy finger when it came to phoning a favorite reporter, any such person would simply be detained until noon tomorrow. The authority for such actions was clear and necessary: In a world of crazy dictators, rogue nations, and blood-soaked ideologies, national security was never to be taken for granted.

"Then do it, Mr. Stanley."

"Yes, sir!"

Next, Spencer buzzed Wormley and asked him to step into the Oval Office.

"I'm sending the helicopter for Mrs. Winston now," he told his scheduler when he arrived. "I'd like you to be on it. Take her from Maury Field straight to the hospital. The ward is being closed off. There'll be a suite for her, a room for you. I want you to make sure she's well tended to, and I don't want you to leave her out of your sight until this time tomorrow, Mr. Wormley. Is that all clear?"

Clear? My God, it was like handing a fifth of Scotch to an alcoholic. Wormley practically bounced his way out of the room. Through the half-cracked door to Kay's office, the President could hear him arranging for drapes, afghans, down quilts, whatever he thought it might take to make Lucinda Winston comfortable.

Spencer was rooting around in his desk drawer for his private address book when Kay buzzed him.

"The protection services, sir—they want to repeat the daily sweep. There have been so many people through."

Of course they would, Spencer thought. It makes total sense that half the emergency-room staffs in Richmond would be riddled with German spies or Chinese ones or Russian ones, just waiting for an opportunity like this to slip a microphone or a miniature camera inside the Oval Office. Christ, Nathan's probably guilty of aiding and abetting the enemy. He had the heart attack, didn't he? Spencer found himself incapable of looking at the two agents as they ran their little satellite dish and mine sweeper through his office. Just get it done, he wanted to shout. Just finish.

When they finally did, he had the White House operator put him through on a secure line to a number in Charlottesville. He'd wanted so much to be able to deliver good news. He had delayed and delayed, hoping that he might have some. Now he would just have to deliver the news he had.

"Lucy?" he said when the phone was answered at the other end. "This is Spencer Lee. I need to speak with your mother."

25

BLUE RIDGE
MOUNTAINS

JOHN HENRY WAS sleeping in his own bed. He'd forgotten how soft sheets could be, how comfortable a mattress and box springs were. He'd forgotten how much he loved to wrap himself in the light down comforter that covered his bed. It was his cocoon, his mother used to tell him; he was a caterpillar waiting to unfold his wings, waiting to fly. Across the hall, he could hear her dainty breathing—in and out, up and down, prim and proper even at rest. Around it curled his father's heavy snuffle. John Henry imagined that he saw a light under his doorway; he imagined it was Lucy's. She had just gotten home from a date, maybe from the library, and had turned on the small china lamp by her bed. Now she closed the door of her bedroom. As she did so, the light under John Henry's own door almost went out. Almost. Not quite.

John Henry went to stand up now. He wanted to go over to his sister's room and talk with her. If she wasn't too tired, they would play Scrabble for a little while. He wanted to smell her room—the lotions, the perfumes. He wanted someone to call him "Germ" again. He wanted to look at her. He didn't know why—it had been so long since he had done so, forever ago. Where had all that time gone?

And then John Henry realized that he couldn't move. He was tied inside his comforter, the comforter itself was tied to the bed, the bed was nailed to the floor, and the floor was firmly bolted to the rock-hard crust of the earth. He looked again under his door and saw shapes moving there in the dim light still cast from Lucy's room. He heard a hand on his doorknob and saw the knob turning so slowly that it seemed time itself would soon have to stand still. Who was it? Cara? Cara? Suddenly, the shapes were inside his bedroom, as if they had slid through the molecules of the door without ever opening it—one, two, a dozen or more of them. And then John Henry heard his name being whispered soft as a breeze: "Johnny. Oh, Johnny."

Two of the shapes bent down to where John Henry's face was being mashed against his pillow—mashed so hard suddenly that it seemed there could be no more space for his eyeball in his head, mashed so hard that his eyeball would have to pop out of its socket just to survive. As they bent down, the shapes pulled back the cowls that covered their heads. And as they pulled back the cowls, John Henry saw who they were: the two Marys, joined now at the ear, it looked like—one Mary instead of two, finally inseparable in whatever half world they had come to inhabit.

Whatever was mashing John Henry's head down pressed harder. His pillow was turning into something else, a cutting board, maybe, as the parade continued past him—one after another of the shapes bending, one after another pulling back its cowl: the woman who had set "Jack Sprat" to opera at dinner that night; Jonah, the Jamaican gnome who had played John Henry's father in the skit; the night-shift worker whom John Henry had helped to the bathroom. Everyone was here, John Henry thought—all except one.

It was a hand that was holding his head down. The hand was kneading his head hard with its knuckles, driving his face into the board—John Henry could feel the hand now, the rough texture of its fingers digging into his scalp. He thought he might not be able to avoid crying. His face, he thought, might just break off. Then the pain would never end; it would only get worse and worse and worse. Suddenly, he was on his back, his head free. The magic cocoon of his comforter had simply dropped off him, disappeared; and the hand that had been on his head was on his throat, kneading that now, gently this time, a caress, almost. Whatever face it was that was attached to the hand—through sinew and bone—now lowered itself to John Henry's own. John Henry could smell the Guinness on his breath. He was certain who it was even before the face—still lost in the shadow of its cowl—whispered in John Henry's ear: "Johnny boy, we know! We know who you are!" Behind him the other shapes went "know" and "know" and "ah, ah, ah."

How, John Henry wondered, could his room be big enough to hold all this? This man? This chorus he had brought with him? The room had always seemed so small. In the end, it hadn't even been big enough for just himself. And now this! Then he felt something cold pressed flat against his throat, and he knew with an absolute certainty what that was too.

"Where are they, Johnny boy?"

"Who? Who?" the chorus sang as if it were reading John Henry's mind.

"Your mommy and daddy, Johnny boy. Your famous daddy. Ah, and your lovely sister, Lucy, too. We'll be wanting to meet her as well. Now, where would she be, charming Johnny?"

Where? John Henry thought. How could they have missed that? It was so simple, so obvious. And then it occurred to him that it wasn't so easy as stepping across the hall. The house on the Lawn—this house, the one he had been raised in—had grown labyrinthine. Only John Henry could follow the light from his room to Lucy's, because it was a light that shone only for him. And now he knew something else: He would never give up the information, never while he lived.

"Tell us, Johnny boy. Tell us." The mouth so close to John Henry that the words formed themselves as moisture on his face.

"Cost me. You cost me. It's time to start paying."

The knife blade was no longer flat against his throat. John Henry felt as if a door were slowly being opened into his neck, into the vast chasm of himself. Like the door to his bedroom, this one was opening so slowly that time had to decelerate. John Henry had expected a trickle of warm blood down his neck—a trickle, a stream, a torrent; he had felt it coming for weeks. Instead, a cold wind was flowing into him as the door opened wider, inch by inch by inch.

Once the door was open all the way, John Henry wondered, would he still be able to keep the secret of the mazes? Would he still own the labyrinthine architecture of the pavilion, his house on the Lawn? Or would all that knowledge just fly out with the breeze, where anyone could grab it? John Henry didn't know. Then a final revelation: Cara was not coming to save him. She wouldn't arrive on time, even if she knew, even if she wanted to. He was on his own, alone, flying solo. And then the door that had been opening so slowly closed with a bang, and the shapes went away, and John Henry was awake.

He blinked, opened his eyes, and wanted to give praise for his deliverance. Outside the window next to John Henry's head, a loose shutter banged again in the evening breeze—the sound he had heard, John Henry thought, the one that had brought him out of his dream. And then he saw him and quickly closed his eyes again. What was dream? What was not?

This time John Henry breathed slowly, deeply, through his nostrils: one, two, three, four times. He cleared his head and thought about where he was in place and time. His left arm was under a pillow; his right arm caught under his chest. He felt the cool mountain air, the thin sheet that barely kept the chill off him. Ready, his self-inventory complete, John Henry gradually opened his eyes again—wide enough to see; not wide enough, he hoped, to be seen—and stared into the circle of light at the center of the cabin. There was no question about it now: It was him—Sean, large as life.

AGAIN, CARA AND he had driven all night, reversing their tracks this time, keeping once again to the gentle mountainous spine of the Northeast Industrial Zone—the "safety of bad roads," as Cara had called it: the Berkshires south to New York Territory and the Taconics; from there tacking southwest to Poughkeepsie and across the thundering Hudson—thundering water, thundering factories, the power lines overhead seeming to crackle and thunder with their load—to the Shawangunks; the Shawangunks to the Kittatinny range; the Kittatinnies into Pennsylvania Territory and the broad eastern sweep of the Appalachians. They'd crossed into the Confederacy proper near Emmitsburg, in Maryland, under cover of the Catoctins. From there, they had wound their way through the Catoctins to the Blue Ridge and Virginia and, for John Henry, something like home. If only he had been allowed to see it.

The going was tortuous, but there had been fewer rests this time. At Great Barrington, they'd stopped briefly to pick up a man who looked so much like Cara that he might have been her brother, her twin. Cara said only that he was to help her drive.

"But," John Henry said, "I—" He was dumbfounded. *He* had

been helping her drive; he thought *he* had become her right-hand man. Whatever else he had been through, John Henry was still a seventeen-year-old, crazy for internal combustion, for the feel of a wheel in his hand, tires on the road.

"No, baby," Cara had answered. "We got to keep you rested." Nothing more.

Hours passed—God alone knew how many—before they stopped again, near Stroudsburg and the Pocono Mountains. More hours passed—an eternity—before they pulled off the road a last time, just south of the Potomac River at Harpers Ferry. Cara reached into the glove compartment, pulled out two packages, stripped off the wrappers and the protective backs, and told John Henry to close his eyes. She leaned over the seat then and fit the pads to both eyes.

"Lie down," she told him as she handed him her jacket to use as a pillow. "It's for your own good, baby. You don't want to know too much. Your Cara's taking good care of you."

Supine on the back seat with his eyes sealed, feeling the car curve its way through the hilly terrain, John Henry felt as if he were regressing in time. He was a man, for God's sake. A man! Going north, his Cara had let him rest his head in her lap. Going south, back into the heart of the world he had known, John Henry wished she would again.

FINALLY: SOMEWHERE. JOHN Henry was led from the car to the cabin. Inside, the pads were peeled from his eyes. While they adjusted to the light, Cara and the man busied themselves with a fire, cans of stew, a plastic jug of drinking water. The cabin, a single large room, had four bunk beds against the walls, a table and three chairs near the middle. At the very center sat an open woodstove with an overhanging ledge for cooking. Cabinets had been built between the beds. Outside, shutters closed off the windows when no one was around. The sun was beginning to set when the fire caught and started driving the worst of the dampness out of the room; the sun was diving into the mountain when the man pronounced the stew cooked and slid three paper plates of it onto the table. Dinner was eaten in silence. Afterward, the man took the plates, their plastic forks, the plastic cups they had drunk their water from, the water jug itself, the cans their dinner had come from, and stuffed them all in a plastic bag. Then he walked out the door with the bag and never came back. John Henry listened for the car—an engine firing, gears shifting—but he heard nothing.

"Time for you to get some more beauty sleep, honey," Cara said to him as soon as the man was gone. "We got to get you to that Mall by five A.M., and you want to look good for your daddy, baby. He's going to be so happy to see you."

While Cara pulled a pillow and a sheet out from a cabinet, John Henry sat on one of the lower bunks and took off his shoes. He left his socks on against the evening cool. A thin dew covered the mattress, but the pillow was soft, and the sheet provided just enough warmth. John Henry watched with one eye as Cara stoked the fire, got it roaring, and settled down with a book. And then? And then the shutter had banged by his head, and he had been brought back from the dead—his throat sawed half open, secrets about to fly from him—and Sean was standing behind Cara, lit by the dying firelight, massaging her neck, running his hands down her shoulders, her arms, across her breasts.

"Soon, baby, soon," Cara was purring.

A bottle of wine was open on the table; two nearly empty tumblers stood beside it.

"Soon."

It was a voice John Henry knew well, a voice that had wound itself around his heart. Inch by inch, millimeter by millimeter—time was decelerating again—he brought his right hand out from where it had been trapped under his chest and ran it down beside him. Quietly, he reached into his jeans pocket and found the stub of a pencil he kept there and the card Daniel Brewster had given him more than two weeks before. John Henry coughed slightly. When no one turned his way, he brought the card and pencil up. Sean was bent over the back of Cara's chair now, chewing on her ear.

"How soon?" His voice a whisper, the whisper a kiss.

"Oh, baby. Any moment."

Sean bent over still further and brought his lips around to meet hers. As he did so, his shirt pulled up above the waist of his pants, and John Henry could see a gun—he had no idea what kind—jammed into the waistband at the small of Sean's back. "Mall," John Henry wrote on the back of the card. "5 A.M." That was all he had, the only coordinates, the only message he could send to the world. Before morning, he would be in Richmond; somewhere among the statuary, his father would be waiting. He knew nothing more than that.

John Henry slid the card between his mattress and the webbing that covered the springs. Why, he really didn't know. Because of Sean, of course—what was he doing here?—but maybe more for the same reason he had left "DRAGO" spelled on his sister's Scrabble board: to mark his life; to assert a presence; to say hello, to say goodbye; to say, if nothing else, that he had been here.

Cara pulled Sean's hands off her, stood up, and poured the last of the wine for both of them. Through the slits of his eyelids, John Henry watched them touch glasses—the thin clink of plastic on plastic—and throw back the wine in a single swallow. And then Sean, too, was gone, as if he had walked out of John Henry's dream into this world and then decided to walk back into the place where dreams come from.

"John Henry, baby," Cara was whispering into his ear. "It's the last little part of our trip." She kissed him on one eye, then the other. As John Henry bent over to tie his shoes, she kneaded his shoulders.

"It'll be over so soon, honey, so soon."

Cara banked the fire, picked up the one tumbler that was left— the bottle had disappeared with Sean—and dropped it in her purse, along with the book she'd left open on the table. She closed the door behind them. No eyepads this time. John Henry had waited inside the door for Cara to put them on. When she hadn't, he simply followed her out. The moon was bigger than he had ever seen it: He could see everything as he climbed into the car beside her. Maybe one hundred yards down a rutted lane, they came to a state highway and turned left. A minute or so later, John Henry looked back and saw a car without headlights, washed in moonglow, emerge from the rutted lane. Another minute or two passed before Cara slowed and pulled over onto the shoulder. The car, still traveling in the dark, roared past them. It was just about out of sight in the distance when its headlights and taillights finally came on.

"Just breathe deep, baby. Breathe deep," Cara said. She rested her hand on John Henry's leg and left it there. "You're going to see your daddy."

And for John Henry, that was all that mattered now. Not Sean, not anything else. He was living in a world that had stopped making sense, a world he no longer could parse. He wanted to see his daddy.

26

THE WHITE HOUSE

THE SECRET SERVICE agent on duty stared forlornly out the window from his small office by the front door of the White House. Had the man no sense whatsoever? It was pouring out there. Not even ducks were leaving their shelter. His colleagues were going to crucify him—he'd be buying them beers for months to make up for this.

"Sir," he said into the phone, searching the hand he had been dealt for a convincing card to play. "Sir, I'm afraid visibility is very poor. I'm not sure we can guarantee your safety even with tighter stationing. Perhaps the fitness center would be a better choice."

"Agent Andrews?"

"Yes, sir?"

"Words cannot adequately express my gratitude for your concern or my sympathy with your position. There are windows in the private wing of the White House as well, and any fool can see that it would be insanity to run in this weather."

"Then, sir, perhaps you might—"

The President cut him off in midsentence.

"In fact, I intend to call Director Stanley as soon as this conversation is concluded and tell him that you went the extra mile and that your conduct during the entire length and breadth of this phone call has been exemplary in every regard. Every regard, Agent Andrews."

"Thank you, sir."

"You needn't thank me, Mr. Andrews. You've earned my esteem, but—" Spencer was going to prevail, at any rate. He was President, commander in chief of everything. Still, there was no sense making an enemy in the bargain.

"But, sir?"

"May I ask your age, Agent Andrews? Thirty-three? Thirty-four?"

"Thirty-four next week, sir."

"Then perhaps you have not yet had occasion, Mr. Andrews, to fully contemplate all the horrors that can overcome a middle-aged body. Cholesterol. General flabbiness. The need to let off steam before it grabs you and sinks you into a depression. The quick decay that a lack of muscle tone invites. The heart." The image of Nathan strapped on his gurney almost overwhelmed Spencer as he talked. Nathan was holding his own, Dr. Ashbury said. The next thirty-six hours would be critical. Spencer went back to his conversation: This much he owed Nathan.

"In other words, Agent Andrews, I need an outlet. I need to get this perilous flesh and bone of mine back into equilibrium."

Agent Andrews wanted to reach through the phone line, grab the President by the throat, and shake some sense into him. What was it with these joggers? Another inch or so of rain, and women and children would be evacuated to higher ground. Bass would be swimming down Broad Street. Noah would be relaunching his ark.

"Sir," he said one last time, owing at least this much to the men on his assignment roster this evening. "The rain—it's expected to move off in a few hours. Maybe a late-night jog, after your dinner? The agents are on duty all night."

"And I need to do it now. The usual door? Five minutes?"

"Yes, sir!" Saluting the receiver, Agent Andrews set the timer on his watch, opened up the daily logbook to note the request, and phoned the Secret Service duty room. He could hear the television playing in the background—a shoot-'em-up, one of hundreds of videos the service kept on hand for rainy evenings. Andrews could practically smell the coffee percolating in the kitchenette to the side. It was going on six-thirty. The White House mess would be delivering plates of something soon—something like everyone's mother used to make on days when the only people outside were the ones without enough sense to come in: chicken and dumplings, a Brunswick stew with fried corn bread on the side, pot roast. When Andrews passed on the President's request—four minutes and counting, *hut-hut,* everyone to battle stations—he could practically feel the walls of his little cubicle by the formal front door of the White House shake with dismay, anger, outrage. What is the guy? Fucking nuts?

Agent Andrews called his backup into the cubicle, grabbed the roster book, and went down to the private Mall exit. His reputation was already shot: There was no chickening out on this one. By the time he got there—double time all the way—the agents were lined up and waiting, wide-brimmed trooper hats pulled low over their ears. The earpieces and crinkled wires that ran from them down into their trench coat collars made the agents look like audioautomatons—beefy androids wired for sound, stamped out at some Martian factory working from a fuzzy image of life on planet Earth.

"Mr. Andrews?"

It was Bishop, at the front of the line. They had entered the Presidential Protection Corps the same year, both fresh out of national service.

"Yes, Mr. Bishop."

"Your insurance premiums are paid, sir?"

"Very funny, Tommy."

"All of them? Medical? Home owners? Disaster? Acts of God? Nuclear strike?"

"We know where you live." It was another voice, deeper and more ominous, farther down the line: Swanson.

"Some of us have even had the pleasure of visiting you in your abode." Mercereau this time. "Way back when. Back when you had a heart."

"Guys, come on." Andrews could see the light start to blink on the elevator that served the private wing.

Quickly, he called the roster: Bishop, Davidson, Evans, Johnson, Mercereau, Pignon, Swanson, on and on. And as he did, each agent punched him once in the right arm—a short, hard punch with the middle knuckle extended, each blow in exactly the same spot, an age-old reward for delivering these awful chores—then sprinted out into the rain and the dying evening light and rushed to his assigned station. That much, at least, they could do blindfolded. Andrews knew from bitter experience what lay ahead: His arm would be throbbing by midnight; by morning, it would be pinned to his side, unable to move. It wouldn't be until the next day that he could even begin to brush his teeth.

Agent Andrews was envisioning a long spiral into tooth decay when the elevator arrived at the door beside him and, as Andrews brought himself to attention and readied for a salute, kept on going, down another floor to P-1, the first level of the parking garage. *Maybe he's changed his mind. Maybe he's thought better of this madness and decided to go for a joyride instead.* The prospect brought Andrews no particular pleasure—there would be still greater hell to pay among his colleagues if he had rousted them out for nothing. *Then again, maybe the President had just punched the wrong button. He needed to have his eyes examined, maybe his brain too.*

Now the arrow reversed itself. The elevator started back up, glided softly into its station, and out stepped the Man himself, in a jogging ensemble Andrews had never seen, one that was testament to the seeming inability to produce miracle fibers in colors the human mind could comprehend: Lycra tights in a magenta that was like a poke in the eye, a blinding chartreuse Gore-Tex parka with its hood pulled up and tied tight at the chin, clear plastic goggles set over his glasses, running shoes in colors the agent couldn't possibly name. As always, he saluted the President; as always, the Man saluted back— two fingers to his brow, somewhere between the Citadel and a fox hunt. Then Andrews opened the door, and this rainbow apparition stepped jauntily into the pouring rain.

At least, Andrews thought, no one is going to have trouble seeing him. He reached into his coat pocket, pulled out the transmitter, and held down on the Send button:

"Condor is soaring."

The most fun part of the job, Andrews often thought, was coming up with names for these odd birds.

IT WAS AGENT Bishop, the first agent stationed, barely into the run, who noticed that the President seemed to be favoring his right foot. By the time the President had crossed over the Mall and started along the path lined with azaleas—their blooms now long gone—that led to the statue of Judah Benjamin, his whole gait seemed to have been affected. He was between agents when he slowed, stopped, bent over, put his hands on his knees, and breathed deeply. When the agent next in line sprinted over to see what the delay was, the President waved him off. He jogged in place for a few seconds before starting on his way. Nothing, though, was right. His stamina seemed to be gone; his gait collapsed again. He was limping now, listing to the right, grabbing his side as if he were suffering a stitch. Word had bubbled up from the agents who had been in the duty room that morning—something about a small medical crisis in the Oval Office, the Vice President, maybe, the President with some kind of muscle tear. Director Stanley sat on the whole thing, but maybe that's what this was about. The rain pounded down, like a physical assault.

The President headed into the canyon between the twin obelisks. Who was going to stop him? Who was going to grab the President of the Confederate States of America by the shoulders and tell him to turn around and walk back to the White House? Who was going to tell him to take a shower, get some rest, get a life? And who was going to turn him in the other direction when he veered right after he came out of the canyon and set off for the equestrian statue of George Washington rather than—as always before—the oratorical statue of Madison Tompkins? Instead, Pignon called back to Agent Andrews and told him to dispatch someone in a golf cart down the jogging line, just in case.

"Now?" Andrews asked, incredulous.

"Now," came the answer. "Fast." Jesus, Andrews thought, another person to make mad, another debt to his colleagues that would be months in the paying.

Just as he was circling Washington's statue—Agent Evans in charge—the President himself solved the Secret Service's dilemma. He was half running, half limping, when he saw a bench off to his left and made for it. By the time Evans came on the scene, the President was removing his left running shoe and massaging his foot. Evans could hear him panting, breathing deeply. Now the President threw his head back and greedily let the rain run into his mouth. Sated, he undid the knot at his chin and pulled the parka hood back from his head. Last, he lifted off the plastic goggles.

"Sir," Evans called. "Sir, you really shouldn't—"

"Oh, Mr. Evans, there's no need to be so formal." The President stood up now and let Evans play his flashlight across his face. "It's just me." Leo Manzini took a step, hobbled on his left foot, and almost had to sit down again. "I seem to have a size eleven left foot and a size ten-and-a-half right one, at least when it comes to jogging shoes. How was I to know? Why in heaven's name do you suppose he does this? It's barbarous. And thank God for that," he said as the golf cart came into view. "I'm not sure I could walk all the way back on my own."

THE THINGS YOU discover about your own house. Spencer had reached the second parking level in the garage under the public wing of the White House and was still descending. He'd never been here and only dimly knew it existed. How many levels were there? How many more cars could there possibly be? And did all these people work here? Spencer had a vision of subterranean rooms chockablock with file clerks, seamstresses, butchers, bakers, candlestick makers. How many of the people employed in the executive branch had he actually met in any meaningful way? Or had the waterway been so expensive that Treasury simply started renting parking spaces in the garage to the lawyers and lobbyists and other hangers-on who cluttered the streets of the capital?

Spencer pulled the collar of Leo's windbreaker tighter around his face and tugged the brim of his Irish walking hat lower on his brow. The heavy black frames of the glasses Leo had found at a drugstore pinched hard against the President's nose, but the magnification wasn't so far from his own prescription that he couldn't see to drive. The hat was an affectation Spencer had not known about, a touch of vanity: Leo had a small bald spot that was getting larger. And speaking of vanity, he thought, what a sight Leo had been when they parted at the elevator a floor higher! This much he had learned in politics: If you're going to tell a lie, tell it big; wrap it in bright colors. In Leo's case, blinding ones. Agent Andrews must have felt he'd had the wind knocked out of him when the elevator door opened and Leo stepped out. Thank goodness Jason had gone through a Day-Glo phase when he was playing on those high-school soccer teams. Who would dare look at that hideous confection long enough to see if the President was actually inside?

Ah, well, he would recommend Andrews for something rosy when this was all over. He had, after all, been absolutely right: No one should be jogging on a night such as this. Worse, no one should have to look out for someone who was.

At the third subterranean level, Spencer turned left down the parking aisle, just as Manzini had drawn it. He ducked his head to examine his keys when two interns came bubbling along beside him, talking about the reception they were headed to: free drink, all you could eat. It seemed a million years since Spencer had been that young. He counted now—three, four, five cars from the far wall— and there it was: a station wagon, maybe five years old. It seemed strange to him that he should have no idea what kind of car Leo drove: Friends knew such things about one another. Still, his was a strange life.

He unlocked the door, slid in, and turned the engine over—easy on the accelerator, Leo had said; let the car do the work. When it was running smoothly, he backed out of the space and began winding his way back up to the surface world. It wasn't until the first level that he remembered to put his seat belt on. It wasn't until he'd cleared the guard booth—a perfunctory wave for those leaving, laser fingerprint reads for those coming in—that it occurred to Spencer Lee that he hadn't driven a car in almost eight years. It had taken him fifteen minutes to find his driver's license; it predated his administration. Strange indeed.

From her perch on the landing of the great entrance stairwell of the White House, Kay winced as she watched Manzini's car bounce over the curb and head along the private White House ramp that would carry it to Lee Boulevard and from there northwest out of the city. She tracked the station wagon as best she could through the downpour. When it was gone from view, Kay walked up the stairs and down the hall. In her office, next to the President's, she called the secretary of state, just as she had been told to.

Had Mr. Sumner received the note the President had asked to be hand delivered to him? He had, the secretary said, only minutes before. Could Kay . . . ? Kay could not, in fact, shed any light. All she knew was that the President would be incommunicado until sometime the next morning, and the Vice President—well, the cabinet had already been informed of that.

"I guess," Sumner finally said, "I'd better drink nothing stronger than wine tonight. I seem to be in charge of the nation."

Kay had just hung up and put a bag of tea to steep when Agent Andrews came storming into her office, with Mr. Stanley himself in tow. Manzini was in the lockup next to the ready room. More agents were surrounding his house.

"Do you have any idea where Manzini's car has disappeared to?" Stanley asked. "And in general, just what the hell is going on?"

Kay shook her head: Sorry. No.

"One more thing," Andrews said to Kay as he and Stanley were leaving. The agent was holding his arm, kneading the muscle. "Do you think you or Mr. Wormley could find some dry clothes in the President's living quarters and take them down below to poor Leo?"

That, at least, Kay had prepared for. The clothes were sitting in a neat pile on the chair beside her desk, the one with the needlepoint cushion, the chair that Mr. Wormley practically owned.

SPENCER LEE FOLLOWED Lee Boulevard all the way to Gaskins Road before he turned north and began angling back to the east. Driving, he supposed, was like riding a bike—once learned, never really forgotten. Leo's station wagon reminded him of a good sturdy boat: Set its nose on the right marker, give it a little gas, and it felt as if it would take you anywhere.

The diner sat just off the highway, a few miles south of Ashland. Behind it was a two-story motor court, as forlorn-looking as the diner itself, both victims of a recent interstate highway. Spencer pulled the car to the back, locked it, and had a good look around. Then he made his way gingerly through the dying rain for the neon lights in the diner windows. Helena was waiting in one of the booths. She'd ordered them both meat loaf and mashed potatoes, with a side of green beans cooked nearly to a mash themselves, dripping with the ham hock they had been simmered with. She was amused to see the President in her husband's windbreaker. Leo's Irish walking hat looked almost hilarious on Spencer's head.

"The things men get up to," she said as Spencer sat down and the waitress pulled their plates from under the warming lamp. "Those glasses don't do a thing for you, but at least you don't look like yourself. And I suppose that's the point."

"Helena, I don't know how to thank you."

"Oh, for heaven's sake," she said, waving it all away. "You help us; we help you. Leo's tied to you like white on rice, and we both know it. Dig in. This place looks awful, but Lord, Spencer, can they cook."

Twenty minutes later, weak in the knees from a second helping of sweet potato pie, the President had to agree. Helena took the keys Spencer had left lying on the table and gave him a room key—212, second floor on the corner—and a set of keys to a rental car.

"I rented the car in my maiden name, Spencer dear," she said, laying a warm hand on top of his. "It seemed best. It's blue, directly below the balcony to your room." And then she rose, gave him a motherly kiss on the cheek, and was gone.

Spencer fell into a panic when the waitress brought him the check. He hadn't carried cash in he didn't know how long. He had only his credit cards, which of course he couldn't use here. And then he remembered that Leo had taken three twenty-dollar bills from his own wallet and stuffed them into the President's shirt pocket before they started for the elevator. He knows me better than I know myself, Spencer thought. Well, it's time I learned a few things.

In his motel room, he set the travel alarm Leo had packed for him to two A.M., giving him enough time to shower. Just as he lay down in the bed—lumpy, miserable, the few remaining resources of this enterprise doubtless having gone to the diner out front—the wind howled once and the rains broke completely and moved on. Filled to the brim with meat loaf and pie, Spencer fell quickly asleep.

27

AFTON GAP

WHERE TO BEGIN? Lieutenant Haddon had driven through sheets of rain, then a steady downpour, a spring rain, a drizzle, and now this: a moon so bright he could read by it, stars such as he hadn't seen since he didn't know when, mountain air so clean and crisp he wanted to bite into it. He had to get out of the city more. There were other ways to live a life.

God bless the spelunkers, he thought. You had to be crazier than a frog to lower yourself into one of those caves. Bats, snakes, blind newts, poisonous salamanders, collapsing walls and tunnels, bears, who knew what else—the inventory of dangers to be found in such places was breathtaking. But the spelunkers knew how to orient themselves. It was more than Haddon could say for nine-tenths of his colleagues.

The lieutenant had found the clearing without a hitch. Just as the sun was going down, he'd run his fingers along the high horizontal streak of quartz and stood in what he thought must be the very footsteps of Joseph Ngubo—figurative footsteps only, the real ones having been nothing more than footfalls on leaves and moss. Haddon had even taken his flashlight and shone the powerful beam into the cave entrance. Something had scrabbled for deeper cover when he did so. Instead of following it, he'd studied the loose dirt at the entrance and quickly convinced himself that if DRAGO wanted to hide in there, he was prepared to let them do just that. He was interested in justice, but his usual beats were horror show enough.

Maybe he should have brought Flannerty and Jenkins after all. He could have ordered them both into the cave, then shot one to convince the other that he meant it. Ah, well. The greatest ideas always arrive too late.

The clearing sat in a small glen not far off the picturesque parkway that winds along the crest of the Blue Ridge Mountains from one end of Virginia to the other and down into North Carolina. No trails were blazed to the clearing; there was no parking designated for it. But it was easily accessible by foot, and the full moon was a godsend. He'd used it to reconnoiter the area. Seven cabins in various states of repair and elegance sat within the general ambit of the clearing. Three of those Haddon had eliminated immediately—roofs staved in, vines growing through the windows, doors swinging loose on their hinges, the whole corner of one building toppled off its cinder-block pier, dragging the rest of the structure down with it.

The lieutenant took a pad and a pencil from his pocket and drew a map of the four remaining cabins. They were arranged in a rough arc that stretched away from the clearing, with maybe a mile of uneasy landscape separating them from one end to the other. Map in hand, he did a mental inventory of his strengths and weaknesses, just as he had been taught to do before heading into any operation.

Weakness: He was on someone else's terrain, not his own.

Weakness: He was without jurisdiction or any other legitimate— in the eyes of the law—reason to be here. He could always flash his badge and hope that in the dark and the rush of the moment it might be credential enough, but he also had little doubt that even if his badge were legal, his jurisdiction clear, half the people who lived in these parts would just as soon feed him to their dogs as look at him.

Weakness: the dogs themselves—the lieutenant could hear them baying at the moon, barking across the distances. He assumed they were the kind of dogs who could strip a tire from a wheel in six seconds flat.

Strength? Well, all you can do is what you can do: "That's why they call it do-ty, men—duty. Got it?" Some had gotten it; some hadn't. It had been a favorite expression of one of the lieutenant's instructors at the police academy, a sallow-faced ex–street cop who used to parade back and forth in front of the class as if he were still walking a beat.

The lieutenant scaled the escarpment behind the clearing and picked his way across the rubble as carefully as he could until he found a high flat rock with a good sight line. He lay down on it and trained his binoculars on the cabin to the far right. A chimney jutted from the middle of the roof, smoke curling from it. As the lieutenant watched, a large, broad-faced white man emerged from the front door, glass in hand, firelight flickering behind him. He walked maybe ten feet away from the cabin, found a log to balance his glass on, and pulled down the zipper of his jeans. Then he let loose a stream of piss into a clump of bushes. The glass he had set down on the log glinted red in the moonlight. Wine, the lieutenant thought. He shifted his line of sight slightly now and saw two cars parked behind the bushes the man was peeing into. A woman appeared for an instant at the door and then turned back inside. That's what normal people do, the lieutenant thought: have two cars, own a country cabin or borrow one, take vacations, have wine with dinner, pee outside in the full moon, have more wine, do what they do. Or maybe it's more complicated than that. Maybe she stays at the cabin during the day while he goes into Charlottesville to the university—academicians, neo-ruralists, weird hours. Maybe it's the other way around. She teaches while he stays home and chops and splits wood. Either way, it might explain the two cars better, the wine—city affectations. Either way, too, Haddon saluted them: Be sure to respect each other in the morning. He was daydreaming again, losing sight of the prize.

Orienting himself by the moon and a chimney rock on the horizon, the lieutenant walked maybe a quarter mile to the west, until he saw a light burning. When he heard a dog begin to growl, he backed up fifty yards into a grove of trees. No high rocks to lie on this time—he circled to his left along the edge of the grove, steadied himself against a tree trunk, and raised the binoculars again. This time it was Bill and Buffy Go Country: gingham curtains framing the windows, hurricane lamps burning brightly on the tables, against the far wall one of those hardy Scandinavian stoves you can burn anything in—wood, coal, peat, bat dung—and cook anything on, from a hamburger to chicken Cordon Bleu. Buffy seemed to be doing something on a counter—kneading bread, choking a baby; it was hard to tell. Bill was draped across a brightly colored butterfly chair, reading a magazine. Except for whatever wolfhound from hell was guarding the house, it seemed a perfect picture of domestic felicity. The dog didn't bother the lieutenant—he would have had one guarding his cabin if he lived way out here, and the meaner the better. The perfect domestic felicity did. Perfect felicity was foreign to the lieutenant's domestic experience.

He moved on to the southwest this time, fighting his way around a thicket of mountain laurel, and found himself walking smack-dab into the front yard of the next cabin on his map. Nothing. No one. The door locked. He thought about kicking it in. Instead, he shone his flashlight through the window. A dozen or more red eyes shone right back at him. The lieutenant nearly jumped out of his skin. He went for his gun, only to recall that he'd left it locked in the car—and a good thing, he thought, given his edginess. He was on his own out here. Shoot and kill someone, and it would be murder, manslaughter at the least. He put his flashlight back to the window again, trying to get beyond those angry eyes. The light had put the creatures inside on edge as well: They'd drawn their mouths back, revealing teeth that looked like razor needles. Long striped tails lolled behind them. Patches around their eyes made them look like furry buccaneers, shipwrecked in the Blue Ridge. Lieutenant Haddon had stumbled upon a raccoon convention. He was glad for the glass and walls between him and the conventioneers, but he had no desire to stick around. The raccoons had gotten in there somehow, he reasoned; they could get back out again. He turned around, hot-footed it across the yard, and almost emasculated himself on a pump handle. Maybe city life wasn't so bad after all.

The last cabin made no sense whatsoever. An expensive all-terrain car—costing nearly what the lieutenant earned in a year—sat in a clearing in the front. Folding aluminum chairs were set up closer to the house, the webbing hanging loose from their frames. Beside the house, an old woman was hanging wash on a line; as near as the lieutenant could tell through his binoculars, the clothes looked like rags. Inside, he could hear an infant crying. Whatever was inside, there was no going closer.

Haddon retreated. Back at the escarpment, he settled himself into a rock that had been worn almost into the shape of a lounge chair. Sometimes the best thing to do when you have no idea what to do is nothing at all. And the stars—my God!—the stars were a sight to behold.

Really, the questions hadn't changed at all: Why had Joseph
Ngubo been here? What was that photograph trying to tell the lieutenant? He'd wait to see if any answers came.

AT A LITTLE after one o'clock by his watch, an answer came. Maybe
two answers. Haddon was balancing his way across Orion's Belt as
if it were a tightrope, getting set to leap for the Big Dipper, when
he heard a car start up near the cabin to his far right and saw a set
of headlights sweep the sky. He was already walking in that direction
when the second car ground once, caught, and began to pull away,
this one without lights.

Haddon found his way back to the same high rock and swept the
house with his binoculars again. A thin curl of smoke was drifting
from the chimney. Otherwise, nothing: Cars gone, no sign of anyone,
no cracks of light drifting from under the door or through the windows, save for a dim glow at the center, which the lieutenant imagined must be the dying fire. Why would two people leave their cabin
at one in the morning? Why would they take two cars? Why would
the second car not turn on its headlights? Everything was explicable:
an emergency, a long drive ahead, cheating lovers heading back to
their separate beds after a rustic tryst. As for the headlights, who
needed them with a moon this bright? Fine, the lieutenant thought:
Let the cabin prove its innocence.

He was standing next to the clump of bushes, standing just about
where the man had relieved himself. Slowly now, careful not to
make a sound, he began circling. He'd gone only a few feet when
he cracked his first stick, a few feet more when he tripped over a
rock. Soon, it seemed to him, he was making enough noise to bring
the neighbors running from miles around. Fine, he'd be a lost traveler. Improbable story, insane hour—together they would be suffi-
cient to get him shot on the spot, he supposed. But what the hell?
The lieutenant righted his direction, made a beeline for the front
door, and knocked once gently, a second time harder. No answer.
The third time he knocked, harder still, the door gave way at his
touch. Haddon stepped in and flattened himself against the wall to
the right of the door, trying to make himself as small as he could.

"Anyone home?" he called.

Apparently, no one was. Haddon ran his flashlight around the room, then lit a candle that sat on a table near the center, by the woodstove. The illumination was barely enough. On the other hand, there was barely anything to see. Instead of a lost traveler, the lieutenant decided to be what he was: a policeman, a cop. He sifted through the ash bucket next to the fire: nothing. Then he sifted through the banked fire itself with a shovel and a poker: nothing again. He opened one of the cabinets that stood between the bunk beds: empty. He opened another one: empty too. The third cabinet yielded a few sheets, a few towels. The towels hadn't been used, but one of the sheets had. There was the smell of a body that had gone too long without bathing. The lieutenant checked to make sure he wasn't just smelling himself. No, this was different.

The lieutenant decided to become one more thing before he gave up on the night: a cop with an attitude. He'd rip the place apart and, if anyone asked, explain that he suffered from some sort of childhood-related stress disorder. And there was this advantage: There was so little ripping apart to do here.

Haddon started with the cabinets again, methodically this time, playing his flashlight in every crevice, into every dank corner of every shelf. He shook out the other sheets, the towels. When that proved futile, he flipped the table over to see if anything was taped on the bottom and then did the same with the chairs. From there, he moved on to the bunk beds—top ones first, in case anything got dislodged and dropped down below while he was searching. He was searching the bottom bunks, trying to figure out what he would use to knife open the pillows, when he lifted a mattress and saw a card lying there, on top of the webbing.

"Daniel Brewster. Congregational Church. Springfield, Massachusetts Territory." And a telephone number. It seemed a long way for a card such as this to have traveled—the lieutenant hadn't heard of a Congregational minister since he threw one in the drunk tank his first year on the force. Then he flipped the card over and saw the handwritten message on the back: "Mall 5 A.M." It was scribbled, really, done in a hurry, he guessed. Innocuous, the lieutenant wondered, or a little cry for help? And if so, what 5 A.M.? And what Mall?

All you had to go on was what you had to go on, Haddon said to himself. All you could do was what you could do—your do-ty. All you had to go on finally was your own gut: My Mall. This 5 A.M.

And not for the first time, it occurred to District of Columbia Detective Lieutenant Clark Haddon that if he were going to make love
to a black woman, kiss a man, or trim off twenty fingertips, there
could not be a much better place to do it than where the two fin-
gertipless corpses that had led him to this spot had first been found.

Turning to leave, he felt the ground shift almost imperceptibly
beneath his feet, as if there had been a flutter in the earth's crust.
Orogeny, the lieutenant thought, earthquake, volcano—whatever it
was that Ridley said had formed this peculiar piece of the planet.
And then he realized: not ground: floor. It was the floor that had
fluttered, shifted ever so slightly. The lieutenant tapped with his
heel—here, here, here—then bent down to examine the floorboards.
When he located the seam, he dug in with his fingernails, found a
tiny purchase, and pried the section of flooring up high enough to
get a real hold on it. After he lifted the flooring and laid it to the
side, Haddon turned his flashlight on the hole beneath it, terrified
of what he might see. The pit was about as big as a shower stall;
five, maybe six feet deep—the top foot of that a wooden collar that
isolated the hole from the crawl space beneath the cabin. Dirt, he
was certain, had been packed around the collar outside to keep sound
in. A chair sat at the bottom of the hold and what looked in the
light like a chamber pot.

No bones. No bodies. Not yet.

The lieutenant checked his watch: 2:15. He'd made it down here
in three hours, driving almost as hard as his unmarked police car
could comfortably travel. If he ran back to his car now, Haddon
calculated, if he didn't get lost along the way, if he didn't get eaten
by a pack of a wild dogs or an angry bear, if he hammered the
engine from Afton Gap to where the Fourteenth Street Expressway
crossed the old canal, if the engine held and didn't throw its rods
like confetti at a Capitulation Day parade—if all that happened, then
he might just get there in time. He'd call Flannerty and Jenkins
from the car. They'd be thrilled.

28

THE MALL,
WASHINGTON, D.C.

"BEWARE OF WHAT you wish for, baby. It might come true. You've been wanting to be a man. Now you're going to have to be one."

They were sitting in Cara's car. Straight ahead, John Henry could see what he thought must be the dome of the old Union Capitol, dimly outlined against the sky. After the long, all-day run down from Massachusetts Territory and then this early-morning drive up from the Blue Ridge, John Henry had thought he might never stop riding in cars. Now he wished he hadn't stopped. He had never imagined it was this Mall she had been talking about. He'd never thought twice about this Mall in his life.

"Tell your daddy what your Cara has shown you," Cara was saying. "Tell him what you've seen. You're our ambassador, baby. You're speaking for us all, all the people who aren't, all the people who can't."

Cara took a brush from her pocketbook and tried to revive John Henry's hair where it gone flat from his sleeping with his head against the car door. She tugged at the neck and shoulders of his T-shirt, trying to get it to sit right on his long bones.

"Go four blocks straight down Constitution Avenue, straight down this street we're on, until you come to the overpass. Walk slowly, baby. Walk along that street like you've been walking on it all your life. You've got lots of time," she told him. "When you get to the overpass, turn right and follow the gravel path right under the elevated highway until you come to the canal. Then, baby, just wait. If nobody comes in half an hour, retrace your steps. Come back here. Someone will pick you up."

"My father will come," John Henry said as he got out of the car. In that he had a rock-hard faith: His father would be there.

Cara reached back to the rear seat, picked up John Henry's sweatshirt, and slid over to the window on the passenger side of the car.

"Take this, baby."

"No." It was cool outside, humid. He could already feel tiny goose bumps rising up on his skin.

"You don't want to catch a cold. Not after everything we've—"

"I'm not taking it," John Henry said, suddenly petulant, cutting Cara off. "I'll get it from you later."

Cara looked at him. She was studying him as if he were a specimen, John Henry thought, an insect in a jar.

"I'll see you soon," she told him. "You can get the sweatshirt then. I've just begun to show you the world. I'll always be your Cara, baby."

Cara leaned out the passenger window and kissed him on the cheek. Then she slid back behind the steering wheel, put the car in gear, and left him standing there. As John Henry watched her taillights disappearing down Constitution Avenue, it came to him with an absolute certainty that he would never see her again. He'd known so, he thought, ever since she hadn't put the eye pads on him back at the cabin. Maybe he had wished for that too: Maybe he had wanted to be free of Cara as much as he had wanted to be with her. If so, he thought, it was one more wish to beware of.

John Henry ached for what he was walking away from, ached for what he was walking toward. He couldn't have felt more scared if he were walking through a pit of cottonmouths. As a schoolchild, he had made the traditional visits to the shrines of northern Virginia: Mount Vernon, the Custis-Lee mansion just across the Potomac, where the blood of the great Washington mixed with the blood of the great Lee; the great Lee's birthplace at Stratford Plantation, farther away on Virginia's Northern Neck, familiar to anyone who had ever studied the back of a five-dollar bill. To the best of his recollection, though, John Henry had never been in the District of Columbia. He couldn't imagine why he might have come, nor could he dream that he would ever want to return once this was over. The street he was walking along was barely lit; the pavement was pocked and broken. Beside him, bordering the Mall, high uncut grasses, clumps of bushes. Within them—God knew—stirrings, hushed words, harsh words, moans, groans. A man walked toward John Henry now—emerged from the gloom, mumbling, with his hand out and an anxious look on his face. John Henry stepped to his left to pass but found the man directly in front of him, the hand almost touching him, eyes burrowing into his own. Shocked, John Henry walked out in the street and quickened his pace. Behind him the man stopped, turned, and screamed after him in a thin, child's voice: "Fuck you! Fuck you! Fuck you!" John Henry didn't turn around. He couldn't imagine what he had done. A few steps later, the "fuck you"s stopped as abruptly as they had begun. Now John Henry could hear eighteen-wheelers thundering above him. He looked up and saw the gridwork of the expressway etched across the sky three blocks ahead, and he started to hurry—to the safety of transportation, internal combustion, the known world. Then he remembered what Cara had told him: Walk slow, be natural, don't draw attention to yourself.

It's not even five o'clock in the morning, John Henry thought. Lunatics are walking the street. The air was so thick he had to push his way through it. Still, he slowed his pace, took a deep breath, and fought the panic. I'm on the Lawn back at the university, John Henry told himself. I'm delivering the morning newspapers. Everyone here knows me. I'm Professor Winston's son, Provost Winston's son, the Vice President's son. I'm in the one place where I'm most safe of all the places on earth. . . . It worked. He could feel the tension easing, his walk loosening up. I'm going to deliver these newspapers, he told himself, and then I'm going to go home, and there will be fresh-squeezed orange juice waiting for me. Lucy will have gotten up early and made pancakes for us both. John Henry could almost taste them now—blueberry, with maple syrup. He could smell the bacon cooking. Above him, the sky seemed to be shaking.

John Henry looked up and saw that he had made it, that he was under the safety of the expressway. He turned right now, as Cara had told him, and stopped. Directly ahead of him was a highway to hell that he knew he could never, ever, walk down. Overhead, trucks droned endlessly, in what seemed a constant parade. Ahead, a blackness, not quite pitch dark. The trestles formed a tunnel of sorts as they diminished in the distance. Somewhere down that tunnel, John

Henry told himself, I'll come to a canal. My father will be waiting there, or he'll come soon. Either way, whether he is already waiting or he's on his way, I have to go there. John Henry tried to take a step and found his shoe was nailed to the sidewalk beneath him. He tried to move the other foot and found it nailed down too. Things— human, inhuman; spectral, real—moved at the edge of the tunnel, just beyond the trestles. Waiting for him? He couldn't tell, didn't know, didn't want to find out. He thought of all the other places this meeting between himself and his father might have been set up, such as the cabin he had left just hours ago, under a full moon, a Milky Way of stars. He remembered the glimpses he had had of his father from inside that warehouse in North Adams, how he had raced from window to window as his father walked the street. Again, John Henry tried to will his feet to move. Again, he found they wouldn't. Enough, he told himself. Enough of this. Grow up. And he took off running into the darkness as fast as he could go.

There was this that really astounded him: Nothing came out of the darkness to stop him. No ooze rose off the gravel path to roll him up in its maw. The anxious mumbling face didn't reappear in front of him, this time with a knife or gun. Gigantic talons didn't drop out of the sky and pick him up like a mouse scurrying for cover. Instead, the semis kept rolling above him; the air kept parting in front of him and closing behind him. One foot went down, the other came up, and John Henry ran on and on until he almost pitched headfirst into the canal itself.

Christ, he said. Christ, I'm here.

The air seemed thicker still now, a living thing. A mist was rising off the river, rolling in over the Mall. In the first faint rays of the morning sun, he found that he was standing on a gravel path, on the edge of the collapsing stone wall of the canal. On the far side of the canal, tall grass and weeds grew right to the wall's edge. On this side, a two-to-three-foot strip of mowed grass flanked the gravel path before the weeds and brambles began. East and west, the path disappeared quickly into the mist. There was a scrabbling in the canal beside him, but nothing living revealed itself—nothing human, nothing otherwise. Still, even the atoms of the air seemed alive with possibilities.

John Henry caught his breath and willed his heart into silence. Cara had told him to wait, but he would do more than wait, he told himself. He would stand so still that he would become a kind of human tree sprouting by this canal embankment. He would live inside himself while he waited, because at that moment he knew of no other way to survive. And he would do so for however long it took. What is a minute, what an eternity, when you're waiting in some urban wild for your father to show up? John Henry was alone, but he had his faith, his sure knowledge: His father would come. He would come.

And then: a crunch somewhere down the gravel path to the west, a footfall, maybe. Another crunch. A foot for certain this time. John Henry turned and saw a kind of density in the mist, a shape undefined. He felt his heart rise, unseal itself, open up. The footfalls were louder now. And now a voice, so faint that it might have been a breeze, but a voice all the same, was calling out: "John Henry? John Henry?"

The shape grew closer and slowly separated itself from its background. The voice got not so much louder as more distinct: raspy, pained, as if someone were trying to whisper the words and was spitting them instead.

Wrong shape, John Henry thought.

Wrong voice.

Something had gone terribly wrong.

THE SEMI HAD overturned just north of Fredericksburg—hit a car or been hit by one. In the pulsating lights of the emergency vehicles, Spencer would see where it had swerved off the shoulder and scraped the embankment on the right side of the road. Both northbound lanes were completely blocked. Along the left shoulder, there was barely enough room to pull around the wreck. When Spencer's turn finally came, he could see a car lying in the culvert that split the median. The car was mostly crushed, mostly burned. He had no idea how many people might have been in it or if any were alive.

Spencer had thought about trying to circumvent the wreck on the right shoulder. Others were doing it, but as he got closer to the overturned truck, Spencer could see that a trooper had set up a roadblock and was writing tickets. Maybe, he thought, he could enlist the trooper to help him get around the wreck some other way— stop traffic in the southbound lanes, reverse the tides so that the

President could get where he was going. But the trooper would probably think him an impostor, a nut—worse, a nut with a badly out-of-date driver's license. The name was famous, but there was more than one Spencer Lee in America, and the address on the license read Tappahannock, Virginia, not the White House. He couldn't afford the delay while he tried to prove his bona fides to a skeptical highway patrolman. He couldn't, in fact, afford to blow his cover. In the end, he chose the only real course open to him: Sit. Wait. Stew.

Spencer was taking his painkiller on the half dose, one every four hours. He wanted to stay alert and found the pain in its own way invigorating. Every time he shifted in his seat, another nuance of agony banged him to his senses. His intention had been to arrive in Washington at four-thirty, drive around a bit, and "case the joint," although he had no idea for what. Then the wreck: twenty minutes idling stock-still, forty minutes inching forward, the inevitable rubbernecking slowing everything down. The President blamed no one. Who could resist driving by such an event slowly, thankful for the grace of God, rejoicing in the sheer fact of being alive?

As Spencer left the wreck in the rearview mirror and picked up speed, the car clock read 4:37. He estimated that he had another hour of driving ahead of him, so he pressed harder on the accelerator. The wreck had rendered a small advantage: Half the troopers in Virginia seemed to have gathered at the scene. That left fewer for the miles that lay ahead, and all Spencer's fellow travelers seemed ready to make up time too.

It was 5:22 when he peeled off the expressway, found the old Fourteenth Street Bridge, and took that across the Potomac. At 5:27 he pulled the car to the curb on the Independence Avenue side of the Mall near Seventeenth Street. Moments later, he took off running, headed for the footbridge that crossed the canal three blocks west of the expressway. The Independence Avenue approach was Spencer's one concession to caution. Nathan had told him the north side of the canal, and the canal cut closer to Constitution Avenue, in any event. But Spencer had had enough training in military logistics to know that you came in from the less anticipated angle whenever you could. He wished he had worn his jogging shoes, tennis sneakers, anything but the loafers he was trying to run in. He also wished that he'd taken more of the damn pain pills. The muscle tear was growing from a needle to a knife. What came after a knife? He didn't want to know.

As he ran, Spencer rehearsed: "John Henry, your father has had a heart attack. I don't know where you've been, what this meeting is about, but he sent me in his place. Let me take you to him." As he rehearsed, Spencer thought: I know so little about this boy.

"John Henry?" he was calling now into the mist. "John Henry?" Stumbling his way forward, trying to rewind the clock by sheer force of will: You will not have left, time has not passed. Dear God, don't let me be too late. And then something like a tree unfolded in the mist right in front of him and took a step toward him.

"You're not my father," it said. "Why? Why?"

My God, Spencer thought, it's been—what?—four months since I've seen John Henry. He's become a man.

"Listen," he said. "Listen, John Henry."

"Who are you? Why are you here? Where's my father?"

The President reached out and tried to fold John Henry in his arms, but he misjudged the distance. The second time he got him.

"Listen to me. There's not much time." As he drew John Henry toward him, Spencer could feel something tear a little more.

Inside the embrace, John Henry panicked. He tried to wriggle free but couldn't. Whoever had grabbed him kept saying, "Listen! Listen! Listen!" in a fierce whisper. To what? John Henry wondered. Why? Where was his father? Why hadn't he come? John Henry had trusted—trusted absolutely—that his father would be here. Now? He worked his right arm free at the elbow, pulled back, and hit the man who was holding him with a short blow, square in the middle of the abdomen. Spencer fell as if he'd been clubbed with a brick. He went down on his hands and knees.

"Listen, please, John Henry," he said, looking up at him now. "Your father—"

And then John Henry realized who it was.

"Why are you here?" It was all he could say.

"I've been trying to tell you that. Maybe if you could help me stand."

And so it was that the President stood on the embankment of the Washington City Canal, one arm over John Henry's shoulder for support, and told him about his father.

"He's had a heart attack, John Henry."

"Is he . . . ?"

"He's in the hospital, in Richmond." Spencer suddenly felt the need to be honest, not to sugar-coat the truth. "Everyone is hoping for the best, but it's hard to say, hard to say. Your dad's in bad shape."

As he talked, Spencer did the math in his head. If Dr. Ashbury had been right, there were twenty-four hours left that would spell the difference for Nathan: dead or alive.

"I don't know what this is about," he said, throwing a hand out to the canal, the Mall, whatever set of circumstances had brought John Henry here, whatever had taken him away from his home. "It doesn't matter to me right now. Let me take you to your father. I've got a car. We need to leave right now."

They were a dozen steps down the gravel path—Spencer's arm over John Henry's shoulder, John Henry's arm around his waist, trying to walk for the President as much as he could—when John Henry heard a metallic click behind him and a voice cry out: "Sean! Sean!" And as he spun out from under the President's arm and hurled himself over Spencer's back, John Henry was sure, absolutely certain, that the voice also was saying: "No! No! Don't!"

The bullet hit him in the shoulder, spun him to the side, and sent him buckling into the grass beside the path. Spencer turned to see the burst of red already blossoming over John Henry's T-shirt and threw himself on top of him just as the gun fired again. My God, he thought, the sound! The sound! Spencer had hunted all his life, but nothing had ever sounded anywhere near this loud. Blood seemed to be pouring down his head.

There was more gunfire now, from the east, back up the path: one, two, three shots. Spencer heard someone running near them, below them. The canal! It came to him in one of those flashes of understanding that exist outside time: They had been shot at from the canal. Whoever was running in the canal was beside them now— had come to a dead standstill. We're going to be shot at point-blank range, Spencer thought, and he scrabbled to gather up John Henry as if he were a mother trying to return a baby to her womb.

"The Lord is my shepherd," Spencer began to say, his lips moving, the words barely escaping his mouth. "I shall not want . . ." He could hear the person in the canal breathing, could almost feel the breath against him. How near can we be? he wondered. Three feet? Less?

Spencer had just gotten to "in the valley of the shadow of death" when he heard what seemed to him like a sharp intake of breath and assumed the person was stilling his nerves. The President found John Henry's head and cradled it against his chest. Then the footsteps began again, turned into a run, and the run went on into the early morning, somewhere to the west, just as the first sunshine from the east fought its way through the mist.

Spencer was contemplating the miracle of it all when the air around him simply exploded. This time the gunfire was everywhere.

THE GOOD NEWS, the lieutenant thought, was that his car had not actually broken down. The bad news was that it was like any car purchased by the District of Columbia and issued to its detective force: bought on the cheap and poorly constructed and maintained. At Culpeper, halfway back to Washington, the engine had begun to buck over fifty-five miles an hour. By Warrenton, twenty-five miles away, he was down to four of his six cylinders and a top speed of just over thirty. Still, it was forward motion.

He had called Jenkins from the car, awakening him from a sound sleep, awakening Mrs. Jenkins too, which was trouble but happily not his own. Jenkins could call Flannerty and suffer his volcanic abuse. The two of them were to position themselves on Constitution Avenue, under the expressway, parked across the street from the Mall. The lieutenant wanted them in place by 4:45. He would meet them there. In the meantime: stay low, take note of anyone entering the Mall from beneath the expressway, and stop anyone leaving it. The lieutenant expected none of the latter; mostly he hoped Jenkins and Flannerty wouldn't get hurt.

It was 5:20 when the lieutenant's car limped in. The street was quiet save for the usual furtive rustlings at its margins. Only one person had entered the Mall down the expressway corridor while Jenkins and Flannerty had been watching: "A black male," Flannerty said, shining his flashlight on a pad, reading from his notes, "approximately six feet tall. Hesitated, then raced in. Time of entry: 4:58 A.M." For crissake, the lieutenant wondered, did he have to read every word?

He sent Jenkins down the right side of the trestles, Flannerty down the left. I've probably watched too many westerns, he thought, as he walked alone in the center of the gravel path. Not for the first time, but rarely before so clearly, the lieutenant wondered what would become of the person who had been Clark Haddon when he was gone: His few possessions, his little pension, his tiny nest egg, would go to his mother and sister. But his mother was nearing eighty; his sister already had beaten the mortality tables for Down's syndrome. Neither was likely to live all that much longer. Curtains, finally, for them; curtains for me; curtains for us all. A tiny genetic strain wiped out. Jenkins wasn't likely to sing the lieutenant's praises to his two sons. Even had he been capable of it, Flannerty wouldn't wax lyrical about his old boss. Haddon's ex-wife would remember him only so long as she needed something to torture herself with, which in her case, granted, might be forever. Who else was there?

Haddon and his two wingmen were halfway down the corridor now, halfway to the canal. Finally, the lieutenant thought, all you have to go on is your gut. All you can do is your do-ty. He slipped his nine-millimeter pistol out of its belt holster and was just thumbing the safety off when the first shot was fired.

To his right, Jenkins flattened himself against a trestle. On the other side, Flannerty rolled once in the gravel, lost his flashlight, and came up in a crouch, fumbling for his pistol. Between them, the lieutenant took off in a run dead ahead—willing to bet his life that the gunfire hadn't been aimed at them. The second shot gave him a line of sight. The lieutenant dropped to one knee, fired at where the flash had been—one, two, three—and was up running again. By the time he got to the canal, he could hear footsteps fading away off to the west, already making for long distances.

The lieutenant played his flashlight after the footsteps and saw nothing. If whoever it was followed the canal, he would already be at the river. From there, he could hide in the marsh or row to Virginia. If he'd left the canal, he could have turned either way, crossed the Mall, and disappeared already into the early-morning traffic. If he was simply waiting out there in the half light of dawn, the advantages all belonged to him.

"Lieutenant, you want us to go after him?" It was Jenkins, suddenly beside him.

The lieutenant emptied his pistol down the canal in the direction of the footsteps; fit in a new clip and emptied that too. He'd be deaf for weeks now; Flannerty and Jenkins too. But deaf beat the alternative. And you took care of your own first.

"Naw," the lieutenant said. "Forget it. It's a fucking rat party down there." What was he going to do? Get them killed? For what?

The sun was just beginning to rise, the lieutenant realized. He had thought the night was never going to end. He looked down the gravel path beside the canal and saw something stir in the mist, a lump of something human. The night hadn't ended; it was just stretching into daylight.

By the time the lieutenant got there, the lump was sitting up, unfolding into two. The lieutenant saw a white man cradling a black teenager in his arms and wondered what the hell could possibly be going on. Then he bent down with his flashlight and saw blood spreading over the boy's shirt, blood matting the white man's hair, streaking his face. Did every illicit love have to end up on his turf? the lieutenant asked himself. And did they all have to come to this? Haddon stepped back now and studied the face some more as it squinted up into his beam. Jesus, he thought, will it never end?

"I'm—"

"Yes, sir," Haddon said, snapping to attention and identifying himself. He'd spent his first three years out of high school in the Marines. Attention is what you stood at in the presence of your commander in chief. "Sir, I know who you are, sir." He thought about saluting and abandoned it as ludicrous.

"Sir? What . . ." Haddon was squatting, half shouting. Everyone was speaking too loud, ears ringing. Like all crime scenes, this one had its own illogic.

"The boy, Lieutenant. Could you have a look at him, please."

Behind him, Haddon could hear Flannerty or Jenkins, he couldn't tell which, saying: "Christ, isn't that . . . ?"

"Check the canal," he called out over his shoulder to them. "Under the expressway." It seemed like an order he'd been giving for half his life.

The lieutenant ripped the boy's T-shirt open from neck to ribs and all the way over to the side. Then he peeled it back as gently as he could, handed his flashlight to the President, and moved in closer. The wound was high on the shoulder and clean as could be. Because it had been fired from below, the bullet appeared to have ripped through only flesh, no bone. A half inch higher, a half inch to the right, and it would have missed altogether. As it was, the entry and exit wounds were close enough together to clasp with a single hand. Blood was trickling out of both now, already clotting. The lieutenant felt his pockets for a handkerchief, then realized that the President was handing him his own. He folded it, draped it over the wound, and told Spencer Lee to press down as hard as he could—heel of his hand on the entry, fingers on the exit. As Spencer did so, John Henry jerked up with a start, as if he'd been having a nightmare. He saw the President and Haddon, half closed his eyes again, then opened them wide and settled back into the Spencer's arm.

The boy would be fine, the lieutenant thought. He was young; he had his health. Most important, he had most of his blood still inside him. The lieutenant had seen too many people about whom none of the above could be said.

"It's remarkable, isn't it, Lieutenant." The President was studying his windbreaker, John Henry's T-shirt. "You can't tell where his blood leaves off and mine begins. It all looks just the same."

"Always has, sir. Blood's blood. It's just a matter of how slow or fast it pours out of you."

Lieutenant Haddon took his flashlight now, shone it on the President, and saw blood, lots of it. By the looks of it, Spencer Lee had been grazed by a bullet right at the hairline. A scalp wound, too many capillaries forced by the skull to live too close to the surface. Playgrounds across America were always filled with little boys bleeding the same way. An inch or two lower, and the President's brains would have been leaking out.

"We were lucky," he heard the President saying, to himself, maybe.

"How?"

"Whoever it was, he was a pretty lousy shot."

"Almost everyone is, Mr. President. Semiautomatics make it easy, but with a single shot, you've really got to concentrate to kill someone. Or just get lucky."

Behind him, he heard Jenkins shouting: "Lieutenant, you got one of them."

SO FAR AS the lieutenant could tell, he'd shot the man in the neck, the carotid artery, something of the sort—the most astounding shot of his twenty years on the force, almost unimaginable, sheer luck.

The man was draining out now. Leave him where he was, and there would be a rat feast rivaling Washington's best. Beside the dead man, on the canal floor: lengths of rope, rolls of duct tape, wire, a black cloth bag with a drawstring. The size of a man's head, the lieutenant realized. A Buck knife, open, sat in the middle of a puddle of blood. A pistol—nine millimeter, like Haddon's—lay on slightly higher ground, next to the dead man's hand. The lieutenant took a pencil out of his pocket, slipped it through the trigger guard, and picked the pistol up. The barrel smelled of cordite; he could still feel the last traces of heat in the metal.

Haddon squatted beside the man now, unwilling to put a knee on the ground here. The man's face was white, broad, strong, going gray in a hurry. The lieutenant dropped his gaze down now, not really wanting to. Something was all wrong with the wound. Bullets rip into flesh, or they slip into it and rip out the other side. This one had done neither. Haddon took a handful of the man's hair, pushed him forward just slightly at the shoulders, and tilted the head back. A line ran across his neck, exact as the horizon. He hadn't been shot. His neck had been slit from ear to ear.

"Sean."

The lieutenant heard a voice above him, turned, and looked up. The boy and the President were standing there, leaning on each other for support.

"Sean," the boy said again, recognizing every bit of it from his shopping trip in North Adams: the rope, the wire, the tape, even the drawstring bag that he himself had finally found while Cara stopped to talk with a millworker she knew. He could feel the weight of the packages in his hand, the hot south wind of that morning blowing in his face.

"His name was Sean," the boy said. "At least that's what he called himself." Then, as the President held him up, John Henry turned and vomited into the grass beside him, gagged once, vomited again, and was done with it. There was that one advantage to having almost nothing in his stomach.

Spencer was patting John Henry with one hand and covering his bullet wound with the other, when the lieutenant scrambled out of the canal.

"Looks like someone wanted to wrap you up like a Christmas present, Mr. President." He was nodding down at the ropes, the tape, and the wire.

"Not me, Lieutenant, but close enough."

"How about the other one?" Haddon said now to John Henry. "The one who got away. Who's he?"

"She," John Henry tried to say. "She—" And couldn't. What did it matter what her name was? What did it matter who she was or where she might be? Cara was going to cease to be Cara, and John Henry would never see her again. Had this been what everything that had passed between them was about? John Henry delivering his father somewhere like a sack of potatoes?

"DRAGO?" the lieutenant asked.

John Henry nodded once: Yes.

At least there's that, the lieutenant thought. He'd picked up a scent, followed it, and come back to where he began. It wasn't quite closure, but at least it was a sane progression. Sometimes two plus two still equaled four.

"She tried to kill you and the President," Haddon said.

John Henry closed his eyes, saw the slice along Sean's throat like a second mouth, and remembered the dream where Sean was cutting into *his* throat, opening it like a door.

"I think she might have saved our lives."

There'd be time for questions later, the lieutenant thought, time to get the boy away from the President, time to see what he could say (a great deal, Haddon suspected), time to see what he would say (less, maybe a great deal less).

"Well, at the least, the two of them seem to have been in the packaging business. That rope and wire—they were planning to take at least one of you with them." But the boy had gone mute.

The lieutenant turned to the President now: "Sorry for the delay, sir. An ambulance is on the way. We just want to run you and . . ."

"John Henry," the President volunteered.

"You and John Henry by the hospital for a quick checkup, dress those wounds, clean you both up. Nothing personal, sir, but you're a sight."

"Wrong, Lieutenant."

"Sir?"

"We're going to a hospital, but in Richmond, not here."

"But, sir—"

"And guess who's driving us, Lieutenant Haddon?"

"Mr. President, it's really none of my business, but does anyone in the government know where you are right now?"

"Only the person you're taking us to see, and right now he's the only person in the government I care about."

THIRTY-FIVE MINUTES LATER, Clark Haddon swung left off the old Fourteenth Street Bridge, caught the entry ramp, and muscled his way onto the interstate, bound for Richmond, one hundred ten miles to the south. He was driving the President's rental car, power everything, including under the hood.

They had gone to the lieutenant's car first—Jenkins and Flannerty practically carrying the President, Haddon practically carrying John Henry. Haddon had soaked their wounds in hydrogen peroxide from the emergency medical kit he kept in his trunk and dressed both wounds as well as he could. The pain of the hydrogen peroxide had jolted John Henry awake and made him scream. Good, the lieutenant thought. He was of the no-pain, no-gain school when it came to doctoring: Medicine had to hurt to achieve its ends. He cleaned the blood away wherever he could. The President now looked less like a serial killer or an escapee from a hospital for the criminally insane, more like a vagrant who had an unfortunate accident with a Mixmaster.

Be thankful for small miracles, the lieutenant thought. In his experience, there were no others.

When John Henry and the President were ready to travel, Haddon had had Jenkins call in yet another murder on the old Mall. The two patrolmen would wait for the medical examiner and the evidence wagon—both knew their way all too well.

"Remember," Haddon had told them, "all you found was the one body. I'll fill in the picture when I get back."

Jenkins nodded. He just wanted to finish this up and get back to bed. As for Flannerty, forgetting came naturally to him.

Just beyond Alexandria, the President reached awkwardly into his pocket and extracted a vial of pills. In the rearview mirror, Haddon saw Spencer Lee tip out two for John Henry, two for himself. They swallowed them dry.

"Your father said to tell he was sorry, John Henry. Sorry he couldn't spend more time with you, sorry he didn't listen more."

Tears started up in John Henry's eyes. "He doesn't have anything to be sorry about," he finally said. "None of this was about that."

"He said to tell you that he loves you."

"I know," John Henry said.

"He made me promise I'd tell you that when I saw you, but he'll tell you all that himself in just a few hours." Spencer said it with conviction and hoped it was true.

The lieutenant drove on. For the most part, he'd always given politics a wide berth. He knew as little about the private lives of the leading public figures as he could, and he had no idea who John Henry's father was or what his passengers were talking about.

Just north of Richmond, Haddon pulled off the road and fed a fresh clip into his police nine millimeter. The nation's capital was no proof against bad people. Then he reached over the seat and shook the President awake.

"What hospital are we going to, sir?"

Spencer Lee looked as if he'd just stuck his finger in a live electrical socket. He'd been dreaming that he was wrapped in coils of heavy rope from his waist to his neck, like a cartoon character. Someone he couldn't see was leading him by a leash through a city he couldn't recognize, a place, by the looks of it, deep in the Northeast Industrial Zone. Nestled against him now—his good shoulder dug into the President's chest, his bad one wrapped in Leo Manzini's windbreaker and cradled against the seat back—John Henry was snoring softly. Chum, Spencer thought: little fish and big fish. Leo had been right all along.

RICHMOND

THEY'D STOPPED ONE more time before the hospital, while Spencer stood at a roadside telephone booth in the roar of the midmorning traffic and called Wormley's cell phone. If the President were a dog, the lieutenant thought, there would be only one thing to do with something that raggedy-looking: one bullet, just behind the ear.

John Henry was awake now. He'd even found a position that didn't cause him too much discomfort. The President's pills, whatever they might be, were powerful medicine.

"That's not a sight you see every day," Haddon said over the front seat.

"Sir?"

The lieutenant signaled out the side window. "That's the most powerful man in the world, son. If he wanted to, he could have you and me packed up in a crate and shipped to Antarctica. Or he could arrange to have our taxes forgotten about for a year or a lifetime, not that it would do me a lot of good. Your own tax situation I don't feel competent to speak for." John Henry smiled—a start, the lieutenant thought. "And there he is, for God's sake, feeding a quarter into the damn public telephone and calling who the hell knows. That's why I say it's not a sight you see every day."

"Rarely, I'd say," John Henry answered, giddy on the pills and amazed at his own survival, "if ever at all."

The lieutenant took a long look at Spencer this time. Though Haddon had been up something like twenty-seven straight hours, he figured he had another ten or fifteen hours in him. If nothing else, insomnia was good training for sleeplessness. Spencer was talking hard into the mouthpiece now. His blood-matted hair was covered by the Irish walking hat. Still, the sight was simply too much.

"You know, come to think of it," the lieutenant said after deep consideration, "it's rarer than a pregnant pope."

John Henry had laughed himself into tears by the time Spencer very carefully settled himself back in place. Pills or no pills, Spencer had had enough of pain. For now, he'd had just about enough of civilian life too. Spencer suddenly missed limousines and soft leather interiors. He missed having his own cell phone at the ready and minions at his feet. I've gotten soft, he thought. Life has been too kind to me. He wondered what in the name of hell John Henry was finding so funny.

"Straight ahead to the next traffic light and then a left, Lieutenant Haddon." The President knew his way to Tompkins Memorial in his sleep. Frannie had undergone her chemo there.

"Mr. Wormley is having the south entrance to the hospital secured. A doctor will be waiting to look at John Henry's shoulder." Haddon had no idea who Mr. Wormley was, but south he could locate once they found the hospital.

Spencer turned to John Henry. "Your father is holding his own. He knows who he is and where he is. That's all good."

Spencer didn't tell John Henry what else Wormley had said: that every time he rallied himself to consciousness, Nathan asked if the President had come yet. "He's coming, dear. He's coming," Lucinda kept assuring him, according to Wormley. Now he *was* coming, and not alone.

At the hospital, Spencer helped Lieutenant Haddon get John Henry onto solid ground. Then he gritted his teeth against the pain, bent forward, and climbed out of the car himself.

"Good God, Mr. President!" Wormley was waiting, stiff at attention. "You never mentioned—"

Wormley looked down wistfully at the exquisite wool, the beautifully muted plaid, of his suit—it had come from an exclusive London tailor—before grabbing Spencer's arm and putting it across his own shoulder. With his other hand, Wormley pulled a cell phone out of his coat pocket and began to punch in a number.

"We'll get Dr. Ashbury over ASAP to have a look at you."

Spencer took the phone out of his scheduler's hand and snapped it closed.

"Maybe afterward, Mr. Wormley."

"After?"

"After we get John Henry cleaned up and where he belongs. I'm going to live. Believe me."

Inside the hospital, Spencer stuck by John Henry's side, watching as the doctor examined and bandaged his shoulder, watching even more closely as an orderly used what seemed like buckets of alcohol to clean the blood off his torso, his arms, his head and hair. When the orderly was finished, John Henry was fitted with hospital pants and tunic.

"Your turn, sir," Wormley said.

"Not yet." John Henry glowed. He was gift-wrapped as well as he could be. It was time to go.

The corridor outside the Vice President's room had been blocked at one end and turned into a kind of waiting room. Lucinda was sitting there when they arrived, a magazine open on her lap. She looked up and gasped.

HE'S BEEN DELIVERED: It was all Lucinda could think. He's been delivered.

She hugged her son—carefully, from his left side—circled him, examined him as if he were a Thanksgiving turkey she was considering buying. She'd been right to worry: He was too thin. He hadn't eaten nearly enough, or any of the proper things at all—of that she was sure. Lucinda placed her head against his chest and listened for the wheeze he'd had as a boy: Thank God, at least not that. *He's been delivered.*

"Mom," John Henry said. "I'm so sorry."

"Hush," she said, laying a finger on his lips and another on her own. "Hush. I don't want to hear sorry right now."

She raised his hospital tunic—dear Lord, how his ribs stuck out—and had a look at his bandage, as if she were Florence Nightingale herself, as if Lucinda Winston had been dressing bullet wounds her entire life.

Satisfied with the hospital's work, she dropped the tunic, hugged

John Henry, and kissed him on the cheek—all from his left, everything from his left. John Henry's right sleeve was pinned to the tunic to support the arm inside; his bandaged right shoulder was sacrosanct. Tears were streaming down Lucinda's cheeks.

"I'll have plenty to say to you later on, young man," she said, "and I may use some words, John Henry, that you didn't think your mother knew." Reaching up now, she grabbed his left ear, twisting it as if she meant to pull it off. "Words, if the truth be known, that I'm embarrassed to know. Words that for the life of me I can't imagine having learned. But for now, you just hush. You just hush."

Lucinda had no illusions that this was the same boy who had left her home seven weeks earlier. She had no idea what he had been through while he was away—she had only Nathan's "apparition" to go on as to where he might have been. She didn't even know why a bandage covered his right shoulder or why his right arm was supported. All that was for later. What Lucinda did know was that her son had been delivered and that whatever he had done, whatever he had seen, and wherever he had been were bound to have made him a different person. You don't erase such experiences; you don't get people back from them. She just wanted to make sure all the parts were there. She'd figure out later on what boy, what man, he had become.

She hugged him again. This time she felt him hugging her back with his good left arm. That was enough, she knew; that was enough for now.

Lucinda opened her eyes and for the first time realized that she and John Henry were not alone.

"Spencer," she said. "Oh, Spencer, how can I ever—" And focusing harder: "Dear Lord in heaven, Spencer Lee, what happened to you? You look a fright."

And then, seeing the man standing just beside the President, Lucinda turned away from her son, held her hand out, and advanced.

"You'll pardon my manners, I hope," she said. "I'm Lucinda Winston. I presume you've already met my son, John Henry."

And for Clark Haddon, at least one piece of the puzzle fell into place. He was "disconnected" from the national news, as he liked to say, disenchanted with politicians generally, in the way that only a career policeman can be, but Haddon hadn't lived under a rock these last seven years.

The lieutenant settled into one of the two chairs in the far corner of the makeshift waiting room and opened up a *Richmond Times* that had been left on the seat.

"GO SEE HIM now, honey," Lucinda was saying to her son. "When he wakes up, I want him to see you there."

As she opened the door to Nathan's room, Spencer saw John Henry take a deep breath before starting slowly forward. Nathan was lying half propped up, his eyes closed, still as still could be. Two tubes ran into his arms; another tube fed him oxygen through his nose. Monitors were everywhere.

"Just wait for him, honey. He'll wake up." Lucinda closed the door again, shutting the two of them inside, granting them privacy.

"Anything new, Lucinda?" Spencer asked.

"No. It stays the same. 'He's doing as well as can be expected.' 'This count is holding steady at so-and-so. That count has slipped slightly.' 'We're upping one thing, modifying another, taking it all under advisement.' All gobbledygook, Spencer, but who can blame them? If I had their job, I'd hide behind language too."

She sank into her chair, exhausted. "How can I ever thank you, Spencer? Dear heavens, what can I possibly say?"

Spencer wanted to tell her that there was nothing to thank him for. He had done it for Nathan, whom he already owed so much, and he had received in return the greatest gift he could be given: He'd begun—only begun—to learn about his own limits. Spencer sat in the chair beside Lucinda's, put his hand over hers where it rested on the chair arm, and said all that it was within him to say.

"Seeing you with John Henry again is more thanks than I ever deserve, Lucinda. It's the happiest thing I've ever seen. I'm sorry I've been such a poor friend."

Lucinda glanced at him, uncertain of what he had meant just as Spencer was uncertain where it had come from. Nathan's heart attack, the stacked deck on Nathan's first visit to North Adams, Spencer's own professional lifetime of compromise . . . Introspection didn't become him. Besides, he was tired and filthy.

"Now," he said, rallying, the campaign spirit back in his voice, "we need to make sure Nathan pulls through. And he's going to, Lucinda; he's *going* to."

The President's voice was suddenly full of that quiet conviction Lucinda had heard so many times before, in so many different places: We're *going* to get this waterway built before our term is complete. We're *going* to carry the Senate even if we lose the House. Well, she thought, Spencer is a politician. He wants the greatest good for the greatest number of people. And he wants everyone to love him. For her part, Lucinda had spent too many of the past eighteen hours at Nathan's side, staring at those monitors, to think that her husband's fate had much to do with what other people wanted.

SPENCER HEARD A slight modulation in the air, a practiced "ahem." When he looked up, Wormley was standing at the door, cell phone in hand.

"Lieutenant Haddon will need to talk with John Henry eventually, Lucinda," the President said as he rose. "He has his job to do."

"Of course," she said, already half asleep. There was one more thing to talk with the President about, but Lucinda was pared down to essences: She was taking her deaths one by one.

"It's the secretary of state, Mr. President," Wormley explained when they were out of earshot in the corridor. "He wants to know if it would be all right for him to have a drink with lunch. 'Something noonish,' he said, 'like a Bloody Mary.'"

Finally, Spencer had a laugh. It's been weeks, he thought, far too long.

"Tell him to have his drink, Mr. Wormley, and one for me. And tell him I'd like a generous dab of horseradish in mine and not to go light on the vodka. And now I think we'd better go spruce me up a bit. If the secretary of state is going to get plastered at lunch, I'd better start looking a little more presidential."

At last! Wormley thought.

SPENCER WAS ALMOST to the examining room Wormley had pointed him toward when he heard a voice behind him.

"Dad!"

Who told him? Spencer thought. There had been no need. Then he turned and found all the explanation he wanted.

"Dad, what happened to *you?*"

Jason had broken into a half run. Lucy Winston was trailing five yards behind him.

"It's a long story," Spencer said, wrapping his son in a bear hug, grimacing as Jason hugged him back. "Too long for now. And I imagine you're not here to see your old dad anyway."

He broke off now and hugged Lucy lightly from the side, afraid of contaminating, with his own filthy clothes, something so pure and beautiful as she looked.

"I'm hopeful, Lucy. I really am," he said. "Your dad's a fighter."

"Have you seen him?"

"Only from the hallway. He was resting." Resting, wired, trussed, Spencer thought. He wanted to prepare Lucy for the surprise of seeing her father, and then it suddenly occurred to him: There would be more than one surprise.

"Mrs. Winston called Lucy this morning," Jason was explaining. "I—I offered to drive her. You shouldn't drive in situations like this, not when you're worrying about your father. Lucy . . ." Jason never ended the sentence, sins of omission tangling in his mind with those of commission. What to say? How to say it? His father rode to the rescue.

"Before you go in to see your father, Lucy, I think I'd better tell you that long story I was going to save." He put an arm around each of them and turned them back up the corridor until they came to an alcove. "I'll try to leave out the whaling chapters." Hearing his dad's old *Moby-Dick* joke, Jason laughed in spite of himself as he sat on a short bench. Lucy sat down beside him as Spencer pulled a metal-framed chair up to face them.

"To begin with, Lucy, your father's not alone in his room."

"Mother—"

"Not your mother, Lucy. John Henry's in the room with your father. He's been shot in the shoulder. Not bad, not bad." Lucy's eyes were wide; she was half out of her seat already. "He'll be fine; he already is. Before you go in there, though, you probably ought to have some idea of what's happened these last few days."

LUCINDA WAS DOZING, a foot in two worlds, when Lucy and Jason slipped quietly through the door. She rose and hugged her daughter, both of them crying silently.

"Your father is hanging on as best he can," Lucinda said, then added a phrase she had come to loathe in the last half day. "He's doing as well as anyone could hope under the circumstances."

Lucy had so many things she wanted to say to her mother, so many things that needed saying, and no idea of how to say a single one of them. She kept quiet and looked for a clue.

"He's been delivered," Lucinda whispered in her daughter's ear. "John Henry—he's been delivered."

"I know," Lucy said. "I know. President Lee told us."

Lucinda caught the "us" and saw Jason standing awkwardly in the doorway. She nodded at him and turned back to her daughter:

"I'd almost given up hope."

Lucinda walked Lucy over to the door of Nathan's room and opened it. John Henry was standing at the foot of his father's bed with his left shoulder held back—a soldier half at attention. The sight was a balm to Lucinda's wounds.

"Go on," she said to Lucy, in a voice so soft you would have thought there was an infant asleep on the bed. She gave Lucy a slight push at the back, had another quick look—her daughter and son together in the same room—and closed the door behind her. Really, she couldn't believe her eyes. If only Nathan could survive . . .

"Mrs. Winston . . ." Jason said when she had settled into her chair, slipping back into the half world she had just risen from.

Lucinda opened her eyes now and shook her head: No. She wasn't dealing with that right now either.

LUCINDA HAD ARRIVED at the hospital a little after three the afternoon before, shepherded by Mr. Wormley. She'd sat with Nathan while he was awake off and on, and when he was awake, mostly lucid. A little after ten, she called Lucy to tell her that her father seemed to be "out of the woods." Lucy would come in the morning, they had agreed.

"I'll have Mr. Wormley arrange something, dear."

"No, Mommy, no," Lucy had answered. "I'll get a ride."

Fine, Lucinda thought. Fine. There were only so many things she could worry about.

At five in the morning, Nathan had awakened and yelled, "John Henry, John Henry, where are you?" before going silent again. A

few minutes later, it occurred to Lucinda that Nathan had nothing
to wear but the clothes he had gone to work in the previous day—
ripped to shreds by the emergency team, or so it looked—and the
pale-green hospital gown he now had on. She called Lucy to tell her
to bring her father's bathrobe, but she got only the answering machine. Five minutes later, she called and got the machine again. Why
wasn't her daughter answering? There were telephones in Lucy's
bedroom, in the upstairs hall, in the master bedroom, the kitchen,
the front hall, Lucinda's office, Nathan's office. There were phones
everywhere, and Pavilion Three wasn't that big a house. If Lucy was
on her way to Richmond, why had she left before five in the morning, an insane hour? By six-thirty—no Lucy in Richmond, no Lucy
answering the phone at home—Lucinda had become distraught.
Lucy had been working with Jason; maybe he would have some idea
of where she was.

Lucinda walked across the makeshift waiting room outside Nathan's door, knocked on Mr. Wormley's door, and asked him for
Jason Lee's number. Wormley seemed to be instantly awake, as if
waiting to see what he could do next for Lucinda. Back in Nathan's
room, she called Jason's apartment and got him on the second ring.
Two hours later, Lucinda could remember every word.

"Jason, it's Lucinda Winston. I'm terribly sorry to bother you, but
I've been trying to phone Lucy at the house."

"Mrs. Winston?" Jason's voice had been cloudy with sleep.

"Do you have any idea, Jason—any idea at all—where Lucy
might be?"

Lucinda could hear Jason picking something up and putting it
down again.

"It's six-forty, Mrs. Winston. In the morning."

"Jason, it's an emergency. I *need* to speak with Lucy. Just think.
Did you work on the paper together yesterday evening? Did she say
anything about travel plans?"

"Emergency?" Jason repeated.

"Yes, Mr. Winston is in the hospital."

"I know, Mrs. Winston. I'm very sorry. Is he doing—"

"I'm calling from the hospital in Richmond, Jason. I need Lucy
to bring some things with her when she comes."

Lucinda heard "emergency" repeated again. Then the phone
seemed to go dead—two, five, ten seconds. Lucinda was about to

hang up and call back, when there was a click and a new voice came on the line.

"Mommy?" It was Lucy, panic in her voice.

How did something like that happen? Lucinda had wondered. What amazing feat of phone technology was this? And then it came to her: No amazing feat. Just proximity.

Now she shook her head again at Jason. No. I'll deal with that later, deal with you later, deal with her. At the moment, Nathan was enough. Lucinda shut her eyes. She had to get some rest.

JASON AND LUCY had gotten dressed immediately and set off for Richmond without even a cup of coffee, or Nathan's bathrobe. Finally, they had forced someone to notice them—to see who and what they were together—and Lucy knew that having once done so, her mother could never forget or just turn away from the knowledge. There was no telling where it all would end.

Jason looked around the small waiting room for a chair as far away from Lucinda as possible. As he sat down, the man next to him handed him the sports section from the *Richmond Times*.

"Something to do," he said, "while you wait."

The man, in his mid-forties or so, had deeply sunk eyes and seemed not to have slept in weeks. If he had been splattered with dried blood, he would have looked as bad as Jason's father.

"Thanks," Jason said, grateful for anyone who would talk to him in the room. "Thanks a lot."

"It's nothing," Lieutenant Haddon answered. "The paper was a freebie. It was here when I sat down." There was no question, he thought. This kid had to be Spencer Lee's son.

"LUCY."

John Henry didn't have to turn around. He could tell by the footfall, the fragrance, the way the molecules rearranged themselves to include her, that his sister had come into the room.

He wondered what he could possibly say to her. Then he felt Lucy's hand on his left shoulder.

"Germ." A word that came out of a dream.

Lucy took a few steps and hugged him from the front. She felt light as air as John Henry put his good arm around her. Cara wasn't much bigger, she couldn't have weighed much more, but she had been so dense, so heavy. Lucy pushed back—barely a touch at all—and stood at arm's length to have a look at him. Like her mother, she poked him here and there. She, too, seemed to have become an overnight expert in diagnosis.

"I've been—" John Henry started to say, but Lucy pinched up her face to look like Lucinda and took a deep, long-suffering breath.

"You've been delivered," she broke in. "Lucy, he's been delivered."

They laughed, then cried. Their lives had gone on for years and years, it seemed to them both, without a single tear being shed except over scraped knees and minor insults to their childhood dignity. Now everyone seemed to be crying constantly, and with good reason.

"I was so mad at you, John Henry. I hated you."

He'd been expecting the word. Still, it nearly buckled his knees.

"I couldn't understand how you could leave us, how you could care so little about us, about Mommy and Dad and me, that you'd just walk away like that."

"Luce, I did it—"

"Then I learned that there's more than one kind of love."

John Henry looked at Lucy. Tears were starting up again in her eyes.

"I learned that love is so much more difficult than I ever thought it would be. God, Germ, it's so complicated."

"Jason Lee."

It wasn't a question, really. Like Cara, John Henry had learned that there's a mode between the interrogative and the declarative—a space where questions and answers are one and the same. He'd known about Jason, now that he thought back, before he ever left—there was something about the way she said his name. Now he knew, too, what edges of existence their love could lead them to.

"Mother?"

Lucy looked at the floor and nodded. "She called Jason's apartment this morning, early. I was there. I'd been there." Looking up now: "We make each other so happy."

"I've seen worlds I didn't know existed, Luce—possibilities I didn't know about. It's just such a hard place to get to. It's so much harder than it should be."

"Breathe with me, Germ," she said, "the way we used to. Let's breathe together until our heartbeat is one."

And thus they stood, the two of them, shoulder to shoulder, breath to breath, heartbeat to heartbeat—co-vigilists, looking at their father in his hospital bed. Behind him, above him, beside him, monitors blinked, whirred, recorded. John Henry and Lucy could count the drips from the IV tubes; they could hear the hiss of the oxygen. Their father had always seemed so large; he'd always been so large. Now he seemed to be shrinking in front of them, fading away so that when he finally did open his eyes—*when*, not yet *if*—there might be nothing left of him.

"I did this," John Henry finally said. "This is what I did to him." The thought had been eating at him ever since he had walked into this room. It was like some gigantic parasite burrowing its way recklessly through his insides. "Christ, Luce, *I* did this."

Lucy took her brother's face between her hands and squared his head to her. "Grandpa Jack had a heart attack, too," she said: Nathan's father, John Henry Winston, for whom his grandson had been named. Lucy had been only six years old when he finally succumbed. Lucy remembered him dimly as drawn, almost speechless, never out of his wheelchair. "It's in the genes," she said, looking into her brother's eyes. "You didn't do this."

Whether either of them was fully convinced—whether John Henry would ever be—was another matter. She was holding his head still, staring into his eyes, when they heard a kind of snuffle, as if someone had gauze packed in his nose. Their father was lying in his bed, eyes wide as saucers.

"Oh my stars!" Nathan said. "Oh my stars!"

SPENCER'S FIRST ORDER of business after leaving Lucinda in the waiting room had been to call his Secret Service chief and get poor Leo out of hock.

"Blame me, Mr. Stanley," he said after listening to a litany of complaint: protocols violated, systems stressed to the breaking point, agents forced to stand out in a driving rain while a valet jogged. "Blame me for every bit of it. I don't know what came over me. But release Leo. Now. And may I congratulate you on the excellent way in which you've contained news coverage of the Vice President's medical problem? The family very much appreciates the peace and quiet."

It took so little, really, to keep people happy, Spencer thought as he hung up. The wonder was that more of his colleagues in government didn't take the time. Dr. Ashbury was waiting in the examination room next door.

"No more than superficial," he told the President when he was through poring over the skull crease. "If I'd been there at the time, I might have put a stitch or two in just to hold things together, but there's no need now. You're going to need a little stronger rinse, though, in your hair next time. Whoever cleaned your wound used hydrogen peroxide on it—that whole corner of your head is already going white."

The President laughed as he stood up—the two of them had known each other for dogs' years. He was almost to the door when Ashbury called after him: "Christ, Spencer, do you have any idea how goddamn lucky you were?"

"Doesn't seem fair, does it?" Spencer answered.

"How so?"

"I've been lucky my whole damn life." Dear God, he wanted a shower. He wanted water hot enough to boil a lobster in.

Wormley had taken over a private room down the corridor that led to Nathan's waiting room and extended the security wall to include this adjunct as well. By the time Spencer arrived, he had laid out the President's clothes on the crank-up bed; next to them was a white silk sleeveless undershirt, navy blue silk boxer shorts with tiny white polka dots, and a pair of almost sheer over-the-calf black socks. Spencer looked at them and cocked an eye at his scheduler.

"Extras," Wormley explained. "I forgot to have Kay send over your accessories, but providentially, I had overpacked myself. Um, should I wait outside?"

"Yes," Spencer said. "Outside probably would be best."

Standing beneath the shower head, letting the water beat down on him, Spencer was thinking of a time when he and Frannie had gone to see his own father at one hospital or another. Cirrhosis was starting to settle in, along with the other decays of a serious drinking man. His father was becoming a familiar of extended hospital stays. Spencer had met Frannie three years earlier, when he was a senior at the Citadel, but he had proposed to her just a week before, a

month away from getting his law degree. Now it was time to do
what he had managed to avoid to date: introduce his wife-to-be to
her future father-in-law. At home, Spencer's father behaved at best
erratically, at least toward the end. During his hospital stays—de-
prived of the usual fuel, mellowed with other medication—he tended
to revert to charm. So it was that Spencer had asked Frannie to run
out to the hospital with him. He had to go in any event; it was time.
And Spencer's father was charming.

They sat in an alcove off the solarium. Spencer and Frannie shared
a small rattan love seat, appropriately enough; his father faced them
in a rattan easy chair. He'd chosen for his text that day his 1942 run
for the presidency—not the ugly parts, not the beautiful speeches
that were ignored, not the Holy Cause lost out on, not the landslide
defeat that had led to the drinking that had led more or less in a
straight line to this solarium, but the fun parts: the comically missed
or misboarded connections (a train, for example, out of Savannah
bound for Miami, when his next speech was to be delivered in
Charleston), the critical names his father had forgotten at key moments (including most memorably the senator who had seconded his
nomination at the convention that year), the convention itself (back
when drinking in such quantities had still been enough to amuse his
father), more. His father had charmed Frannie indeed and been
swept off his own feet in return. He was to love her until the day
he died—a wife like that might have made him a champ.

He and Frannie had been so young then, Spencer thought, just
twenty-four and twenty-two years old. They'd wanted to spend every
moment with their fingers intertwined, their bodies warmed against
one another. He remembered the heat of the two of them squeezed
into that rattan love seat, how he had wanted to put his arm around
his fiancée but thought it improper in front of his father. Still, his
hand kept starting to reach for hers, and hers for his. There had
been an almost electric crackle between them. And then? And then
decades had passed, and Frannie had started coming three times a
week to the oncology wing of this hospital, and little by little she
had faded from life. Spencer suddenly wanted to smash something,
to beat his fist against the wall. Love was so sweet and so perilous,
all at the same time.

Frannie had worn her raven hair long and loose. It flowed over
her shoulders as they sat on that rattan two-seater. Spencer could

still feel it brushing against his head when she turned. He could smell the shampoo. When you really love someone, you risk everything, he thought, even loss. Now that the hole in Nathan and Lucinda's life had been filled, he could feel the hole in his own.

He was putting on his tie, shaping the knot, slipping it up tight against his throat—a President again—when another thought hit him: the way Jason and Lucy, sitting opposite him, had been as he told them of Nathan's trip to North Adams, the note, the heart attack, the gunfire on the old Mall, the rescue, and the trip down here. Spencer had thought it was just nerves—Jason's at hearing of his father's close call; Lucy's at her fear for her brother's safety, her father's health. She seemed to use Jason as shelter from the story Spencer was telling, while Jason's hands seemed almost disconnected from the rest of him. But nerves were only the beginning of it—he realized that now.

Not until he was walking back down the corridor to Nathan's sitting area did the full import hit him: Jason and Lucy were in love. It was as if he had been shot again, this time in broad daylight and by a better marksman. He wanted to sit down on the floor and pull the hair from his scalp. Jason was the fruit of his loins, the sole survivor, his every hope. How much were the two of them willing to risk? How much more could Spencer bear to learn about himself?

LUCINDA WAS JUST coming out of Nathan's room when Spencer walked into the sitting area. Her hair was once again pinned back, the circles under her eyes appeared to have retreated, and she'd put on fresh lipstick. In the corner of the room, Lieutenant Haddon seemed willing to outlast eternity. Next to him, Jason had his nose buried in the front section of the newspaper. Spencer squatted beside him—a flash of pain raced along his stomach wall—and squeezed his son's knee. Lost in reverie, Jason was taken completely by surprise.

"Jase," his father whispered, patting him on the leg. "Jase." He couldn't think of a single thing more to say.

"You know?"

Spencer nodded once. "Yes." Again it was only a whisper, as if he were afraid to say it out loud.

So, Jason thought, the downhill slide has a bottom after all. He put an arm around his dad and kissed him once on the forehead. The relief—the sheer relief of it!

As Jason kissed him, Spencer opened his eyes and saw Lucinda staring at them from her chair on the opposite wall, measuring Jason, measuring them both. "No." She just formed the word for him with her lips. "No." It had worked thus far—a totem word, a bit of magic.

Spencer was about to rise and go sit by Lucinda, when Lucy stuck her head out of her father's room.

"President Lee, Mom," she was saying. "Dad wants you. Someone better bring chairs."

At the door, Spencer Lee turned around and signaled to Jason and Lieutenant Haddon to join them.

"HER NAME WAS Cara," John Henry began, and Spencer Lee knew without being told that it was Cara who had slit Sean's throat and stood beside them at the edge of the canal, their lives held in her blood-soaked hands. It was a day for things revealing themselves instantaneously.

"Her skin was"— John Henry stopped, held his black arm against the fair skin of the President's hand where it stuck out from his cuff—"it was almost exactly halfway between President Lee's and mine. I thought that if God ever wanted to produce a new race, Cara is what He would make.

"I thought she—" He stopped again, worked through a sentence in his mind, and retreated to safer ground. "I thought she cared for me. I thought she wanted me to join DRAGO because I was who I was, not because I was part of you." John Henry was looking now at his father, propped up in his hospital bed, the oxygen tube feeding into his nostrils. "Now I'm not sure. She said it was about power— not me, not her, not you. It was about who had power and who didn't."

He choked and fought back a tear—what power could his father possibly have now, shrunken in this bed? John Henry leaned into his chair and stared blankly ahead. He and the President were sitting to the right of the Vice President's bed. Lucinda and Lucy were sitting side by side opposite them, Lucinda holding Nathan's hand, Lucy holding her mother's. Jason was leaning against the wall behind his father. Haddon had taken a dark corner near the door—as invisible as he could make himself.

"That's the thing, Mr. President. You have no idea how many people don't exist in America, no idea how many of them there are."

And then as they sat there, with his father's hand covering his own, John Henry told them all—father, mother, sister, President, Jason, and the lieutenant—about the world Cara had shown him, about the life he had led. Finally, Cara had been right: John Henry was a perfect spokesman, a perfect ambassador for all the people who weren't in the Greater Confederacy of the Confederate States of America.

"I saw you, Dad," he finally said, "the time you visited North Adams. I guess I didn't know what I would have done if you'd seen me. I still don't know. I just knew that I had to tell you something. I had to tell you that I love you."

Nathan leaned back, closed his eyes, went somewhere else. Above him, the monitors marked his regular heartbeat, his pulse, the intake and outflow of his vital gases. There was a tiny rumble in his throat that soon settled into a steady snore. John Henry slipped his hand out from under his father's, stood up, turned to the others.

"Cara," he said. "It was her idea that I write Dad the note. I didn't want to do it, but so much had been done to bring me there. The two waiters who had been killed—the white one, Randy, had taken Cara in when she was just a girl, almost; he and Cara and a few others had founded DRAGO."

"Killed themselves," Spencer said, as gently as he could.

"I don't understand."

"The two waiters killed themselves, John Henry. Cyanide. The capsules were found in their mouths. They were already dying when they were hit."

The news stunned John Henry. The lieutenant had told them about the corpses in the canal—the doubles for the waiters, the bodies without their fingertips. How, John Henry wondered once again, could he possibly have been worth so much death?

"I didn't think—" As John Henry looked at his father, he imagined him bound and gagged, hidden away in that hole beneath the cabin that Haddon had told them about on the drive to Richmond. "I didn't imagine it would lead to this." A gesture: his father, the

President, himself. "I don't think she did either. Sean was the violent one. Cara—" John Henry said it as if something were snapping inside him. "Cara said that Sean wanted too much, that Randy didn't want enough. She called me her Mr. In-Between."

John Henry's voice broke as he said it.

So there's that as well, Lucinda thought. The two of them had made love, had sex. She knew enough about what had happened by the canal in Washington to realize that Cara had probably saved her son's life and the President's. Lucinda also knew that if she could ever get her hands on Cara, she would try to rip her apart bone from bone, limb from limb, flesh from flesh, like a leftover Sunday chicken.

"No one comes home exactly the way they left," Lucinda said, "even if it's just for a walk around the block."

30

TOMPKINS MEMORIAL HOSPITAL, RICHMOND

AT 2:11 A.M., such event never to be recorded, Nathan Winston saw his father, Jack, and his mother, Phyllis, walking hand in hand down a sun-dappled country lane. His father was carrying his doctor's bag in his free hand, as if they were going to visit a sick patient. His mother was swinging a bonnet with her other hand, singing softly. What was the song? What was it? Nathan couldn't quite hear. The scene struck him as odd; "passing strange" was the phrase that jumped into his head. His mother had been a serious woman who rarely sang. She was also a city girl, and she abhorred bonnets. And his father had been a surgeon, not a general practitioner. He kept an office on the bottom floor of their nineteenth-century town house in downtown Richmond and spent his entire career between that office and the hospital. To Nathan's knowledge, his father had never made house calls, certainly not in the country. Indeed, Nathan couldn't imagine what kind of house calls a surgeon might make, country or city. And yet. And yet they looked so happy.

A few minutes later, Nathan began to feel the weight fall away from him and was amazed. He'd been battling extra pounds ever since his late teenage years. He opened his eyes to find Lucinda, his wife of almost twenty-five years, dozing in the chair next to his bed. Dear God, the sight of her! He squeezed Lucinda's hand, felt her squeeze back, and tried to imprint her in his memory: her touch, her feel, her smell, the sound of her as she turned over in her sleep, the taste of her breasts. Nathan closed his eyes again and found that—yes!—there she was, inside him. There with Lucy. There with John Henry, the boy miraculously delivered. There with his own brother, Oscar, dead—what?—a dozen years now. There with his mother and his father, walking down an improbable country lane.

Oh, and the light. The light!

AT 2:16:32 A.M., such time duly noted on the hospital log and delivered to a shocked and saddened nation, Nathan Albert Winston, the Vice President of the Confederate States of America, died of the complications of a massive heart attack suffered nearly forty-two hours earlier in the Oval Office of the White House. He was completing his second term of office, the obituaries read. He'd been a political neophyte when Spencer Lee selected him as his running mate, but he had had a long and distinguished career in university administration, most notably as provost for almost a decade of the National University of the South. In an interview televised earlier in the year, the Vice President had called his university work excellent training for his current position, although, he added, "only a career as an undertaker could have prepared me for all the funerals I've had to attend." The Vice President was celebrated for his dry wit, the obituaries noted, and occasionally mordant humor.

The Vice President's wife, media accounts reported, had been by his side at the time of his death. His wife, media accounts had no way of reporting, had been asleep when she felt the squeeze of her husband's hand and had squeezed back, still asleep. Their last connection had been nothing more than a reflex action, the culmination of a quarter century of practice. It was the monitor alarm that had awakened Lucinda, just seconds before the nurse on duty came racing through the door. In addition to his wife, the Vice President was survived by his children, Lucinda—known as Lucy—and John Henry, both students, both living at home.

"SECRECY IS ALWAYS regrettable in a democracy," Sheila Redmond was saying in the White House briefing room that afternoon. "But it had been the family's wish to spend its hours with the Vice President in seclusion, and without the security precautions that were taken, I think we all know that Tompkins Memorial Hospital would have been turned into a three-ring circus."

Redmond was dressed in black. Farley, seated in his usual spot in the front row of the press contingent, had pinned a black square to the lapel of his blue-and-white seersucker suit. There hadn't been time to change to something more appropriate.

"Yes," Redmond said in response to a question. "The President had approved the plan, of course. He was certain that you ladies and gentlemen of the press would understand and that the public would too. As the President frequently notes, the public is the court in which we ultimately are judged in this business."

"Why was the Vice President at Tompkins Memorial?" a reporter from one of the back rows called out.

"Dr. Withers was out of the White House when the Vice President was stricken," Redmond explained. "He'd been called away on pressing professional matters. Mr. Winston was expertly attended by Dr. Ashbury, who holds admitting privileges at Tompkins, but Dr. Withers was in close consultation.

"And before anyone asks, yes, President Lee was in the Oval Office when the Vice President took ill. The President and his longtime valet, Leo Manzini, used cardiopulmonary resuscitation to revive Mr. Winston after his attack. Unfortunately, it was not enough."

"Sheila?" Redmond looked up from her notes. Farley had half risen from his seat, as he always did when he delivered a question.

"The funeral service. You haven't given us the details."

Redmond took off her glasses and pinched the bridge of her nose before answering. It had been a long day for everyone. "First things last, I suppose, Mr. Farley. My apologies. The funeral service will be held at noon on Wednesday here in Richmond, at Saint Paul's Episcopal Church. President Lee will address the nation afterward, at a time still to be determined. Vice President Winston will be interred privately later in the day at University Cemetery, lot number two, in Charlottesville. As many of you know, that's the lot reserved for the most prominent faculty members and alumni of the West Campus."

Redmond was gathering her notes, a sign to the press corps that the briefing was ending. Notepads were snapping shut as she spoke into the microphone a last time.

"The President regrets not being able to appear before you in person, but he's in mourning. Vice President Winston was—"

There was a commotion in the hallway to Redmond's right, a rustling from the press corps. She looked up to see Spencer Lee entering the room. He was wearing a dark-gray suit, a black tie; there was a butterfly bandage at his hairline.

"Ladies and gentlemen," Redmond started to say, "the President of the Confederate States—"

Spencer put an arm around Redmond as he leaned in front of her.

"I think everyone here knows who I am, Miss Redmond, but thank you all the same."

He stood quietly for a minute while the reporters resumed their seats, then he began again.

"Vice President Winston was not only a close personal friend of many years' standing, ladies and gentlemen. He was an invaluable counselor to me, as well as a selfless public servant. Only the evening before he was stricken, the Vice President had returned from a grueling unannounced inspection of conditions in the Northeast Industrial Zone, undertaken at my request. Naturally, I deeply regret now that I sent him on such a mission, but his inspection revealed structural flaws in the Patriation Program that we are even now beginning to address."

Spencer paused to wipe away a tear and clear his throat.

"I also want to say, ladies and gentlemen, that I had the honor of visiting with Vice President Winston in what were almost his last hours. Even as life ebbed from him, the Vice President was making suggestions that I believe will make this glorious Confederacy of ours an even greater nation. Over the final months of this administration, I intend to do everything I can to bring the Vice President's last wishes to fulfillment.

"Now, if you'll all join me in praying for Lucinda Winston and the two wonderful children Nathan Winston has left behind . . ."

Spencer had no sooner said "amen" than a question was shouted out of the press pack:

"Mr. President, the bandage on your forehead? What happened?"

But Spencer Lee was already leaving the briefing room.

31

THE NATIONAL MALL

"HE WAS DETERMINED to join the angels that day," the President was saying, "but the angels seem to have been determined to welcome him too."

He grabbed John Henry by the right elbow—his shoulder had long since healed—and half dragged him across the floor of the rotunda. Spencer had to tell the story one more time, and Jason was far too preoccupied to listen. Besides, Spencer felt like something of a father to John Henry these days. He had helped rob him of his own father and owed him something in return, and God, what the two of them had been through! Maybe most important, John Henry had no place to hide. He laughed and let himself be dragged along by the President. His mother was resting on a folding chair, waiting for the ceremony to begin.

"Here," Spencer said. "This scorch mark here. This is where the fire first leapt to. It jumped out of the small circle of flame that surrounded Jefferson Davis—there, that scorch mark, and that one, and that one there"—leaning back as far as he could, pointing with one hand, with the other adjusting John Henry's head upward with each new marking, as if it were some kind of telescope.

"Once on the balcony, the fire streaked around the railing of the balustrade like a race car, like something possessed. People were screaming, of course, running for the stairs. Federals were trampling their own, as Federals would, but really, who could blame them? They were Yankees, and the fire was building up its strength, its

speed. It had something even greater in mind. A gigantic leap—
right there!—to the dome, where it roared until the skylight itself
began to melt. What other cause could there be for such a fire than
divine providence, John Henry?"

Spencer turned now, grabbed John Henry by both shoulders, and
stared straight into his eyes. Sweat was running from his forehead;
his voice had settled into a gospel cadence.

"Surely, God's hand had been guiding Jefferson Davis as he lit
that match. Surely, it had to be God's own countenance that shone
down on Jefferson Davis as he stood with perfect calm at the center
of that conflagration, his flesh sizzling—oh, yes, *sizzling*—certain of
his place in the great Kingdom to Come. And don't forget, John
Henry—don't forget: It was the Sabbath when all this was happen-
ing. The Lord's work on the Lord's day!"

My God, Spencer thought, what a tale! He could almost hear the
panic and crackle. As he talked, he could feel his own flesh melting.
And the story could never be told the same way again. The gold
disk that marked Spencer's great-great-grandfather's martyrdom was
encased in an impenetrable plastic. Above it, the skylight that
crowned the dome of the old Capitol had been removed. A grapple
hook descended through it, suspended from the long arm of a crane,
ready to lift the disk from where it had sat for nearly the whole
history of the nation. What fire and nature had failed so long to do,
satchel expolsives would soon accomplish. By tomorrow, the wreck
of this place would be cleared and the disk returned to its place of
honor, uncovered, alone—a simpler monument to a heroism of almost unbearable complexity.

This was it, Spencer thought, the end. He took a handkerchief,
and as he mopped his brow, he heard Jason applauding lightly from
across the rotunda. He bowed slightly in Jason's and Lucy's direction
and threw an arm over John Henry's shoulder.

"Or so the story goes," he said.

"Oh, I believe, Reverend! Hallelujah!"

Who would ever have known the boy had a light touch? Life
these days was nothing but surprises.

Across the rotunda he saw Lucinda rising, John Henry at her
elbow now.

"Mr. President."

It was Daniel Brewster, dressed in a blue suit, a white stole thrown over his shoulders, with gold crosses embroidered at either end.

"Mr. President, we're about to begin."

What to make of this, Spencer had no idea. Nor any idea of what God himself might make of it. Very little, he suspected, but very little might be enough. Spencer Lee was down to grasping at straws.

LUCINDA HAD BEEN surprised to find a pasty-faced minister at her door one afternoon three months before, in mid-July. He'd introduced himself as Daniel Brewster, a name she vaguely recognized from somewhere. Then, as she stood there, trying to decide whether to let him inside her home, he'd looked over her shoulder, seen John Henry emerging from the kitchen, and called out, "Johnny."

Johnny? My heavens, wasn't it enough what they had done to him? Did they have to change his name too? But John Henry had seemed so happy to see the man, and in the month since his return—his deliverance, as she still thought of it—happy days were too rare in her son's life.

"I'm on a new circuit now," Brewster had explained as he sipped iced tea at the kitchen table. "We Congregationalists are trying to tend directly to our flocks, such as they may be." Lucinda nodded but didn't smile. The intricacies of the Congregational denomination held no interest for her. Why had he come?

"I saw the funeral service," he said, looking at John Henry and his mother. "I'm sorry, of course, sorry for you both. I was an admirer . . . And then a Lieutenant Haddon from the Washington police force called me. My card had turned up in an investigation."

John Henry relaxed for a moment and smiled. What would he have done without Brewster's card? Written on his own skin and torn it off for someone to find? Black graphite on black skin? A low probability of success there. You never knew how one event was going to affect another, how one kindness might play itself out in someone else's life.

"There's a daughter too, I believe?" Brewster asked.

Is . . . was, Lucinda thought. We'll see, we'll see. She hoped the former with all her heart. She missed Lucy deep to the bone.

. . .

THE BATTLES HAD begun as soon as Nathan was in the ground and the TV cameras were turned off. Lucinda felt as if her world had turned upside down. Her son, with whom she had had so many arguments, now sat quietly, lost in his own thoughts and memories, while she and Lucy picked at one another and passed each other icily in the hallway. Sometimes they fell to uglier moments and more heated exchanges; the worst—and last—of them had come two weeks after Nathan's death.

It was just after dinner. Lucy had come into the kitchen to get the car keys and say goodbye.

"Where are you going, dear?" Lucinda had asked from the sink.

"Out."

"I assumed that, Lucy. Out where?"

"Mommy—"

"Where?"

"Mother, I'm—"

"What? You're almost twenty-one? You know what's best for you?"

Lucinda put the dish sponge down, wiped her hand, and walked over to face her daughter. For a moment, Lucy thought her mother might slap her. Instead, she reached out, grabbed the car keys from Lucy's hand, and threw them in the corner of the kitchen.

"Why can't you let me live my life?"

"You mean why can't I let you ruin your life? Why can't I let you take every opportunity, every chance that life has afforded you, and throw it all away because you can't stay away from—" Lucinda stopped.

"From?"

"You know what I'm talking about. You know who."

"No, Mommy. I want to hear you say it."

My God, Lucinda thought, it sounds so much like herself and John Henry not long ago. She imagined herself stuck in some kind of eternal argument loop—first the one child, then the other.

"I'll say what I want to say, Lucy. When I want to say it. And I will not take direction from a young lady who runs off to some boy's apartment like a dog in heat the minute her father takes ill."

"That's what you think, Mother? Is that it?"

"Oh, Lucy, Lucy, I'm sorry." Lucinda was stunned by the things that came out of her mouth these days. She sometimes felt as if an alien lived inside her. "This can't go on. It just can't go on."

"If Daddy were alive, he'd at least try to understand. He'd try. Why can't you do even that?"

"Well, that at least is one thing we can agree on."

"What's that?"

"Your father, Lucy. He's not alive. He's not alive at all."

Lucy had run up to her room after that, while her mother sat at the kitchen table and cried once again, as if there were no bottom to grief. The next day, Lucy had been sent to Clarisse's house in Atlanta for the rest of the summer. She could minister to the elderly and abet Clarisse in her other charitable schemes, Lucinda explained. Mostly, Lucinda just wanted to keep "them" apart—"them" being the way it was easiest for Lucinda to think of her daughter and Spencer Lee's son: not as Lucy and Jason, not as her flesh and his blood, but as some abstraction, chemicals that needed to be kept in separate jars, separate rooms, labs, worlds. Watching the train pull out of the station in Charlottesville nearly killed Lucinda. It was like swallowing lye, she thought. A terrible bitterness settled deep inside her.

For his part, Jason had simply come "home" to the White House once the semester ended and Lucy had been sent away. What was the point of Charlottesville without her there? With Kay's connivance, Jason studiously avoided all state functions, formal dinners, informal palavers, anything that had the slightest stamp of officialdom on it. Evenings, if his father was free, the two would jog on the Mall together—or rather Jason would run ahead of his father, double back, then run ahead again. Otherwise, he holed up, read, grew sallow, and lost weight, until Leo finally had made it his special duty to ply Jason with an almost endless parade of milk shakes, hamburgers, french fries, grilled cheese sandwiches, ice cream, chocolate cakes, pecan pies, anything the White House kitchen could throw together to tempt a new twenty-one-year-old with a sweet tooth the size of Georgia and a wooden leg for junk food.

Jason was willing to keep to the routine until September, until school was back in session and there was a reason to go somewhere else. One evening, as he and his father were stretching after their jog, it became apparent that Spencer had other ideas.

"You need to get out of here, Jase. You're morbid. Look at you— you don't have nearly enough sun. It's not the way a young man should live. All you do is mope around and think about—"

"About?"

"Jase, you know what. You know who. Lucy. Let's face it. I've talked to Uncle Davey. They've got that old cook's bedroom off the kitchen at Pawley's. . . ."

By mid-July, Jason had decided Pawley's wasn't such a bad idea. The cook's bedroom was comfortable enough. Mornings he taught soccer at a youth center not far north, at Murrells Inlet. By two o'clock, the mail was waiting at the post office out on the main road. Jason made retrieving it his duty. Davey was on his boat if there was any hint of sunshine, and his wife, Jason's aunt, had a metabolism made for such a climate. She drank milk punches for lunch and sensibly slept away the hottest part of the day. That gave Jason the late afternoon to read Lucy's letters, and reread them, and read them again.

They wrote every day, of course—wrote despite the fact that Lucinda had asked Clarisse to refuse Jason's letters and to confiscate them if they did get through. Though she had never married herself, Clarisse knew even if her sister didn't: You can't stop a tidal wave by putting tape over the mail slot.

DANIEL BREWSTER STAYED four days that first visit. He and John Henry took walks or sat in the kitchen, sipping Lucinda's iced tea while they talked about North Adams, the world they had briefly shared. On the last day, Brewster suggested that they sit in the garden. "To get the air" was his euphemism; John Henry translated it, "so I can smoke." Still, the crape myrtles were blooming, and the fountain near the back of the garden bubbled softly. John Henry had always been indifferent to this space, uninterested in nature as decoration; now he felt almost proprietorial.

"DRAGO seems to be gone," Brewster said. "The house is still there and pretty much the same people when I last checked in. But no Cara. No Sean. One of the Marys told me they were going to call the group something else, even though it will still be the same thing, a way to look out for each other."

"Sean won't be back," John Henry answered.

"Won't?"

He nodded his head. Nothing more.

"Cara?" Brewster asked. He seemed to be saying a prayer, some kind of benediction just under his breath.

John Henry shook his head this time: He didn't know. He didn't want to know.

"It's eating you, Johnny," Brewster said, a hand now on John Henry's knee. "It's gnawing at you. You could pray about it—ask God about whatever it is. I could help you with that."

As John Henry looked down at the gravel walk, he sagged inside himself.

"Or you could tell me, Johnny. Just tell me. Maybe . . ." Brewster let the word hang, hoping it was filled with possibility.

John Henry closed his eyes, saw Sean's slit throat, and imagined the dead men in the canal in Washington weeks and weeks before he had ever been there. He saw the two waiters fall to the floor of the hotel ballroom in Richmond. He saw—he couldn't help it— Cara. He saw his father laid out that last time, before the casket was sealed, impeccably dressed, impeccably dead. He felt the bullet hit his shoulder and Spencer Lee covering him, trying to absorb him.

"What have I done?" he finally said, looking up at Brewster, tears in his eyes for the first time since his father's funeral. "What have I done, Daniel?"

John Henry was shuddering now, lost. Daniel Brewster stood him up, wrapped both arms around him, and held him until the shaking stopped.

"You went looking for truth, Johnny. What's the harm in that?"

Watching from her office window, Lucinda could almost feel the weight lift off her son. He wouldn't open like a flower—be nothing one moment, be blooming the next. That wasn't John Henry. He had to think each moment through. But there would be air now; there would be light.

BY THE TIME Brewster returned to Charlottesville, in mid-September, John Henry was a freshman at the university. He'd celebrated his birthday just at the end of August and was allowing the possibility of fun in his life, maybe for the first time. There was a girl in his English class—Phoebe, goddess of the moon—his first real girlfriend, from a fine old Charleston family. Lucinda was thrilled. For now, it was enough to have John Henry smile, even occasionally blush. Lucinda could lie in her bed at night and hear her son and daughter playing Scrabble at the board in Lucy's room— a sound that once had been as common as wind, a sound she had thought she might never hear again.

My world has not collapsed all the way, not yet, Lucinda thought. The six weeks at Clarisse's did not change Lucy—maybe nothing would—but it had at least given tempers a chance to cool down. What was Lucinda going to do? Scream at her daughter for the rest of whatever life they had together? Instead, she had decided to take her joy in John Henry—in having her son restored to her—and in the moments when she could be with both her children and pretend, at least for a little while, that life was as it had been. To Lucinda, it seemed the only real hope.

It was time, too, for Lucinda to reenter the world, to get back to her teaching and writing, to tend to her friendships and responsibilities. A memorial scholarship program had been established at the university in Nathan's name, richly endowed by the Manufacturers' Coalition, the National Agricultural Association, the Lee Family Trust, and others. Lucinda chaired the board.

And then there was Jason: Nothing short of a bullet in the heart seemed likely to discourage him. He'd shown up at the Winstons' pavilion door almost his first day back in Charlottesville, holding a box in his arms.

"My father has been going through his office, Mrs. Winston," Jason had explained. "He's trying to clean things out for, well, the next person. He thought you might like to have these. I think they're papers that Mr. Winston sent him."

Lucinda glowered as she thanked Jason, then took the box and closed the door in his face. He was back two days later with a bouquet of flowers the size of a small town, shifting from foot to foot as he waited for someone to answer the door.

"Yes, Jason?" Lucinda asked when she finally did.

"Flowers, Mrs. Winston."

"And the occasion? The reason?"

"Oh, none. There won't be that many more, you know. Not fresh.

It's fall." Jason turned and was gone before Lucinda could close the door.

Half a week later, Lucinda opened the door to find Jason standing there with a flat rectangular package that she recognized all too well.

"Leave it right there, Jason," she said, pointing to the top of an antique milk box that sat by the door. "There."

"It's Dad's—"

"Oh, dear Lord, boy, I could smell your father's famous smoked mackerel miles before you got here. Miles, Jason."

Jason smiled as he put it down.

"It keeps well underground, Mrs. Winston."

"We'll see. We'll see."

Soon, too, there were drafts of the paper he and Lucy had written on transmigration, now destined for a very minor academic journal. Still, the excitement!

Like his father, Jason made up for his faults with perseverance. Like his father, too, he was hard to dislike. Even Lucinda had to admit that. And he was willing to use any excuse to get near Pavilion Three.

Lucy meanwhile had gone back into the fast-food delivery business, for real this time, although only two hours a day, at dinnertime. Jason was having pizza sent in every evening.

"They're doomed, John Henry," Lucinda said one day as the two of them sat over drinks in the kitchen—wine for Lucinda, a cola for her son—waiting for Lucy to return from her food-delivery chores so the three of them could have supper.

"Doomed?"

"They are, you know. They are. I've been trying to get used to the idea of losing Lucy—just like I tried to get used to the idea of losing you. I'm not good at this." Lucinda looked at the clock on the microwave—8:15, and still no sign of her daughter.

"If worst comes to worst, they can go away. The territories—"

Lucinda winced as he said it, and John Henry understood that the territories were outside his mother's code of civility, outside her realm of the possible. She might still be able to see Lucy, but Lucy would be lost, gone forever. Having been there himself, he wondered how his sister could even survive. Could she and Jason love each other enough to withstand a life that nothing in their own lives had prepared them for? Or would it all just go bad? John Henry was too new to this sort of love to have any real idea.

"Maybe, Mother, I could have Daniel talk to them. He's met them both, and he's had lots of experience with these kind of things. Daniel understands. . . ."

Lucinda went to the counter and poured herself a second glass of pinot noir. "If Reverend Brewster is willing, John Henry, I'd be very grateful."

Good heavens, she thought as the front door opened and she heard Lucy call from the hallway, who would ever have guessed I'd come to be asking favors of a Congregationalist?

BREWSTER MET WITH Jason and Lucy at a restaurant in downtown Charlottesville that was actually three restaurants in one—a black bistro that was entered from one street, a white family restaurant entered from the next block over, and a basement restaurant that could be entered from either of the others. John Henry had found it, just as he had found other places and seen other possibilities since his return, his deliverance. Cara had been right. If he opened his eyes—really opened them—the world he lived in was far more complex than he'd ever imagined.

He and Lucy came in through the bistro and found Jason and Brewster already waiting for them at a table along the side of the room. John Henry stayed only long enough to seat his sister and say hello. This was their event, not his. Still, it struck John Henry as "passing strange" that his journey through the NIZ should have landed him here: considering medicine as his father once had, inflaming his mother with visions of a "successful" match for him, trying to help his sister—who had always protected him, always walked the straight and narrow—to survive along the margins of the possible.

Lucy saw John Henry lingering at the door and made a sweeping movement with her hand—out, out, go see Phoebe—and he laughed and was gone.

"Look around," Brewster was saying. "Take a moment. Just look around the room."

Locked so long in their own company, convinced that their love was unique, Jason and Lucy were amazed to see mixed-race couples sitting nearby, holding hands, deep in conversation, some side by side with their arms thrown over each other's shoulders.

"I didn't know this was possible," Lucy said.

"Oh, it is," Brewster assured her, "and not only here. There are restaurants all over the country like this, even motels and hotels with mixed-race wings, even churches. You find out. You learn. Word spreads."

"Then it's possible," Jason said. He reached beside him on the table, put his hand over Lucy's, and felt his arm jump back. What are you doing? his brain seemed to be screaming. What? Then he reached over again and took her hand in his, squeezed it, and felt her squeezing back.

"Yes, it is possible, Jason. There's only one price," Brewster warned.

"Price?" It was Lucy this time.

"Whatever you do, whether you're praying, eating, whatever"— a gesture that included everything, even those mixed-race motel wings—"when you're through, you always have to leave by the same separate doors you came in by. Is that what you want? To always come and go by separate doors? Because that's the price of existence in this Confederacy of ours."

Jason and Lucy looked around the room, measuring the architecture of what their lives would be like.

Finally, Jason spoke for them both: "Yes." He put his arm around Lucy's shoulder and hugged her tight against him. "It's not what we want, but it's where we're willing to begin."

Brewster held his beer glass high for the waitress—another, please—then he looked to see if Jason and Lucy wished to join him. Jason nodded and held up two fingers of his own to the waitress.

"Good," Brewster said, shaking a cigarette out of his pack. "I've got something that may help, then—something we've been working on developing at the seminary."

Three hours later, Jason finally got his father on the phone.

"There's a minister, Dad. Daniel Brewster. The one whose card John Henry used. . . . Lucy and I were talking with him." Jason could almost feel his father's apprehension. "He wants to meet with you and Mrs. Winston, Dad, sometime early next week, before he has to leave for the North. He has an idea...."

God, the joy in his son's voice, Spencer thought. The happiness. But where would it lead to?

"I'll listen," Spencer said. "No promises."

"WE CALL IT a 'service of conciliation,' " Brewster was saying. "It's something we Congregationalists have been working on—a way to recognize commitments beyond the bounds of the allowable, to encourage support and understanding on the part of the families of those involved. There's nothing binding about it, obviously; nothing in law—church law or state law—that recognizes what we'll be doing. It will all be done in private."

Brewster stopped, weighing his audience. "It's a way—Mr. President, Mrs. Winston—to open a small bridge, a tiny connector between the recognized and the real."

Spencer and Lucinda were sitting in Nathan's office at the pavilion, on the same leather sofa where Lucinda had sat with her husband when he told her about what he had seen in North Adams. Here, she thought, were the worlds of gray Nathan had tried to explain to her: a service that neither was nor wasn't, a relationship that couldn't be yet was, a kind of half existence that might be her daughter's only chance for happiness. What had her whole professional life been, Lucinda wondered, if not a quiet fight against just this sort of thing—this bending, this accommodation?

"No," she said quietly to Brewster, who was sitting across from them. "No. I appreciate all your efforts. I'm deeply grateful for the help you've given my son and the help you are trying to give Lucy. But I can't take part in this. No."

Beside her, Spencer was still trying to digest what Brewster had told him earlier. He had been amazed when Jason told him the minister was a Congregationalist; he thought the Congregational Church had been banned after the War of Dissolution. Now, as he felt Lucinda settling into a shell of resistance, Spencer asked the simplest question he could think of: "Why?"

"Why the service?" Brewster asked.

The President nodded.

"Because without something like this, Jason and Lucy might simply disappear—go off and become part of the world that is not. Because the sum total of misery of keeping people like Jason and Lucy apart is greater than the sum total of benefits of doing so. Because they will need you and Mrs. Winston to support them. The question to me isn't 'Why?' Mr. President. The question is 'Why not?' "

Whether the sum total of misery exceeded the sum total of benefits, Spencer had serious doubts. The Confederacy seemed to have survived quite fine for most of its hundred and thirty-four years. But this was a son, not a regressive analysis, and dear God, he didn't want to lose Jason, couldn't bear the idea of it. Spencer still thought of Jason's love for Lucy as some sort of killer disease that had dropped out of the sky and afflicted his son—one of those horrible, remorseless cancers that gobble up life an organ, a bone, a cell at a time. And so he did finally what any father would do with a dying child who had so far resisted every standard remedy and protocol: He reached for the miracle drug, the bizarre powder, the folk cure. He reached for life—not for himself but for the light of his existence. First, though, he reached for Lucinda's hand. Spencer could feel her delicate bones begin to quake.

"You've lost a husband, Lucinda, and almost a son. Don't risk losing your daughter. We have to fight. For their happiness. For our own."

"No, Spencer. Biequality, the separation of the races, racial purity laws—there's a reason for them, and the reason is that they work. Look at what they've given us. Look at this nation."

" 'Two-bit dictator,' " Spencer suddenly remembered.

"Dictator?"

"That's what Nathan called me the morning of his heart attack, Lucinda. They were practically his last words to me. He was telling me about the suffering he'd seen in North Adams. Funding the waterway, he said, had fallen hardest on the people in the territories, the ones we don't see. But the waterway justified the suffering, I argued—so many benefits ultimately would come back to all of us. 'That's what every two-bit dictator says,' he told me. 'The means never justify the end. Never.'

"Is biequality worth it, Lucinda, if we have to sacrifice Jason and Lucy to make it work? Is that the world we want?"

Lucinda buried her head in Spencer's shoulder as her tears began.

"There's a place, Reverend Brewster; a time," Spencer said. "There's a chance to do this right."

THEY STOOD, ALL six of them, at dead center in the rotunda—contained within the almost thirty square feet of the gold disk, now encased in plastic, that marked the heroic self-sacrifice of Jefferson Davis.

At the center of the disk—the true center of this central structure of the history of the nation—stood Lucy and Jason. He was wearing a red-white-and-blue tie, as his father did, but in vertical stripes. Jason had consulted Leo Manzini on the suit; Manzini had consulted Wormley. Spencer couldn't remember seeing his son dressed so carefully since Frannie's funeral.

Beside Jason, holding his hand, Lucy stood in a tan dress with thin straps across the shoulders, small black buttons all the way down the front; a matching tan hat had a wide brim that shaded her eyes.

Behind and just to her daughter's left, Lucinda had taken John Henry's arm. She was dressed in black, still mourning in public. A veil dropped from her own wide-brimmed black hat. She was crying, Spencer assumed, but softly—the shake of her shoulders just noticeable. John Henry looked over and caught the President's eye: What do I do with a crying mother? Spencer shrugged: He had no defense against tears. They were simply one of the many mysteries of womanhood.

Brewster, standing directly in front of Jason and Lucy, facing them head-on, began to speak. "We are gathered here not to unite this couple. We freely acknowledge that we lack that power, that it is not within the laws of this state or this nation to so do. If God in His infinite wisdom chooses to change those laws, we have faith that He will guide us. Rather, we are gathered here to celebrate the greatest of God's gifts to us."

As Brewster talked, Spencer sidestepped to his left, took Lucinda's other arm in his own, and put his hand on hers. Frannie's voice seemed to have lodged itself in his head: You've got to learn to let go, Spencer. Of history? Of his son? If he only knew which.

"And then abidest these three," Brewster was saying, "faith, hope, and love, but of these the greatest is love."

High above him, Spencer could hear a plane going by. How different the light and sound were at ground level without the skylight in place.

"For finally love is stronger than hate." Brewster was looking at Jason and Lucy. "It is stronger than tradition." Shifting his gaze to Lucinda. "Stronger even than history." Looking now directly at the President.

Mumbo-jumbo, Spencer thought, but maybe not. God had favored this nation—of that he had no doubt: The Confederate States of America was His gift to all mankind. But maybe it was a gift with an expiration date, and a world lay ahead in which America would have to change to survive. Perhaps this beautiful experiment of the Confederacy was as doomed in the eyes of history as every other system mankind had ever devised for living together, one race with another. If so, Spencer didn't want to be around when it ended. He wanted nothing more than for Jason and Lucy to find some level of happiness in the here and now, not in the sweet hereafter. He wanted them to find a way to exist without having to cease to exist. What are the odds? Spencer wondered.

"Lastly," Brewster was saying, "we are, in fact, gathered here for a kind of union."

Beside him, Spencer could feel Lucinda start—her alarm bells suddenly at full alert. His antennae were rising as well.

"We are gathered here to unite ourselves into a caring community, a place where this love can grow outside its own hothouse, away from the few dark corners where it is allowed to be. We are gathered here to recognize its right to exist, to pledge our support and our own love to nourish this one.

"Please," Brewster said, stepping between Jason and Lucy, taking a hand of each, "let us all join together."

It was what Spencer disliked most about modernism in the church. His life was public enough. Still, he reached to take Jason's hand, took Lucinda's with his other, and closed the circle as he did so.

As an absolute silence settled over them all, Spencer found himself wondering precisely how many laws and customs he might be in violation of. He had taken over the rotunda under false pretenses. For all anyone else knew, the two families had gathered to pay a final tribute to Spencer's great-great-grandfather. Spencer was using Secret Service personnel to guard the doors outside—a gross misuse of public servants to serve private ends. And he was standing now, linked through this chain of hands, with a minister who, if not DRAGO himself, had aided and abetted the enemy. The President was about to call the proceedings to an end when he raised his eyes and saw Jason looking at him, and Lucy looking at Jason beside her. As Spencer joined eyes with his son, he felt a kind of energy flowing through him—not quite an electricity, but a current, a connection. And then from beneath him, a voice seemed to rise up out of the disk itself, through the impenetrable plastic, out of the gold, the ashes it encased: "Be brave. Be brave."

"Amen," Brewster said at last as he stepped forward to embrace Lucy and Jason, and then to hug Lucinda—who, maybe even to her own great surprise, let herself be hugged—and John Henry. To the President, he offered his hand, but Spencer stepped inside it and gave him a hug himself.

"I've been speaking to my great-great-grandfather all my life," the President said as they broke away. "He finally spoke back." Then, as Spencer watched, Brewster disappeared through the far door, out the private eastern entrance, with his stole and Bible wrapped and stowed away.

The sky as they exited was one of those fall blues that Spencer hadn't seen in a year, the air was football crisp, the sun dazzling, and after the quiet of the rotunda, the noise of the crowd was almost deafening. Lord, Spencer thought, as he squinted into the distance and across the Mall to the crowds that filled Ninth and Twelfth streets as well. So many people.

SPENCER HAD ACTED unilaterally to change the name of the government air base from Maury Field to Winston-Maury Field. But privately, and particularly within the councils of his own party, he had argued that the airfield was hardly tribute enough for Nathan Winston's selfless service. The Vice President had had a dying wish, he said—a wish delivered personally to the President from Nathan's hospital bed, only an hour before his death. Spencer's eyes glistened as he told the story. He could hear the monitors whirring, the hushed clatter of a hospital ward in the middle of the night as he bent over, straining to hear what were to be Nathan's final words in this world:

"The old Capitol, Mr. President. Its time has come. Demolish it, Spencer. Knock it down."

The story, of course, was not entirely accurate, but it partook of the nature of truth, and in politics that is often as much truth as you get or want. Historians were free to sort it all out later on. More to the point, the story worked, and in politics, utility counted for everything.

Walking across the Mall arm in arm with Lucinda, Spencer wondered how many in the vast crowd present actually cared about the issue, how many were simply here for a good time. More of the latter, he suspected, probably far more. Like the multitudes that gathered for public executions in the few states that still allowed them, most of this crowd had come for the spectacle: if not to hear a neck crack, see a body crumple from gunshots, then to watch the past blown to smithereens. And why not? Spencer thought. Why not?

Behind him, the crane began raising up the great gold disk. Inside the rotunda, technicians were making the final microadjustments to the explosives scattered throughout the hulk. Spencer turned briefly when an "ooh" swept the crowd, and he saw the disk rise in the sky, a circle of light. Beneath it, lit by its glow, the old Capitol looked more than ever like a temple, and maybe, Spencer thought, that, too, is part of the problem: We're forever confusing God and man in the Confederacy, forever losing sight of the fallible nature of humankind.

"Nathan . . ."

The name of the late Vice President seemed to fall out of the sky, materialize out of the air—it was a day, Spencer thought, for voices searching him out from the beyond. Then he realized that Lucinda was talking to him. He bent slightly to give her his ear.

"Nathan would have liked this, Spencer," she said. "I think if he had known his last words could accomplish this much, he would have said them himself."

Lucinda smiled up at the President, patted him on the hand, and said more softly, "There are no secrets, Spencer. In Richmond, even the walls speak."

Behind him, Spencer could hear Jason, Lucy, and John Henry yammering away as the party approached the raised platform. What they were talking about, Spencer suspected he did not want to know. In truth, though, his windows of deniability were quickly closing around him. Ah, well, what was he to do? He was a father too, and if all this had taught him anything, he was a father primarily.

ON THE PLATFORM, the usual luminaries were waiting: Toby Burke; the Senate Majority Whip; the secretary of the interior; church dignitaries; others, nearly all of them easily identified, even Leo Manzini, who was well known to the press from his foreign travels with the President and who was sitting today with his lovely wife, Helena. Only two people stumped the celebrity watchers; both were seated at the far right, next to the chair reserved for John Henry. One was a somewhat grizzled-looking white man in his early forties, his Sunday suit barely holding together; beside him was a woman of perhaps thirty, dressed to the nines and completely agog with anticipation. As was widely noted, she bore the unmistakable identifying characteristics of Down's syndrome.

It had been two months since Haddon was last in Richmond. On that earlier occasion, he had been invited to the Oval Office for a get-together that had left his colleagues in the District police department stunned. Haddon? Detective Lieutenant Haddon? The meeting had begun as a kind of mini-reunion. John Henry had been there when the lieutenant arrived, and the three of them had traded memories like war buddies.

"Do you want to know?" Haddon finally had said.

"Know?" John Henry asked.

"Who they were? The bodies in the canal that started all this? It was all routine discovery once the President here unsealed the investigation and the federal coronor gave us our John Does back." John Henry nodded. He'd needed to know for weeks and weeks.

"The black one had been released from prison two months earlier, after serving five years for grand larceny. The white one was a drifter, who liked to spend winter nights in a jail cell. Someone had to book him. We found the clerk who let Sean page through the mug books. She didn't know a thing."

"And Sean?" John Henry finally asked, reluctant to say his name.

"Brendan O'Connor," the lieutenant said. "He was wanted on two counts of murder in Ireland—his wife and her boyfriend. Dublin was glad to close the case."

"So many bodies," Spencer said. "So much blood."

"They were people, Mr. President," John Henry said. "They were people before they were just bodies and blood." He stood and walked over to the windows that looked south along the Mall. It was where his father had been standing, Spencer thought, when he had his heart attack—the exact spot.

"So that's it, Lieutenant?" the President said. "Case over?"

"Not quite, sir. There's still the woman. Cara." He looked at John Henry's back as he said it. The boy's shoulder blades were clenched together. He's got a way to go, Haddon thought. She's still inside him.

The President had wanted Haddon to meet with John Stanley about a position with the Secret Service; but Haddon wasn't interested. Policing was what he knew, and there was that apartment high up in Georgetown where he could talk with the stars late at night and hear the mad people screeching in their asylum, their lovely, loony "Castle" on the old and tattered strip that once had been the national mall.

"Well, then," the President said as their meeting wound down. "What can I do for you, Lieutenant? John Henry and I, we owe you so much."

His sister, Haddon answered: It would be wonderful if the President could invite her to some kind of function. And here she was. Doris couldn't have been more excited if she were sitting in the cockpit of a space probe, waiting to be launched from Cape Canaveral.

Haddon saw John Henry smiling as he edged his way down the podium to the seat next to him. He looked so much looser. The kid's going to be all right, the lieutenant thought. He's edging Cara out of his life, bit by bit. That's all you can do.

AT THE CENTER of the podium, Spencer introduced one of the church dignitaries, who delivered a short prayer in praise of the weather, fall itself, and the wonders of nature as a whole. Another church dignitary asked God to continue shining down His special favor on this great nation. Still another got more to the point, thanking the Divine for his son Jefferson Davis, who, one hundred thirty-five years ago, had set the course that delivered the Confederacy from the Great Satan Lincoln and the Dominion of Darkness he presided over.

Next came a famous actor to recite Strother Bowman Pinckney's "Fire of Heaven, Light Our Way." And then it was Spencer's turn. The President raised both hands over the plunger box that had been set on a table by the lectern, looked long and hard at the crowd for effect—should I or shouldn't I?—and then shouted into the microphone, "Is everybody ready?"

When the response reached a roar and the roar itself seemed ready to do the work, the President of the Confederate States of America brought both hands down on the plunger, radio signals were activated, signals raced at the speed of light to the satchel charges that were waiting a quarter mile away to receive them, and the Confederacy's most famous structure shuddered, collapsed, and disappeared into itself, obscured by a cloud of dust that rose into the crystal-clear afternoon sky.

Spencer felt as if a part of himself had imploded as well—tradition, family, blood. Maybe it was the best part; he didn't know. He'd have to wait to see what was left of himself to go on with. But he felt light. He felt as if his feet were barely held down by gravity, as if he himself might rise forever into that afternoon sky. The dust had just started back down when John Henry saw an apparition rise up in front of him. She had mocha skin, tiny curls tight against her scalp—she seemed to have slipped out from under the podium they were sitting on. As John Henry gaped—it's her!—she smiled, drew back her arm, and tossed something in the direction of Jason and Lucy. John Henry was halfway out of his seat, ready to throw himself on them. He would lick their wounds, beg for forgiveness, take whatever Cara had hurled onto himself, bear all the suffering, pay all the cost. Then he saw what it was that was rolling along the stage: uncooked rice, a tiny gift for the happy couple. Let the celebration begin. He turned back in her direction, but Cara was gone. She once again wasn't.

Clark Haddon, beside John Henry, saw him start and followed his eyes. When John Henry looked over to his left, Haddon was gone too, and Doris was sitting all alone at the far side of the stage.

As he slid over into the lieutenant's seat, John Henry felt Doris reach for his hand. He took it, squeezed, and felt Doris squeeze back. She was sitting on the edge of her chair now, barely able to contain herself. What was going to be there when all that dust settled? Anything?

The rubble that had once been the Capitol of the Confederacy was just becoming visible when John Henry saw his sweatshirt folded on the floor of the podium, in front of his seat. It had been laundered, and even ironed.